MY BROTHER THE KING

עהויע ישוע

BY MIRANDA SHISLER

*For my brothers and sisters who walked
with Yeshue on the same dusty roads.*

*Who heard the voice of God speak, the
love of God reach and the hand of God
save.*

Our faith has been born of yours.

Part One

MY BROTHER THE CARPENTER

*"Is this not the carpenter, son of
Maryam and brother of Ya'achov, and
Yose and Y'hud and Shimon, and are
not his sisters here with us?" And they
were suspicious of him. And Yeshue said
to them, "There is no Prophet who is
despised except in his city and among
his kindred and in his house."*

-Mark 6:3

PROLOGUE

Jerusalem, spring of A.D. 14
Talia

טליה

"I see it!" Talia cried in the childish delight of a six-year-old Jewish girl viewing the Holy City for the first time.

Talia ran ahead of the sluggish caravan, trailed by her little sister, Hannah. As they crested the hill, the mountain of Zion came into view. She stopped short in awe and beheld the city of kings. The temple was within those walls. It was the very dwelling place of Yahweh, the name that should not be uttered. Her cheeks flushed just for thinking it. Little Hannah danced around her, not knowing what they were celebrating but happy nonetheless.

Abba came up from behind and swung Talia up in his arms. "Ah, my little daughter. There is nothing like seeing Jerusalem for the first time. You were here five years ago, but now you are old enough to remember."

Talia beamed as other family members approached. Two older brothers, Ya'achov and Yose, and her older sister, D'vora, walked with the caravan of neighbors and relatives, but her mother and her oldest brother, eighteen-year-old Yeshue, came near. Yeshue grinned. Her father set her down, and she ran to her brother, grabbing his hand and pulling him along so he could see it.

"I don't ever get tired of that sight." He squeezed her hand.

But the happiness was short-lived. A man's cry startled Talia, and she turned to see a young man covered in blood and nailed to a wooden beam.

She screamed and turned her face into Yeshue's robe. Her mother reached for her and her sister, pulling them toward the city gates, but there was no way to avoid the scene. The image of the young man would be burned into her memory forever.

"Please," the dying man said as they passed. "Help me."

She looked to her parents, but they were silent, their heads bowed. They pulled her along on the opposite side of the road. When she looked back, she realized Yeshue had stopped.

He was standing directly underneath the cross. Its shadow passed over his body, and the man's stream of blood nearly touched the rims of Yeshue's sandals. He watched the man with a solemn expression. Talia wondered what he was thinking. She wished he would move away. That he wouldn't let the blood touch his feet.

"Yeshue," she whispered. Why must she live in a world where young men were killed on crosses outside the Holy City of Alaha? All of her excitement faded. Fear struck her young heart as an infection that would begin that day and grow, spreading like wildfire, setting her ablaze with terror. She was afraid for herself, for her family...

For Yeshue.

ONE

Nazareth, A.D. 20

"I know you are there, little girl."

The familiar clinking of metal to stone went silent. Yeshue's voice brought a flush to Talia's cheeks as she hovered behind the table in the evening shadows of her father's shop. She pushed against the wall and rose from the packed dirt to approach him. He was holding a chisel as he turned to her.

"Aren't you supposed to be sweeping?"

She nodded. She had been sweeping, but could no longer bear the arguing. She had slipped through the passage that adjoined their cramped home with the workshop.

"I'm sorry," she said in a soft voice that seemed to be swallowed up by the stone walls and low ceiling.

"Finish your work and then I'll tell you a story," he said. She nodded before she rushed back to the abandoned broom in the living space. Words assaulted her ears as they flew back and forth, cold and sharp as ever.

"Are we to do all his work, then?" Ya'achov, her second-oldest brother, snapped at their mother. "I have a family of my own to feed. Yeshue has the responsibility to care for you and the little ones now that Abba is gone. Especially since he hasn't bothered to take a wife and raise his own children."

The steel of his words brought the sadness from the dark place inside Talia's mind. They were all unhappy and torn apart. Abba was dead.

She panicked at the thought of being twelve and fatherless. A girl her age needed a father's protection. She was old enough to realize she was vulnerable without him, and young enough to ache to crawl into his lap. To press her ear to his worn tunic and hear the comforting rhythm of his heart.

But Abba was gone. He was not there to reign in the bitter words of her siblings, who had always been prone to disagreements. Not there to stand between her and the darkness.

Abba had always spoken words of reproof to the dark speakers living in her mind. They had always fled at his command. Had Abba's love died along with his body? Did everything he had been lie lifeless in that tomb outside of town, forever lost? Or did his spirit yet live, watching over her and her family from a distance? Would that she could pull the veil aside and see for herself.

She closed her eyes and let Abba's voice speak into her mind. At least she had not forgotten his familiar tenor yet.

You must trust Alaha, little one. Only he is stronger than the fears that plague you.

Instead of the image of her father, strong and robust, standing at their head, now she saw the image of him on his pallet, frail and white and gasping for each breath. Then, with a ragged final draw of air to his lungs, the sound of silence. His vacant eyes. She easily recalled the pungent scent of the spices her mother, sister and aunt had rubbed on the body as they wailed with sorrow the day after Abba left them. Though it was meant to be a pleasant scent, to stifle the stench of death, the spices always accompanied sorrow. Her nose hated the smell.

Her mother, Maryam, appeared to have aged ten years in the space of a month. Her mother rubbed her hands over her pale face. Ama had been ill almost continually since Abba died, which worried Talia. Ama's hair had turned dull; her dark eyes were overwhelmed by deep, dark circles. Her once busy life had been reduced to basic duties, followed by the tears. Many tears. Tears that Alaha stored up in a bottle, remembering the bitterness he had dealt her. At least that was what Ama said. What if she died of sadness and joined Abba in Sheol? What would become of Talia?

Ama's voice interrupted her thoughts. "Yeshue does as he should. He has responsibilities in the prayer house. He teaches the children, including your brothers. Would you have him ignore his duty to the Torah?"

"Life is more than the Torah! Mouths must eat!" Ya'achov threw his hands in the air and shouted the words. Talia grimaced. Why must he yell? The neighbors already gossiped enough about their turbulent home.

"You dare give me a look of disrespect, girl? I'll take a stick to you!"

Talia cowered away from Ya'achov' outstretched arm as Yose grabbed him. "Leave her alone. She's just a stupid girl."

Ya'achov turned back to his mother. "Do you understand that Abba is dead? You have four children to take care of, all under the age of ten. The work Yeshue is doing will not feed you all. He has to stay home or Yose and I will be forced to leave our jobs to do his."

Talia knew all her brothers worked long and hard for the meager living they earned. Ya'achov and Yose made the four-mile trek to Sepphoris every day, hauling the stones that Yeshue carefully chiseled. They were purchased mostly by Herod's workers.

Herod Antipas had it in mind to build a glorious city, dedicated to himself, and his endeavor required quite a bit of stone. Whenever she visited Sepphoris, which wasn't often, she felt tiny in the presence of the huge buildings he was crafting. A massive theater towered over the small houses of the common people. A breathtaking arena played host to the violent gladiator entertainment, which was a common delight in every part of the Roman Empire. She was horrified by it, though she had wondered what it must be like to be so wealthy one could build anything they wanted.

"Yeshue is going to be sorry when we end up having to sell some of these children as slaves to the Romans." Ya'achov huffed, collapsing onto a chair and accepting a cup of watered wine from D'vora.

"May it never be!" Maryam spat on the ground.

Talia's mother had always been full of faith; passionate. Sometimes her passion made her cheeks flush and her heart race. Abba had been able to steady her. Would she lose her mind from her feelings, or her grief? Talia hated what their family had become. Why had God taken Abba? Wasn't it obvious they needed him?

"We're only concerned for you, Ama," Talia's older sister D'vora said to Maryam, fanning herself in the hot, crowded room as she bounced her baby, Omer, on her knee. She was married and lived in the home of her husband's family, but she often came by when her husband was in the city selling his pottery. "We all know you think Yeshue is the M'sheekha—the Anointed One. But so does every Jewish mother! I have that same hope for my Omer. You should let the dream go. Yeshue isn't any different than the rest of us."

As D'vora spoke, her brothers lost interest in the conversation and turned their attention to the animals that needed to be fed in the front portion of the house. They were still within hearing distance. Talia heard Ya'achov grumble as he pitched hay into the stone manger.

Maryam stood and paced the room, pulling her cloak tight around her shoulders. "Why has Alaha given me such foolish children? When will you open your eyes?"

Talia finished her task and replaced the broom as the baby began to cry. She reached into the cradle to get him, but her five-year-old brother, Y'hud, suddenly ran in front of her. Talia stumbled and fell over the division between the rooms and landed in the hay. Ya'achov almost ran her through with the winnowing fork.

"Clumsy girl. You'll be the first to be sold," Ya'achov said, hissing at her.

She scrambled to her feet and went to scoop up the baby. She hurried back to the shop, rocking little Shimon in her arms to quiet him. She sat down in the corner against a pile of rough stone. She bounced the toddler and hummed a haunting lullaby Ama always sang.

Talia liked watching Yeshue at work.

No one other than her mother seemed to notice anything unusual about her twenty-seven-year-old brother. He had the same brown hair and beard, strong nose and dark eyes that every other Jewish man possessed. His daily task of moving heavy stones had made him strong and muscled. His skin was lighter now than Ya'achov's and Yose's since he no longer made the trek to Sepphoris in the hot sun, but he looked every bit the average industrious Galilean man.

No, it wasn't his appearance that made him different. It was the way he held the chisel in his hand, making sure every stone was perfectly proportioned, as if it mattered that each one was done well. It was the tender way he knelt by old Ezra in the vineyard each morning on his way to the prayer house. He would squeeze the man's hand and tell him that Elohim saw, though everyone else ignored the ancient man with so many physical troubles. It was the way Yeshue brushed away tears when the neighbor's mule was mauled and killed by a wildcat. It was how he hugged her tightly, just the way Abba had. It was his measured voice in the midst of the anger and arguing of their home.

He glanced at her as he chipped away bits of rock. She brushed her tears away as Shimon whined and fought for his freedom. The baby crawled toward a scrap pile in search of diversion. It was past time for him to nurse, but she didn't know if she should take him to Ama yet.

"You can tell me your troubles," Yeshue said.

"I don't know why everyone fights all the time since Abba died." The words spilled from her mouth and tears reappeared. Yeshue stopped. He set the chisel on the table and held his arms out, and she came to him. She wished she was small enough to climb into his lap, but it helped to lean against him and feel his embrace.

He sighed in a weary way. "They are heartbroken."

"You are heartbroken, but you don't fight."

He didn't bother to hide the tear that rolled down his cheek. "Neither do you."

They were silent for a long moment. Shimon came to the stool and reached his hands up to his brother to be lifted into his lap. Yeshue obliged him and held him close, fingering a soft baby curl. Shimon caught his finger and squealed. Hunger could be forgotten with the attention of his older brother.

"What do you miss most about Abba?" Yeshue asked.

"His smile. His voice. I miss the way he never let Ya'achov speak against you or Ama. I miss watching him work here in the shop."

"As do I." Yeshue's voice was so soft she barely heard him. "Sometimes I think I sense him near me, but when I turn around there is no one there."

"Brother…" Talia hesitated, unsure whether she should say what she was thinking. He smiled sadly, as if he knew what she would ask him.

"Go ahead," he said.

"I heard Ama say when Abba died that you could have saved him, but you didn't. What did she mean?"

Yeshue leaned his head against hers. "She didn't mean to say that, Talia. She was upset."

"But what did she mean? Could you have made Abba better?"

"Yes." He spoke the truth plainly, as was his custom. She searched his dark eyes, friendly despite his hard life. His eyes smiled even when his mouth did not.

"Why didn't you? We needed him, and you let him die."

"I could tell you you're a child and you wouldn't understand, but I know better. You are a truth seeker. Never stop searching for truth."

"I promise," she said. She waited for his answer. He stood and went to the window where the sun was setting behind Mount Tabor.

"I could not save him, because it was his time to go. God willed it, for so many reasons it would be impossible to try to explain them all. Everything happens to bring about God's plan for those that love him and follow him."

"If I got sick, would you let me die?" Talia frowned. He looked back at her.

"It's not your time. God has a purpose for you."

"Me?" Talia laughed, shocked by his unexpected words. "What would Alaha want with me? I'm a stupid girl who will never have a husband because I'm too quiet and skinny."

"You are repeating your brother's words." Yeshue shook his head, reaching for her again.

"Elohim loves you more than you can imagine," Yeshue whispered close to her ear. "I hope you will grow to know and trust your Creator."

"Me too," Talia murmured in reply. "Yeshue?"

"Yes, child?"

"I love you. I hope you never change."

She heard the smile in his voice when he spoke. "You can count on that."

She nodded. "Please don't ever leave me."

She wanted him to say he wouldn't, but the slight hesitation caused her hopes to plummet. Fear rose like bile in her throat as she waited for him to answer.

He set her back so she could turn around to look at him, and he put his palm against her cheek. "My Spirit will always be with you. Even when I am not."

"I'm afraid," she said. She wanted him to promise never to leave Nazareth. To never be more than a Sabbath day's walk away. But something had warned her he would not be able to promise it.

"I can't do what I need to do for you if I stay in Nazareth for the rest of our lives, Talia." Yeshue looked toward the southern facing wall where a small window gave light to the shop. He was quiet for a long time as Talia played with the baby. Shimon babbled his infant speech, reaching out to pull on Yeshue's rough cloak of woven sheep's wool. The movement brought Yeshue's attention back, and he caught the little fingers in his hand.

He smiled again, a soft, sad smile that did nothing to ease the anxiety welling up in Talia's heart. "Never fear," he said gently. "I will find you a good husband in a couple years and you will be too busy carrying babies to wonder where I am."

She frowned. "May it never be. I will go where you go."

He watched her, thoughtful. "Don't make promises you can't keep, dear one. The road I must walk will not be easy."

"I will go where you go," she repeated stubbornly. She didn't care if he went as far as Britannia. She would go, too. It would be a welcome change from the darkness that clung to their little dwelling, anyway. Yeshue was the only good thing about the house, the family or even their town full of conniving relatives and gossiping know-it-alls.

He didn't admonish her or argue. He smiled as if he was looking at a different version of her, someone far more beautiful. "Talia." He breathed her name and it sounded like a song. "Your name suits you. *Dew from Alaha*. You are refreshment to my soul."

She felt tears sting her eyes as she gazed at his warm brown eyes. "Let me always follow you."

"Amen," he said. "So be it."

TWO

Three Years Later, A.D. 23

Talia searched her surroundings. Everywhere was darkness. Shadows. Something slimy crawled near her feet and water splashed at her legs, as if she was standing in the Jordan River in the middle of the night.

A whisper spoke into her ear, words she didn't understand and a tone that terrified her. She jerked away from the unseen speaker. It only laughed and spoke into the other ear.

She screamed in terror and closed her eyes tightly, hoping that she would be home and safe when she opened them again. But as her eyes opened, she saw she was standing outside Jerusalem.

A terrible storm was brewing in the sky, flashing and swirling blackness that caused a chill to work its way down her back. The hill outside the city she remembered passing when she was little, where she saw the man on the cross, suddenly rose up out of the ground, towering over her with a rough-hewn post protruding from the top.

"Yeshue!" She called as the wind tossed around her tunic and slapped it against her legs. Her scarf blew off her head and her hair fell down around her shoulders. "Where are you?"

At that moment she realized the post was occupied. A man hung on it, his head lolled to one side, his eyes staring straight ahead yet seeing nothing. He was dead.

She could not make out his features, he was so disfigured and the darkness so heavy. But her heart knew who it was.

She screamed again, holding her head and falling to her knees. "Let me die!" she shouted into the darkness. Her voice was swallowed by the silence. She could not live in a world that had defeated *him*. He was the only good thing about this life.

Suddenly her eyes opened and she sat up straight on her pallet, breathless and hoarse, but safe, in the cozy upper room of their home.

"You woke me up, Talia," Twelve-year-old Hannah said irritably as they lay together on their pallet in the dark. "Why are you crying?"

Talia tried to swallow back her sobs, which made her chest ache.

Hannah made a sound of disgust and flipped over, pulling the thin blanket with her. Talia got up and tiptoed across the mud plaster. She climbed down the ladder, causing a sheep in the corner pen to stir in its sleep and make a noise.

"Talia?"

She turned to see her mother sitting by the hearth stove, rotating grain in the stone grinder so they would have bread in the morning.

Talia rushed to Ama's side and kneeled beside her, resting her head in her mother's lap.

"Did you have a bad dream?" Ama stopped her grinding to push away the loose, damp curls around Talia's face.

"He was dead."

Maryam's face paled, but she shook her head with resolve and her eyes darted upward. "No," she said, as if she was also assuring herself. "Yeshue is up on the roof praying. He's fine. Don't say such things!"

"I can't help what I dream," Talia said helplessly. "And I can't stop being scared. Ever since Abba died, I can only think of losing Yeshue, too."

"Oh, Talia," Maryam said with a soft sigh. "You must stop being so selfish. You are not the only one who grieves."

Though Maryam spoke tenderly, Talia heard the reproof in her voice. She considered going to Yeshue and sitting at his feet until dawn. He never seemed to mind her presence and his hand on her head never failed to calm her, even when he was fast asleep.

Maryam stopped her. "You must not bother your brother during the night anymore. He has much work to do and needs his sleep. I wish he wouldn't get up this early to pray, but he said he had things on his mind when I asked if I had woke him. Don't go up there."

Talia gulped back disappointment. "Yes, Ama."

Maryam hesitated, then returned to her grinding as she spoke. "I know you feel scared and sometimes sad, and you don't understand why. It is partly a symptom of growing up and becoming a woman. It will ease as you get older. You must learn to accept it and not let it keep you from sleep. Trust Alaha, as we all must. We have nothing else to trust in."

Talia didn't answer, but went to stoke the fire they would need to bake the bread. She considered how her brother had changed, only in the past few months, it seemed. He was still the same Yeshue he had always been, but he was quieter than he used to be. When he was younger, he had laughed often, enjoying children's play and exploring creation. But as he drew near the age of thirty, she noticed he had become contemplative. Not sad, as Talia or her mother, but thoughtful. As if he knew things that no one else knew, and those thoughts troubled him in ways he couldn't begin to explain to anyone else.

Without his levity, the conflict in their home had only increased.

Dawn eventually came, and sleepy faces began to appear at the ladder. Y'hud and Shimon ran out the door before their mother could stop them, and Hannah went to fetch the water from the well at Maryam's insistence, though she wore a look of insolence as she took up the water jar.

Talia helped her mother knead the bread dough into round cakes and set them in the oven. She watched them as they inflated with pockets of steam and browned around the edges. She was pulling them out when her sister returned from the well.

"Ama, those boys are fighting in the street again!" Hannah called in a singsong voice as she came in with the water jug. She was known for her tale bearing.

Maryam made a noise of frustration as she attempted to throw the hot bread on the coals. Talia saw her mother's eyes dart to the workshop where Yeshue had more orders than time to complete them. When the bread was safely on the table to cool, she stormed out the door.

"Shimon! Y'hud! Get up off that ground and get the sheep up to the pasture. Do you think everything will be handed to you on a platter while you roll around on the ground like a pair of dogs?"

The boys ignored her and continued their angry brawl.

"Must I call your brother from his work? Have you no respect for anyone?"

Talia heard desperation in Maryam's voice. She knew as well as Maryam did that Yeshue could hear her words.

Yeshue did not make Maryam come and find him. He appeared in the passageway and went through the door to the street. He took the boys firmly by the arm and marched them to the shop to be disciplined. Talia knew they would clean up wood chips and gather firewood along with their daily chores. At the young ages of four and eight, they respected Yeshue's authority without question, as if he was their father. They had no memory of Yosef, their true father, and even called Yeshue *Abba*.

"Alaph, Beth, Gammel, Dalath, He ..."

The sounds of her younger brothers reciting the familiar letters came from the shop, causing Talia to smile. "He's determined those boys learn to read."

"If it means they have something to do besides destroy my home and each other, amen, so be it," her mother murmured from across the room. "Why he was so concerned that you and Hannah learn—that is another question."

"Some girls learn to read. Some families even send their daughters to the school at the prayer house."

"Foolishness," Maryam said, but she smiled as if she did not mind as much as she claimed. "What use will letters ever be to a girl who must bake bread and weave cloth and have babies?"

Talia shrugged. She didn't tell her mother how much she enjoyed being able to read. Language fascinated her. Seeing the very words of

God in Scripture for herself felt like an honor. She was thankful her brother had been willing to sacrifice his precious time to teach his sisters.

"Ama, if Ya'achov and Yose do not learn to respect Yeshue, I worry that Y'hud and Shimon will learn to disrespect him as well. Hannah has even been impudent with him at times." Talia's words tumbled from her mouth and caused her mother to look up sharply. She knew it was not her place to question, but she did not understand her siblings' rebellion. The rare times Yeshue had been disappointed in Talia, her world had crumbled.

Maryam's face softened, and her shoulders slumped as she set the tray of dried fish and fresh bread on the table. She went to get the pitcher of watered wine and the jar of olive oil.

"Let your brother handle it," was all Maryam said in reply as the boys burst back into the room. They saw the bread on the table and went running for it until Yeshue stepped into the room behind them.

"Wait, boys." He did not speak angrily. It was not Yeshue's way. He spoke firmly at times, but he never lost control. His quiet instruction made the boys stop in their tracks.

"We will wait for our brothers."

Most of the farming families they lived alongside in Nazareth didn't make time for a morning meal. They took bread, dried fruit or nuts along with them in their pack to eat as they worked. Yeshue had long ago decided the family should have provisions in the morning before they went their separate ways.

"It is good to start the day with nourishment and thankfulness," he explained cheerfully when Ya'achov complained about losing time in his work day. "Besides, sometimes you do not come home from Sepphoris until the children are asleep. Do you not want your children to know you?"

Ya'achov grumbled, but eventually he gave up and heartily ate his breakfast.

Today, Ya'achov and Yose had a big delivery of stones to load onto the carts they would pull into the city for sale. Most of them were already contracted to go to Herod's workmen building a theater. When they finally loaded the last one, the brothers appeared in the doorway, already sweaty and out of breath though the sun had barely risen above the horizon and the air was still cool.

"Let's thank Alaha," Yeshue invited. Everyone bowed their heads and the little ones kneeled on the dusty floor. Yeshue took the bread from the table and broke it into pieces as he spoke. "Praise you, Adonai, for this food you have given to nourish and strengthen us this day. May our thoughts and actions be reflections of our trust in Yehovah Yireh—our God who provides."

A chorus of *amens* followed his prayer and then everyone reached for the food. Maryam passed chunks of bread to little ones as Ya'achov' and Yose's wives handed cups of goat's milk to their husbands.

Besides Y'hud and Shimon, Ya'achov and his wife, Nava, had a daughter, Amaris and a baby boy, Caleb. Yose's wife, Ariel, was heavy with child. Talia had noticed she was starting to support her large stomach with her hands as she moved around the house. She remembered that Maryam had done that just before Shimon was born.

The room was barely big enough to hold all of them. They usually ate in the courtyard, but when Ya'achov, Yose and their wives were in a hurry to get to Sepphoris for Market Day, they barely took enough time to sit and chew their food, let alone gather in the courtyard outside Maryam's tiny kitchen area.

Talia surveyed the room as she ate the fresh warm bread dipped in a grape and nut sauce. The chamber was the original room of the house Yosef had built when the family had moved to Nazareth from Alexandria, Egypt. When Yeshue, Ya'achov and Yose were old enough to help, Yosef had added a second story. When Ya'achov turned eighteen, he already had his extra room built, connected to the main house by the courtyard. He married Nava as soon as the marriage contract could be made by the scribe in Sepphoris. Yose had followed suit by building his own room and marrying Ariel.

You boys marry so young because of all the stone we have in our shop! Yosef used to tease them, knowing the boys had an advantage because of access to free building materials.

The adults besides Maryam and Yeshue left, and Yeshue went to the shop to work. Maryam sat down in a cool corner of the house to card wool that they would later weave into new tunics for the men, whose clothes were beginning to look threadbare.

Talia and Hannah were responsible for the younger children, and in usual fashion, Hannah disappeared after they took the children to the olive grove to play. Talia didn't mind. She sat under an olive tree and helped the neighbor separate the olives that had been shaken out, showing her little brothers and her niece how to help.

They went home when the sun was high overhead and Talia put the children in the upper room of the main house for a nap. Y'hud escaped and took off down the road to find his friends, but Talia didn't chase after him. She went to help Maryam instead.

"Talia, you are a good girl," Maryam said as she handed Talia a length of wool. "I will miss you when you leave us."

Talia's eyes flew up to meet her mother's. It was the first time her mother had mentioned it, though Talia had been dreading the conversation.

"I don't want to leave."

"You became a woman over a year ago. I'm sure Yeshue is thinking about finding you a husband. It is the way of things. You know that."

Talia felt hot tears sting her eyes and a lump form in her throat. Maryam shook her head and was about to say something else when Yeshue appeared in the doorway between the house and the shop.

He smiled at Talia. "Yeshue is thinking about it, but Yeshue will not make any decisions without talking to you first."

The twinkle in his eye helped her relax. She had no right to expect him to include her in the decision. Fathers made matches they thought were best; rarely did a daughter have any say in the process leading up to a marriage. It was another way Yeshue showed himself to be different than everyone else around him.

"Yeshue, Talia has no idea what she needs in a husband," Maryam admonished softly, though her tone was respectful.

"Talia knows more than you think, Ama." Yeshue came to stand behind his mother and placed his hands on her shoulders. "She is my little *n'vee*."

Talia frowned. "Why do you think I am a prophetess?"

He pulled his cloak around him and tied his belt. With a wink, he left and walked in the direction of the prayer house.

The memory of the dream returned as she watched him go. She tightly closed her eyes against the image of her dead brother.

Why did he call her a prophetess? Would the dream come true? She clutched at her chest as fear tightened its grip around her anxious, weary heart.

When the sun sank below the tops of the trees and the air cooled; when farmers headed in from the fields and rowdy boys ran home from rabbi school, it was somehow easier to forget her worries. Talia enjoyed suppertime best.

As she and Hannah filled the courtyard table with bowls of steaming lentil soup, their brothers came through and sank to the ground around the low table. Hannah served wine and barley cakes, though she set a cup of water in front of Ya'achov. He was under the Nazarite vow, so he did not drink wine. Ya'achov took it and gulped it down. He set down the cup hard and pushed his unruly, sweaty hair behind his shoulders. Ya'achov' hair was always an impossibly long, tangled mass. His wife often tried to loosen the snarls in the evening, but hair that had never been cut was not easily tamed.

"I can't remember a day as hot as today," Yose complained before he took a long drink of wine.

"It was awful heat," Ya'achov grunted. "Did you get the order done for tomorrow, Yeshue?"

"I have two stones left." Yeshue sat beside his brothers and offered the evening prayer, breaking his cake and handing half to Shimon, who sat in his lap.

"I was hoping we'd get the full order in for once." Ya'achov eyed his older brother. Yeshue met his gaze evenly.

"I learned about Jonah today in school," Y'hud said, either not sensing or ignoring the adult tension in the air.

"Did Yeshue teach you?" Ya'achov shared a look with Yose.

"Yes," Y'hud said blankly, as if he wondered who else would do it.

"This has gone far enough!" Ya'achov threw down his bread as his voice got louder. "You must finish your work before you go to the prayer house, Yeshue!"

Yeshue didn't respond right away. He finished his bite of soup and took a drink of wine. "You forget the Shema, Ya'achov," he said calmly.

"I know the Shema. You forget I am a Nazarite. I say the Shema every time I go to worship and I say it with all my heart. But I don't say it when I'm supposed to be working!"

"What does the Shema tell us?" Yeshue looked at Y'hud and Shimon with a smile. "Do you remember, Shimon?"

"Hear O Israel, the Lord our God, the Lord is one." Shimon recited proudly.

"What is your point? How does the Shema excuse you from work?"

"The Lord is one. There is no separation. I must be about my Father's business."

"That's exactly what I'm telling you to do!" Ya'achov made a loud sound of irritation.

Yeshue smiled again at the boys. "Take your meal up to the roof and be careful to stay away from the edge."

Y'hud and Shimon happily complied, walking carefully so they did not spill their soup or drop their bread.

"Watch your temper, Ya'achov. The boys need strong examples."

"Oh, you're one to talk," Ya'achov replied with a sputter. "You seem to think the only thing to life is hanging around the prayer house with the rabbi and telling your little stories. I hate to be the one to tell you, but no one's listening! Everyone wishes you'd just go home and do your job. You're a joke! Do you hear what the neighbors say about you?"

Yeshue didn't answer. Talia stood near the doorway of the courtyard and clenched her fists at her side.

"When is that crazy Yeshue bar Yosef going to take a wife and have

a family? Why does he spend so much time studying the Torah like a rabbi?" Ya'achov mimicked the voices of the alleged gossiping villagers.

Yeshue still didn't speak. Ya'achov smirked and Yose shook his head.

Talia turned to her mother. "Ama, they must stop!"

Maryam shook her head, the grim lines of her mouth hard as she set dates and figs with grapes on a plate to serve the men. "What can we do about it? They're grown men. Yeshue knows how to take care of himself."

"But they're wrong! How can they not see it? He is so different from them."

"They're sinful. They don't know what they're doing."

Talia sighed. "I'm sinful too, Ama, but I know better than to speak against the M'sheekha."

Maryam squatted next to the fire and pulled the fish from the pot to plate them. "The M'sheekha can handle himself without a girl's interference, don't you think?"

Talia took the plates she handed her and went out into the courtyard to place them on the table.

"Thank you, Talia," Yeshue said in a cheerful voice. She could see his smile was strained, but his thankful attitude was genuine. She nodded.

"Get out, girl, we're talking." Ya'achov shooed her away.

"There is no reason to be unkind," Yeshue said firmly.

"Don't tell me what to do," Ya'achov shot back. "Since Abba died you think you can order everyone around."

"Your father would not be pleased with your attitude," Yeshue reminded him.

Ya'achov exploded. "He's only *my* father now? You're too holy to have a father? I suppose you really believe our mother's hysterical little tale of your miraculous conception?"

Yose looked uncomfortable. "There's no need to bring all that up, Ya'achov."

"I didn't bring it up, Yeshue did! Anyway, it's time someone says it aloud." Ya'achov turned his attention back to Yeshue, who had set down his soup and was staring at it. "Women don't have babies but for one reason. There's only one way you were born, and as much as no one likes to talk about it, I'll be bold. Our parents came together before they should have. They made a good story to cover their shame. It worked at the time, but we're all grown now. You're grown. You haven't saved your people. You've taught a few children in the prayer house, and you've chiseled a few stones for Herod's monuments. That's it. No wife, no family. You haven't amounted to anything."

Talia watched as Ya'achov pushed back from the table and got up. He stormed out of the courtyard. He pushed past his wife and went into their small house.

Yeshue placed his hands on his face and sighed deeply.

THREE

Ya'achov

יעקב

Ya'achov didn't dare look his wife in the eye or cast a glance in the direction of his mother's kitchen. He felt guilty enough for the way he had spoken to his older brother. He thought the words so often, and once or twice he'd muttered them to Yose, but he had never said them so openly to Yeshue before this night.

He went through the house and out into the neighbor's olive grove. He sunk to the ground next to an old gnarled olive tree. The winding strands of wood tangled up and bound together were his thoughts, he mused as he ran a hand over the rough surface.

"Someone had to say it," he said to no one. *I was doing him a favor by telling him the truth. He's been told his whole life by our mother that he's the savior of the world. Who wouldn't want to believe it?*

So why did guilt still plague him?

When Ya'achov was very young, he'd followed Yeshue everywhere and believed every word he said. But as he got older it started to irritate him that Yeshue was never punished. Ya'achov had been disciplined almost constantly by his father, mostly for losing his temper. And as their parents told the boys about Yeshue's miraculous birth, Ya'achov secretly began to resent the *miracle son*. The bitterness lived inside his heart, festering and growing as he grew taller. Now he could hardly stand to look at Yeshue. Everything about him was so deceivingly perfect. He never lost his temper and he always knew what to say. Yeshue had a way of making Ya'achov feel like a failure without saying a word.

His considerations sparked a memory he didn't like to think about. But the scenes returned to him without his permission. A bad taste filled his mouth.

Ya'achov had been nine when Yeshue brought the injured animal home.

"Yeshue! That's a filthy dog on my table!" Ama said loudly.

"Someone hurt him. I found him in the street. He's just a pup."

Ya'achov felt embarrassed when his brother's eyes filled with tears.

"He's in pain," Yeshue said.

"I'll take it outside and end its suffering." Abba reached for the whimpering animal. It was covered in dirt and leaves and its leg was bent at an unnatural angle and bleeding.

Yeshue took the animal in his arms before Abba could reach for him. "Wait."

They all stood around and gawked at Yeshue while he whispered words Ya'achov couldn't hear. He rocked it gently like Ama rocked her sleepy babies in the cool of the evening. The sound of his voice was like a melody never sung before. A prayer never prayed before. Suddenly there was an audible snap.

"There." Yeshue set the dog down and it wagged its tail and stared at Yeshue. It was well. It turned in a circle and looked down at the leg that had been broken as if it didn't understand what had happened.

"What did you do?" Maryam stepped forward, her eyes large and afraid. "What did you do, Yeshue?"

"I wanted it to be well. I was thinking about him whole and happy, and I guess I must have pushed the leg back into place." Yeshue chuckled as the dog jumped on him and licked his hands.

The family stood there and stared at him. None of them knew what to say. Ama looked like she might burst into tears.

"You're a sorcerer," Ya'achov accused.

"Ya'achov!" Maryam cried in disbelief. She spat on the ground, as if to cleanse the room of the evil he had unleashed.

He didn't say anymore. And though dogs are vile creatures who are a nuisance to everyone, Yeshue kept his dog as a special pet. The animal followed him everywhere and slept outside their dwelling as if to protect its master from harm. Yeshue took the scraps from his own plate to feed the dog, and taught it how to chase sticks in the meadow.

"That thing will bring disease into our home," Maryam complained day after day, but she never made him get rid of it. Eventually everyone came to accept it as part of the family. Neighbors made fun of them and gossiped about strange Yeshue who put spells on dogs. What sort of magic would he do next?

One day Yeshue got to go with Abba on a special trip to Sepphoris. Abba said he had an important rabbi in the city who wanted to talk with Yeshue. Ya'achov fumed inside.

"You have outgrown the rabbi here in town," Abba said to Yeshue, unaware of Ya'achov's dark thoughts. "I'd like you to study with this man in Sepphoris when I come to market."

Ya'achov continued to rage within as he was sent to clean up wood chips in the workshop. He didn't dare question his father, but the unfairness of Yeshue's special treatment plagued him all afternoon while he worked.

Suddenly, Yeshue's dog came through the door and looked at him, wagging his tail.

"Go away!" he yelled and went after the dog with a broom. The dog yelped and ran out the door.

Ya'achov picked up another chip, but a thought took hold of him and wouldn't let him go.

I could get rid of the dog. No one would ever know it was me, and that would show Yeshue.

At first, he dismissed the idea, but by suppertime he had convinced himself that no one would be sorry to see the ugly mutt go. People killed dogs all the time if they were a nuisance. It was the way of things.

That night, before his father and Yeshue returned from the city, Ya'achov found the creature and grabbed it by the legs, shoving it into a sack while it cried in protest.

"What are you doing, Ya'achov?" His mother called from the courtyard.

"Nothing," he said, and stole out the door before she could come to check.

He ran down to the well. It was late in the day and no one was there, so he took the bag and held it over the opening. Before he could change his mind, he let it go.

A final yip and a splash signified the end of Yeshue's dog.

Ya'achov had smiled at the time. He felt a certain victory. He'd done something to control his brother's life instead of his brother always controlling his. He'd had the final say. And no one but Yeshue would ever care that he'd done it.

When Abba and Yeshue came home a few minutes later, Yeshue excitedly told Ama about the day he'd had in Sepphoris and all the things he'd learned. When he finally stopped, he went to the workshop door and whistled for his dog.

"Poor thing must be hungry," he said to himself. Ya'achov stood back and watched him, trying not to smile at his prank.

When the dog didn't come, Yeshue came back into the house. "Ama, I am going to walk down the path and try to find my dog."

Maryam nodded from where she sat rocking the baby.

Yeshue didn't come back until after the sun had set, and Maryam was calling him from the door. He wasn't smiling when he came inside. His eyes were red and swollen and he held a wet bundle in his arms.

"Someone threw him in the well," Yeshue said to Maryam.

Maryam took the bundle and set it on the ground, then took her son in her arms and held him while he cried.

"He was just an animal," Yeshue said, his voice muffled against her tunic. "Why would anyone be so cruel?"

"That well is our drinking water," Maryam said in disbelief. "What were they thinking?"

Yeshue cried. And Ya'achov felt the wound on his soul bleed and fester. Suddenly, he could see what he'd done.

Sorrow eventually hardened into bitterness. He blamed Yeshue for what had happened, because if it hadn't been for his "perfect" older brother, he'd have never done it in the first place.

Ya'achov saw his mother approach as he heard the steady pounding of hammer to stone begin in the shop. Apparently Yeshue would make use of every last bit of daylight to finish the stones he had left.

"I suppose you're going to tell me I should be ashamed of making Yeshue feel guilty." Ya'achov folded his thick arms across his chest, feeling like a pouting child. He stared straight ahead as his mother sat down beside him.

"Yeshue doesn't feel guilty, Ya'achov. He was already planning on finishing those after dinner. He said so earlier."

Ya'achov seethed.

"You haven't had an easy life, have you?" Maryam smiled and reached for Ya'achov' unruly curls, smoothing them back behind his ear. "Always in the shadow of your brother."

Ya'achov was surprised by her words, though he didn't say so. He couldn't remember a time either of his parents had ever recognized his internal struggle. It soothed his anger, if only a little.

"Well, none of us have an easy life," he said gruffly.

"I wish there was some way I could prove the stories your father and I told you about Yeshue's birth."

Ya'achov shifted uncomfortably. He could imagine his accusations had hurt her. He was glad he hadn't mentioned the village gossip about how Yeshue didn't look like the rest of his siblings. His skin was a different shade of olive and his hair and eyes were a lighter brown. He wondered if Maryam had given herself to another man before Yosef. As much as he didn't think Yeshue was Spirit-born, he didn't like the town making fun of Yeshue or Maryam, either.

Ya'achov made himself look at her.

Maryam was in her early forties. Her hair had not turned to silver and her skin was still relatively smooth. But something in her eyes made her seem older, as if the inner struggles of her life had aged her beyond what they should have.

"You look tired, Ama," Ya'achov spoke gently.

She glanced at him and nodded. "I am tired with years of anxious prayers for my children."

Ya'achov considered her words. "I'm sorry. I spoke too harshly."

She nodded, meeting him with a direct gaze. "If what you suspect was true, I would have told you."

Ya'achov knew the passion his mother had for her story. She had probably told it so fervently for such a long time, she sincerely believed it was true. He patted her hand. "True or not, I had no place to say anything. You are to be respected. Would that I could take my words back."

Maryam sighed at his evasive answer. Ya'achov stood up and headed back to his house, unable to bear any more conversation about Yeshue's supposed divinity. It had divided their family since the first time Maryam had spoken of angels and prophecies and stars and wise men bearing gifts.

It wasn't fair. Ya'achov felt he should be treated as an equal to Yeshue now that they were grown. And Yeshue shouldn't be above correction. How could he mature without discipline? It was why he was shirking his duties now, and why he didn't give anyone else consideration. He only did what pleased him. And what a dreamer he was! Always posing questions and thinking up stories better left to the old rabbi with no responsibilities.

Ya'achov was afraid he was going to lose everything trying to make up for Yeshue's carelessness. And he didn't like to think about it, but he sensed and dreaded a truth becoming clearer every day. Yeshue was pulling away from them. Ya'achov suspected he would leave the family. And that would put all the burden of their care on Ya'achov.

Maryam's voice stopped him before he stepped back into the house.

"Think on something, Ya'achov," she said. "What if God does not mean for Yeshue to be a *tekton* and fashion stone and wood all his days?

What if God means for him to be a rabbi and fashion men instead? Who are we to argue with Elohim, whether it suits us or not?"

Ya'achov avoided her eyes. "Why was I put under the Vow?"

His abrupt question surprised her. She hesitated.

"It was your father's wish."

"Why? Did he give you a reason?"

She nodded. "He said he felt it was the will of Alaha."

"Was one special son not enough?" Ya'achov asked, hearing the impatience in his voice.

She shook her head. "Your brother being special does not mean you are worthless. Maybe that was why Yosef willed you to be a Nazarite. Maybe he hoped you would understand it is for all of us to do the work of God, not just the rabbis. Not just the *M'sheekha*."

Ya'achov wanted to argue, but Maryam left. He exhaled, running his fingers through his tangled hair. Would Alaha go against the accepted order of things? Would he call a builder to be a rabbi if he had little ones needing bread and a business that needed to be run? What could be so important that Adonai would change the rules?

In the twilight, Ya'achov heard the clanging stop. Candles had been lit, and Ya'achov saw his brother's form as he came to stand in front of the window. Yeshue's eyes turned heavenward and Ya'achov heard his whispered prayer.

"Father, let your will be done. Accomplish what you desire."

Ya'achov had to strain to hear the softly spoken words. He shook his head. "If only you truly meant that."

Dawn came before Ya'achov was ready for it. He moaned as his wife rose and rolled her pallet away. She went to the beds of their children to wake them.

"Wife, I feel a hundred years old this morning." He yawned loudly.

"You look more like two-hundred."

He laughed and rolled his mat to the side of the room. He grabbed his wife around the waist and kissed her on the mouth.

"Would that my husband was this affectionate every morning," she said as she pushed him away with a smile and went to the fussing baby.

"Abba!" Ya'achov's little daughter screeched with delight. She wrapped her small arms around his neck and tangled her fingers in his hair. Her large dark eyes were framed by beautiful brown curls. Ya'achov swelled with pride every time they went to the prayer on the Shabbat, for everyone loved to compliment the small child's beauty. Ya'achov had been disappointed his little Amaris was not a son when she was born, but now he wouldn't trade her for ten sons.

Once they reached the courtyard, he remembered why he hadn't wanted to get up that morning. Yeshue was already reclining at the table, drilling Y'hud on some obscure part of the Torah. Ya'achov grabbed a handful of figs and a cup of water and went to the shop to finish a table he was making for a rich man in Sepphoris.

As he worked with the smooth olive wood, his idle mind returned to a memory from Passover in Jerusalem when he was just a boy—ten or eleven years old. When the feast was over, the family had left with the caravan headed north to Galilee. Ya'achov played with his cousins, unaware his brother had been left behind in the city. In fact, he was happy to be free of Yeshue's presence, wherever he'd gone. He wasn't going to question it. But three days later, his mother came running.

"Ya'achov, have you seen Yeshue?" Her brows were tense with worry.

He shrugged. "No."

"Yose?" Maryam turned to the younger boy desperately, as if he was her last hope. He slowly shook his head, his eyes large with the fear he saw in her eyes.

"I thought he was with you boys! He's nowhere in the caravan!" Maryam wailed, and Ya'achov frowned. It sounded like she was accusing *him* of losing Yeshue. When had he been responsible for his older brother? Was he Yeshue's personal guardian now?

"I'm sure he's fine." Ya'achov tried not to let his mother see his bitterness.

"Why are you still sitting there?" Maryam pulled him up by the arm.

"Spread the word that we are looking for him! *Azal*! Go!"

Ya'achov knew she wasn't interested in discussion. He went, unwillingly, to ask if any of the relatives had seen Yeshue.

When the word came back that no one had seen him, Ya'achov's parents broke with the caravan, sending the boys and four-year-old D'vora home with Maryam's sister and her family. They returned to Jerusalem to search for their missing son.

They rejoined the caravan several days later with Yeshue in tow. Apparently, they'd found him in the temple. Most boys, finding themselves free, would be expected to run wild in the marketplace or play in one of the pools located around the city. It was what Ya'achov would do. But his strange older brother found it more exciting to spend his freedom with the old men in the temple, discussing theology he had no business thinking about at the age of twelve.

"You should have seen him, answering their questions. They were astounded at all he already knew," Yosef told the other men while Ya'achov fumed. If he'd stayed behind in Jerusalem and his parents had to come back for him, he had little doubt he'd receive a sound beating. Why did Yeshue have a different set of rules than the rest of them?

Ya'achov couldn't figure it out. Yeshue was *no* different. He had the same worn clothing and sandals that made all the city dwellers turn up their nose. His features matched every other Jewish boy. He ate the same diet of barley bread and lentil soup, slept on the same mat in the sleeping loft with Ya'achov and Yose, went to the same prayer house and learned his reading and writing lessons from the same decrepit rabbi. What made Yeshue so special?

Ya'achov had pondered the question his entire life, even to this very moment as he sat carving a table leg. He realized his anger had caused him to strip away too much of the soft wood, and now the table would be lopsided. He uttered a curse and threw it across the room where it smashed to pieces against a stone block ready to go on the cart.

"What troubles you, brother?" Yeshue stood in the doorway, obviously witness to his outburst.

"Cursed thing didn't turn out right," he mumbled. He got up to start loading stones before Yeshue could give him a lecture about curses.

"I'll fix it later this morning," Yeshue offered instead. He helped Ya'achov pry the heavy blocks onto rolling logs that would get them to the reinforced ox cart. Sweat quickly poured down their faces, soaking their clothes as the sun beat down on their skin.

Another day had begun.

"I hate work," he complained to Yose when they were on their way to Sepphoris. "Did Adonai really put us here to move stones, eat, sleep and have sons? Are we going to be moving these blocks from here to there until the day we die?"

Yose made a face and shrugged, content to let his brother complain. It was their way. He leaned back and chewed on a stalk of wheat as they passed the prayer house. The rabbi lifted a weathered hand in greeting.

"He gets to sit in the shade and rest. What I wouldn't give to have that kind of life. I should have enjoyed it more as a boy. When you become a man all you have is work." Ya'achov huffed.

It was noon when they reached the city. The marketplace was loud and crowded when they came through the gate. Sounds of building echoed everywhere. Structures had grown taller even since the day before. Herod's prized theater looked nearly done when they climbed the steps and surveyed the progress. They waited for the foreman to see them. It didn't take him long.

"Just in time! I'm almost out of stones. I've come to depend on you," he said as he followed them to the oxcart. He ran his hand over the blocks and nodded his approval. "Your brother does meticulous work. I wish all the tektons who bring us stone made them as well as Yeshue does."

He motioned for workers clad in girded tunics to take the blocks before he counted coins into Ya'achov's hand.

"If you ever want to earn some extra money, I'll hire you or your brother to work on some of the details inside the theater. We always need skilled workers."

"We'll keep it in mind." Ya'achov nodded. "Yeshue and I worked on this very theater with our father years ago."

"Ah, yes. No wonder it is so sound! Your father will have to come see it when it is finished."

"He's dead." Ya'achov squeezed the coins in his hand and headed for the well to refresh his water skin, leaving Yose to say parting words.

Ya'achov tried to ignore the merchants on either side of the road, shoving wares in his face and eyeing the money bag he was still tucking inside his belt. Yosef's family had no need to buy anything in Sepphoris. Nazareth was an agricultural village. They had olives, grapes, grain and sheep in abundance. Especially during the harvest. They made their own clothes with animal skins and wool. They made their own pottery and household tools. Everyone took responsibility for their neighbors and relatives. After all, the people of Nazareth shared a common ancestor. They had all come from the line of King David. Their ancestors had journeyed from Persia to make their home here on these Galilean cliffs after the exile. Most of the two-hundred people living in the village were the descendants of those pilgrims. They were dependent on one another, and fiercely proud of their heritage. Though the city dwellers and foreigners looked down on them for their simple life and reclusive ways, they ignored the outside world as best they could. After all, they had come from kings.

Ya'achov knew what the prophets had said about the house of Judah. The M'sheekha would come from their family. It was hard to be objective with King David's royal blood running through his veins. He was every bit as much a candidate to be the M'sheekha as Yeshue.

He must have been smirking, because Yose gave him a look. "What?"

"I'm just thinking. I could be the Promised One, you know." He snorted as Yose rolled his eyes.

"Great. Now I've got two brothers who want to claim the throne," Yose said with an exaggerated sigh.

"I'll have you know I'm of the line of David."

"I'll have you know I am, too," Yose said. "I guess we'll have to fight for it."

"Done!" Ya'achov grabbed his walking stick and wielded it in the air, shouting a battle cry. Yose grinned and did the same. They engaged in a mock swordfight as they had seen Roman soldiers do in Sepphoris from the time they were small boys. Finally, Ya'achov bested Yose by poking him in the chest with his stick.

"I win. Bow to me, you filthy Nazarene. You should have known better than to challenge a man under the Vow. I have miraculous strength, you know. Like Samson."

Yose chuckled and gave a mock bow. "You have my allegiance, oh wise M'sheekha! I didn't want to have to go up against Herod or Caesar, anyway."

Ya'achov grunted as they got back on the wagon. "It would take more than a few Jewish rebels. Enough have tried it to know that."

Their voices were hushed as they spoke, and both of them glanced around the cart to make sure there were no soldiers nearby who might overhear their careless words. It would not do to be arrested on suspicion of inciting a rebellion.

"Remember old Judah? He was so sure he was going to be the one to defeat them," Ya'achov said as they rolled the cart out of the city. "The garrison completely destroyed them before they even started the battle."

"He was a fool," Yose said. "As any of the other fools before him who have tried. It's better just to live quietly. Not make any waves."

"You speak like a new husband and father," Ya'achov teased. "Don't you want to be free like any other good Jew in Israel?"

Yose shrugged. "Of course. But I don't want to put my family in danger over it."

Ya'achov clapped his shoulder. "Me either, brother. But I sure would like to see someone beat them, wouldn't you? Can you imagine living without worry that we won't have enough to pay our taxes to the emperor? Without having to keep our heads low lest some soldier decides to take our wife or daughter? Alaha intended for this land to be our inheritance. Yet it's overrun with heathens."

Yose nodded. They drove in silence for a time.

"What if Yeshue really is the M'sheekha?" Yose suddenly asked a few minutes later. His tone was quiet. Contemplative.

Ya'achov nodded. "I've considered it. But it doesn't make sense. What is he going to do against a power like Caesar? He'd be crushed if he tried, just like all the others. He's not even a fighter; he never has been."

"I guess that's what I'm afraid of," Yose admitted. "That he's going to get himself killed. He doesn't seem to be able to let things go. I know he's impossible sometimes, but he *is* our brother and I don't want to see him get hurt."

Ya'achov had nothing to say in reply. They lapsed into silence again. When the village of Nazareth was visible on the horizon, Yose spoke again. "If he makes a stand, will you stand with him?"

Ya'achov felt blindsided by the question. And yet the question had always been there in his mind. What *would* he do if Yeshue stood up to Rome?

"I don't know."

"I don't either."

Ya'achov shrugged off the uncomfortable tension his brother's question had caused. "Well, hopefully we'll never have to make that choice. We have a life in Nazareth. People mostly leave us alone there, as long as the harvest is good and we can pay our taxes. Maybe Yeshue will come to his senses, find a woman to marry and get over his wild ideas."

"Amen. May it be so." Yose raised his water skin and took a long drink.

Although he smiled, Ya'achov felt hollow within. What was he saying? Didn't every Jewish man have within him the innate desire for freedom? Had he not prayed for M'sheekha to come his entire life?

But that was when M'sheekha was a nameless, faceless entity with limitless power and authority. If M'sheekha was a simple stonemason from a tiny village, who had the Torah memorized but didn't own a sword—what did that mean for their people? For their family?

FOUR

Hannah

חנה

"Ya'achov and Yose are returning!" Twelve-year-old Hannah peered off into the distance. She turned back to the well and watched Talia dutifully put down the water jug and reach for the rope that raised the bucket inside the well.

"Some days I hate being a woman." Hannah tossed her jug in the dirt and fell beside the stone well, kicking off her sandals to rub her dusty feet.

"And you think being a man would spare you work?" Her older sister Talia turned the lever and brought up the bucket full of water. Hannah glanced at her sister. Talia was tall and quiet. Meek as a lamb and boring as the old rabbi. Her only interesting features were her large dark eyes.

"I never said I wanted to be a man." Hannah huffed in disgust. "I want to be a queen. Like Esther."

"Queen Esther was a refugee orphan who was torn away from the only family she had left to enter a harem devoted to a pagan king."

Hannah scrunched her nose. "Maybe not Esther." She tossed her hair behind her and reached for cool water from Talia's jug to splash on her face. Talia regarded her evenly before she reached for Hannah's jug to fill it up.

"Cleopatra," Hannah decided.

Talia gasped in shock. "Hannah, why would you want to be a pagan?"

Hannah laughed at her sister's expression. Talia was so innocent and wholesome. It was fun to tease her. "I think it would be interesting to be a pagan for a while."

"You shouldn't say that," Talia said, her tone urgent and her eyes wide. "Do you understand what happens to pagans?"

Hannah rolled her eyes. "Of course. I have the same brother as you who wants everyone to know what happens to pagans."

"Don't talk about Yeshue that way." Talia's eyes flashed with anger, making Hannah wish she hadn't brought him up. The conversation was starting to bore her.

"Sorry," she said, not out of true remorse, but so Talia would drop the matter. As Talia drew up the second bucket of water, Hannah wandered to the edge of the path and looked up the hill, catching a flirtatious smile from Reuben, son of Jonah who was coming down the path from his father's vineyard. Reuben was seventeen and had a reputation as a troublemaker in the village. Hannah liked him. He always smiled at her as if she was beautiful, and she thought he was handsome.

"I can't wait until the harvest celebration next week." Hannah thought ahead to the party when all the villagers would gather at the vineyard to stomp the grapes used to make wine.

"Hannah, stop smiling at him," Talia said, shaking Hannah's arm and handing her the jug. "He was caught stealing from Uncle Ezra. He's should be thanking Alaha he wasn't sold as a slave."

"All boys steal sometimes, Talia," Hannah said loftily, turning and following her sister down the path, though she looked back to meet his gaze one more time with what she hoped was a coy smile. He raised an eyebrow.

"If I catch you talking to him, I'll tell Yeshue," Talia said.

Hannah shrugged. "Yeshue is busy enough he won't care. I'm going to convince him to let me marry Reuben."

Talia nearly dropped her water jug. She stopped and turned around.

"Hannah, no!"

"He'll be eighteen in a month. And I'm already a woman." Hannah made a face at her sister and stalked down the path toward the carpenter shop.

She set the jug down and went into the shop, eager to get to Yeshue before Talia did.

Yeshue glanced at her as she ran her hand along wooden beams that had been tied together and plastered. "What's this?"

He chiseled at the rock he was working on. "It's a piece of roofing. Ezra's was damaged with the rain last week, and I've made a new section for him."

"That's so nice of you, Yeshue," Hannah gushed. "You're an excellent builder. Abba would be proud."

Yeshue set down his chisel and gave her an even expression. "Little girl, I suggest you say what you came to say or take your flattering tongue elsewhere. I have no use for it."

She pouted. "I wasn't flattering. I meant it. You are the best tekton in Nazareth."

"We are the only tekton shop in Nazareth," he reminded her, his voice stern, but his eyes lit with amusement.

"Well, you're better than Ya'achov and Yose."

"Hannah."

"Fine." She took a deep breath. "I wanted to speak to you about Reuben."

"The son of Jonah?" Yeshue returned to his chiseling.

She nodded. "Talia calls him a thief, but it was just one time. We need to give him a chance to prove he's learned better."

"Are you trying to say you want me to arrange a marriage for you to Reuben?"

She nodded. He didn't speak for a time.

"If you were thirteen or fourteen, I would give you the reasons why he is not a good match for you. Since you are twelve, I will only say you are too young."

"I'm not!" Hannah protested loudly. "I became a woman two months ago!"

"I'm aware," Yeshue said as he carefully chiseled out an edge of stone block. "But physical maturity is not the only consideration."

"Abba would let me," she said in a savage tone. "You're so unfair!" She ran from the shop before he could stop her.

Hannah pouted the rest of the day. When she took the bread and wine to the table in the courtyard at supper, she refused to look Yeshue in the eyes.

"Why are you so quiet?" Her mother asked when she returned to the kitchen.

"I have nothing to say," Hannah replied with dramatic flair she hoped left an impression. Maryam let the matter drop. She mumbled something under her breath about preferring boys to girls at this age.

Dinner was loud and crowded as usual, so it was easy for Hannah to sneak away. She went down the path at dusk as a comfortable cool settled over the village. Children came out in the streets to play. Older men and women sat outside their homes on benches and debated over what the weather might be the next day, or reminisced about the old days or argued about points of contention in the Torah.

It was too dull for Hannah to linger. She had more interesting things to do. She walked further up the path, close to the hill where Reuben lived. The terraced grapevines were full of luscious grapes ready for harvesting. The huge vat for crushing grapes stood ready near the house, as if calling the villagers to come and be a part of the feasting.

Hannah's heart fluttered when she saw Reuben watching her. He sat on the ground in front of the watchtower, carving a piece of wood with a small knife.

"Hello, little Hannah," he said with a smile. The dangerous glint in his eye thrilled her.

She approached and stood near the structure. Watchtowers were built near the fruit when it was ready for harvest. Their family depended on the protection of the vines, so they stayed close to deter thieves.

Hannah noticed the knife and bit of wood in his hands. She was surprised. Their people did not carve images. It was akin to the pagans making gods to worship, a disregarding of the second commandment. "Aren't you afraid you'll get caught?"

He laughed. "I'm not a coward. It's just a little bird. For good luck."

Hannah tried to stifle her initial response, which was fear. What would Yeshue say if he heard Reuben's careless words? But the thought caused a delightful chill to travel up her spine.

"You're brave," she said, glancing around to see if anyone had seen or heard her words.

He jumped up and handed it to her. "For you, little girl. Maybe it will bring you some good luck, no?"

It felt heavy in her hands. For a moment she wished to toss it away from her in fear, but instead she tucked the gift into her robe so no one would see it.

"Shouldn't you be getting home soon? The children are going to bed."

"I'm a woman, not a child." Hannah raised her chin and glared at him until he chuckled.

"A pretty one at that," he admitted. "Better get on home, woman, before your rabbi brother has me stoned."

"I wouldn't let him," she scoffed, but she headed back down the path before Yeshue came looking for her.

"See you at the harvest celebration," Reuben called.

Her heart raced with joy.

The week passed slowly, each day a drudgery. She sat in the prayer house during the hot afternoon as the rabbi droned on and on. Yeshue could not come this week to teach the children, since he would have much work to do before they closed the shop for harvest time. Every able-bodied male in Nazareth stopped his own work and joined the farmers and the women and children in the harvest of the olives, grapes and figs.

I don't know why I have to come to the prayer house if Yeshue doesn't. She thought to herself as she looked around and saw the thin showing of girls compared to the boys. Yeshue had always insisted his sisters go to school until they were thirteen, no matter how many of their friends and family laughed at him for it.

Why does a girl need school, Yeshue? Yeshue had been asked many times. Most of the families in Nazareth sent their girls when they were five or six so that they might have a basic understanding of the laws and prophecies, but no one else kept them there until thirteen. Only more proof that her brother was completely unfair.

Finally, the rabbi dismissed them. That meant it was time for the harvest party.

A joyful group of neighbors and relatives hurried up the hill to the vineyard that stood above Nazareth. Men carried tents, poles and ropes. For the next few days, everyone would camp in the vineyard. All would eat from the harvest and drink the sweet juice their labors produced. It was a welcomed break from the difficult, daily tasks of survival.

Before long, a large group of young girls gleefully jumped on the grapes in the vat. To the sounds of the lyre and flute, the girls sang and danced with abandon. Talia and Hannah kicked off their sandals, rinsed their feet and jumped in. Hannah held on to her sister's arm and laughed as the cold, slippery fruit squeezed through her toes. Soon, their feet up to their ankles were stained with the purple juice. Often someone fell— or was pushed in— and everyone laughed at their expense.

More than once, Hannah raised her gaze and met Reuben's, who seemed to watch her with more interest than he ever had before. She felt her face flush hot. She was glad no one would notice. When they finally climbed out in exhaustion, a new group was ready to take their place. Talia and Hannah ran, laughing, to the tent Yeshue and Ya'achov were constructing close by.

"I'm going with my friends," Hannah announced. Before anyone could protest, she joined a group of girls huddled together and giggling.

She glanced behind her to see if Yeshue would stop her. His features appeared sorrowful. Worried. Part of her regretted for the way she'd acted, and she considered turning back to apologize. But she couldn't. If she did, he'd think she'd lost interest in Reuben. She decided to ignore him. She told the girls about the looks Reuben gave her during the grape-pressing. Their envious expressions were satisfying.

Afternoon faded into evening. The noise of music and celebrating increased as wineskins appeared. Lamps were lit, and people gathered in groups, talking as they sipped sweet red wine from their cups. Girls Hannah's age eventually walked back to their family tents, called by their parents. Hannah saw her family sitting around a fire. Yeshue seemed distracted, peering into the darkness with a concerned crease in his forehead. He was looking for her.

She ducked behind the watchtower to wait until he looked away. His eyes remained fixed in her direction, though she knew there was no way he could see her behind the stone structure.

"My little Hannah-bird has come to keep me company."

She gasped and looked up. Reuben leaned over the side of the watchtower ten feet above her, smirking.

She smiled up at him.

"Are you coming up or what?"

She only hesitated for a moment. Carefully staying near the back so Yeshue wouldn't see her, she nimbly climbed the rope ladder and reached for his hand when she got to the top.

He pulled her inside. She was surprised by how close his face was to hers. It wasn't proper, and he should know better. But she saw the thickness of wine in his eyes and knew he was drunk.

"I'll get in trouble," she said, backing away from him and reaching for the ladder. "I better go."

He grabbed her wrist so tightly she winced. "Don't, lamb. You're always teasing me with your hair peeking out of your scarf and your eyes sparkling like waves on the sea. Tonight, you tease no more."

"Let me go," she said, panic rising in her throat. She wasn't sure what he meant, but she knew she didn't want to be there anymore. The flirting and suggestive glances had been one thing, but the force of his grip and the look in his eyes scared her. She opened her mouth to scream, but he silenced her with a hand and pushed her down onto the rough wooden floor of the tower.

"This is what you wanted, isn't it?" He laughed as she tried in vain to scramble away from him. "You were begging for me to love you, just admit it."

She shook her head and tried in vain to make noise louder than the rustling of the trees in the wind. She needed to alert someone. Hot tears sting her eyes.

"Just listen for a minute, Hannah. If you promise to be quiet, I'll take my hand away."

She hesitated, then nodded. He relaxed his grip.

"Will your brother give you to me if I ask him?"

"Yes," she lied. "I'll talk him into it."

He studied her for a moment. He shook his head. "You're lying. The only way I'll have you is to take you now."

She tried to plead with him. "Just wait until I am thirteen. Then he'll let us marry," she whispered.

"That's too long to wait. This is the best way. Trust me."

He kissed her then. She felt embarrassed, but enjoyed the nearness more than she expected she would. She squeezed her eyes shut and banished all thought of consequences, and she let him have his way.

The villagers were quiet and the night only lit by dying embers of fires and the half-moon in the sky. The chill traveled up her legs as Hannah climbed down from the tower. It reminded her of the cold she felt inside. Icy terror spread over her mind as she considered what she was now. Who she had become in the space of a few stolen minutes.

She couldn't face her family, so she silently slipped down the path to their home, now empty because of the harvest feast. A few sheep standing in the pen eyed her suspiciously as she came in. Was her shame that obvious?

She climbed the ladder and went to her pallet, curling into a heap in the corner, wishing she could curl up so tightly that she disappeared and was never seen again. How could she look her mother or her sister in the eye, ever again? Would Ya'achov and Yose beat her when they found out? Would they kill Reuben, like the vengeful brothers of Dinah when she was violated by Prince Shechem? Would she be stoned?

But no thought was as horrifying as considering what Yeshue would say. How he would mourn when he discovered her foolish actions.

Why had she done such a thing? She turned her head into her robe and sobbed.

Fear consumed her like a great black cloud, choking her. When she heard a creak on the ladder, she gasped.

"No! Don't come in!" she cried. Yeshue stood at the top of the ladder. She could tell he knew. Yeshue always seemed to know, even if there was no way.

He crossed to her and set his lamp in the alcove of the wall. She cowered in the corner as his shadow moved over her. Neither of them spoke. When she finally dared to peek at him, he had covered his face with his hands.

"Brother?" she whispered, venturing from her corner and crawling on the floor to touch his feet. He uncovered his face and she saw the evidence of tears under his eyes. She had been afraid of his anger, but she realized his pain was much harder to bear.

"Hannah, what have you done?" His voice broke with emotion.

"I have sinned!" She sobbed again, wishing she could lower herself further than the floor beneath her.

"Why?" he asked, his voice barely more than a whisper.

Why? How could she tell him why when she had no idea? Should she lie and tell him Reuben forced her? Should she reveal Reuben's plan to convince Yeshue to let them marry? She had no idea how to explain herself to her brother, not with tears of disappointment and betrayal in his eyes. It would have been far easier to come up with a defense if he had responded in anger.

Yeshue gave a ragged sigh, as if her sin caused him physical pain.

She had no response, so she waited quietly, resigned to whatever he would decide. He could easily convince the town to stone both Reuben and Hannah. She'd never seen it happen, but the old rabbi had warned the children about God's prescribed punishment for this kind of sin. She knew her people did not take it lightly. She had never imagined the line between an innocent virgin and a ruined sinner was so thin. So invisible she hadn't even seen herself stepping over the threshold.

The only other option Yeshue had was to allow them to marry. He was quiet for what seemed like hours. She waited in the dirt, not daring to move a muscle.

"Hannah, do you have anything to say before I do what I must do?"

"I'm sorry, Yeshue. I'm so sorry."

He was quiet for another long moment. "Reuben will pay the bride price and take you as his wife immediately."

Hannah felt a whole new terror. It was as if she had been blinded and now she saw clearly. She would have to leave her home and her family. She would have to live with Reuben and his family and depend on them for her survival.

She saw clearly why Yeshue had denied her request and said she was too young. For as she faced the prospect of becoming a wife, she knew she was nothing more than a terrified child.

Two days later Reuben came with coins and harvested fruit, enough to cover the bride price. Hannah watched the somber exchange between Yeshue and Reuben in front of their home, witnessed by neighbors and relatives. They all shook their head and clicked their tongues, murmuring about the sad state of the two youths who had broken Alaha's law.

Yeshue arranged her dowry by presenting Reuben with their family's two goats, a mother and her kid. Hannah realized with a pang of regret that her family would have no milk or cheese until Yeshue could afford to replace the animals.

Her mother pushed a basket filled with bread, olive oil and blankets into her hands. "You must leave your family, but Adonai be with you." Maryam's words were soft, as if she wasn't completely sure they were true, but Hannah appreciated her saying them, anyway. She wished to run into Maryam's arms and feel the tender embrace of her mother one more time, but Maryam stood back and crossed her arms across her chest.

Talia reached for Hannah's hand and squeezed with tears trailing her cheeks, but she said nothing. What could gentle, innocent Talia say in light of Hannah's great shame?

She walked outside to Yeshue, who was speaking sternly to Reuben. "You will treat her as your honored wife. You will not withhold from her food, shelter, affection or children. She is your responsibility now."

Reuben kicked at the stones of the path and shifted. "Let's go, Hannah."

She stared at him, seeing for the first time what everyone else had seen all along. Why had she been so blind? Reuben was nothing but a selfish troublemaker. She cast a desperate glance at Yeshue. He appeared sad, but his expression was tender.

"Trust in Elohim," he said quietly, so only she could hear him. "He is your refuge, your rock. Your help comes from Adonai, maker of heaven and earth."

Hannah almost asked Yeshue to forgive her. The words were on the tip of her tongue. But before she could speak them, a darkness settled over her. Why should Yeshue send her off with a man who would not be a good husband? She had made one mistake. Should she be judged for the rest of her life? Couldn't he think of a single way to save her?

Yeshue watched her sadly. "Be a good wife."

She walked away from her family without another word.

The months that followed were difficult. Hannah learned quickly that she was not welcome in her new husband's home. His parents and sisters blamed her for what happened at the watchtower. They treated Reuben as if he'd been a victim, forced to marry Hannah against his will. Reuben's mother treated her with disdain and heaped chores on her while she refused to speak to her. Reuben's thirteen-year-old sister spoke of her upcoming wedding often, obviously trying to hurt Hannah's feelings.

"My husband is pleased I will present myself to him without blemish," Abigail said haughtily. "We will be able to have a true wedding, not just an exchange in the street."

Hannah did much growing up in the months that followed. She realized what a carefree and happy childhood she had known. She tried to remember why she had been so dissatisfied. Her family had argued, but it hadn't been her fault or her concern. She was never hungry at home, but in her new house she was only allowed scraps when everyone else was done eating. Her own mother, Maryam, had lovingly crafted her beautiful, sturdy tunics and cloaks that lasted a long time; now her clothes were threadbare and she was not allowed material to patch them.

She rarely saw Reuben. He was busy with work in the vineyard, but she knew he was also using it as an excuse to avoid her. He spent his free time on the terrace carving his animals. He ignored her when he came in for the evening meal. When she asked him questions, he only gave short answers without looking her in the eyes. He hated her. Hated that she'd stolen his freedom.

In rare moments when Hannah found herself alone, she watched the little tekton shop down the hillside. Sometimes Y'hud and Shimon were playing outside; sometimes her mother was fanning herself on the stool beside the doorframe. She ached for her mother's arms. Maryam's eyes turned often toward the vineyard, her mouth moving, as if in prayer. Hannah took comfort in her mother's prayers.

She had a partial view of Yeshue from the doorway of the vineyard home. He worked long hours on the stool in front of the blocks of stone he patiently sculpted. She could almost hear his soft humming. Though she still harbored anger over being sent away, she couldn't deny she missed him. She hadn't considered her brother much before she left home. She had thought him boring. An obstacle to her getting her own way.

Under Yeshue's roof, she had longed for romance. She wanted Reuben to love her like Isaac loved Rebekah or Boaz loved Ruth. She had thought there was perfect love between a man and a woman. But maybe such a thing didn't exist. Maybe she had traded the only love she'd ever know for a life of misery.

FIVE

Y'hud

יהוד

Y'hud squinted up the road toward the vineyard as Shimon threw a rag ball toward him.

"Catch the ball!" Shimon complained. "What are you gawking at?"

"Hannah's house." Y'hud pointed. "I think she's watching."

"Ya'achov says Hannah sinned." Shimon picked up the ball. "And she gets what she deserves."

It had been almost a year since Hannah left. Neither of the boys had spoken to her, and they rarely saw her.

"I don't think she's allowed to leave the house."

"Shimon! Y'hud! Come eat your dinner." Talia's voice made Y'hud realize how hungry he was, especially with the enticing aroma of spicy lentil soup wafting out into the pathway. They hurried to wash their hands as they had been taught and went through the house to sit in the inner courtyard with the men. Ya'achov and Yose didn't speak as they drank deeply from their cups. Talia brought bread and the soup from the room with the oven just behind where they reclined around the table on worn cushions. She paused in the doorway to look up at the sky, causing Y'hud to look up as well. The sunset glowed with brilliant hues and brought a comfortable cool to the dry air.

Y'hud listened to his sister and mother speak together as he slurped his soup. Their voices were hushed, but since none of the men spoke, he could easily make out their conversation.

"Y'hud and Shimon saw Hannah up at the vineyard."

"Poor girl," his mother said in a mournful tone. "I hear a baby crying when I pass by on the way to the market. It must be Hannah's."

Y'hud's ears perked up at that. He listened more intently.

"They never let her come outside. They all came with the caravan for Passover, but they left her at home by herself. It's not fair." Y'hud heard the thick sound of Talia's throat, as if she was about to cry.

"Life isn't fair," Maryam said. "Especially when we sin."

Y'hud saw Yeshue glance back at the women, as if he was also listening to the conversation.

"Talia?" Yeshue asked in his gentle tone. She gave their brother a brave smile.

"I'm sorry, Yeshue. We were talking about Hannah."

"I think she has a child." Maryam stepped into the courtyard, drying her hands on her cloak.

He nodded. "I think you're right. I've heard a baby crying."

"Isn't there anything we can do?" Talia followed her mother out the door.

Yeshue gave them a sorrowful smile. "You can pray." He looked at Y'hud. "We all can."

Y'hud nodded, ripping a chunk of bread and eating it in one bite. He felt strange talking about such a sad thing. He didn't like the way his eyes felt swollen.

"I will talk to Jonah and see if she might bring the child for a visit," Yeshue said to their mother.

"Thank you, Yeshue." Y'hud watched as his mother visibly relaxed. He was glad Yeshue had made her happy again.

"In fact, I will go right now. The family will be at supper and will welcome a guest."

"No, eat your dinner, son," Maryam urged. "It can wait."

"It's important," he said as he got up and went to her. He held his hand against his mother's cheek for a moment before he went through the house to the front door.

Ya'achov and Yose said nothing after the prayer of blessing for the food. They ate, unconcerned with the plight of their younger sister. Y'hud watched the door, waiting to see Yeshue again. He wasn't gone long. And he didn't smile as Y'hud had hoped.

"Jonah said Hannah is well, but she cannot visit tonight. She will be sent over when they finish pulling in the rest of the harvest."

Y'hud frowned.

"The girl deserves what she gets," Ya'achov said.

Yose seemed more interested in his bowl of figs. "Maybe the soldiers will burn down their house."

"We will not wish evil on them." Yeshue didn't look at Yose, but his voice was firm. "We will pray for them."

Y'hud turned around and stared at Yeshue. "Why would we do that?"

Yeshue put his hand on Y'hud's shoulder. "Because God would have us pray for our enemies. It is his way."

"It certainly isn't man's way." Ya'achov made a scoffing sound.

"We will pray," Maryam said, eyeing Ya'achov with narrowed eyes.

The family finished dinner. Maryam called Y'hud and Shimon to her and washed their feet, hands and faces before she helped them take off their cloaks and sent them up to bed with a kiss and a blessing.

Y'hud lay on his straw pallet above the main room, listening once again to Talia and his mother talk as they cleaned up.

"We must listen to Yeshue, Talia," Maryam said. "Even when his words sound strange. He is the one sent from God."

"I know, Ama. I believe. But it is hard for my brothers to see it."

Maryam sighed. "I suppose I am most blessed. I know truths no one else could know or believe. I know without a single doubt in my mind that Yeshue does not have an earthly father. I saw the vision of the angel who came to tell me I would bear the M'sheekha. I saw the star shining above Bethlehem the night Yeshue was born. I knew Herod's fear that Yeshue would steal his throne. We ran away to Egypt in the night before the soldiers came and killed all the baby boys in the town."

Talia gulped back her sorrow that such a thing had happened. What must those mothers have suffered as they sacrificed their little ones to save Yeshue's life?

"I believe he is the M'sheekha," Talia said again. "But knowing scares me."

Y'hud leaned over the side of the loft and peered at them down below.

His mother cast Talia a tentative glance. "Why?"

"Because of the prophecies." Talia pulled her knees up to her chest and hugged them.

"Let's not speak of it, Talia," Maryam said, busying herself by putting jars away in their alcoves in the wall.

Y'hud lay back on his pallet, considering his sister's words as if he was poking at a snake with a stick. He didn't want to get too close, for he feared something dangerous in the words, but at the same time, he couldn't leave it alone.

He was oppressed, and he was afflicted, yet he would not open his mouth; like a lamb to the slaughter he would be brought.

Yeshue had taught the children the passage from the Isaiah scroll the last time he had come to the prayer house. He had explained what it meant – that Isaiah was talking about the M'sheekha, who would come and save them, but Y'hud had trouble remembering everything his brother had told them. He hadn't really considered it before. He had believed his mother when she told them Yeshue was the M'sheekha God had promised hundreds of years before, but he had assumed M'sheekha would be a conquering king. Why did the Torah speak of him that way? It made him sound like he would be killed. Like he wouldn't be able to stop it.

Was that why Talia was scared? Did she think Yeshue would be killed because he was the M'sheekha?

He frowned into the darkness. He'd like to see the soldier, king or emperor that tried to kill his brother. He wouldn't let that happen to his abba. And Yeshue was strong. Yeshue wouldn't let anyone kill him. He'd stop them.

He sighed, satisfied that Talia had nothing to be afraid of. He put his arms behind his head and let sleep claim him.

SIX

Talia

טליה

Talia went to the roof. She couldn't sleep. Visions of prophecies turned in her head, taunting her with truths she didn't want to face but couldn't escape.

"Talia."

She heard Yeshue's voice as she stared up at the brilliant night sky and hugged her cloak tightly around her shoulders. She looked up, startled. "I'm sorry, Yeshue. I didn't know you were here. I'll go to bed."

He stopped her by touching her hand. "God has opened your eyes to truths most people do not understand. You have wisdom, and with wisdom comes responsibility."

She hung her head, chastised. "I shouldn't have worried Ama."

She saw the faint outline of his features as he spoke. "No, that's not what I'm saying. I just want you to understand that Elohim will use you if you allow him the space to work through you."

Talia didn't answer for a long time. "Part of me wants that. I want to bring glory to Alaha with my life. But I don't know how to handle this constant fear I carry in my heart. Fear for our family, fear for our people—but mostly fear for you."

Yeshue came closer and slipped his arm around her shoulders. "Elohim is bigger than your fears. You do not have the ability to overcome them, but he does. Remember this, no matter what happens, no matter how things may fall apart and seem hopeless: Elohim is trustworthy. If it seems evil has won, you must remember that he will always do what he said he would do. All the prophecies will come true— *all* of them—in Adonai's time."

Talia was quiet for a long time as she considered his words. She said them again and again to herself so she would remember.

"Ama is afraid to look at the truth."

Yeshue nodded. "She is my mother. That is understandable."

"Ama is like Hannah from the Scriptures. Isn't she? She has to be willing to give her son to Alaha's service. Hannah had to take Samuel to the temple and leave him with Eli. He must have cried and begged for her not to go, like Shimon did after he got lost in the Sepphoris market a few months ago."

"Remind Ama of Samuel's mother if she seems like she might lose her way."

"I will," Talia said solemnly.

They were quiet for a few moments, and Yeshue looked to the stars. Suddenly, he spoke again.

"When you were a little girl, you said you didn't want to marry and have a family. Do you remember?"

"I told you I would follow you instead," she said softly.

"Our family is about to experience some changes. If you want me to find you a good husband, you must tell me now. Yohanan bar Simeon asked about you a while ago."

"What will you decide?" she asked, her heart skipping a beat. Yohanan was a decent young man, hard-working and quiet. She did wonder what it would be like to have children of her own when she saw her old schoolmates carrying their infants to the well. But her desires seemed trivial. And risky. She waited for his answer.

"I won't decide. You will. You know your own mind."

She gave a soft laugh and shook her head. "What father or brother gives a woman's opinion any thought? I've never heard of such a thing."

He smiled and squeezed her hand. "I believe everyone should have choices. Freedom. Especially when it involves the choice to follow me."

"You should join the Zealots if you think freedom is so important— maybe I don't want to have to make that decision for myself." She smiled at him to let him know she really did appreciate his trust.

He chuckled, but he waited for her answer.

"I don't think I could bear to be apart from you. I want to follow wherever it is you are going."

"Then let it be so," he said quietly, as if Adonai were witnessing a solemn oath between them. "Now get some rest. Morning comes early."

Talia tried to sleep, but she felt the weight of the words she had spoken to her brother. She felt a dread she could not identify. His face had been so serious. She understood the path would not be easy, and to be safe, she should have chosen to stay in Nazareth.

But she couldn't imagine a life away from Yeshue. She knew she must go. And nothing had ever scared her more.

SEVEN

November, A.D. 25
Ya'achov

יעקב

"Foolishness!" Ya'achov slammed the hammer on the rickety workshop table, which wobbled precariously in response. "We've been in Nazareth our entire life. Why would we move to Capernaum?"

"Because you trust me to make the right decisions as leader of this family," Yeshue said.

"First you go off on some pilgrimage to the desert, leaving Cousin Levi to take your place in the shop. When you get back, you bring two men, which means more mouths to feed. Now you want us all to pack up our life and follow you to Capernaum, for no other reason than you're the leader of this family?"

"Ya'achov!" Maryam hissed from the passageway where she was watching them. "You forget yourself."

"No one else is going to challenge him!" Ya'achov roared at her. He immediately felt sorry for his outburst, but pride kept him from apologizing. He went to the doorway of the shop and breathed in and out of his nose as he looked on the village he loved. How could Yeshue ask them to leave for his own personal crusade?

It started after harvest when Yeshue found their cousin Yohanan by the Jordan, dunking people in the dirty river and proclaiming them "clean." Yeshue asked to be dunked as well, after which he'd decided to take some pilgrimage into the desert to fast and pray. Ya'achov hadn't missed him a bit, but the business had suffered. They weren't meeting their quotas for stones, because Levi wasn't as fast as Yeshue. Not that Yeshue was by any means "fast." Because of that, Ya'achov wasn't sure now they'd have enough for taxes. He didn't want to contemplate what might happen if they missed payment. Roman soldiers were ruthless.

Yeshue put a hand on his shoulder. "I know you're frightened, Ya'achov. But you must trust me."

Ya'achov shook off his hand. "I don't trust you! You seem to care more about your holy mission to save the world than you do about taking care of your own family. Go off to Capernaum with your disciples. They can be your new family. I'll take care of this one."

He turned his back on Yeshue. He felt the catch in his voice and was afraid Yeshue would see how afraid he really was. Yose still stood by the wall, his arms crossed over his chest. He stared at the floor. He hadn't said a word since Yeshue had broken the news to both of them.

"I would rather you do what I say because you trust me. But since your hearts are weak, I'll explain. I am concerned that we will not be able to feed this growing family on the work we can do in this shop alone. You both have children on the way. Sepphoris is too far to walk every day and still have time with your families."

"We have women to look after them," Ya'achov argued. "When they're older, the boys will work with us. That's what our father did with us. Was his way not good enough for you?"

"It's important to be a part of their lives when they are very young. The older they are, the more influenced by this world they will become. You must teach them how to be men and women devoted to Elohim. If I can find a way to help you do that, I will do it."

"So that's the only reason you want to move to Capernaum?" Yose asked.

"No. I also must keep in mind the work Elohim has given me to do. I must go to Capernaum because Peter and Andrew live there, and they have resources we can use."

"Your disciples? You want us to be dependent on strangers? How could you ask that?" Ya'achov's voice was high and tight and he hated the sound of it. "While you take off after your destiny, I suppose."

"Ya'achov," Yeshue said in quiet admonition. Ya'achov heard his mother sniff in the passageway. He must have set her crying again.

"I won't leave you on your own unless I am sure you are able to take care of the family. But I also cannot accept your disrespect. There are so many things you are not considering. Trust me to act with your best interests in mind, because I promise you I always will."

"You'll do what's best for *you*, like you always do," Ya'achov said bitterly. The harsh words seemed to echo off the walls, and none of the brothers spoke again. Eventually, Yeshue left with his new followers, who glanced back at them awkwardly but didn't speak.

Whether Ya'achov wanted it or not, and no matter that it broke his heart to pack their belongings and their families and leave his father's workshop to sit empty – a few weeks later, that's exactly what they did.

Talia

טליא

Talia secretly fumed as the villagers lined up to say goodbye to Yeshue. How many times had they hid their gossiping mouths behind the back of their hand as they giggled and clucked at his expense? How many times had she been asked why Yeshue was at the prayer house instead of the workshop, or why Yeshue hadn't taken a wife, or why Yeshue didn't act like other men his age? Now they carried on as if they had believed all along he was destined for great things.

Hypocrites. People always said one thing and did something else. Why couldn't they just say what they meant? Yeshue knew their thoughts anyway. He seemed to know the minds of his family members better than they knew it themselves sometimes.

Yohanan, the son of Simeon, who had asked for her two years before, was married now and had a son. They came to say goodbye as well, and it made Talia wonder what life might have been like if she had chosen differently. She might be the contented mother holding a baby on her hip. But then she would be saying goodbye to Yeshue, and that would have been too hard to bear. She could see now she'd made the right decision. She was only surer when she saw D'vora's tears as she clung to Maryam. D'vora and Hannah would be left behind.

D'vora came to her and hugged her tightly. "I will miss you, little sister. You know you can still change your mind. No one will think less of you if you ask Yeshue to find you a husband here."

Talia hesitated only for a moment before her eyes found Yeshue. He was watching her. She saw within his heart, in a way she couldn't explain to anyone else. Her intuition told her that following Yeshue could not be half-hearted. If she had promised to go, anything less than the fulfillment of her end of the deal would disappoint him.

"I can't," she said, her weak whisper betraying her attempt at confidence. "I can't hurt him."

D'vora gave her a strange look. "Why would Yeshue care what you do?"

Talia shook her head. She wouldn't attempt to explain it to her sister. She gathered her courage and took a step toward Yeshue, toward the family caravan heading out of town for the long journey to Capernaum. But Yeshue surprised them all by stopping outside the vineyard.

Jonah answered Yeshue's knock. He frowned at Yeshue, but he heard him out. Talia was far enough back that she couldn't hear what they said. Jonah suddenly waved his hand as if he was relenting to something he didn't want to approve.

Hannah flew out of the house and into the arms of Yeshue. He practically carried her down the hill to the waiting family.

Maryam and Talia both ran to her. They hugged her. It was a bittersweet moment, knowing they might never see Hannah again, but they were thankful for the chance to at least say goodbye.

Hannah was different. She looked as if she had aged ten years, though it had been no more than three. No longer the precocious, friendly child, she was hardened into the adult role she had earned through her actions.

Ya'achov and Yose wouldn't look at her. They turned their backs and waited for the goodbyes to end. But Yeshue held her tenderly, tears shining in his eyes.

"His name is Y'aqim," she whispered to the three of them. "He is a sweet baby, though he is my only joy. I don't know what I'll do when he is weaned. Reuben's father hates me and tries to keep me from my son. He blames me for everything."

"Oh, my child!" Maryam brushed away tears. Yeshue put a supportive hand on Maryam's back. Hannah only looked away, a passive expression on her face. Like she had accepted her fate.

"There is hope, little girl." Yeshue lifted a finger to her chin. "Sin destroys peace, but there is always hope. Trust in Elohim, and he will make your paths straight."

"Would that I could go with the family," Hannah said after a moment, as if she didn't know what to do with Yeshue's words.

He touched her cheek, and then he stepped back. "Are we ready?"

Talia's heart jumped with anticipation and anxiety. They waved to the well-wishers and set off down the well-worn road with everything they owned. Yeshue led the way, forging a path into the unknown. He seemed determined to walk it, as if he *must* walk it.

And she was determined to follow.

Hannah

חנה

Hannah tried to focus only on the cooing child she tended, rather than the hateful words buzzing in her ears.

"Why I ever allowed you into this household…" Her father-in-law, Jonah, stood over her, his hands on his hips and his dark eyes flashing fire. "Your brother should have had you stoned. The last thing we need in this village is a harlot."

Hannah cringed. *I hate you,* she screamed silently. *I wish you would all die.*

"You ruined his life." Jonah pointed across the room at Reuben, who reclined at the table eating the rest of the grapes from dinner. Hannah wanted to roll her eyes. For her to ruin her lazy, selfish husband's life, he would have to actually acknowledge her existence.

Her mother-in-law refilled Reuben's cup with wine and patted Reuben's cheek. Hannah's stomach turned with revulsion. As the woman came back her way to return to the oven where bread was baking, she pushed past Hannah, knocking her off balance. She jostled the baby and made him cry.

"Stupid girl," her mother-in-law muttered.

She took a deep breath, swallowing the lump in her throat. She gathered her crying baby to her chest and turned to take him to the room that had been added—eventually—by Reuben when they had married. Hopefully he would stay with his horrid family and give her some peace for the rest of the evening.

Hannah had been trying to work up the courage to tell her husband that she was expecting another child. She hadn't been able to speak the words aloud. The innocent life growing inside her womb would be safe from his family a little longer. She wanted to keep the precious secret for as long as she could. She held Y'aqim to her breast as he continued to fuss.

"Maybe the soldiers will take her," she heard Reuben say from the other room. "Then she won't be my problem anymore."

Hannah had always been terrified of Roman soldiers, like any other young girl in town, and for good reason. Soldiers didn't enter Nazareth very often, but they would stand on the outskirts by the well and frighten the young women getting water for their families, laughing obnoxiously when the girls screamed. If a family was unable to pay their taxes, which didn't happen often because the townspeople met each other's needs, the occasional daughter was ripped out of their parents' arms and dragged off to become a slave—or worse. Hannah had always worried that their family would not have enough for the emperor's tax and the village would not help them because they did not approve of Yeshue. As the youngest daughter, she would have been the first to go.

"I'll put a curse on her and send her a deadly plague," her mother-in-law said indulgently to Reuben. Angry tears stung Hannah's eyes.

She held the baby so tightly he tried to wriggle free. Several families in Nazareth had sickness already. No one went outside in the rainy winter weather for fear of it—it had already killed two infants and an elderly woman.

"Amen," Jonah laughed. "Even better, send her to the house of Shimeon. They have sick there. We'll send bread."

"Oh, Hannah," Reuben called. "I have a task for you."

She avoided them as long as she could, but eventually they came. His mother pushed a basket of bread into her hands and grabbed the baby, who began to wail pitifully and reach for Hannah. "Ama!"

"Go and feed the sick, Hannah. Your brother would want it. Didn't he always visit sick people?" Jonah gave a cruel laugh and went back to the table for more wine. Reuben joined him.

Her mother-in-law leaned into her face. "Don't come back until you are sure you aren't sick," she seethed into her face. "Stay in town until Shabbat."

"But I must nurse Y'aqim!"

"He's nearly a year old. He can have goat's milk."

She could no longer contain her fury. She gave a last, desperate look to her baby and angrily grabbed the breadbasket, dumping it on the floor and screaming with rage.

Her mother-in-law only laughed at her. She picked up the bread and returned it to the basket without even dusting it off. "Go."

She could hardly see through the blinding rage that gripped her very soul. She stomped out of the house and down the hill, obeying because she had no other option. She could hear their laughter as far as the end of the vineyard. She went down the hill toward the house of Simeon. She approached with trepidation. One of the brothers stood outside the door.

"You can't go in," he said with a firm shake of his head.

She lifted the basket of dirty, soggy bread. "A miserable gift from the miserable house of Jonah." She left it on the ground and walked away, through the mud.

She reached the end of the main road and saw her father's house and shop up on a small knoll. It invited her in, as if Abba himself were opening his arms to her. She looked around to make sure no one was watching her before she entered the abandoned house.

The rooms were dark and cool. The house smelled damp with the recent rain. Memories lived in every corner. She learned against the stone wall and fell to the ground, pressing her face into her headscarf.

She fell asleep there, praying for her child to be protected from his hideous family. When she woke, the night had fallen and the room was chilly. She shivered and went to find some kindling in the woodshop to start a fire. A jug outside the door was filled with rainwater, so she put water in the kettle that had been left for travelers who might want to use the home. She found leftover vegetables and herbs in the courtyard garden and put them in the water. She was hungry for bread, but her simple stew would have to do for a few days.

When it was done, she sipped the soup and dreamed of her mother's hands, lovingly planting and cultivating the food she was eating. It was almost as if her mother had made the soup for her. The thought made it a comforting meal.

She lay down in front of the fire to sleep on the bare ground. Her eyes fell upon an old stool that had been left behind, too rickety to be of any use. The sight of it triggered remembrance.

"Daughters, come near," Yosef said weakly from his pallet on the floor. He had been thrashing back and forth all evening. The girls had been huddled in the corner together, watching his face grow white and his desperate breathing become a tell-tale rattle in his chest. They knew death, and they knew their father was close to it.

They came to him and knelt beside him. Talia buried her head in Yosef's tunic, crying.

"Save your tears for mourning, little Talia. I want to go to Sheol with the memories of your beautiful smiles."

"Please don't go, Abba," Talia begged as she tried to stop her tears. Her sobs only grew deeper.

"Be silent so I can speak," Abba said tenderly, lifting a trembling hand to Talia's cheek. When she quieted, he spoke again. "When I am gone, little lambs, you must do something for me."

"Anything, Abba," Hannah leaned over him and squeezed his arm. "Just say the words."

Yosef smiled at her and reached a hand to smooth back the hair from her face. "Little Hannah. Only eight years on this earth and you wish to be a grown woman. Don't be in such a hurry. Womanhood will come all too soon."

"Amen," Hannah said without thinking. She took his other hand. "May you be there to see me as a woman."

"I will not be there," Yosef said decidedly. "I want my daughters to be strong. Help your Ama in her grief."

They hesitated, exchanging glances, then nodded.

"Whatever happens, you must both follow Yeshue. Not only in matters relating to the family, for he will be the head of this house, but in all things. He is the M'sheekha, and you must follow him."

Yosef's voice became urgent, almost as a plea, as the spirit ebbed away behind his warm brown eyes. "I have told your brothers the same."

"Yes, Abba," they both said in unison.

"If only I had the time to tell you..." Yosef's voice faded and Hannah thought he had died. A cold chill spread over her.

"I must speak to Yeshue," he said suddenly, squeezing their hands with his little remaining strength. "Send in the one they call my son."

They sprang up from his pallet, crying as they descended the ladder and ran to find Yeshue. Hannah found him in the courtyard, sitting against the wall, his head in his hands. She was not sure if he was praying, or crying, or both.

"Abba asks for you," she said. He jumped at the sound of her voice, as if he'd been surprised. Very rarely did anyone surprise Yeshue. He must have been deep in thought.

He stood and motioned for her to come to him. He kissed her head. "Go to your sister, Hannah. She will need you to hold her while she grieves."

Hannah nodded, a lump in her throat.

"You are a strong one. A brave girl." He squeezed her shoulders before he went to Yosef.

Instead of going to Talia, Hannah followed Yeshue back into the house. She sat in the doorway and listened to their words. She had to strain her ears to hear Abba's words over Ama's sniffling.

"Son, my time has come," Yosef said.

Yeshue said nothing. After a moment, he nodded.

"I know we haven't spoken of it in a long time, but I want to remind you of your birth. Make sure you understand."

Hannah would have laughed if it had been any other circumstance. Yosef and Maryam had talked often of Yeshue's birth. Sometimes Hannah wondered if they could speak of anything else.

"I understand, Abba." Hannah heard Yeshue's soft answer.

"Ah, let an old man speak his memories," Yosef chuckled, which made him cough.

"If he must," Yeshue sat down on the stool made by Yosef's own hands. "I will be glad to listen."

"You indulge me," Yosef said, and Yeshue chuckled in response.

"Your mother was the most beautiful girl in town. Have I told you that? Long dark hair, shiny brown eyes full of innocence…"

"You describe every young woman I can think of, Abba," Yeshue teased him mildly.

Yosef reached a hand to lightly slap Yeshue's arm. "You are employed here only as a listener."

Yeshue nodded and bowed his head in deference.

"I was taken with her from the moment I arrived in town. You know I came from Bethlehem, but our family had come to Nazareth for the wedding of my cousin. We ended up staying for several weeks, and I wanted her for my wife, if her father could be convinced to let her marry an old bachelor."

"An old bachelor at twenty-four. You wound me. I hadn't realized at twenty-five I was useless and elderly."

Yosef wheezed a short laugh. "Well, I seemed an old bachelor to

Maryam. She was barely thirteen. But there was something about her. Wisdom beyond her years. She wasn't flighty or silly as the other young women. She had a peace about her I found very attractive."

"As you should have." Yeshue looked at his mother across Yosef's pallet and nodded.

"I decided not to ask for her, though. Surely she deserved better than a poor carpenter."

"What made you change your mind?"

"In the end I didn't need to. Her father's olive crop was destroyed by flies and they had no money to pay the tax. He would have had to sell her to save the little ones, so I paid the bride price. He asked me to wait a year before I took her to my home because she was so young, and I agreed.

"Not two months after this, Maryam was visited by the angel."

"Gabriel," Yeshue said with a nod. As if he spoke of an old friend.

"Imagine my shock when she came to me with wild stories of angels and heavenly messages! I pulled her aside to hear what nonsense she had dreamed up. When she told me she was going to have a baby, my blood ran cold."

Hannah sneaked into the animal shelter underneath the floor. She watched them through a small hole in the floor of the upper story. She knew her parents would make her leave if they knew she was listening to such a conversation. But she was intensely curious about the part of the story no one would speak about when she was around. Her brother Y'hud played nearby, banging on a pot with all his strength. She glared at him, and he gave her a toothy smile.

"You did well to hear her out," Yeshue said.

"I was like one possessed," Yosef continued, his voice softer and weaker. "I wanted to rage and find the man who had defiled her. I would give him justice. But she went on about how the baby would be born of the Spirit of Alaha. He would be the M'sheekha."

"Did you believe her?"

"Yeshue, surely you know every woman who has come to be with child in the last four hundred years has claimed to be carrying the

M'sheekha."

Yeshue smiled. "Ah, but it is true."

"Well, I marched her right back to her father's home and left her there, too angry to say a word. Then I paced the rest of the day, trying to decide what to do."

"You did well not to have her publicly shamed."

"I did not want to run ahead of Adonai." Yosef closed his eyes, his words slurring as he tried to gather strength to finish the tale. Yeshue put his hand on the older man's arm, and the gesture gave Yosef strength to continue.

"I was going to put her away from me without anyone knowing. I wanted her life to be spared, at least. I thought maybe the father was a Roman soldier that had cornered her and taken advantage of her innocence. Maybe she'd come up with the angel story to cover the horror of what had happened."

"You were a man of integrity, thinking the best of her."

Yosef shook his head. "A good man would have stood by her and believed her story. Alaha had to send an angel to me before I would accept it."

"You did, though. You didn't question after that."

"No, I didn't. How could I question the word of Adonai?"

Yosef was quiet for a long time. When Hannah thought maybe he had died, he suddenly spoke again. "I am going to die."

Hannah expected Yeshue to disagree—to urge Yosef to fight the illness and stay with them. After all, he had eight children and other relatives to care for. What would their family be without him?

"I know." Hannah heard the catch in Yeshue's voice and imagined the tears swimming in his eyes.

"You will be head of this house."

"I understand."

"Do you have any questions? Do you know what to do for the girls when they come of age? Do you understand how to balance family and the business, and still have time for your studies?"

"I think so," Yeshue said simply.

Yosef nodded, visibly relaxing in the quiet confidence of his eldest son. "Don't misunderstand me. I know you are here for a higher purpose than looking after the poor family of a tekton. You must be about your Father's business, as you have reminded me."

The words didn't make sense to Hannah.

"I will do what I have come to do," Yeshue promised.

"No man has ever left his family in better care. That I should be so blessed..." He stopped speaking and took a deep, laboring breath. "I am so tired, my son..."

Her father's voice trailed off, and moments later, she heard the wails of her mother begin. Yeshue gathered his mother in his arms and wept with her.

The vivid memory ended abruptly. Hannah sat up in the home she had grown up in, but it was no longer warm or comfortable. She thought of her son alone on the hill with those people.

If she hadn't left Yeshue's house, she would still be under his care. She'd be safe.

She huddled in the corner of the dark dwelling with nothing but her threadbare cloak to give her warmth. Even though she could see no one, she felt the echo of a tender presence. A love. Why did the love of Alaha always seem synonymous with the love of her oldest brother?

And yet she had thrown it all away. There was no way Yeshue could ever change her fate now. She had gone too far for even his reach to bring her back.

EIGHT

Talia

טליה

The Capernaum marketplace was closing as the family entered town. Talia drew close to her mother when the Roman soldiers stared at her from their positions on either side of the busy road. Yeshue must have noticed as well, for he slowed to walk beside the women.

"What do you think, Talia?" he asked, smiling. She stopped and looked around. The sun was just beginning to set, and it cast a lovely glow over the Sea of Galilee, nestled within the valley. Male voices bantered over law and religion outside the spacious house of prayer. Women laughed as they gathered outside their houses. Fishermen headed to the harbor to prepare their nets for the night fishing. She took a deep breath. The air smelled fresh and exhilarating—a mixture of fish and the sea, hearth fire and oil burning in lamps. The village was obviously much larger than Nazareth, but it wasn't overly crowded, and almost everyone was Jewish. The houses were closer together than in Nazareth, but they were more carefully built with larger complexes. She glanced at Yeshue and saw the peace in his expression. This was a good place to live.

"I like it here," she told him.

He seemed delighted by her response. "I do, too." He gave her shoulders a quick squeeze before he stepped back in line with the men. Yeshue's disciples, the brothers Peter and Andrew, came across the road to meet them, bringing others. Yeshue greeted them as if they were kinsmen, but they bowed in awe. Ya'achov made a sound of disgust, and all the family members stood awkwardly outside the circle.

It was an uncommonly large group to move to a new town. Even Talia's old Uncle Amos had come with them. He was her father's brother and at least eighty years old, hardly able to walk or speak anymore. His mind had been absent for years now. He spent most of his conscious hours in confusion. Yeshue was patient with him even when everyone else ignored him. He answered the same questions over and over as if Amos had not asked them a hundred times.

"Where are we going? To Jerusalem for the Passover?" Amos struggled along the path on the main road of Capernaum.

"No, Uncle. We are going to live in Capernaum now," Yeshue answered as he guided him over a rut in the road.

"Not going to Jerusalem?" Amos's eyes were covered by cataracts, so he gripped Yeshue's arm like a lifeline.

"No, Uncle. We aren't going to Jerusalem this time."

They came to stand in front of a large family insula. Peter said it had been his father's dwelling, but both his parents had recently died. Peter's family consisted of his unmarried brother, his wife, several young children and his wife's mother, who was a widow. She was often ill.

"My brother and I built our own insula for our families when my parents still lived in the main house. We are comfortable in our rooms and we would like your family to have the main house," Peter told Yeshue.

Yeshue sent the families to different rooms. He gave Ya'achov and his family a smaller set of rooms off the main house. Yose and his bride were given a room beyond the courtyard, with plenty of space should their family grow any larger. Talia would share the main house with her mother and brothers. Uncle Amos would live with them.

Talia watched the children dance with excitement over the new, larger home. They sang a song of praise in Hebrew. Yeshue sang along.

Talia felt a sting of sorrow, realizing that she would never know the joy of having her own children. From her earliest memories, Talia had wanted to be a mother. She had mothered Y'hud and Shimon as if they were her own. Ya'achov's wife and Yose's wife already had four children between them, causing Talia to feel out of place. What purpose could she serve if she didn't marry and have little ones? Was she wasting the life entrusted to her from Alaha? Had she made a mistake in coming?

Following a good night's sleep, Maryam woke Talia where she slept on her pallet. "Come. We have work to do."

And they did. The day was filled with work, just as it had been back in Nazareth. They began by making the customary breakfast of flatbread with fresh fish and figs.

"We will eat fish for every meal now that we live by the sea, until we are sick of it. Like our ancestors when Alaha sent them quail," her mother joked as they scaled sardines Yeshue brought from his disciples' early morning catch.

Talia considered the almost continuous harvests back home. The olives, grapes and figs were always plentiful. She felt a pang of sorrow for their loss.

"I will miss the fruit of Nazareth." Yeshue seemed to read her mind. Everyone agreed heartily, and took a little extra time chewing the treats they had brought since they would soon be gone and would not be as easily found in the fishing town.

After breakfast, the women set to work cleaning out the house as the men repaired what was in need of attention.

Yeshue fixed several holes in the roof by tying together bundles of straw and pasting mud into the gaps left by weather and time. Shimon and Y'hud were sent to repair broken stalls in the front room reserved for the animals.

Ya'achov and Yose built several simple bed frames for the families to sleep in. There were no second stories on the houses of Capernaum, and no one wanted to sleep in the dirt. They built the frame and smoothed the wood before stretching rope across the surface where the pallet would lie.

Talia set to work cleaning the mikveh. As she removed the dead leaves and dirt from the bottom of the empty reservoir, she thanked Alaha for the blessing of having a place of ritual cleansing in their home. Not many homes did. This home was near the prayer house and had been used by a priest's family before Peter's family moved from Bethsaida. The priest had relocated to Jerusalem to work in the temple. It was no surprise he would have a mikveh in his home.

When she finished scrubbing the stone walls and stairs, she had Shimon mix mud and straw to plaster the holes in the wall. By the time they finished, the mikveh looked new.

Yeshue leaned over the side as he balanced bunches of straw on his back. "A fine job you've done! At the rate you're going, we will be ritually pure by sundown."

Talia laughed at his teasing. She climbed out. "I'll have Shimon and Y'hud carry water from the well and fill it up."

When nightfall came, the family stopped working. It was Shabbat. There would be no more work done until the next day's sun had set. Maryam, Talia and the other women filled lamps with olive oil and lit the wicks. The flames cast warm shadows on the family room where a newly constructed table stood ready for their meal. The men sat on the floor around the table while the women served clay bowls filled with dates, olives and barley bread still warm from the dome-shaped oven. After Yeshue gave a prayer of thanksgiving, he broke the bread and passed it around until everyone had a piece. Cups were filled to the brim with sweet Nazareth wine and passed by Yeshue. The family listened to Yeshue tell the story of Jonah, a favorite with the children. Yeshue animated the tale until everyone was crying tears of laughter near the end as Jonah stumbled into Nineveh in the foulest of tempers, covered in slime and fish stench. Even Ya'achov smiled once or twice.

Talia leaned back against the wall by the warm oven and sighed in contentment. She wanted life to be like this always. All of them together and happy, enjoying the plentiful goodness of Alaha's creation. She didn't always enjoy change, but she felt they were where they belonged. She hoped the family would stay in Capernaum.

Her thoughts went to her younger sister, left alone in Nazareth with Reuben and his spiteful family, poor little Y'aqim caught in the middle. Tears filled Talia's eyes.

"What is it?" Maryam asked next to her.

"Hannah. It hurts to think about the life she is living while we are all here, well-fed and happy."

"Would that I could take her place," Maryam said with a sad sigh. "Alaha be with my child tonight."

Talia stood in the doorway and looked up at the night sky. The light that glowed from the olive oil lamps didn't quench the strong light of the moon and stars. She traced the lines between the stars as she had as a child, wondering at the world around her. Maryam caught her hand and kissed it.

"You are my comfort, Talia. I'm glad you're here."

"You don't wish I'd stayed and married Yohanan?"

Maryam smiled and watched the blanket of twinkling lights above them. "Yeshue would say there is more to life than marriage and babies."

"Did you want to marry Abba?" Talia asked suddenly.

"I was young. Much younger than you. I had no idea what I wanted. It didn't matter, though, because my father needed the dowry Yosef would pay more than he needed my mouth to feed. Your father was a good man. Sent from Alaha at just the right time. I won't complain."

"Would you have chosen differently if you had a choice?"

Maryam hesitated, and Talia was sorry she had asked. But Maryam chuckled softly. "You sound like your brother. Always speaking of choices in a world that gives us precious few, especially as women." She sighed. "Yes, I would probably have chosen to wait longer and stay with my family. But I'm not sorry for the way things happened. Alaha knew better than I did."

"You mean how Yeshue came to you?"

Maryam nodded. "He was more important than my comfort. I am first of all the servant of Alaha."

"I want to be his servant, too." Talia gripped her mother's hand. "But I'm scared he can't use me. I'm afraid to fail him."

"If he can use timid little Maryam of Nazareth, he can use anybody." Her mother squeezed her hand. "Just rest in Alaha and be ready when he comes to you."

"Will he send an angel?" Talia smiled.

"Oh, Talia," Maryam said, her tone heavy with reflection. "You have no need of angels. You have the M'sheekha himself sitting just beyond the wall."

Hannah

חנה

Somehow Hannah made it through the long days of solitude in the abandoned house as the rain poured outside. No one in the town walked the streets, afraid of sickness. Early on the morning of Shabbat, Hannah gathered her basket, put out her fire and headed back up the hill with urgency in her step. She needed to see that her son was okay.

As she approached the stone house, she knew something was wrong. Y'aqim wailed in terror. She dropped the basket and ran up the terraced hillside. She pushed open the door and fell to the ground where her baby sat alone in the middle of the room, crying pitifully. She pulled him close to her and rocked him back and forth. Her anger toward her miserable in-laws was so furious she saw white in her vision.

"Hush, now, I'm here. I'm here. I'm sorry," she said as she sat back against the wall to nurse him. He desperately nursed, obviously ravenous with hunger.

"Did they not feed you?" Hot ire coursed through her, lighting her cheeks on fire. His soiled, wet clothes soaked through her tunic. A cup lay on the ground nearby, the contents spilled out. She cried as she thought of her baby all alone with nothing to eat. Where in the world was the miserable family who should be caring for him?

"I'll never leave you again," she promised. She would not stay here. She would take her son and run away. She didn't know where she would go or how far she would get before they dragged her back, but she would try. She would try for Y'aqim.

"I'll go to Yeshue." She was desperate enough to grovel at her brother's feet, even though he had sent her to this awful place. But wouldn't he send her back? After all, she was the property of her husband. Legally, Yeshue had no right to interfere.

Eventually, Y'aqim finished nursing. She took a bucket of water by the stove and bathed him. She found fresh clothes and put the soiled ones in the bucket to soak. She set Y'aqim on a blanket on the floor with a few carved animals Reuben had made. She hoped the baby left plenty of teeth marks in them.

She filled the basket with bread, olives, figs and grapes. She took a measure of barley and another of oil and dried fish from the clay bowl above the oven. She reached for Jonah's wine skin, glad to find it full.

She didn't know where the family was, but she didn't question it. She grabbed her sleeping son and wrapped him in a sling where he could nap against her.

"Adonai be praised for your safety," she whispered. She hurried down the terraced vineyard as fast as she could without careening down the hill.

A couple approached. Hannah forced herself to slow down, to appear nonchalant.

"Where are you going, girl?"

It was Jonah's younger sister, Miriam, and her husband Micaiah.

"I'm going to visit my family in Capernaum. I want to get the baby away from the sickness." She held Y'aqim firmly against her chest. Let them try to take him from her arms. They'd have to kill her.

"You can't travel on Shabbat. And you can't travel alone." Miriam eyed her suspiciously. "Abba didn't say you could go, did he? You're sneaking away."

Hannah tried to feign an indifferent expression. "Why should I care what you think?"

"Why didn't Abba and Reuben come to the prayer house today?" Miriam asked as if she suspected Hannah was at fault. "Are they sick?"

Hannah shrugged, unable to keep the bitterness from seeping into her words. "How should I know? He sent me into the village days ago to get me sick. I came home this morning and found the baby alone and starving."

Micaiah looked to the house on the hill. He ran up to the door and pushed it open. Miriam followed him. Hannah felt panic settle in her chest. She wanted to run, but her feet seemed planted to the spot.

When she heard the telltale wail of grief pierce through the rain, she ran.

Talia
טליה

Talia woke with a start. The early morning sky was dark and gray through the rough-hewn window. Rain was falling again. She had noticed it rained more in Capernaum, though rain was common during the winter anywhere in Galilee. Already in the weeks they had lived there, they had seen several violent storms rise up out of nowhere over the sea.

"Hannah," she whispered when she identified the reason for the dread and the restlessness of her soul. Something had happened to her sister. She was sure of it.

"Adonai, Hannah is in trouble. Please be near. Guide her steps. Bring her and her child to safety."

The whispered prayer gave her a measure of peace. When she sat up, she heard Yeshue somewhere, probably on the roof, reciting a passage from the Torah in a hushed, fervent voice.

"And he shall stand and lead with the might of the Lord, with the pride of the Lord, his God: and they shall return, for now he shall become great to the ends of the earth. And this shall be peace."

She climbed up the stairs to the roof. Yeshue's knees, hands and face bowed to the floor as he spoke the words of Scripture. He sat up and looked at her, but did not stop his recitation. "And the remnant of Jacob shall be in the midst of many peoples—like dew sent by the Lord, like torrents of rain upon vegetation that does not hope for any man and does not wait for the sons of men."

"What does that mean?" Talia sat down opposite him and pondered the familiar words.

"Abba spoke that passage the day you were born. That is why you are called *Talia*, which means *dew from Adonai*. Abba knew peace would come, and the remnant would be saved, like dew from above."

"I'm glad my name can honor you," Talia said.

Yeshue nodded. "You will honor me with more than your name, little girl."

He said the words in a tender voice, but she couldn't help but tremble.

Talia went about her duties as was expected of her, but her mood continued to plague her as much as the dark weather. The voices of her sisters-in-law grated on her. They prattled on about neighborhood gossip.

"Did you see that Babylonian robe Salome wore at the prayer house? I can't believe she would be so bold. She is always trying to get attention."

Nava turned when Talia came into the room to get the broom. "Talia, I saw Shimei look at you several times in the market yesterday." She smirked, her tone teasing. "I think his father asked Yeshue about you."

"I didn't notice," she mumbled. She took the water jug instead of the broom and escaped to the well. She heard the women laughing behind her.

Tears burned her eyes as she made her way down the sloped dirt road toward the well. She regretted her decision to come to the well as soon as she saw the gathering of women, so many more than she'd ever seen at the well in Nazareth, and none with a familiar face. She stopped short and turned toward the harbor instead. She sat down on the beach to watch the boats come in after a night of fishing.

She sat far enough away that no one would notice her. She liked seeing the young men jump off their boats and proudly pull in their catches to take to the fish market. The sea must be alive with fish. No wonder the fishermen of Capernaum had enough to live comfortably. She breathed in the briny air and watched the sun rise high over the waters, waves catching the light and shining like jewels.

"Galilee must be your special delight, Adonai. It is surely mine," she whispered.

After she had been there for some time, she noticed Yeshue sitting down on the dock, smiling at his young followers with amusement. Another pair had joined the first two. She watched her brother curiously. She wished she could be more like him. Though he had no problem being by himself, lost in prayer or study, he also came alive in the presence of others. He always knew what to say to make someone smile or laugh or think. His words flowed from his mouth like a fountain of life. Even now the young men eagerly gathered around him. She heard his distant voice and knew he would ask them about their catches, about the best weather for fishing, the types of fish they caught or any other number of questions that showed his genuine interest in their work.

Yeshue had always been intensely interested in others. While most men worried about themselves and their own family, Yeshue was outward-focused, as if he was trying to soak up every bit of knowledge about people as he could. And it was the people that drove his interest. His eyes would light up with energy when he was around others. Not the high and mighty, no, not the ones everyone else assumed were important. He had no use for emperors, kings or rulers. In fact, the lowlier, the more downcast and the more socially unacceptable, the more interested he was in their perspective.

That was Yeshue. Unexpected, inexplicable Yeshue. Talia considered for one holy moment the possibility that her brother, whose arms she could feel strong around her and whose friendly eyes and gentle smile were more familiar than her own mother's—was Elohim. Alaha. Almighty God. Come to earth disguised as a commoner, loving the lost.

Though the air was warm, a shiver passed over her body.

Yeshue chatted cheerfully as his brothers ate their soup and fish. They largely ignored him, but Talia had noticed their animosity lessen since the move to Capernaum. Ya'achov and Yose had their own tales to tell of all the work they'd found in their new town, repairing boats and some of the houses that lined the main street of the city. Talia waited to hear them belittle Yeshue for spending his time with the young fishermen rather than looking for a job, but they hardly said a word about it.

"Who were those men you spent the day with, Yeshue? I know Peter and Andrew, but who are the others?" Maryam spoke as she poured their wine.

Yeshue looked at her as he spoke. "Ya'achov and Yohanan, sons of Zebedee. They are youngsters. Full of dreams, ready to take on the world like someone lit their tunic on fire."

He smiled at the boys, and Y'hud and Shimon laughed.

"I enjoy their company and their youthful energy," Yeshue explained.

"You speak like an old man," Uncle Amos said, wheezing as he spoke.

Yeshue put his hand on his uncle's arm, obviously glad for his moment of lucidity. "I *am* old compared to them."

"Would that I could be as elderly as you, Yeshue," Uncle Amos said with a loud snort before he returned his attention to the meal before him.

Yeshue laughed. "And would that everyone could have the wisdom of your years, Amos."

"What do you want with a bunch of kids?" Yose spoke around the mouthful of bread in his mouth. He took several gulps of wine. "They don't exactly look like the typical Torah gang."

"I want to teach them God's ways. They are ready to learn." Yeshue looked at his brother. Talia saw the yearning in his eyes. She knew he would rather teach his brothers, had they any interest.

"Ah, of course." Ya'achov glanced at Yose, but he let it go.

"There are many rabbis who do the same," Maryam said from the doorway. All the men except Yeshue ignored her.

He nodded. "Yes, it is common for a teacher to choose young

students. Sometimes they learn more easily than one who has studied on his own too long. I intend to call these young men to follow me."

"Fools. You'll only inherit trouble with that bunch." Ya'achov waved his hand. "Look, I don't approve of all this nonsense and I think your time could be spent in better ways, but if you're going to do this, you may as well do it right. If you call those boys to be your students, you'll spend more time breaking up fights and getting them out of trouble than anything else. Teaching them will be impossible."

"Anything is possible with Adonai." Yeshue shrugged and returned his attention to his supper.

Talia smiled, proud of her brother for once again looking beyond the normal and expected. He wouldn't be Yeshue if he didn't do the complete opposite of what they thought he would do. He was always surprising them.

She definitely hadn't foreseen what he would bring home for her the following day.

NINE

Hannah

חנה

Hannah's feet were blistered by the time she finally walked within sight of the Sea of Galilee, glimmering in moonlight. She adjusted the sling that held her sleeping son and hurried toward the city with new determination. She considered herself fortunate that it was the Sabbath, and no one in Nazareth had cared enough about her to follow after her.

The city was bedded down for the night by the time she reached the main roads of Capernaum. She searched for an inn, knowing a city that size would have accommodations for travelers. She saw a small sign on a building next to the fishing harbor.

"Sh'lam lak," she called through the closed curtain that hung over the front entrance.

"Sh'lam lek," someone called back. A man pulled back the curtain and stared at her. "What are you doing? The hour is late and you and your child are alone. You want the spirits in the sea to rise up and pull you into the abyss?"

She hoped he was teasing, but his face was solemn. She reminded herself that her people were often given to exaggeration and superstition. Reuben's mother had been incredibly superstitious, constantly burning incense to prevent dark spirits from entering her home. What good had her delusions brought her except death?

"Alaha protects me," she said with a wave of her hand. He shook his head as if he doubted it, but led her to an empty sleeping pallet. A scowling woman came and handed her a bowl of nearly-cold lentil soup and barley bread.

The man's features softened as he sat back at his place in front of the fire and began to carefully sand a small cradle. He saw her watching him.

"My daughter will give birth any time," he explained gruffly, but his eyes smiled.

"My father was a tekton."

"Was?"

Hannah shook her head. "He's dead."

"May his spirit find rest," the man murmured. "My name is Tavi. My wife is Marte."

"Hannah."

"What brings you to the city, Hannah?"

Hannah laid Y'aqim down on the pallet and ate the soup, realizing how hungry she was from her journey. Most of her food and wine was gone.

"My family moved here. My husband and his kin are all dead from sickness, so I came to find my brother and his household."

"I'm sorry for your loss. What's your brother's name?"

"Yeshue bar Yosef." She watched the man's face, hoping to see signs of recognition. He only shrugged.

"I haven't heard of anyone by that name. Plenty of Yeshues though."

She nodded. "About as common as my mother's name, Maryam."

"If you went to the top of the hill and called *Yeshue* and *Maryam*, many people would come running." He laughed at his joke.

Hannah didn't know why the man was so talkative with her, since she was a woman, but she liked his friendly chatter. "My brother said that Yeshue and Maryam are so common because the people of Israel are calling to Alaha for the savior to come."

"Your brother sounds very wise. I hope you find him."

"I'm sure I will," Hannah mused, lying down next to her son. As she listened to the rhythmic sound of the planer, she considered whether her brother would even want to see her. She knew Ya'achov and Yose would reject her, and she wasn't sure Maryam would welcome her back into the family, either. She knew she had broken her mother's heart.

A big part of her didn't want to go back to Yeshue. She wouldn't grovel. She wouldn't. If he wouldn't take her as she was, without humiliating herself over decisions she couldn't change now, she wouldn't try to stay. She'd had enough punishment for her sins. Enough for a lifetime.

The next morning, she took some bread and cheese from Marte, who still did not speak a word to her. She asked Tavi about payment, but he waved his hand.

"I suspect you have nothing to pay me, little girl. Go find your brother. Bring him by sometime and we will settle up."

"Yishar," she thanked him. She did not tell him she was beginning to second guess her decision to go back to her brother.

She wandered down to the market by the harbor. The largest part was dedicated to fish, but there were booths selling spices from Damascus or Persian robes, shimmering with golden thread. She touched the smooth painted pottery and colorful beaded necklaces. The smells of roasted lamb teased her nose as the sounds of people bartering and animals protesting the close quarters exhilarated her. She had only been in Sepphoris or Jerusalem a handful of times, and the local Nazareth market had never been as large or varied as this one.

"A beautiful necklace for a beautiful woman," the merchant came toward her with the beads she had fingered. He had a wide grin on his face.

"No," she said, stepping back and waving him away. She had no money, and the alabaster jar she had stolen from her mother-in-law's things would remain hidden in her pack. It was probably worth nothing, just a pretty trinket, but it was all she had.

As she wandered, she tried to think of a way to make some money. If she didn't look for Yeshue and her family, she would have to find a way to feed herself and her son, and they would need shelter. She glanced around Capernaum. It was not a large village by any standard, and the locals were mainly Jewish. But because of its location on the edge of the sea, the trade route from Egypt passed by and made it popular for commerce. Greeks, Romans and Egyptians stood side by side and sold their wares. Dark-skinned people from Africa stood tall and proud in the sunshine, dressed in richly colored clothes. Hannah glanced down at her own simple tunic and cloak, which boasted only the color of the sheep who had given their wool for its creation.

Lost in thought, she didn't see the collection of Roman soldiers standing in a group on the edge of the market. She almost ran into one of them, and got an eyeful of the iron breastplate he wore. She stepped back with a gasp. The man looked superhuman in his armor and the plumage rising off his shiny metal helmet. His hair was cut short and he wore no beard like Jewish men.

Fortunately, the men didn't notice her. They were laughing raucously at a joke.

She started to turn the other way, but one of them glanced over.

"Junius, look at this pretty little Jew, staring at you like you were Zeus himself?" The soldier laughed.

"Who says I'm not?" Junius shrugged haughtily. They all laughed again.

Hannah hurried away, her cheeks on fire. Yet if she was being honest, there was something about the imposing presence of the soldiers she found exciting. Terrifying, but somehow compelling. She glanced around, afraid someone had read her thoughts. After all, Yeshue always had.

The military presence was stationed to the east of the town. It was a large Gentile complex Hannah had seen as she came into town. She knew Jews would avoid it because it was ceremonially unclean. She stopped and surveyed the tops of the buildings, curious about the garrison behind the wall. She had heard Reuben discuss the Roman way of life, with their gymnasiums and bathhouses. Places her people would say were vulgar and immoral.

"Now this is a sight. Why would a good Jewish girl stare at the soldiers' bathhouse?" A man spoke in Greek next to her. She jumped back. A Roman Centurion towered over her on the back of his stallion, his position clear by the animal he rode and the three-foot staff in his hand. The horse nickered and shook his shiny black hair in the breeze as the man kept his eyes on her. She expected him to start harassing her, as the soldiers in Nazareth always had. She remembered them threatening one of her neighbors with crucifixion for not being able to pay his tax. She would never forget the terrified wails of his wife and daughters as the soldiers held him by the tunic and shouted in his face.

She glared at the man and held her son close as he fussed.

"Don't be afraid," he said. She frowned, stepping back. Had she misunderstood his Greek?

"I know, you have every reason to fear me," he said, switching to her language of Aramaic. "I won't hurt you. I was just surprised by your interest in the military base. Most Jews who come along the Via Maris act like our compound doesn't exist."

Hannah relaxed a bit. She wasn't ready to speak to the man, but she didn't think he would hurt her.

"Are you in trouble?" He eyed her and Y'aqim. Did he see her pack that held their meager belongings and the remainder of their food and wine? Did he wonder why a young woman with a child traveled alone?

"No," she said in a small voice.

He jumped off his horse and loosely held the reins. "My name is Lysander. You can tell me the truth."

She lifted her chin. "My name is Hannah. I'm looking for my brother."

"Where's your husband?" The soldier nodded at her child.

"Dead," Hannah said, expecting to see his pity. If he knew her husband, he would congratulate her.

He only watched her with an even expression. Y'aqim reached for her headscarf and pulled some strands of hair loose.

The soldier sighed. "I'd like to help, but anything I could offer you would be unthinkable to your people."

She lifted her head in interest. "Like what?"

"One of my servants has need of help in the bathhouse. But if you are any sort of faithful Jew, I doubt you will be able to accept."

Hannah hesitated. "What about my child?"

"A woman looks after the children of the servants and slaves in a separate house. He would be cared for."

"And my duties?" She cringed, unsure she wanted to hear the answer. Yet, if she had survived being Reuben's wife, she could probably survive any man, Roman or otherwise.

He smiled sardonically. "Any job the *balneator* finds for you." At her expression of confusion, he interpreted the word. "The bath keeper."

He was probably expecting her to immediately decline his offer. He had a bemused expression, as if he wasn't sure why he had even said it. She studied him more closely. He was not a youth; his hair was already starting to show signs of gray. He was maybe a few years older than Yeshue. His eyes revealed a gentleness she wouldn't have expected from the commander of a hundred Roman soldiers. Especially toward her, a Jew.

"If I accept and later find it to be too much, will I be able to change my mind?"

He considered her words. "Possibly. It would be up to the balneator. But you would be a hired servant, not a slave."

"Why are you showing me this kindness?" Hannah narrowed her eyes.

He shrugged. "I don't know. I don't like to see mothers and children go hungry. This is a peaceable village. I've had no trouble with the inhabitants, and I'd like to keep it that way."

She took a deep breath, considering the offer.

"You know, if you'd rather, you can give me your brother's name. I can find him for you. I'm on good terms with the Jewish people here."

"His name is Yeshue."

He chuckled. "He and every other man on the streets of Capernaum.

What is so special about that name?"

"It means *he will save his people*," Hannah explained before she thought better of it.

Lysander laughed. "That makes sense. Well, the odds of me finding your brother by that name are not as good. But I will do my best."

She bowed respectfully, hoping he wouldn't try too hard to find Yeshue. Yeshue and the rest of her family would have nothing to do with her after she set foot in the Roman garrison.

He motioned toward the barracks. "Go to the gate. Tell the guard that Lysander sent you to be put to work under the balneator. Tell him you are not to go into the baths themselves."

She adjusted Y'aqim on her hip. "Why not?"

"Woman, you do realize the baths are where soldiers swim without clothes, don't you?"

She felt her face flush hot. But she was determined not to be some shrinking little Jewess. She needed to prove she could do the job. "Well, that is why they call them the baths."

He raised his eyebrows, surprised, which gave her a measure of satisfaction. She started to walk toward the garrison, but she turned back suddenly and called to him. "Lysander, sir, you don't need to search for my brother."

"Why not?" He asked, stilling the horse so he might hear her answer.

"He would not claim me here."

Lysander watched her for a moment, as if he was torn, and then gave her a short nod before he rode away, the red of his cape flapping behind him in the breeze.

Part Two

MY BROTHER THE RABBI

And he left Nazareth, and came to dwell in
Capernaum, by the side of the sea ...
From then on, Yeshue began to preach.

Matthew 4:13, 17

TEN

Talia

טליה

"Talia!" Yeshue called her name before he even got to the doorway of their house. She ducked past the curtain and met him in the courtyard. His eyes were shining and he grasped her hands excitedly.

"Yeshue?" She eyed the long line of young men who were standing behind him. She counted two more besides the four she had already met. The sight of one of them required a second glance. He was tall and lanky, with tousled hair and a dusty robe. He had a sort of introverted, awkward look, but his eyes were friendly and his expression thoughtful.

Yeshue smiled at her as if he were keeping some sort of secret. "We have guests for dinner. Please make them comfortable."

She nodded even as she looked at him with silent question. His grin remained as he moved past her into the courtyard, where he greeted his niece, nephew and brothers and introduced them to the young men.

Talia hurried inside to tell her mother and sisters-in-law they would need more food than usual. Yeshue led his men to the table in the courtyard and had them sit. None of the men appeared more than twenty years old. Talia could not keep her eyes from finding the tall one, no matter how many times she told herself to stop being silly. As she brought cups and poured wine from a jug, she felt his inquisitive eyes on her.

"She is my sister, Talia." Yeshue answered the silent question, though it was not the Jewish way to draw attention to a woman during a supper of men. She blushed and wished she could hide behind her headscarf, which she could not because of the large jug in her hands.

Yeshue's smile only grew wider. "Talia, you know Peter and Andrew. These fine brothers here are Yohanan and Ya'achov, and then Philip, who is from Bethsaida, and Nathanael bar Tolmai. He is from Cana."

Yeshue had saved the tall one for last, and if she wasn't imagining things, he had emphasized Nathanael's name.

The other four nodded quickly to her and returned to their conversation, but Nathanael's eyes stayed locked on her.

"Sh'lam lek," Nathanael gave her the traditional Jewish greeting.

"Sh'lam lak." Her voice was barely more than a whisper. She did not know what else to do or say, and every man had his cup full with sweet wine, so she turned and rushed back to the house.

She thought she heard Yeshue chuckling behind her and made up her mind to give him a lecture later on the impropriety of introducing women to young men during dinner.

Yeshue was sitting in the cool shade of the house watching the evening activities of the household when Talia found him. She sat down next to him on the bench.

They sat in contented silence for a few minutes. She leaned back and took in the sounds of Capernaum. Rabbis argued nearby on the steps of the prayer house, their conversation animated as they discussed fine points of theology. Young women visited at the well, frequently bursting into giggles. Young men and boys played games in the street. Children laughed as they romped and dogs barked. Babies fussed as they grew tired.

"This is a good place, no?" Yeshue sighed in contentment.

She looked at him. "You always see the good no matter where you are."

And he did. From her earliest memories, Yeshue became animated over the tiniest details. An ant carrying a leaf. A bird circling overheard. A flower bud that suddenly burst into bloom. As he grew older, he would often stand over the Nazareth cliff with his arms outstretched, drinking in every detail of sound, smell and sight, as if he was storing them up to take with him on a long journey.

Nathanael came from Peter's house to the gate of the courtyard, catching her eye. He looked at her with a solemn expression she didn't understand.

Yeshue noticed her spying and smiled. "What are you thinking?"

She shrugged, pretending she didn't know what he was talking about. "Do you think it might rain tomorrow? If we were back home it would be time for barley harvest."

He was amused at her evasiveness. "I suppose it's possible it might rain, even if the old men didn't prophesy it."

She made a face at him. "Why do you keep smiling at me?"

He chuckled. "I think my little sister is far more interested in a certain young man than she is in the weather. A certain young man trying not to let her see he is watching her."

Talia frowned. "Don't tease."

He scooted closer and put his arm around her shoulders. "I'm not teasing. I just enjoy your youthfulness. I enjoy seeing the heart of young people as they look around, trying to find that special person that can be their *beloved*, as Solomon wrote."

"Yeshue!" she protested with a chuckle of disbelief. "I already told you I would follow *you*."

He nodded. "But it is possible to follow me ... together." He winked before he raised his hand and waved to Nathanael. Nathanael acted like he had just noticed them sitting there and waved back.

"He's a good man. I found him under a fig tree." Yeshue grinned.

"He's a good man because you found him under a fig tree?" Talia quipped.

He bumped his shoulder against hers. "No, he's a good man because he has a great interest in the things of God. He has studied the Torah well and tries to follow it. His thoughts run deeper than most men his age. He sees problems and wants to solve them."

"He's a good man because he's following you." Talia sat up and glanced at the man standing in the gate.

"But does he follow me because he believes in me or because I have a beautiful sister?" Yeshue looked at her with a twinkle in his teasing eyes. "I wouldn't fault him for the latter."

She blushed and shook her head, determined not to let his words sidetrack her. Was he testing her resolve? "Yeshue, I promised you."

He nodded. "I believe you will hold to that promise no matter what direction Elohim leads you. And I would not have either of you hide an attraction. It wouldn't do us any good, now, would it?"

Talia shook her head, her hands starting to tremble. She hid them in her lap. "I don't think I could ever be brave enough to speak to him." Her admission was a whisper, meant only for Yeshue to hear.

He nodded in understanding, and she appreciated how easily he let it go. They sat in silence for a time. A thought occurred to her, a question. In all his endless hunger and thirst for life, she had never seen Yeshue making eyes at the pretty girls, though she'd seen more than a few look his way. "Did you ever think to take a wife, Yeshue?"

He didn't answer right away. His warm brown eyes reflected the light of the moon and stars above. Then his eyes searched and found Nathanael, still sitting by the gate. He was talking to Philip, the one who spoke Greek fluently.

"Yes, I did."

She was surprised by his answer. She sat up and stared at him. "When? Who?"

"I was seventeen. The girl was fourteen. She was graceful and humble, so creative and passionate. I talked to her once or twice by the well. She was much like you, actually."

"I'm not so graceful," Talia said. "And I'm surely not very humble."

"You are more than you realize, Talia. Your beauty grows every day."

She shook her head, but she didn't argue. "Tell me more. Who was she?"

"Her name was Maryam."

"As every other girl born in Israel," Talia said with a chuckle. "You'll have to be more specific than that."

He looked at her, his eyebrows raised and his smile pulling at one side of his mouth.

"You mean not to tell me who she was," Talia realized.

"Of course not." He sat back against the wall intertwining his fingers across his chest. She pushed him lightly. "You are unfair, brother."

"I had it in mind to marry her. I even asked Abba to talk to her father. But when he did, he found out Maryam was loved by another and arrangements had already been made."

Talia watched her brother's voice grow serious. There was no sign of regret, but she saw the pain of rejection any man would feel in the same situation.

"I'm sorry, Yeshue. I didn't know."

He shook his head. "I was young. Eloi protected me and preserved me for other purposes."

"Such as ..."

She didn't like how sober his face became at her question. She could almost feel the tightness in his throat when he spoke. "What should *Yeshue* do?" He stared at her.

"Save his people from their sins," she answered according to the meaning of his name.

"Amen. So be it."

Hannah

חנה

The first step Hannah took into the military outpost was a careful one. She half expected the earth to break open and swallow her along with her baby boy. She breathed a sigh of relief after she safely placed a small sandaled foot on the unholy ground of the Roman garrison.

Immediately she felt the interested gazes of men. She had some idea of what a Jewish girl was to the average Roman soldier. There had been several incidents in Nazareth where drunk and rowdy soldiers had ruined young virgins. The poor girls crept along the streets in shadows or stayed hidden away in their family insula, covered in ashes and shunned by the community. It didn't matter that they hadn't had a choice. No one would share in their uncleanness.

Anger seeped into Hannah's spirit. Men were men, no matter what country they hailed from. The arrogant pagans who trampled on carefully protected righteousness were akin to the Jewish religious leaders who were so quick to condemn those without any choice. Did Alaha also judge them?

She wondered for a passing second what Yeshue would think of her now. He would probably have plenty to say about her sinful choices.

A voice interrupted her thoughts. "What are you doing here, girl?"

She looked up into the leering face of a Roman soldier. His entire person from the top of the plumes on his helmet to the toes of his golden sandals overwhelmed her senses. She faltered and stepped back over the threshold of the barracks.

"I've been sent by Lysander." She found her voice and her confidence and boldly stepped forward again. "He said I should be hired by the balneator, and I am not to enter the baths themselves."

"You want Felix." The soldier scoffed and jerked his head toward a man across the path, arranging jars of oil on the shelf just inside an open door. The soldier's eyes resumed an appreciative study of her figure.

The older, shorter man with silver hair and an embroidered toga came out of the shop when he noticed her standing there.

"Optio Lysander sent her." The soldier nodded toward her. "She's to work for you."

"*Abscedo.*" Felix waved the soldier away. He gave Hannah a hard stare. "Child, why would you want to work here?" Felix sounded tired, and she could tell he suspected her motives. "Your religion forbids it."

"I need to work to feed my son," Hannah said. Her voice was stiff and she forced herself to stand tall.

"This is the only work you could find?"

"This was the work offered to me," Hannah said.

Felix regarded her. "You realize that I am under no obligation to release you once I have taken you on as a hired servant. You will stay here until I don't need you any longer."

"I understand," Hannah answered.

Felix shrugged. "I'm innocent of your transgressions," he absolved himself. "The baths are directly outside the gate to your right. You can take your child to the *infantia* room in the first building you see before the door of the bathhouse. Then report to the towel and lotion room in the bathhouse. Cassia will tell you what to do."

She nodded and followed his instructions.

After Y'aqim had been taken into a separate house by a woman who gave him a look of disgust, Hannah went to the bathhouse. She entered through the arched doorway and found herself in the most beautiful room she'd ever seen. Richly colored tile covered every inch of the floor, walls and ceiling. Erotic frescoes had been painted on the walls. Steaming water sparkled in the sunlight from the skylight and windows. Male voices echoed through the chamber.

She heard laughter and as she looked around, she realized where she was. Naked men stood around the water, talking in Latin and pointing at her. She stumbled backward, fumbling for the exit and trying to breathe.

"What are you doing in here?" A male voice behind her demanded. She whirled around and found herself an inch from a man's bare chest. She was relieved he at least had a towel wrapped around his waist. She gasped as he grabbed her arm. She tried to pull away, but his hold was too powerful. She stared into his face, suddenly possessed by his features. She'd never seen a more handsome man. Her cheeks warmed.

"I was told to come here by Felix. That Cassia would tell me what to do," she said hotly.

"Felix didn't tell you to come in here." The young man eyed her suspiciously. "The servants' entrance is around the back. Get out before you get devoured by the lions."

His words brought a chorus of laughter, but Hannah saw he was serious. She dared to take another moment to study his face. The strong Roman nose and chin were obvious, as was his intense masculinity. She found herself tongue-tied.

She shook off the reaction and ran for the door. She could feel his piercing gaze on her as long as she was in sight.

A young woman she assumed must be Cassia stood behind a table inside the servants' entrance, arranging small green flasks of scented olive oil. The woman placed a long metal tool with each flask on the table. A stack of linen towels waited next to the flasks.

Cassia looked up, but did not seem interested in Hannah's presence. Hannah was astonished at the woman's obvious beauty. Uncovered black tresses cascaded down her back, and a clinging linen dress thin enough to see through displayed her shapely figure. Her black eyes were lined with kohl and her lips painted, accentuating her sensual features.

"Cassia?"

The woman nodded with no further interest than she had already expressed. Hannah felt childish in her presence. "Felix said you would tell me what to do."

Cassia regarded her with haughty disapproval. "What is he thinking, sending a little Jewish girl in here? You'll make everyone uncomfortable. You should leave."

Hannah fumed. "Felix has already claimed me as his servant. I can't leave, so you might as well get used to me."

Cassia banged the table, causing a flask to fall with a loud clank. "Fine. Strip off that dreary tunic and put on a dress from the room in the back. Come back here and fold these towels."

Hannah gave a short nod before she went to the back room. A row of dresses similar to the one Cassia wore hung on the wall. Putting on a dress like that went against everything Hannah had ever been taught about modesty. But she was in a different world now. Oppressive Jewish rules hadn't protected her, so why look back? She took off her tunic and cloak, removed her headscarf, and snatched one of the gauzy dresses from the row.

The white linen was soft and cool against her skin. The golden strand woven into the edges made her feel like a princess from Egypt. She couldn't deny a certain pride at wearing such an outfit. She brushed her hair and returned to Cassia.

Cassia laughed at her. "You think putting your arms over your chest will hide anything in that dress? Your gods will see everything."

Hannah let her arms drop to her sides. "I only have one God."

Cassia gave another derisive laugh. "One god? Don't your people have any imagination?"

Hannah went to fold the towels, but Cassia wasn't finished. "You aren't just here for your amazing talents at passing out towels and flasks. You're to be viewed by the men for their pleasure. You aren't allowed to hide yourself."

It was at that moment Hannah realized the full scope of what she'd agreed to do. She was certain she would never, ever see Yeshue, Maryam or Talia again. None of them would be able to look at her now.

"Give me another towel for my hair, Cassia." A man entered the room. Cassia didn't hand him a towel, but instead pushed him onto the stool and leisurely dried his wet hair with a towel. He sighed at her gentle touch. Hannah realized it was the same man who had banished her from the tepidarium. She glared at him.

"Who's this?" the man asked without opening his eyes.

"I don't know. Some Jewish girl Felix sent."

The man's eyes opened and he sat up with a frown. Did he recognize her now? "What's your name?"

"Hannah." She folded her hands in front of her.

"Where are you from, Hannah?"

"I come from Nazareth."

He laughed. "Nazareth? That figures. Some little Jewess you are. If they could see you now ..." He glanced at her dress.

Hannah lifted her chin and sent him a look of disgust. "I did not realize I would need to wear this."

The man said nothing in return, but she saw his stance soften, if just a bit. He folded his arms across his broad chest. "Didn't your mother and father explain what heathens we Romans are? Of our wanton behavior?"

"Yes," she said. Her honesty brought the curve a smile to his mouth. She found she liked his smile, and it made her relax, if just a little.

"You are beautiful," he said, though he didn't ogle her figure. He was looking at her face, which surprised her.

"You only say it because I am wearing this dress." She met his eyes in challenge. Did she notice a hint of sadness behind the rough exterior? He sat back and received Cassia's ministrations.

"Before you took your clothes off, I only saw your religion." He gestured to her figure. Hannah felt ashamed and wished she could cover herself. He watched her with interest.

"If it bothers you so much, why did you do it?"

"Because she wanted the great Ennius to prove himself to her," Cassia said next to his ear. Hannah heard the jealousy in the other woman's voice. Ennius ignored Cassia, which irritated the woman.

"Why did you do it?" he asked Hannah again.

"To feed myself and my son." Hannah shrugged, as if she thought the reasoning clear. He didn't answer right away.

"A worthy cause. But was it your only option?"

"As I said, my lord, I didn't know what would be expected of me. I was not raised to even think of such…"

"Evil?" Ennius smirked.

"…lifestyles," she said instead.

"I'm beginning to understand. You are a scared little Jewish widow who didn't realize Rome was so inclined toward things you've been taught are wrong. Even though plenty of Roman soldiers go through the Nazareth outpost on a regular basis, you hadn't understood how adept we Romans are at stealing life, purity or anything else we can get our hands on."

Cassia laughed and slid her arms around Ennius's neck. Hannah realized she was being mocked.

"I am a widow, but if you would ask my village, they would call me a harlot."

The room was quiet. Cassia still smiled as if she did not take a word Hannah said seriously, but Ennius seemed surprised at her words.

"A harlot, you say?" He shook off Cassia's arms and came to stand close to Hannah. She swallowed back terror as she tried not to cower at his stance. He leaned close to her face, so close she could feel the heat of his breath on her mouth.

"Sell yourself to me then, if you are a harlot. I'll pay you fifteen sesterces."

Shock mingled with repulsion. She stepped back until she hit the wall, panicking as he advanced and put his hands against the wall on either side of her.

He scoffed. "Some harlot you are."

With his words, he left the room.

ELEVEN

Talia

טליה

Grain slowly turned to powder as Talia worked the little grinding mill. The device had been handed down by her grandmother. Ama cherished the heirloom.

"You have been cheerful these past days," Maryam said with a knowing smile as she sat cross-legged in front of the oven and tested the bread baking inside. "Does the sea agree with you so much?"

"Oh yes, Ama. I'm sure that's it." Talia smiled.

Her mother chuckled. "You think your mother can't see you making eyes at that young disciple of Yeshue's."

Talia glanced at the courtyard where Yeshue was praying with the six men who had committed to follow him as their rabbi. "Shh! He'll hear you."

Maryam waved off her concern. "Don't be foolish. No one is listening to women's chatter. Not with all these children underfoot and making noise, anyway."

Y'hud and Shimon were having a mock swordfight with sticks while the younger children cheered them on. Maryam shushed their screams of laughter and set food on the table for their breakfast.

"Go wash those dirty hands!" she said as she inspected the boys.

Talia looked back to the courtyard where the men sat around the larger table. From the shadows of the kitchen, she could be bold enough to study this man who had possessed her thoughts lately.

Nathanael was a quiet man, approaching on brooding. He often questioned Yeshue or one of the other men. She could appreciate his methodical ways, even if others said he was too careful. He was quite handsome as well. His chest and arms were thick from hard work as a fisherman and his skin was tanned by the sun. He wore a turban around his head and a blue linen cloak over his simple tunic.

"Has Nathanael spoken to Yeshue yet, Talia?" Her mother spoke with a smile.

"Ama!" Talia protested. "I promised to follow Yeshue."

"Yeshue would understand. Women don't follow rabbis, Talia. They have babies and run households. Did you think you would sit at his feet and learn Scripture instead of serve his meals and wash his clothes?"

"Yeshue has never stopped me from sitting at his feet and learning," Talia said with a frown in her mother's direction. Maryam nodded as she poured water into a cup for Ya'achov.

"That doesn't make it your place. You must show Yeshue proper respect, especially now with his disciples here."

Talia bit her lip to keep back her retort. Her mother didn't understand. Maryam set down the water pitcher and put a hand on Talia's shoulder. "Talk to Yeshue, Talia. There's nothing shameful in marrying a good man."

Yeshue sought her out later that afternoon as she sat in the shade by the sea watching her brothers play. He wasn't alone. Nathanael walked beside him.

Her heart started pounding wildly as she stood up and waited for them. When they had almost reached her, she realized she'd taken off her head covering. She quickly grabbed it from the ground and pulled it over her long curls. She hoped no leaves or dirt were caught in the folds.

"Sh'lam l-kon." She lowered her eyes respectfully.

Yeshue took her hand. "Sit, Talia. Nathanael."

They sat, and Talia stared into the dirt, her cheeks on fire.

Yeshue didn't waste any time getting to the point. "Nathanael finds he cannot stop thinking about you," he said, casting a smile in his disciple's direction. "I have had time to judge his character. He's an excellent match for you, Talia."

Talia's heart fluttered. She quickly met her brother's eyes. "I cannot!" she whispered to Yeshue. She felt Nathanael's eyes on her, but she resisted looking at him. Was he disappointed? Would he argue with her reasoning?

"Sister, I have already told you I will honor your desire to remain unmarried if that is truly what you want, but not under false pretenses. If your heart's desire is to be with this man, I will only have trouble keeping the two of you apart while I am ministering, and that isn't helpful to me. If there is something between you that can't be ignored, we need to talk about it now."

Talia considered his words. She hadn't thought of it that way. She tried to speak, but no words would come.

Y'hud and Shimon called to Yeshue, wanting to show him something they found in the water. He jogged over to take a look, and before long he was deep into an explanation of some sort, using animated hand gestures and picking seaweed from between the rocks.

Talia was mortified. She had no idea what she should say to the young man seated beside her. "Yeshue loves nature," she managed, hoping her voice didn't sound as high and tight as it seemed to her.

Nathanael smiled as he watched Yeshue chase the boys into the water and splash them. "I've noticed that."

She felt his eyes on her. He cleared his throat. "May I speak freely?"

She wanted to run home, but she stayed still and gave him a small nod.

"Will you look at me, please?" he asked in a gentle voice.

She gulped, but found the courage to lift her eyes.

"I didn't expect this any more than you did. I came here to follow your brother because I believe he might be the M'sheekha. But I can't deny you've been in my thoughts. You're beautiful, but you're also humble, gracious, giving … I guess I would just like to know if you feel the same way."

"This isn't how things are done," Talia said, nervously drawing in the sand with her finger. "I shouldn't even be given a choice in the matter."

Nathanael chuckled. "If anyone is allowed to change the way things are done, I guess it would be Yeshue."

She couldn't help but smile. "True."

"I like that he gives you a choice. I don't want to force you to do anything. And I respect your desire to follow your brother as the M'sheekha. But we could follow him … together."

Her heart demanded she relent at his vulnerable tone.

"I would not lie, Nathanael bar Tolmai. I have thought of you, too."

She couldn't believe she'd spoken those words aloud. But when his face broke into a relieved smile, she did not regret them.

"Yeshue—he knows things. He has power, I can sense it. I've never been one to believe in these things, but I do, now, Talia. He's convinced me."

"Me too."

"Then can I ask you to be my wife and serve your brother as my Lord at the same time?" Nathanael almost seemed to be speaking the words to himself. She remained silent.

"I would be a good husband to you. I will provide for you even if I am not always with you," he said.

She frowned. "Where would you be?"

"Wherever Yeshue is."

"But he is here," she said, gesturing to the village.

"He is now. But he will be traveling when he begins his ministry."

Talia considered the words, and finally nodded. "That makes sense. But I want to be with him, too."

Nathanael hesitated, which didn't comfort Talia. She wasn't surprised. What she was asking was unusual, to say the least. Men had a right to go where they wanted, women did not. Women were to be busy at home. But Talia longed for more than that. She wanted to be a part of what Alaha would do through her brother.

She summoned her nerve and tried to explain. "I know it is a strange thing to ask. But as you said, Yeshue is one who could change the way things are done. Yeshue and his disciples will need someone to cook and wash, though. Wouldn't it make sense to have a woman come along?"

Nathanael nodded in understanding. "My family lives in Cana, and they are good people. I'm sure you won't mind living with them. But as long as Yeshue doesn't mind, you could come along sometimes."

It was not the promise she had hoped for. Was it enough?

Nathanael must have sensed her hesitation. "Talia, I'm a simple man. My family and friends would be quick to tell you I'm the last one to try something new. But I believe one thing almost as much as I believe your brother is the Son of Alaha. I believe we are meant to marry. If we didn't, I would regret it the rest of my life. I can see my sons in your eyes. Your beautiful eyes, pure and deep and dark. If you marry me and you want to be with Yeshue, you will be with Yeshue."

Hope made her chest ache. Did he mean it? Would Nathanael love her in the unselfish way Yeshue had always said a husband should love his wife? Such men were not common. Talia had observed enough to know. She gave him a shy smile, finally meeting his eyes with her own gaze. He caught her meaning and grinned. He quickly rose.

"I'll be right back."

Talia expected Nathanael to go tell Yeshue, who was now as soaked as his two younger brothers and happily splashing in the waves. Instead, Nathanael ran back toward Peter's house. He came back a few minutes later with Talia's mother and a cup of wine.

Her heart fluttered as she understood what he was doing. It was the betrothal ceremony. Yeshue and the boys met her under the tree, and they waited for Nathanael and Maryam to climb the hill.

Yeshue reached for her hand with his wet, wrinkled fingers and squeezed. "Don't be afraid," he whispered.

She nodded and took a deep breath. Nathanael came straight to her and pulled out a small bag that was tied to the belt of his tunic. He took out a simple ring and reached for Talia's hand.

"Behold you are consecrated unto me with this ring according to the laws of Moses and Israel," Nathanael said the traditional words with a gentle smile. He offered her the cup of wine. She took a long sip, symbolizing her willingness to become his wife.

"Amen!" Maryam, Yeshue and the boys clapped their hands. Yeshue put his hands on their shoulders and offered a blessing, breaking with tradition. When Talia opened her eyes, she found Nathanael gazing at her with joy. She put a hand over her chest, feeling breathless.

She was betrothed.

Yeshue and Nathanael went to a scribe later that day to write a marriage contract. When they came home that night with the *ketubah*, Nathanael said he would go home to Cana the next morning to tell his relatives and plan the wedding. Talia's family would arrive the following week.

"Aren't you a lucky one," Peter, the disciple, laughed at Nathanael's excitement. "I had to wait two years to take my bride home."

"I thought I had been fortunate to only wait a year," Ya'achov agreed.

"My father's insula is spacious," Nathanael explained. "He is a scribe in Cana. There will be no need for me to build onto the house."

Nathanael led Talia out into the quiet street as neighbors were beginning to go inside for the night. He made sure no one was looking before he intertwined his fingers with hers.

"I will miss you," he whispered.

"Me too," she said. Her cheeks were hot.

"Don't worry. My parents are good people. You won't find life with them difficult. My mother is cheerful and giving. She'll love you as I do. My father is fair, and I have no other brothers. They will like having your company."

Talia wanted to remind him of his promise to allow her to go with

Yeshue, but she decided not to press the issue. They could talk about it after the wedding.

The entire family left for Cana three days later, on the morning of the first day of the week. Yeshue's other disciples came along, invited by Nathanael.

Talia felt herself beginning to panic as they came closer to Cana. Several times on the nine-hour walk she fought the urge to turn around and run for home. She reminded herself it was too late. The ketubah had been signed by Yeshue and Nathanael's father by now. The bride price had been paid, proved by the jingling sound of coins in her bag. Nathanael had handed the seventy shekels to Yeshue, who had given them to her. She had tried to give him part, saying it should be used for his ministry, but he had only smiled and said "Yehovah Yireh will provide."

When Cana came into sight, her stomach lurched with fear. She wrung her hands together and stopped walking. "I shouldn't have done this. We shouldn't be here," she said to her mother. How she wished she was in Capernaum helping her mother make dinner for Yeshue and the disciples!

Her mother smiled and took her hand, leading her on. "It's marriage, Talia, not the grave," she reminded her, chuckling.

"I can't!"

"Yes, you can. You will go into that house and bow before his mother and ask how you may serve her. We will have the celebration and you will give yourself to your husband as you promised. You will have the joy of becoming one with the man who gives you his life. You have nothing to fear. I promise."

Talia turned toward Cana. The town was nestled in a valley. Limestone buildings centered around an old well. It was not as small and out-of-the-way as Nazareth, but somehow it felt familiar.

However she felt about it, she realized then and there the truth. She was home.

TWELVE

Ya'achov

יעקב

Ya'achov swung his daughter up into his arms so she could see what was happening in the doorway of Tolmai of Cana's home.

"Doesn't it remind you of our wedding, wife?" He put an arm around Nava and pulled her closer. She smiled and leaned her head against his chest.

"Long ago and only yesterday," she agreed.

As was the custom, Nathanael had come by night to the place they were staying. Talia had waited outside with a string of maidens from the town. They had giggled and held clay lamps as they followed Talia, who walked silently beside her husband. Ya'achov had thought Talia would never have the courage to go through with it, but she'd proven him wrong.

Nathanael had led the entire procession to his home, where they stood now. Shouts from children filled the night air. "The bridegroom is coming!"

Nathanael turned to Talia and kissed her as they entered the house. Tolmai and his wife, Ruth, welcomed Talia with open arms. Ya'achov watched his little sister, so nervous her face was as a tunic bleached by the sun, bow before Nathanael's mother.

"I am your servant," she said in a small voice. Ruth pulled her up and hugged her so hard Talia gasped for breath. Tolmai couldn't have smiled any bigger as he went around and greeted all the men.

"She'll be well looked-after," Nava said.

The *huppah* ceremony began immediately. The entire community had come to the house until it seemed to be bursting its seams from the rooftop to the courtyard to even the vegetable garden on the side of the house.

As Ya'achov had suspected, Yeshue was chosen to lead the ceremony by saying the traditional blessings over the couple who stood under the shelter of flowers.

"Baruch atah Adonai, Sovereign of the universe, who created joy and gladness, groom and bride, mirth and song. Soon, Adonai Elohim, may there ever be heard in the cities of Judah and in the streets of Jerusalem the jubilant voices of those joined in marriage under the bridal canopy, the voices of young people feasting and singing. Blessed are you, Adonai, who causes the groom to rejoice with his bride."

Everyone started to talk at once, but stopped as Yeshue continued beyond the traditional words. "Adonai, may Nathanael and Talia consider each other better than themselves. May Nathanael love Talia with the kind of love you inspire, and may Talia serve her husband with respect. Give them children to teach your ways and spread forth the seed of your love to all the earth through this union. Amen."

"Amen," several repeated somewhat awkwardly. Ya'achov grimaced, embarrassed. He watched Talia's new husband take her hand and lead her to a private room in the back of the house, which was most likely decorated with tapestries, myrtle leaves and roses.

"That boy will be lucky if she doesn't faint before they get past the curtain," he said to Nava, who laughed.

As the crowd began to converse while they waited for the couple, Ya'achov surveyed the turnout. He'd never seen such a well-attended feast. He remembered the day he had taken his wife. Nava had been a beauty. Sixteen, but full of youthful spirit.

After a time, Nathanael came out and sheepishly gave his announcement with a red face. "The marriage has been consummated."

Laughter and blessings went up from the crowd and the festivities took their full swing. Music played and food and wine were laid out in the courtyard. Young girls took to dancing in the street in front of the house and children were underfoot everywhere.

Ya'achov went to sit with the other men in the courtyard. He was greeted by several of Nathanael's relatives as he sat down at the long table, noting its sturdy construction. It was probably made especially for the event.

Yeshue was already there, reclining beside the town rabbi and eating grapes as they discussed the Torah with enthusiasm. Ya'achov fought the sudden pang of envy as he watched Yeshue. He had not been feeling as hostile toward his brother since their move to Capernaum. He had to admit now it had been a good thing for their family. But his emotions turned on him. Why should Yeshue always be the one everyone wanted to discuss religion with? Was not Ya'achov a Nazarite? Hadn't he been kept pure from birth? Surely he had special insight from Alaha as well.

But the truth taunted him. Ya'achov didn't understand the law and the prophets like Yeshue did. His mind couldn't fathom the concepts that came to Yeshue so easily. Knowing it made him angry. Maybe Yeshue just made it all up to get recognition.

Why did Yeshue always have to be the center of attention?

Talia
טליה

Talia snuggled next to her husband. He spoke softly, so quietly she could hardly hear him over the loud celebration on the other side of the curtain.

"Are you glad we are married?" Nathanael asked, running his hand through her long strands of hair. He wound a curl around his finger.

"Yes." She was glad for the noise outside, lest someone hear their conversation. "You?"

"I think marriage suits me," Nathanael kissed the top of her head.

She closed her eyes and rested on the elegant cushions behind them. The heady scent of myrtle and roses hung in the air.

"Your mother did well decorating," she said.

"I helped," Nathanael said, sounding somewhat wounded. Talia giggled.

"Can you believe we'll be in here for three days?" Nathanael asked as he looked up at the ceiling, covered with tapestry.

"Some stay in *yihud* as long as seven," she reminded him. "I don't mind being in here."

"You like the quiet," he said, kissing her again. "Why are you so afraid of others? You even feared me until we came in here."

"I don't know," she said with a shrug. "I have always been afraid of things."

"We are not to fear man," Nathanael said firmly. "It is like saying a man is as powerful as Alaha."

Talia felt the sting of his reproof. "I know. You may be a disciple of Yeshue, but I have been his sister my entire life. I know the Scripture. But I don't know how to overcome my fears."

She sat up, feeling agitation. Nathanael took her hand and stroked it tenderly. "I'm sorry, Talia. We shouldn't quarrel. Yeshue will help us with our weaknesses, I'm sure of it."

"I hope so." Talia relaxed.

"To think Alaha would be incarnated as a man," Nathanael said in awe.

"How do you know?" She leaned back and looked into his face. "How are you so sure my brother is the Son of Alaha?"

Nathanael took a long moment before he answered.

"Just before I met him, I was sitting under a fig tree outside Capernaum. Thinking. Wishing my life made sense," Nathanael began.

"What didn't make sense?"

"I was a fisherman. I came to Capernaum to start my fishing

business, even though my father wanted me to be a scribe like him. But it didn't fulfill me like I'd hoped. It was hard work. I got tired of mending nets and staying out all night and getting caught in storms. I missed my family and friends here in Cana. Truthfully, that day under the tree I was pouting."

Talia smiled. "So what happened?"

Nathanael stared out the small window at the dark sky full of stars. As he did, the music outside ceased. People were leaving for the night. They would return in the morning as the feast continued. The night air became an eerie stillness. Talia had always been fast asleep at an hour like this.

"Philip came," Nathanael said in a hushed voice. "He was so excited, almost jumping for joy. I calmed him down and asked what was going on. He said 'We have found the one Moses wrote about in the Law and the one the prophets wrote about!' 'Who?' I asked. 'Yeshue bar Yosef of Nazareth,' he answered."

Nathanael laughed. "I said 'Nazareth? Can anything good come out of Nazareth?'"

Talia sniffed. "I come from Nazareth," she said, but she smiled, for she knew the saying.

Nathanael nodded. "You are proof that it is possible."

Talia shrugged. "Nazareth is nothing unless you've lived there your whole life."

Nathanael continued. "Anyway, Philip told me to come see for myself. So I did. He led me to the docks where Yeshue was talking to two pairs of brothers—also fishermen. As I came up to him, he looked straight into my eyes like he knew me. He stood up and said 'Here comes a true Israelite, in whom there is nothing false.' I was uneasy because I knew there was plenty of false in me. But I asked how he knew me. He said 'I saw you under the fig tree before Philip called you.'"

Talia noticed the shine in her husband's eyes as he recalled the event.

"I can't describe what that moment felt like." Nathanael's voice was hushed with emotion. "I felt like I'd been blind for nineteen years and suddenly I'd opened my eyes and saw the most beautiful sight. I knew he was no ordinary man. He'd been a good two miles away and inside a house while I was sitting under that tree. He couldn't have seen me unless he was divine."

Talia nodded. "Yeshue has always been special. Sometimes I think he can read my mind. But I've never seen him display powers like that."

"Not once in all the years you lived with him?"

She shrugged. "Yeshue doesn't draw attention to himself."

He nodded, sitting up and grabbing her hands with excitement. "And that's what makes him so special, Talia! What mere man would be humble about power like that? Only the one who has no need to get attention."

"I see what you're saying," Talia said, although her mind did not want to accept such a strange notion about her brother's power. It made him less familiar to her. It could change her view of him. Her hesitancy must have frustrated him, for he stood up and paced the small area.

"I'm sorry, Nathanael. But imagine if you heard for the first time your brother had powers you've never seen yourself. It seems ridiculous."

He looked out the window, a faraway glint in his eye. She stood and came to him, putting her arms around him and leaning her head against his chest. He held her and sighed deeply.

"So what did you say after he told you he'd seen you under the tree?" she asked.

Nathanael didn't answer for a moment. When he did, she heard the break of emotion in his voice. "I said 'You are the Son of Alaha. You are the king of Israel."

Talia considered the implications of his statement. It was one thing to honor a man as rabbi or teacher. It was quite another to call a man the Son of Alaha. Even more frightening was daring to proclaim a man king of Israel.

"You're scaring me," she whispered. "If Herod heard what you just said ..."

Nathanael turned to her and grabbed her shoulders, staring at her. His face was completely solemn. "It doesn't matter," he said with conviction. "I would die for him."

"No." Talia felt the sting of tears. "Don't say it."

"Would you have me say anything less? Would you have me follow your brother with half-hearted conviction and turn and run when he is confronted by his enemies? I will fight with him. Did you not expect that?"

Talia could not speak. Her tears fell. She didn't want to hear it. She didn't want to imagine that her new husband and her brother she loved more than anything were both willing to give up their lives for revolution.

Men bent on revolution always ended up dead at the hands of Herod or Rome.

"Talia, when I told him I believed in him, he said something else. He said I would see greater things than that. He said I'd see heaven open and angels descending on him."

"What does that mean?"

Nathanael shook his head. "I don't know. But I intend to find out."

"At any cost?" she asked dully.

"At *any* cost."

THIRTEEN

Three days together in the wedding chamber passed quickly. The third morning, they heard whispers and giggles outside their door. Trust the littlest children to remember every part of tradition. They would not be given a moment of extra time alone together.

Talia donned her wedding veil that Nathanael would symbolically remove when they came to the celebration, so everyone could see her beauty. They shared one last private kiss and then he pulled back the curtain.

Talia didn't like having everyone's eyes on her. It didn't matter that they were smiling, and it didn't matter that almost everyone her age and older were also married. She was still embarrassed by the attention.

Nathanael didn't seem to mind. He pulled away her veil and stood back proudly so everyone could see her face. "Behold, my bride!" he said. Everyone cheered. Talia's cheeks burned.

They were shown the place of honor at the head of the long table in the courtyard. Food was passed in a flurry of excitement.

"There should be more food than this," Nathanael whispered in her ear. "There must be more people than they expected. My poor mother will be so embarrassed."

Talia felt a wave of sympathy for her new mother-in-law. She wished she could help. As she was thinking it, she heard her mother speaking to Yeshue, who reclined near them on cushions. Maryam's voice was low and Yeshue bent close to hear her.

"They have no more wine."

Talia looked at Nathanael's parents. His mother was wringing her hands and staring at her husband with wide eyes. He shrugged helplessly. Yeshue watched them with a kind smile on his face. He kissed Maryam on the cheek. "Dear woman, why are you involving me? My time hasn't come yet."

Talia watched them with confusion. His time? What was he talking about? What did Maryam want him to do?

There was a long silence between mother and son as they regarded each other in a sort of stand-off involving affectionate smiles. Finally, Yeshue sat up, and Maryam's grin grew wider. She turned to the servers about to pour plain water into cups for the thirsty guests.

"Do whatever he tells you," she said discreetly. The servers turned to Yeshue in expectation. He looked over to the entrance, nodding toward the six large stone jars standing by the door. They were kept for ceremonial washing upon entering the house.

"How many gallons do you suppose they hold?" he asked thoughtfully.

"I'd say twenty to thirty, my lord," a male server answered.

"Fill every one of them to the top with water."

Talia watched them comply, drawing water from the cistern in the courtyard until every jar was full. She wondered if the servers were as curious as she was. The rest of the crowd continued their noisy chatter and music, unaware of a certain buzz of anticipation in the air, sensed by only a few who were paying attention.

A cold tremor shook Talia's body. Something important was about to happen at her wedding. Everything would change. It was a lightning bolt realization.

When the jars were filled, Yeshue nodded his approval to the server who returned.

"Good man. Now draw some out and take it to the master of the banquet."

The man hesitated. Talia was sure he didn't want to have to present

Nathanael's father with a cup of water. But he took one look at Yeshue, and his hesitation faded. He nodded and went to do as Yeshue asked.

Tolmai took the cup presented by the servant with hesitation. But when he looked inside it, his eyes widened. He took a long sip.

Tolmai was not a subtle man. He hurried over to Nathanael and clapped his son on the back. "Everyone brings out the best wine first at a wedding, saving the cheaper wine until everyone is drunk. I thought we were out of wine. You saved the best until now?"

Nathanael, who had also been watching Yeshue, could hardly find the words to respond. "The best?"

Tolmai thrust the cup toward his son, who sipped what he was convinced was water from the stone jars. His face paled and his eyes shot to Yeshue. Talia's heart fluttered at the look on his face. "This is wine!"

Yeshue nodded, as if he'd just picked up some wine at the market and brought it back so the party might continue uninterrupted. Talia pulled her husband's hand toward her so she might also look in the cup. She brought it to her lips. Not even a hint of poor man's wine, watered down until it barely tasted of fruit. It was the sweetest, smoothest wine she'd ever had.

Her hands trembled as she let go of the cup.

"Praise Alaha," Maryam murmured. The other disciples went to fill their own cups to taste the wine. No one else at the party even noticed what had happened. They were only happy to see the wine flowing again.

Maryam brought Yeshue a cup of the wine he had created out of nothing. Talia watched his eyes close in appreciation as he sipped it. A smile spread across his face. Not one of surprise or awe at what he had just accomplished. It was the same smile he always had when he was eating or drinking. Like he was savoring every last drop or bite. Storing up the memory of each taste.

Prophetic Scripture flooded her mind. She gasped and shook her head in desperation. She wouldn't allow it. Not now. Not here, at her wedding. This was all just a misunderstanding. A trick of the mind.

But there was little she could do to comfort herself. Her brother had just turned water from the cistern into the strongest, tastiest wine ever made. In seconds.

There was no doubt now. Her brother was a miracle-maker.

Hannah
חנה

The shout inside the barracks signaled the end of morning exercises for the soldiers. Hannah sighed, knowing the bathhouse would soon be flooded with men. She stacked the towels and set up lotion and oil bundles for those wishing to purchase them. She ignored a hard look from Cassia.

"Don't pull your Jewish modesty act today," Cassia said under her breath as they heard the men's laughter outside the door. "No one believes you are pure."

Hannah tried to ignore her. Cassia's harsh words continued all day, every day, and Hannah was weary of her. It was hard not to see herself as Cassia saw her—a second-rate prostitute willing to give up her religion and family. Was that really all she was? Something occurred to her from all her hours in the prayer house listening to the rabbi or Yeshue talk about the Torah. Didn't Alaha love all equally? It must have been Yeshue who had spoken the words, because any good Jew would not want to believe Alaha loved pagans as much as his people. But it was something to give her a small measure of hope, anyway. If Alaha loved the people she was with, maybe he wouldn't judge her quite as severely for living among them.

Even as she thought the words, other Torah lessons came to mind. The rabbi's creaky voice wasn't hard to remember.

Do not intermarry with them. Do not act like them.

She pushed every thought of religion from her mind and found her false smile as the men poured into the room. They grabbed towels and whatever else they could get their hands on. Hannah cringed as one man grabbed her and held her close. Another openly spoke to his friend about her body without looking at her face. By the time the last man had come through, Hannah felt unclean. Burdened with the sin of the men she served.

She sank back to the stool as Cassia scoffed at Hannah's reaction. But before Cassia could attack her with words as she did every other day, a shadow passed over the door. Hannah looked up to see Ennius.

She went to get him a towel. He took it from her, but his eyes studied her face. "What's wrong, Hannah?"

Ennius had come through every day, and every day he asked Hannah some personal question. At first, she thought he was teasing her, but even if he was, she looked forward to attention that had nothing to do with the shape of her figure.

His eyes were as dark and grim as ever, his manner as harsh as any self-respecting Roman soldier. He had held Cassia enough for Hannah to know he had nothing against such things. But at least his supposed kindness gave her one small thing to anticipate each day.

"Nothing." She tried to smile in the seductive way Cassia did. Ennius ignored Cassia's haughty snort and touched Hannah's arm. "I expect you to tell me if anyone mistreats you."

She stared at him in surprise, but he stood waiting for a response, so she nodded. "Yishar ... I mean, thank you."

"I've been searching for your brother, you know. So far, every Yeshue I have found has claimed no sister your age named Hannah."

She was surprised. "How did you ..."

"I spoke with the centurion, Lysander."

"Oh," she said, her voice faltering. How could she explain to him she no longer wished to find her brother? What if he actually came across Yeshue? What would she do then? "Thank you."

"You don't sound very thankful." He seemed thoughtful, not wounded, so she didn't respond. He watched her for another moment, and she recognized a yearning in his eyes. She knew she was beautiful, no matter what Cassia tried to say about her long arms or big ears. Her pregnancy had given her curves that made her appear older than she was. But for some reason, Ennius never acted on the feelings she was sure he had for her. He never treated her like property, or acted like she owed him something.

"Has anyone hurt you?" he asked in a quieter tone meant only for her.

She lowered her gaze. "No."

"You are to tell me if they try anything."

She nodded.

As he strode purposefully into the bathhouse, she wished she could run after him and jump into his arms. No one had hurt her beyond repair, but she had been forever altered from the moment she had stepped into the military complex. She was damaged. She had the sense he would be disappointed if he knew she had given in to the pressures of the soldiers, offering their sesterces for an hour alone with her. She had rationalized it. She must feed her son. She had closed her eyes and pretended herself far away from the filthy stench of sin that hovered over the Roman camp like a dark cloud. She'd focused on the brass coins in her hand. Her mind had become numb to the evil. She no longer hesitated or blushed when they came to her dwelling.

The only time she felt any regret was when Ennius spoke to her. Why should she care what he thought? Perhaps it was because he treated her as if she was someone to protect. Did he look after her because she was Jewish? If he only knew what her family would think of her now. He might not bother with her if he had any idea.

She certainly didn't intend to tell him.

Ennius leaned his head back into the room. She looked up expectantly, ready to get whatever he had forgotten.

"Would you take a walk with me this evening?" he asked her. His manner was tentative, as if he wasn't convinced it was a good idea. She longed to agree to it, but she knew it was impossible.

"If my people in Capernaum were to see me dressed this way, they could have me stoned. Especially today. It's Shabbat."

He nodded abruptly. "So wear your tunic and head covering. I'll meet you in front of the baths when midday rest is over."

He didn't give her a chance to argue. He was gone, leaving only a faint masculine scent behind.

FOURTEEN

Later that day as midday rest ended and the camp came alive again, Cassia watched Hannah change into her worn Jewish clothes.

"Don't think for a minute Ennius is in love with you. He doesn't love anyone except himself," Cassia said. "Even if he did, when he found out you were as much a common whore as I am, he'd despise you for deceiving him."

Hannah sighed loudly in frustration. "Why must you always be so cruel? Just be quiet."

"The little Jewish princess doesn't like to hear the truth. No one forced you to be this way. You chose to put a price on your body. Your God means less to you than a few coins that bear the face of Caesar."

Hannah reached out and slapped the lovely face of Cassia as hard as she could, before she thought better of it. Cassia fell back, holding her red cheek. "You are worthless, Jew. Your *virtue* is nothing but lies."

Cassia left, still holding her mouth. A lump gathered in Hannah's throat. She started to pull her veil over her head, but she couldn't bring herself to do it. She sat on the stool, staring at the covering that was meant to keep her pure and safe. She had no right to wear it. But she had no choice, for she didn't want her family to recognize her. In shame, she finally put it over her head and got up to meet Ennius in front of the building.

She saw that he was standing in the door, watching her. He gestured to the head covering she wore. "The opinion of others means that much to you?"

"It might to you as well if they had the ability to stone you."

"You'll be with a Roman soldier. Do you really think anyone will hurt you?"

He turned abruptly and left. She had to hurry to catch up with him as he took large strides toward Capernaum.

He said nothing for a long time, seeming agitated for reasons she could not decipher. She kept her head down, feeling the harsh stares of her people.

"Maybe it's not their opinion that bothers you. Maybe it's your god. Are you afraid he'll strike you down for your sins?"

Hannah felt irritation. What right did he have to judge her morality? He was a Roman soldier!

"You're thinking I have no place to talk," he said with a smirk. "At least you're a Jew and not a Roman, right?"

"Where are we going?" She tried to change the subject, afraid of his ability to discern her thoughts so accurately.

"I want your opinion about something."

"My opinion? You would respect the judgment of a fallen Jewish woman?" Hannah laughed, though not with humor.

"My people may be pagan idol worshipers, but at least we respect the thoughts of our females," he said, his tone rife with irritation. "Your Jewish leaders seem to think women are less important than the stray dogs that roam the streets. Some god you serve."

"Alaha says that women hold value." At least that's what Yeshue had said. Though he had been challenged for his ideas, no one had been able to stand up to his defenses. He had maintained that women were as significant as men, with different purposes.

But he had been speaking of pure women, not women like her. Even Yeshue would agree she had thrown away her value with her integrity.

"So, your priests and teachers don't tell you what your god says? They make up their own rules?"

Hannah felt uncomfortable speaking for the religious leaders of Israel. "I should not say anymore."

Ennius made a sound of disgust as he perused the table in the market, his hands behind his back. "I see it every day. You like to make yourselves out to be happy and devoted to your god, but I know better. I see a miserable lot tossed around by every idea the rabbis and leaders think up and call your god's idea. You've given them too much power. They hold it over you. Just as the Romans do. Maybe even more so."

"Stop!" She considered pushing him into a pen crowded with lambs. "I will not defend my people or my God to a pagan."

He went silent as they continued out of the market and past the prayer house, where men stood in groups discussing the portion of the Torah that had been read in the prayer house that morning.

Hannah eyed them. They seemed more animated than usual. Excited. She had never known her fellow Jews to become *that* enthusiastic over anything taught in Shabbat prayer house.

She stopped and listened to their words.

"He told the evil spirit to come out. The spirit obeyed! You could almost see the darkness leave his eyes."

"I've never seen anything like it! Who can this Yeshue of Nazareth be?"

Hannah balled her hands into tight fists under the sleeves of her tunic. She felt breathless. Another loud conversation between two women toting babies drifted her way.

"That old woman had the fever. Everyone said she would die. And all he did was take her hand and help her up. She's completely well!"

"She must have been pretending," the second woman said with skepticism.

"I've never known their family to spread falsehood. They're honest people."

"You're right about that, I admit."

Hannah took several small steps backward. Ennius finally realized she wasn't at his side and turned around. "Come on," he called, motioning impatiently.

"I can't," she said. "Something has happened."

"I know," he said. He came back to her and grabbed her arm. "That's why I asked you to come. I don't speak your language very well and I want you to interpret. It's important."

Hannah narrowed her eyes, offended by his ulterior motives in asking her to walk with him. She allowed him to pull her down the road a bit further until they came to a large crowd gathering in the dim light of dusk. A sense of foreboding haunted her until her ears heard the familiar tones of a tender voice.

"No," she begged, pulling against his grip. "Please don't make me go any further."

Ennius turned and saw recognition in her face. "You know who this man is, don't you?"

"Yes." When he let her go, she turned back toward the military complex. He caught up to her outside the main road by the market and grasped her hand to stop her.

Several Jewish merchants eyed him with suspicion, though they didn't challenge him.

"Please don't run away. I have to know who he is."

She stared at the ground. The image of *his* dear face seemed written in the grass at her feet. She looked up, and imagined *he* smiled from the clouds. Arms open. Hands beckoning. To everyone but her.

Her voice trembled as she spoke. "His name is Yeshue."

"Yeshue your brother?"

She didn't respond.

"Hannah, is he your brother?"

She met his eyes, surprised to find a measure of tenderness there despite the gruffness in his tone.

"Yeshue of Nazareth. My brother the rabbi."

He didn't speak for a long moment. "But you don't want to speak to him?"

"No," Hannah said. She shook her head and traced the dust with the toe of her sandal.

Ennius crossed his arms over his thick chest. "Well, do you know what he's doing?"

She shook her head and took a step backward and leaned against the trunk of an old olive tree.

Suddenly several women ran past them with crying children in their arms. Hannah watched them go, concerned because of her own little one waiting for her at the complex.

Ennius must have seen her interest kindled, for he motioned for her to follow him back. "Come. We'll stay hidden."

When they came to the house where she had spotted Yeshue, the women were there, fighting the crowd.

"Rabbi Yeshue! Please save my baby, he's so sick!"

Hannah frowned and searched for her brother. What was happening? Everything was strange and new, and she wondered for a moment if it really was her brother or if she had mistaken someone else for him.

Ennius motioned her closer, and they climbed all the way to the roof. They moved to the other side where Yeshue was sitting on a bench below them. She leaned over as far as she dared, hoping no one, especially Yeshue, would see her there.

"Your faith has made you well. Go in peace," Yeshue said gently to a crippled man.

The man suddenly stood up straight and laughed in disbelief. "I'm healed!"

Hannah's hands began to tremble violently, and Ennius pulled her back from the edge of the roof before she fell over it. She took deep breaths, trying to will away the flashes of hot light in her vision. "What's happening?" she managed.

His arm stayed around her, supporting her. "Is this common? Do your rabbis heal sick people?"

She shook her head, dumbfounded. "I've never seen anyone ..." her voice trailed off as she held her hands to her forehead. When her mind began to recover from the shock, something else occurred to her. "We are taught that people get sick and die because they have sinned. Even if a mere man could reverse sickness, why would he think of intervening with the judgment of Alaha?"

Her mind was a tangled mess of thoughts. She could not begin to process what he was doing. More overwhelming was the fear that he would see her and find out what she had been doing. He would be so disappointed. He would have no choice but to see to her judgement this time, immediately. She had scorned his first act of mercy. She'd sinned again—and worse this time. She'd sinned until she no longer felt the sting of it.

"I have to get out of here," she pleaded. "He'll kill me."

He hesitated, regarding her evenly. "Don't you want to know what he's doing?"

She only shook her head. She thought she saw a flicker of kindness in his expression. He finally nodded and they climbed down from the roof and returned down the hill to the army post as she veiled her face with her head covering.

Once they returned to the bathhouse, Ennius sat down on the step. Not knowing what else to do, Hannah did the same. The evening air had a chill to it. Ennius fidgeted and ran his fingers through his short black hair. Hannah watched the sun disappear over the horizon as the night sky began to twinkle with the light of thousands of stars. She only had one thought as she stared into the sky.

Yeshue.

He'd always been different. She'd noticed because he embarrassed her sometimes. But even with his quirky ways, it had been obvious others were jealous of him. He just had a way about him. Ideas and concepts came easily to him. He could solve any problem they came up with in the shop, and he could answer any questions posed at the prayer house with all the confidence of Moses himself. Even with his great understanding and wisdom, he was humble and unassuming. Even when he was so tired he could barely keep his eyes open long enough to climb up to his pallet, he would never turn away someone with a question or a need.

But most of the villagers had made fun of Yeshue behind his back. Some of the children had been cruel, saying that their mothers had told them Yeshue was possessed by demons. She hadn't understood why until now.

What kind of man drove away sickness with a word? She'd never seen that kind of power. She'd not thought it possible.

Yeshue would say it was the power of Alaha, but Hannah had her doubts about that, as well. The only thing she'd ever gotten from Alaha was silence. She'd come to believe that he didn't care anymore. That he'd left them to suffer, tired of their sinful ways.

A whimper behind them returned her to reality. Aemilia, the infant caretaker, dumped her son into her lap.

"Next time you leave him late I'll whip him until you return." She snarled at Hannah before she turned on her heel and left them. Hannah hugged Y'aqim tightly.

"She's cruel to him," Hannah said to Ennius, who had silently watched the exchange.

Ennius reached a finger to Y'aqim's chubby legs and traced red welts. Hannah felt a sudden and forceful need to sob.

"I'm sorry, baby," she whispered, rocking him back and forth and pressing her mouth against his soft dark hair. He snuggled against her, putting his thumb in his mouth and closing his eyes.

Ennius got up and left without saying another word. As soon as he was out of sight, she could take the pressure no more. She despised tears, so she raged instead. She set her son on the ground and pounded her hands against the side of the building until they were red and painful.

When her strength was spent, she was startled by a dark form standing over her.

Ennius had returned. And he had a chunk of bread in one hand and a cup of watered wine in the other. His expression surprised her. His eyes were large and dark in the dim light of the torches at the doorway.

"For your boy." He handed her the snack and sat down next to her.

Y'aqim ate the bread so fast he nearly choked on it. Hannah helped him sip the wine.

"Does that woman even feed him?" Ennius said in disgust.

She felt the lump in her throat again.

Y'aqim squirmed away from her and began to play with a stick on the step. Ennius scooted closer to her and put his arm around her shoulders. She gratefully leaned into his chest.

"Don't cry," he said gruffly, patting her back. "It won't change anything."

She quickly wiped her eyes and scoffed at him. "I'm not crying."

As she looked up into his face, she was startled by a feeling she'd never sensed before. It came over her like a powerful wave. She wanted to be loved. Loved by Ennius. In whatever way he would.

It's wrong, she said to herself. *In so many ways.*

But what did it matter? She'd already sinned so badly the damage would never be repaired. Aliaha, wherever he was, had given her up to her rebellion. There was no use trying to be anything but what she really was.

She made her willingness evident, leaning toward him and giving him what she thought was a seductive smile. He frowned, but he didn't pull away from her. He leaned closer and kissed her. It wasn't the greedy, selfish kisses she'd received from her husband or the soldiers in the bathhouse. It was tentative. Sweet.

He pushed the covering from her head and let his fingers trail through her hair. His kiss became more possessive, more what she had come to expect from men. As he moved his mouth against hers, his hand traveled down her side.

He leaned back suddenly, glancing down at her abdomen. "You're with child."

She lowered her gaze and nodded to confirm his accusation.

"By whom? One of the men in the bathhouse?" he demanded.

She narrowed her eyes and pushed him away. "By my dead husband, you filthy Roman!"

He stood up. "Don't take that tone with me, Jew. You think I don't know what you've been doing for money while your child is beaten?"

She seethed, hot anger spilling over her as she stood and grabbed her son. She tried to pass by Ennius, but he caught her arm with a pinching grip.

"Don't walk away from me," he said harshly.

"Let me go! You don't know me. You know nothing about me," she said fiercely.

"So tell me," he said, letting go of her arm. His eyes remained dark and cruel. "Tell me why a girl, who has a brother that can heal sick with mystical power, wants to live in a dung heap like this and trade favors for Roman coins."

She screamed with fury. "Because I don't know what else to do! Because my husband was a cruel man who hated me, and it was my fault I was stuck with him. Because I miss Yeshue and my family, but he will never see me again. Because I'm never going to get out of this. My son, my baby and I will all die because of my sin. Why believe in what is impossible?"

The fight left her, and her shoulders sagged. She turned from him and went to her room. She shut the door and barred it. He knocked, but she refused to open it. She put Y'aqim in their bed and crawled in next to him, hoping that neither of them would wake up and that oblivion would swallow them and end their misery.

FIFTEEN

Talia

טליה

Talia stood at the window long after the men had departed over the hill and left her view.

"They'll be back," her new mother-in-law said cheerfully.

"I know. I thought Nathanael would let me come along."

Ruth wore a confused expression. "Why? Following the rabbi is the duty of young men. Your duties are in your home. Your place is here with me now."

Ruth had no annoyance in her tone, only an inability to fathom why Talia would want to leave. Talia didn't try to explain. Ruth would only say the same things Nathanael had been saying every time she asked.

It will be a lot of walking and we may have to sleep under the stars. How would I look as a husband if I let you wander all over the Galilean countryside? What if you were with child? It's just not a good idea right now.

Talia turned from the window with a sigh. She took the old wheat grinder her mother had given her as a wedding present. She held it in her hands for a moment, remembering happy times spent preparing meals with her mother. Why had she traded everything she knew and loved for this lonely little town?

"In time you'll get used to us and call Cana your home," Ruth said, patting Talia's hand.

Talia didn't answer. She didn't want to have to tell her mother-in-law she would never think of Cana that way. She couldn't. Yeshue wasn't there.

"I'm so glad Nathanael found you," Ruth continued as she set fish in rows on a platter to dry on the roof. "He's always been so careful and studious, so afraid of doing something wrong and displeasing Alaha. I've been secretly afraid he'd never find a wife that met his expectations. You must be an exceptional girl, Talia."

"The only thing exceptional about me is my brother."

"Well, your brother certainly is special. I never imagined I'd meet a miracle worker. I wouldn't have believed it if I'd hadn't seen it with my own eyes. Do you suppose the M'sheekha has really come?"

"I know he has," Talia said, hearing the hint of impatience in her voice and resolving not to talk anymore. The words brought a fresh reminder of all she was missing. Had she made a mistake—marrying Nathanael? Would Alaha have had her follow Yeshue instead? Had she been too afraid to follow him as her heart told her she should?

I've gone back on my promise. All because I was too afraid to follow him. He must be so disappointed in me.

She had gone on one trip before Nathanael had said she should stay home. She had accompanied the family back to Nazareth. Ya'achov and Yose hadn't been able to go, having too much work to do, but Maryam and the boys had come along with the disciples and Yeshue.

They went during harvest so they might be of some use to their friends and relatives in Nazareth. But the villagers had met them with sad news. Sickness had come to the town during the winter. Two families had died of the disease. One of them was Hannah's.

Maryam had been about to break forth in a mourning wail before her aunt grabbed her arm in assurance. "Hannah and her son didn't die. They ran off the morning the bodies were discovered."

Talia felt a rush of relief when she was sure Hannah was alive. Maryam looked to Yeshue. "Where could she have gone? She's so young. My baby girl."

Yeshue had put his arm around her and spoken in whispers into Maryam's ears. Maryam took a deep breath and steeled her expression. Talia heard her brother's words.

"Trust me."

Maryam nodded, her face changing slowly into one of resolve. "I do, my son."

Talia watched her mother's face soften and her shoulders rise in sudden courage. She wished she could believe so easily.

After the harvest celebration and the hard work that followed, a peaceful Sabbath day dawned. The family followed Yeshue down the road to the old prayer house, which seemed small and drab compared to the spacious, attractive building where they worshiped in Capernaum.

Nathanael had leaned over to her as they were walking. "Your village people are odd. They act distrustful of Yeshue instead of excited for his new ministry. I've overheard men saying he should *prove himself.* Have they always treated him this way?"

Talia had to be honest. "Our people have never believed Yeshue was the M'sheekha, and they have resented my parents for claiming he was. It is something no one really talks about, but everyone knows."

He nodded. "It's too bad. Yeshue told us last night he was shocked by the lack of faith here compared to Capernaum. And we both know it takes much to shock your brother. He hasn't been able to do more than heal a few sick children here. It has disheartened him."

Talia's heart went out to Yeshue for the treatment he'd received by his own kin. Not that he was a stranger to such animosity.

They entered the prayer house, which was crowded because of the visitors. Talia and her mother stood by the door, watching the service. There was a time of greeting and then they sang several Psalms together. When the time came for the scrolls to be brought out and the Torah read, the old rabbi, not sensing the tension in the group, smiled proudly and handed the Isaiah scroll to Yeshue.

Instead of asking what portion he should read, Yeshue unrolled the scroll, obviously hunting for a certain passage. The villagers exchanged uneasy glances with one another. Talia knew they had heard of Yeshue's miracles and teaching in Capernaum, for she'd heard them whisper to each other about them. She was sure that was why no one challenged him when he broke with the traditions of their Shabbat service. But she could feel their apprehensive reaction.

"The Spirit of Yehovah Adonai is upon me, and because of this he has anointed me to preach the good news to the poor; he has sent me to heal broken hearts and to proclaim liberty to captives, vision to the blind, and to restore the crushed with forgiveness, and to proclaim the acceptable era of Yehovah Adonai."

Yeshue handed the scroll to a boy who assisted the rabbi. Then he sat down on the first step.

Everyone waited for him to speak. Every eye watched him carefully. Talia could hardly breathe as she both anticipated and dreaded what might come from her brother's mouth in the next moment.

"Today this scripture is fulfilled in your ears."

A collective exhale sounded throughout the room, then the murmuring started. Talia looked at her mother and D'vora, who leaned against the column bearing the weight of her toddler. D'vora shrugged, but Maryam seemed happy.

He's saying he's the M'sheekha, she wanted to shout to the slow minds around her. *Your hearts are so hard you can't see the truth!*

But some of the things she heard weren't negative. In fact, most seemed more hopeful than she gave them credit. Maybe they'd heard about his miracles, and they were impressed. Ready to see some proof and accept him as their M'sheekha.

"Isn't this Yosef's son?" an old woman in the back asked loudly, hard of hearing. Her daughter shushed her, but others nodded and asked the same question.

"It is the carpenter's son. I hear he has quite a ministry in Capernaum."

"Will he do miracles here, too?" someone else asked in a loud whisper.

"He can heal me," a man said, further away. "I wouldn't mind a leg that worked right. It would sure make harvest easier."

Others agreed, and the noise level rose as the conversations grew. Yeshue spoke again, in a voice of authority, to give the morning lesson for the meeting.

"Doubtless you will say to me this proverb: 'Physician, heal yourself,' or maybe you might want me to do here what you are hearing I have done in Capernaum.'"

Laughter followed his words, as well as agreement from the elders sitting in the front row on either side.

Yeshue continued. "Assuredly, I say to you, there is not a prophet who is received in his town. For truly I say to you that many widows were in Israel in the days of Elijah the Prophet, when the heavens were shut for three years and six months, and there was great hunger in all the land."

Talia frowned, wishing Yeshue had taken a different approach. Hadn't they said they were willing to see what he could do? Why didn't he just prove himself to them? It felt more like he was admonishing them.

Yeshue took a lingering look around the room, making sure every eye was turned his way and every ear would hear his words. "And Elijah was not sent to one of them, but to a widow woman. And there were many lepers among Israel in the days of Elisha the Prophet and not one of them was purified except Naaman the Syrian."

Talia cringed. Her brother had chosen specific words as if he was goading them. He knew how they would react. He knew their pride and stubbornness. Why offend them on purpose?

The protest began as a low murmuring, but it got louder. Yeshue sat calmly in his place as men stood around him, demanding explanation. They gave him no chance to clarify his words. One of the more hotheaded neighbors grabbed Yeshue by the arm and yanked him to his feet.

Maryam and D'vora gasped. Talia's heart skipped a beat.

Confusion reigned over the next few minutes. Somehow the entire group of them ended up outside. The shouting grew louder.

The prayer house was the furthest building in the village, set apart from the main rows of houses, close to the Nazareth cliff. Mothers were forever warning their children not to play near the sharp drop-off.

Talia held on to Maryam in the madness and called for Nathanael. The mob of men had backed Yeshue all the way to the drop-off. They stared him down with victorious smirks.

Any second he would be pushed off by the forward pressure of the crowd, and no man could survive that fall.

Talia and Maryam pleaded with them to stop as most of the other women stood back, holding children and watching the proceedings with guarded expressions.

But as quickly as it had started, it was over. Yeshue suddenly walked through the crowd and left them standing in confusion on the cliff. Surrounded by his disciples and the family that moved in behind, they walked out of Nazareth and set their sights toward Cana.

It was a quiet couple hour's walk. Yeshue spoke softly to his disciples, trying to encourage them after the disheartening trip to his hometown.

Talia was embarrassed and ashamed of her people. She knew they were a stubborn lot, but to attempt to kill Yeshue just because he told them he was the M'sheekha revealed the darkness of their hearts.

The most disturbing part about it was that Talia knew she possessed the same stubborn, restless heart. How could anyone follow Yeshue with their sin ever before them?

Later, as Talia had been tucked away in Cana and left with her in-laws, as Nathanael had moved on, she fought anger. Irritation with him, yes, but mostly anger with herself.

The nagging voice in the darkest part of her soul revealed an ugly truth she could barely face. If she were to be completely honest, she was relieved they had moved on without her. It was too hard. Too much. She was too afraid.

But realizing the truth caused her to despise her own weakness. She'd failed Yeshue. Broken her promise.

Ya'achov

יעקב

Ya'achov stood in the market and called to customers to look at the samples of his recent pieces of furniture. Already this morning he'd been approached by time-wasters who only wanted to *touch the cloak of the brother of the M'sheekha*. He had told them with certainty to move on or buy something. Meanwhile, the jealousy he had been struggling raged worse. It ran hot through his veins—hotter than the cursed sun hanging overhead and drenching the town with unrelenting heat.

Perhaps he should tell the next Yeshue seeker that he was the one who had taken the vow. He was the one praised all through prayer school for his exceptional memory of the Torah. He'd been dutifully concerned about the decline of morality in their people. Of the Hellenistic and Roman influences that threatened their very way of life, dragging the young away from the pursuit of Elohim. He'd prayed on his knees daily for Alaha to draw them back.

Yeshue knew how to make people feel good. That was his only gift and the only thing that made him special. He was a big talker.

Well, that and the fact that a word from his mouth healed the sick.

Ya'achov slammed a chair on the ground too hard. He would have broken it if it wasn't so well-made. He sighed and ran his fingers through the tangle of his hair and looked out over the sea.

He'd heard from Maryam the story of how Yeshue had almost been run over the cliff on Shabbat in Nazareth. He could understand their frustration. They knew. They knew how Yeshue really was. And no one else was smart enough to figure it out.

If you have to move to a new town to even begin a following, what does that tell you, oh brother, he thought, his eyes narrowing.

Even as he thought the satisfying words, a memory came to him. He'd been ten, Yeshue twelve. They had been playing after prayer house one afternoon, throwing a rag ball as they did often. Ya'achov had run to get it and ended up losing his balance and going over the cliff.

He hung on frantically, trying to climb the jagged rock with his bare feet. As he tried not to lose his grip on the stony overhang, he cursed himself for being so stupid. Hadn't he been told to mind the cliff since he was a toddler? Now his mother would lose a son and it would be his fault. He called out a swear word as loud as he could.

As he looked up, he saw Yeshue's face peering over the side. He didn't seem upset at all. Ya'achov supposed he'd be glad to get rid of his annoying little brother. There'd be more attention left for him.

But Yeshue held out his hand, his brows knit together in concentration. "Grab on."

Ya'achov shook his head. "Are you crazy? If I let go, I'll fall and die. You won't be able to hold me."

"I'm not going to let you fall. But you have to let go and grab my hand. Trust me. I will rescue you."

Ya'achov snarled. "I don't want you to rescue me! I can do it myself. Just back off and let me climb up."

"If you try to climb up on your own, you will die." Yeshue said calmly. Seriously. Concern filled his dark eyes with moisture, but he did not cry or move away. He kept his arm extended. "Let go and grab on to my hand."

'I don't want you to rescue me!" Ya'achov said again, and his hands began to slip as he yelled. Pebbles fell on his face and landed in his mouth. He spit them out and tried to lift his body with his fingers. He couldn't.

"Ya'achov, I don't want to lose you. You must let me do it."

Ya'achov hung there for a long time. Until he lost most of the feeling in his fingers. His pride raged, insisting he couldn't live with owing Yeshue a debt. Worse still, he couldn't live with his parents if something happened to Yeshue. They'd probably turn him out and disown him. No, nothing good would come of letting Yeshue save his life.

"I won't," he seethed as his fingers slipped further.

Yeshue didn't speak again, but his hand stayed where it was, extending toward Ya'achov.

It wasn't until one of Ya'achov's hands lost grip that Ya'achov *realized he was too scared to die. He swallowed his pride, let go of the rock and grabbed Yeshue's offered hand.*

Yeshue lifted his brother up and onto the rocks at the overhang. It took several moments for Ya'achov's heart to stop beating so fast and his breathing to become regular again.

"I suppose you're going to hold this over me from now on," he snarled.

Yeshue gave a small sigh. "I'm glad you're okay, Ya'achov."

Ya'achov had never thanked his brother for rescuing him. Never. He'd never mentioned it again and neither had Yeshue. But it was another notch on the tally of debts. Ya'achov would never be able to pay them back. He'd always be a step behind.

And it irked him more than he wanted to admit.

SIXTEEN

Y'hud

יהוד

    Ten-year-old Y'hud sat on the front bench of the large Capernaum prayer house, swinging his legs. His mind was lost to childish thoughts as the rabbi taught Torah to a group of boys his age.

    I hope we can play ball again in the clearing this afternoon. He squirmed on the stone seat. He eyed the girls across the room, sitting quietly on the opposite side of the prayer house, their hands folded in their laps. How did they do it? They didn't squirm once.

    He looked above him, examining the ornate building. This prayer house was much better than the one in Nazareth. The outside was made of the dark basalt stones that Yeshue said had formed from a volcano's eruption. The stones had been cut for a perfect fit, just like his brothers did in the shop. Just like he would do himself one day. Inside the large room were fresh white plaster-covered walls. Smooth limestone made up the floor. He ran his sandaled foot over the cool, hard surface. The stones were almost straight enough to come from Yeshue's meticulous hand. Around the center of the room rose huge pillars, from floor to ceiling, and large windows around the top of the building flooded the room with sunlight. He liked all the light. Nazareth's prayer house had been gloomy. It had been hard to read the Torah scrolls in the dark. Yeshue had often taken them out in the sunshine under the olive tree to read.

"Y'hud, please tell us the laws regarding the sin offering sacrifices." Rabbi Jairus, a man a few years older than Yeshue, stared at him hard. He must have noticed Y'hud was not paying attention. He heard a few giggles from the girls as he tried to rein in his wandering mind. Fortunately, Yeshue had quizzed him often enough that there was little of the Torah he couldn't easily recite, even the most obscure points. He delivered the sin offering sacrifices in record time.

Jairus was surprised. "You are young to know the laws so well."

Y'hud couldn't help a proud smile. He enjoyed the attention. The second youngest child in a large family didn't get much of it. He glanced around and saw the other students regarding him with awe.

"My brother taught me."

"Ah, yes, your brother is Yeshue?" The rabbi nodded with understanding. "He is a wise man. A traveling rabbi of sorts, is he not?"

"I guess so," Y'hud said. He hadn't really stopped to consider what exactly Yeshue was doing as he walked all over the countryside with those followers of his. He was only miffed his mother hadn't let him tag along.

Y'hud tried to answer the question. "He's that kind of teacher—what do you call them? They can give new interpretations."

"Your brother is s'mikeh?" Jairus said, astonished. He must *really* be impressed with Y'hud now. The boy was encouraged to go on.

"Yes, that's it," Y'hud said airily, as if he was bored of always talking about something so commonplace. All eyes were on him now. He peeked just to make sure.

"Yeshue healed my cousin's infected leg," a child behind him said.

"My grandmother got healed of a fever," Y'hud's friend Mattiah bar Peter said in excitement. Y'hud lived on Mattiah's father's complex.

The students began to talk at once until Rabbi Jairus tried to get them all to settle down and speak one at a time. In the chaos, Y'hud looked over to the girls' side again, where they were all sitting quietly, of course. One of the girls looked at him. She was pretty. He liked her large brown eyes. She was one of the older girls, probably a year or two older than him. Girls that old didn't usually come to prayer school anymore. Too busy making food and weaving.

Jairus managed to quell the talking and get back to the Torah lesson. He began the story of Ehud the judge, to the great delight of all the boys. There was nothing better than a left-handed warrior who got to plunge a dagger into a fat king while he was relieving himself.

Y'hud looked at the girl again. The other girls wore disgusted expressions, probably because girls didn't favor the disgusting story of Ehud. But the girl he was interested in was still looking at him.

He wondered why. He liked the attention, whatever her reason. He grinned back.

When Rabbi Jairus released them that afternoon, she was waiting on the steps for Y'hud.

She stepped forward and looked him straight in the eye. "Your brother—he heals the sick?"

Y'hud was surprised at her boldness, but not put off. "Well, he's really more my father than my brother. My father died when I was very young. And yes, he heals sickness, and even sends evil spirits out of people."

Her eyes widened. She looked afraid, but maybe a little bit hopeful, too.

"Why, is someone sick?" Y'hud asked, curious. She lowered her eyes.

"I have to go," she mumbled. She headed the opposite way on the street. He watched her until she disappeared around a corner.

Shimon hit him on the arm. "Come on, Y'hud, let's get our chores done so we can play!"

Y'hud followed his brother toward home, but he couldn't stop thinking about the girl the rest of the night. He didn't even know her name. Y'hud saw Yeshue in the street talking with his disciples and went to them. He sat among them and listened to his brother speak. Yeshue nodded at him but kept teaching.

Y'hud liked listening to Yeshue. He was proud of his brother as he looked at the disciples faces, all enthralled with what Yeshue said. He caught the eyes of Nathanael, Talia's new husband, who gave him a smile but quickly returned his attention to Yeshue.

Y'hud studied Yeshue. He wasn't sure what to make of him lately. Up until about a year ago, Yeshue hadn't done much besides work in the shop and teach in the prayer house. He was quiet and sensible. He enjoyed nature and family and the laughter of children playing in the streets. But he had gone away for a few weeks after harvest, and when he returned, he seemed different. More focused and determined than Y'hud had ever known him to be.

This worried Y'hud. Yeshue was the only father he'd ever known, and it felt like he was losing him.

He would never forget the afternoon a few months ago when Yeshue had called him up to the rooftop with him. They had sat together, talking of school and of friends and of nothing in particular, until Yeshue put his arm around him.

"Y'hud, you know how much I love you, don't you?"

Y'hud only nodded, embarrassed at his brother's tender words.

"Elohim has given me a special job to do. You understand I must do it."

Y'hud turned and looked him in the eye. "I know. You're the M'sheekha."

Y'hud's mother had told him the same since he had been old enough to understand what she was saying. But the words weren't alive. He couldn't fathom the impact of them, they were just words. Yeshue was the M'sheekha. It meant nothing more than a reason for family pride.

"Yes. But that means there will be some changes."

Y'hud's face fell. "You're going to have to leave us, aren't you?"

Yeshue nodded. "I will still be close by for a time. You'll be practically a man and no longer need me when I have to go away for good."

"Go where?" Y'hud gulped, feeling a big lump in his throat. He didn't want to hear the answer. It was like a dark spot in his mind that he wished he could ignore and it would go away.

"I will go to my Father."

"But our father is dead!" Y'hud's heart started to race. Was Yeshue saying he was going to die? Why would the M'sheekha die? He had to defeat their enemies and set Israel free!

Yeshue only smiled. His eyes were a little misty as he pulled Y'hud close for a moment. "You're going to do well, Y'hud. Your road will not be easy, but you'll do well, even after I'm gone. And in a very real sense, I'll always be with you. I'll be more with you then than I'm able to be now."

Y'hud stood up, wildly looking his brother in the eye. "Tell me you aren't going to die, Yeshue!"

Yeshue wouldn't say the words. He only watched Y'hud, thoughtful.

"Little Y'hud, son of my heart, I promise you if I die, it won't be the end of the story. Don't forget that."

Y'hud frowned, not comforted by Yeshue's strange words. But he lowered his head in respect. "Yes, Abba."

"Remind the others, too."

"I will," Y'hud said, but his frown deepened and the dark spot inside grew bigger.

Yeshue stood and embraced Y'hud. "Ah, brother. If I were free to do so, I'd never leave you. You fill my days with happiness. Teaching you gives me joy like nothing else. But there are others who need me, too. Desperately."

Y'hud swallowed his protest and nodded.

Yeshue kissed his head, sending him off to find Shimon and do his chores. When they came back later, he was still on the roof. They sat with him in the crisp night air and listened to him sing. The melody was a mournful one—David's sorrow at his sin and hope for restoration.

"Everyone will know who you are, won't they?" Y'hud asked suddenly, after his older brother lapsed into silence. He didn't know why he had spoken the words. Of course they would know him! Yeshue would be king.

"You don't have to understand everything now." Yeshue had continued the song. Y'hud wanted to beg him to answer the question, to confirm that he would truly be the M'sheekha and set his people free. Why wouldn't everyone know?

He thought of all the Torah lessons in the prayer house. Of the prophecies.

"Zechariah said, 'They shall look unto me …'" Yeshue began reciting the familiar passage, his voice trailing off so Y'hud and Shimon could recite it.

"They shall look unto me because they have thrust him through; and they shall mourn for him, as one mourns for his only son, and shall be in bitterness for him, as one that is in bitterness for his first-born."

Y'hud wondered why Yeshue had chosen the strange passage. What did it mean?

Yeshue continued. "In that day there shall be a fountain opened to the house of David and to the inhabitants of Jerusalem, for purification from sin and impurity."

Because they have thrust him through.

Because they have thrust him through.

What did it mean? What was Yeshue saying? Who would be thrust through?

As if Yeshue could hear Y'hud's wild thoughts, his song changed. He sang a beautiful melody Y'hud had never heard before, almost like a soft lullaby Ama might sing in the evening. His words came from Zechariah again.

"'Sing and rejoice, O daughter of Zion; for I am come, and I will dwell in the midst of thee', says Adonai. 'And many nations shall join themselves to Adonai in that day, and shall be my people, and I will dwell in the midst of thee; and thou shalt know Adonai hath sent me to you. And Adonai shall inherit Judah as his portion in the holy land, and shall choose Jerusalem again.'"

Y'hud was drowsy from the long day and difficult conversation. The last thing he heard was Yeshue's gentle whisper that seemed to rise on the breeze and be carried off into the watches of the night, hungry for his words, for his voice.

"Marana tha."

Y'hud considered the words as he drifted off to sleep.
Come, O Lord.

SEVENTEEN

Hannah
חנה

Hannah's eyes opened. The sun was warm on her face, and dreams still lingered in her consciousness. Yeshue was there, laughing in that way of his that made the very birds of the air sing with joy. He was swinging her around and around as he had done when she was little. He held her, and she breathed in his fresh scent of grass and earth and rain and wood chips. She knew peace, even if it was a stolen and surreal moment.

She sat up. The atmosphere dulled, and the sound of marching soldiers outside the dwelling replaced the birdsong. Y'aqim stirred beside her, whimpering. He gave her a pleading look. If he was old enough, she knew he would beg her not to take him to the horrid Aemilia. He would beg for real food for breakfast, bread and cheese and dried figs, not the crust of bread she'd saved for him from her dinner the night before.

He ate the bread as Hannah peered out of her doorway toward the gates. She dreaded having to leave the sanctuary of their tiny room. She wished she could sneak away and be done with this evil place.

Her mood darkened further. It wouldn't happen, so there was no use dwelling on it.

With heavy steps, she crossed the paved pavilion to the bathhouse. Cassia looked up with a cold glare as she entered. Hannah tried to step through to take Y'aqim to Aemilia, but her feet would not obey. She could not cause him more pain.

Please, Alaha, for my son. Not for me. I realize I don't deserve any favor, but Y'aqim has done nothing wrong. Save him from that woman.

She felt shame for speaking to Adonai. She had no right.

"Girl," Felix said before she stepped into the room reserved for the children. She turned around with a small sigh. What now?

"I've had a request for you to be moved to haircutting." Felix was out of breath from coming after her and obviously not in good humor.

"Requested by whom?" she asked in surprise.

"I don't know. Someone close to the centurion Lysander," Felix answered as he moved to return to his work.

"What are my duties?" she asked after him.

"To cut the soldiers' hair," he said with impatience. "Someone will teach you. Your child may stay with you."

"I don't have to take him to the Aemilia?" She stared after him in shock.

"It was part of the request," were his last words before he disappeared.

Ennius.

Had he spoken on her behalf? She walked to the small haircutting room at the end of the bathhouse which was not connected to the rest of the building. It was like a small shop, and the front opened to sunshine. A clear view of the harbor and the crystalline sea met her eyes.

She gave a small laugh of disbelief.

"Are you the new girl?" a voice said behind her. She turned around to see a young Nubian girl, tall and shapely. Her dark skin and features were unreadable.

"I am," Hannah said.

"Thank the gods," the Nubian muttered. "I've been stuck in this room staring at this dull town for months. I'd much rather work in the bathhouse."

Hannah shook her head, wondering why anyone would aspire to such a place. "Why?"

"Why do you think? For the money, Jew." The girl spat the name as if it were a curse. It might as well be. But it was worse to earn her severances in the bathhouse.

"I'm supposed to show you how to cut the hair before I leave. I'll take the next one, then you're on your own."

"Fine," Hannah said with a nod. They waited in silence as Y'aqim played on the floor with sticks, whining every now and then, probably because of his grumbling stomach. The Nubian stared at him in disgust until a soldier finally entered the shop.

"Ennius!" the other girl welcomed him in a suggestive tone. "You finally came to visit me."

"I've come to see Hannah," Ennius said, meeting Hannah's gaze. "But you may cut my hair."

The girl glared at Hannah, but she reached for the razor and quickly cropped Ennius's dark curls close to his head. Hannah felt sorry to see the locks fall to the floor. She secretly loved his curls. When the Nubian was done, she threw down the razor and left without a word.

"She scares me," Ennius said, and Hannah chuckled at his comical expression.

She picked her son up. "Thank you for this." When she met his eyes, she had the same strange feeling as the night before—a blend of desire to please him, desire to be loved, and an awareness of his strength and his kindness. "I wasn't sure you'd want to speak to me again."

Ennius sat down in the chair again and crossed his foot over his knee. "Beautiful view."

It was quiet for a long moment. Y'aqim babbled, which caused Ennius to sit up.

"I brought him food." He removed a parcel from his belt. He tossed it to Hannah, who exclaimed for joy at the sight of the fruit and dried fish. She broke it into pieces and set it on the tile floor next to the toddler, who immediately tried to pick up the entire haul and stuff it into his mouth.

Hannah laughed softly. "One at a time, baby. Don't want to choke." She spread the pieces further away from each other to slow him down. When she looked up again, Ennius was watching her with a faraway look in his eyes. Almost as if he was trying to remember something.

"I wasn't angry at you." He spoke abruptly, but she was beginning to see it was his way. "You're barely more than a child, aren't you?"

She blushed at his scrutiny, but huffed and stuck her chin in the air. "I'm a woman."

"How many years?"

She frowned. "Fifteen."

"My anger is toward the men who used you. Your brother should have protected you."

Hannah shook her head. "It's not Yeshue's fault. He tried to warn me. I went against him. My brother is honorable."

Ennius shook his head stubbornly. "If I ever have occasion to meet him, I'll have words for him."

Hannah sighed, wishing she knew how to explain the way things were. Every attempt she could think of painted herself in a very bad light.

"He could have stoned you," Ennius said. "I've seen Jewish men turn in their own kin over trivial matters Romans don't get excited about. I'm surprised your people have lasted as long as they have when you are always destroying one another."

Hannah wanted to defend her religion, but she didn't know where to start. She could see his point. "It might seem that way to an outsider."

Ennius stood up, his thick arms settled across his chest. "It seems that way because it is that way. I live in your town. I have for years. I know what goes on."

Hannah did not respond.

He came to sit next to her on the ground. "I can't stop thinking about you, little Jewess." He spoke with a sigh, as if his feelings for her were an inconvenience. She dared to look at him and saw tenderness. But she saw hesitancy as well. She couldn't blame him. She was a Jew; she had a child and was expecting another. Not to mention her life was in danger if her people found out where she was.

He was a Roman soldier, probably born to wealthy Roman citizens who had every hope for his future. He was respected. It was humbling to recognize that fact, since he was a pagan.

Jews didn't intermarry with Romans. It was an outrageous thought. But was it any more absurd than a Jewish woman cutting Roman soldiers' hair inside their military complex?

She felt his warm breath on her face, and she turned to meet him. He tenderly touched the tip of his nose against her cheek. Then he kissed her.

At least she could be something to him.

But even as the thought crossed her mind, another followed. A story her brother had told at prayer house. It wasn't a very nice story. One of King David's sons, Ammon, had wanted his half-sister Tamar with the same desire. He had gone through quite a series of lies to get what he wanted. After he was done with her, even though she had been pure only a moment before, he had hated her in her ruined state with as much energy as he had loved her.

Hannah leaned back and studied his eyes. She didn't want Ennius to hate her. In fact, it would devastate her. He wasn't any Roman soldier standing in line with a handful of coins. For some reason, he had taken care of her and her son.

"Hannah," Ennius reached for her and tried to pull her closer. She felt heat rise in the pit of her stomach. She wanted to surrender to Ennius. She had never wanted to give herself to anyone before. Not her husband, not any of the men who used her.

But she didn't want to be Tamar. Unloved, abandoned Tamar.

"No," she said, pushing him back. He stared at her, breathing fast, trembling.

"What?" he said in disbelief. "You're telling me no?"

"I can't do this anymore." She shook her head. "I can't be the harlot."

His face turned red and he stood up. She tried not to let him see her fear, but she trembled as he hovered over her, his fists curled tightly at his sides.

"How could you think I was using you? I've tried to provide for you.

Don't you understand that this—" he motioned to the space between them, "Can come from love as well?"

"Not this way," she pleaded, backing away from him. "I don't want you to hate me."

His fists relaxed, and his face softened into confusion. "I don't hate you," he said in a thoughtful tone. "I think I am beginning to love you."

She shook her head, though her heart did a little dance at his words. "That doesn't make it right."

He glared at her for a long moment. She could tell he had no idea what she was talking about. He had taken it personally.

"I don't understand you." He turned and left the shop as curtly as he had entered.

Hannah gave a deep sigh. She couldn't hope to keep Ennius by her virtue. She had none.

Talia

טליה

"You'll be taken by soldiers, Talia," Ruth said, wringing her hands with worry. "I don't understand why you want to go."

Talia packed food in a cloth and wrapped it. "I'll be with the caravan the whole time. Everyone is going to hear Yeshue speak."

There had been news of a group leaving from Cana. Everyone who wanted to hear the teaching of Rabbi Yeshue was to meet at the east corner of town at dawn on the first day of the week. Talia urged her in-laws to come with her, but Tolmai was recovering from illness and Ruth didn't want to leave him. Talia tried to be patient. And she tried to ignore her own fears.

"Nathanael won't forgive us if something happens to you," Tolmai reminded her.

She nodded and kissed his weathered cheek. "I will be ever so careful, Abba."

"Give him our love."

"I will." Talia went through the front of her house and packed her things onto the donkey waiting outside. The light was just starting to streak across the morning sky and the air was cool and clean. It would be a good day to travel.

Suddenly, fear struck her without warning. Her stomach began to churn and she felt faint. She gasped and crouched on the ground lest she keel over. What made her scared? Dangers on the trail? There weren't many with a large group. They only had to be careful of Roman soldiers and there was no reason for soldiers to bother a group of travelers on the short trip across the hills to the sea.

But she was only pretending not to recognize the source of her fear. It remained there, in the locked part of her heart she didn't have the courage to explore.

Despised and forsaken of men ... we did esteem him stricken, smitten of God, and afflicted ... wounded because of our transgressions, crushed because of our iniquities ... as a lamb that is led to the slaughter ..."

"No," she whispered. The images came to her when she least expected them. Her brother, bloody. Beaten. Dying. When the thoughts tormented her, she wanted to die to be free of them. She cried out and hurled herself on the ground, scraping the dust and pouring it on her head.

"Talia, what is it?" Ruth came out of the house, kneeling beside her.

"She's gone mad," Tolmai said from the doorway.

"Don't you see it?" Talia cried. "He's going to die. He's going to be murdered!"

"Who?" Tolmai came to her and pulled her up, shaking her shoulders. "Who is going to die? Nathanael?"

"No," Talia moaned. "Yeshue. Yeshue is going to be killed."

Tolmai smiled and shook his head. "Why would anyone kill Yeshue? He's the most popular man in Israel. He heals and casts out spirits. He teaches Torah as if he were the Son of Alaha. No one will kill our M'sheekha. It wouldn't make sense. Where is your faith?"

Talia shook her head. She knew his words were empty, but she took comfort in them anyway. If only enough to let her breathing calm.

"Maybe she has an evil spirit," Ruth said to her husband. "Should we take her to Yeshue?"

Tolmai considered the words of his wife. Finally, he nodded. "Go pack our things."

They traveled together to meet the caravan. Talia was silent, unwilling to share her terrifying thoughts lest her poor in-laws deem her completely insane.

By oppression and judgment he was taken away ... he was cut off out of the land of the living ... and they made his grave with the wicked, and with the rich his tomb; although he had done no violence, neither was any deceit in his mouth.

Panic mounted within her troubled mind at the terrible words. Why was she the only one who could see it?

"Talia!" Maryam saw her daughter and ran from a far off. Talia collapsed in the arms of her mother and suddenly felt peace. She heard Ruth's hushed voice behind her.

"Yeshue should speak to her. She's been beside herself with worry for him."

Maryam pushed back and looked into Talia's eyes. "What's wrong, my daughter?"

"I can't keep the visions away," Talia said. Maryam sighed.

"I'll see if Yeshue can come." Maryam put on her head covering. "He's just over at Peter's house."

It wasn't long before Maryam returned with Nathanael and Yeshue following behind her. Her husband came to her, kneeling beside the pallet and taking her hand. "Talia, what are you doing here?" he asked softly.

"I needed to see Yeshue. Your parents brought me. They are going home in the morning. Your father has been ill."

"Come, see your brother," Nathanael led her through the courtyard to the bench in front of Peter's house. He mctioned to Yeshue.

Yeshue came and sat beside her. He took her other hand.

"What is it, my little sister?" he asked.

"I can't stop thinking of the prophet's words. All the horrible things he said about you. Visions come to me without warning and won't leave."

Yeshue glanced around and his eyes focused on Maryam. "Ama, we need some privacy."

She nodded and shoed away the family and disciples who lingered. Only Nathanael and Yeshue remained.

"Tell me which passages bother you," Yeshue said quietly.

"Isaiah. He said M'sheekha would be rejected, smitten, pierced, crushed. His face marred beyond human likeness; his life poured out to …"

"Go on," Yeshue said. "Finish it."

"Poured out to death," Talia said, and tried to swallow back her sob, which only made her hiccup.

"Is she mad?" Nathanael stared at Yeshue helplessly.

Yeshue put his hand on Nathanael's shoulder. "She's not mad. She has wisdom she doesn't know how to handle."

"Help her, Master," Nathanael pleaded.

Yeshue looked back at Talia. "The word of Elohim is not meant to be taken apart this way, Talia. It must be read as a whole."

Gradually she ceased her panting and gulping and took a deep breath. "What do you mean?"

"Say the entire passage. Don't leave anything out. *Yet it pleased Adonai …*"

"*It pleased Adonai to crush him, and though the Lord makes his life an offering for sin, he will see his offspring and prolong his days, that the purpose of Adonai might prosper by his hand. Therefore, will I divide him a portion among the great, and he shall divide the spoil with the mighty; because he bared his soul unto death, and was numbered with the sinners; yet he bore the sin of many, and made intercession for the transgressors.*"

Yeshue smiled as Talia tried to understand the contradictory words. "Do you see?"

She wanted to see. For him. For Nathanæel. But the answer seemed just out of her grasp. "How can death be a good thing?"

"Ah, little one." Yeshue brushed the hair away from her face. "*Zion said, The Lord hath forsaken me, and my Lord hath forgotten me. Can a woman forget the baby at her breast, that she should not have compassion? She may forget, yet will I not forget you. Behold, I have graven you upon the palms of my hands.*"

Talia was comforted by his tone and his gentle touch, but she couldn't understand what he was saying.

He smiled again. "Do you trust me?"

She nodded. "You know I do."

"Then trust that those who hope in me will not be disappointed when all has come to pass."

He brushed a kiss against her forehead. The visions left her mind.

But fear still burned as embers. They seemed unquenchable.

EIGHTEEN

Hannah

חנה

When spring came, Hannah remembered Nazareth. The almonds would be in bloom, and the flax and barley would be nearly ready to harvest. She wondered what her family was doing. They would probably go to Jerusalem for the Feast of Tabernacles. She closed her eyes and imagined the close quarters of the homemade booth she had shared with her family during the festival. It smelled of sweat and wine and sounded like laughter. Abba or Yeshue always told the story of how Alaha brought his people to the Promised Land. How everything they had was a gift from Adonai.

Now, Hannah's days were all the same. Her one joy was Y'aqim, who started to say simple words, including *Ama*. He flitted about the small shop pretending to be a Roman soldier, poking her with sticks in place of a sword. She laughed at his antics, but worried about his future.

She was heavy with child. She knew her time was drawing near, but no one else seemed to care. She had all but disappeared into the complex of Roman military schedule. Ennius had not come for weeks, and no one else acknowledged her presence except to come for haircuts. She longed for days she had at least been noticed by the men, however shameful a thought it might be.

She wondered what she would do when the pains started. How would she care for Y'aqim? Aemilia? She shuddered. She must speak to Felix. Before the sun set.

When her work was done, she balanced Y'aqim on her hip and went to the bathhouse to find Felix. When she found him, he noticed her round figure with a look of repulsion.

"You're with child," he said, his tone accusing.

"Yes," she said. "And my time is near. I will need a time of seclusion."

He sighed. "And you're going to need attention. I don't have time to arrange it. There's the hospital, but the doctor is in Rome right now. Why didn't you tell me from the start?"

Hannah shrugged. She hadn't been thinking that far ahead.

Felix frowned. "Was the child sired by one of the soldiers? If you had said something, we could have had this dealt with long ago."

Her hands went protectively to her stomach and she took a step back. "I only require a reprieve from my work," she snarled.

He rolled his eyes and waved her off. "Fine. Take to your room. I'll see if I can find a midwife. But I don't know what use we'll have for you with two children. You'll have to get rid of them or leave."

Felix turned his back on her. She seethed as she made her way back to her room. The nerve of that callous little man. Suggesting she get rid of her children!

She pouted long after she'd blown out the lamp and lay listening to Y'aqim's soft snores. She had nowhere to go. No one to help her. If she returned to her people, they could stone her.

Where was Ennius? Why wasn't he here to help her?

The next day as Hannah and Y'aqim napped in the early afternoon, loud banging sounded on the doorpost. Y'aqim started to cry and Hannah picked him up. She stumbled to the door, her gait awkward with her large stomach.

She pushed back the curtain and gasped in surprise. "Ennius!"

He examined her round abdomen. "Good. I'm not too late."

"Too late for what?" she asked, confused. She set Y'aqim down, too uncomfortable to hold him up. He continued to fuss and pull on her tunic, so Ennius reached down and picked him up.

Hannah wished she felt like smiling when she saw the picture they made. "Too late for what?" she asked again.

"I've been hunting all over Galilee for a midwife," he said, walking into the room without being asked.

She was shocked that his absence had been on her behalf. "There were none in Capernaum?"

He eyed her, raising a brow. "You want a Jewish midwife?"

Hannah sighed, remembering her circumstances. "I want my mother and my sister. But I didn't have them the first time, either. I had my mother-in-law, who taunted me the entire time and then took my son away from me. She wouldn't let me see him for hours. At least this time I'll be alone."

"You won't be alone. I'll see to it."

She smiled and touched his arm. "Thank you for trying."

"I didn't find any Roman midwives willing to travel here. I offered them money, clothes, even my horse, but no one would do it. I'm sorry, Hannah. I haven't given up yet."

"Thank you, Ennius. But right now, will you just stay with me? I've been so lonely." Her confession required a dose of humility. She was as surprised by it as he was.

He set Y'aqim at the table with raisins and bread. He turned back to her and leaned forward, taking both of her hands in his as she settled at his feet and leaned her head against his knee. She closed her eyes, savoring the awareness of his nearness, enjoying the flutter of her heart.

He was quiet for a time, though she sensed he had something else to say.

"I wasn't just looking for a midwife," he admitted. "I've been following your brother around."

"Yeshue? Why?" Hannah frowned. She hoped Ennius was not about to tell her Yeshue was in trouble with Rome.

"I've been listening to him teach."

Hannah didn't answer for a long moment. "Why would you be interested in what he has to say?"

Ennius shook his head, his eyes focused on something she sensed wasn't present with them in the room. "Truthfully, at first, I just hoped to have a chance to tell him what I think of his rules and his treatment of his sister. But now that I've heard him speak ... I find I can't stop thinking about your religion."

Hannah gave a mirthless laugh. "Don't you have enough gods of your own?"

He didn't smile. He stood and went to the doorway, his hands on his hips and a scowl on his face. He was clothed in a short red tunic that revealed muscled legs, and he wore a breastplate that made his chest seem inhumanly strong.

Finally, he spoke. "I've had enough of Rome's idea of religion. Do whatever you please, then offer coins to the gods and ask them for whatever you want. My people don't believe in guilt. They don't seem to even understand right and wrong anymore, unless it's some foreigner trying to undermine our power."

He shook his head, making a face as if he had just eaten something spoiled. "I don't like how we tread on the backs of hard-working people. I don't like the entitled, spoiled attitudes of our leaders. I don't believe in the Roman way of life anymore."

Hannah was shocked at his words. She apprehensively checked the window for anyone who might have overheard him.

"Ennius, if someone heard you—"

He turned to face her. "I know. I'm a traitor. But I'm disgusted enough with it all to risk it."

"For what? What do you hope to accomplish by this talk?" Hannah whispered, sure someone would overhear their conversation.

He shrugged. "I don't know. I can't stomach Jewish religion, either. It's all rules. No one could really be expected to keep the law you're supposed to live by. And Jews don't invite Romans to join their religion, anyway. The idea is laughable."

Hannah nodded. "It's true."

"Your rabbis flounce around, puffed up and judging anybody and everybody. They're hypocrites. So full of pride they can't see the stench of their attitudes."

"Some," Hannah agreed. "But it's not how Alaha intends for it to be."

He eyed her in surprise. "I didn't take you to be a religious Jew."

She nodded. "For good reason. But Yeshue taught me the Torah."

"Your Yeshue says things that make no sense to me." Ennius rubbed his chin and ran his hand through his curly dark hair.

"Such as?"

"He talks about repentance. He says to repent because the kingdom of heaven is near. Talk like that makes the soldier in me want to pick up my sword and prepare to fight."

Hannah didn't know how to respond. She fumbled for words. "I never heard Yeshue speak like that. Are you sure you heard him right?"

He nodded. "I heard him."

"Well, that doesn't sound very much like the religion of my people. But I do know that a sword taken up against Alaha is a waste of time. You won't win." *And I don't want to see you destroyed.*

"Rome has already won. We have defeated your people and we hold you as ants under our thumb."

Hannah raised her eyebrows at his blunt statement. But she knew what Yeshue would say. "You have no power except what Alaha gives you. He uses enemies to punish his people for not keeping their promises."

She felt sad at the words. When would the punishment be over? When would Alaha smile in favor again? When they stopped sinning? That wouldn't happen. They were only people. Imperfect and broken.

"We need help, Adonai," she whispered.

Ennius watched her, thoughtful. "I want you to come with me," he said suddenly. As she began to shake her head and back away, he grabbed her shoulders. "I need you to explain to me what he's saying.

Your Greek is excellent after being here for so many months, and Yeshue speaks mostly Aramaic. I'm not fluent in that language."

"They'll kill me," she said in protest. "Is that what you want?"

He swore. "Disguise yourself."

"You are infuriating," she said hotly. "One minute you're acting as if I matter to you, the next I'm convenient. Which is it, Ennius? Because you've seen as well as I have how cruel my people can be."

Suddenly she doubled over, gripped by a strong, familiar pain. She cried out. It felt as if her muscles were pulling apart.

All the fight left his eyes as they widened in concern. "Is it time?"

She knew this pain. How many hours had she writhed on the floor of Jonah's house with the same? "Maybe ... Yes."

He ran from the house. She rolled her eyes. Who knew if he'd be gone five minutes or five days? But he returned within minutes, dragging Aemilia in with him.

"Her time has come," he said, pointing at Hannah, who still stood by the table, breathing through another contraction.

"I don't know anything about delivering babies," Aemilia said in disgust. "And I wouldn't help her if I did."

She left, and Ennius ran ahead of her to the bathhouse. If Hannah had thought it would do any good, she would have called after him not to bother. Cassia wouldn't come, either.

She tried to reassure Y'aqim and interest him in something else. He finally fell asleep stacking sticks in the corner. She set the stool next to her pallet resting on the low bedframe. She put a bowl of water and a jug of olive oil, along with some swaddling clothes and salt she had taken from the cook's building only yesterday. She set everything on a towel next to the stool. Then she lifted the hem of her toga and sat on the end of the stool, placing her arms on the bedframe to brace herself. The pains grew stronger and came closer together. She managed every one of them without making a sound, fearing she would wake her son.

An hour later, she panted through the contractions, sweat pouring down her face. She writhed in agony but refused to scream. The time must be close. She glanced at the dirt floor beneath her and tried to reach for a blanket to set down, but another contraction hit her and this time she cried out. Y'aqim began to cry and came to her, reaching his arms out. She patted him desperately on the back and bit her lip so hard it bled.

Ennius came past the curtain, shoving it aside and ushering someone else inside. Had he found a midwife?

She gasped in dismay as she realized the centurion, Lysander, commander of the entire outpost, had joined her in her birthing room.

"Please help her," Ennius said. Lysander hesitated for a moment, staring at Hannah uncertainly, but as he looked to Ennius, his gaze softened.

"See to the child," Lysander said, nodding toward Y'aqim who clutched Hannah's arm and screamed. Ennius quickly picked him up and bounced him until his cries turned to whimpers.

Meanwhile, Hannah's whimpers became cries. "Adonai!" she wailed. "Help my child!"

Lysander's weathered brow creased in concentration. "I've attended several births. My wife had a way of giving birth so quickly the midwife didn't arrive in time."

Hannah nodded, feeling a measure of relief. Lysander kneeled in front of her, giving occasional instructions. Soon he told her to bear down. Hannah only pushed once, and the baby came.

"A boy!" Ennius wore an expression of awe. Hannah leaned back on the side of the cot in exhaustion. Lysander expertly washed, oiled and salted the wee one before wrapping him in the cloths.

"There you are. Good enough to eat," Lysander teased as he handed her the baby and tended to the afterbirth. Hannah smiled at the wrinkled, oily face of her second son. She'd been sure this one would bear the ugly reminder of her husband and his family, but this boy looked every bit as much like Yeshue as Y'aqim did.

"What will you call him?" Ennius asked, bringing Y'aqim near to touch the baby's head.

"Perhaps Lysander?" Hannah suggested. She hadn't even considered what she would call her baby before that moment.

"I think your son might appreciate a Jewish name," Lysander said with an uncomfortable half-smile.

"I guess I'll call him Yosef, then. After my Abba."

A hard knot rose up in her throat at the thought of her father. She had not thought of him in many days. Maybe because his memory made her feel shame, and shame wouldn't change anything. He would be devastated to see how far his little Hannah had fallen.

Ennius must have noticed the darkness pass over her face like a cloud. He kneeled beside her pallet, his imposing figure awkward in the small space. He took an extra cloth and folded it to wipe the sweat from her brow.

Lysander watched them for a moment, frowning. "Ennius, I would like to speak to you outside."

"Yes, my lord," Ennius said and rose to follow him.

They stood outside the doorway as Lysander wiped the blood from his hands with a towel. Though he spoke softly, Hannah wondered if he meant her to hear his words.

"Ennius, don't get involved with that woman. Her situation is bad."

"From the childbirth?" Ennius asked, concerned. There was a long pause.

"From life," Lysander finally said. "If she sets one foot outside this camp, her people will tear her to pieces. Within our walls, she is no longer useful. We aren't in the practice of housing Jewish prostitutes out of mercy. We're the Roman army. I've gone to great lengths to build a relationship of trust in this town, and I won't have this woman coming in the way of that."

More silence.

"Why did you bring her in, then?" Ennius asked, sullen.

Lysander sighed. Hannah saw him rub the back of his neck uneasily. "I didn't know she was with child. I wouldn't have brought her if I did. In fact, I knew at the time I was making a mistake. I had pity on her because she was so young. She was alone and worried about her boy. But did I do her any favors in the end? I only prolonged the inevitable."

Hannah watched Ennius pace in front of the window, his hands held behind his back in thoughtful repose. Why did the two men speak so freely? Why did the centurion talk to Ennius tenderly, as if afraid to hurt his feelings? They didn't seem like centurion and soldier. They seemed like father and son.

"It's too late, isn't it?" Lysander said.

Ennius didn't answer.

Lysander shrugged in a helpless manner. "Then do what you must do."

Ennius looked up. "And what is that? I've been trying to think what to do. Anywhere I could take her in Galilee she'd be shunned or stoned."

"Then take her to Rome."

Ennius hesitated. "You would allow me to do so?"

"You are like my own son, Ennius. I wouldn't hold you back from a woman you have come to love, no matter who she is. I can have you transferred to the homeland with one document." Lysander sounded weary.

"I won't be a burden!" Hannah called to them stubbornly.

They turned to look at her through the door.

"And I'm not going to Rome."

NINETEEN

Hannah watched her newborn son as he nursed. Y'aqim slept on the cot next to her. It was midnight, but she didn't feel tired. Her mind whirled.

Felix had declared she must leave. In the morning she would pack her things and go.

As Yosef let go, asleep, she kissed his head and set him next to his brother. She fastened the makeshift pocket she had created in her tunic for easy nursing, and felt a wistful sting when she remembered her mother had done the same thing.

Hannah wandered out into the chilly night. She pulled her cloak around her and stared up at the immense sky of stars. The gentle wind blew her loose curls around her face. She remembered Talia saying once that a cool night breeze was like the gentle kiss of Alaha.

Not that she would ever know. She'd traded her soul for worthless things. Would that time could repeat. But it was pointless. She'd make the same choices again.

Worse, she couldn't make herself care. Here she was, no idea what she would do, where she would go, with two babies to feed. She felt the empty, hollow apathy of her heart. They would all die, she supposed.

Ennius had disappeared and gone silent again. He had been angry that she wouldn't go to Rome with him and had sworn he'd never darken her door again. He'd stormed off in a fury, mumbling about how much he'd done for her with no gratefulness or cooperation in return.

She was beginning to see it was his habit when he didn't get his way. She put him out of her mind, telling herself someone that childish wasn't anyone to put her hope in, anyway. He might have a handsome face, but he couldn't be counted on.

"Adonai," she said, her voice startling in the quiet of the nighttime. It was strange to be whispering to a deity she had scorned with her actions. "I don't ask you for anything on my behalf. Yeshue always said we were responsible for our own personal sin, not for the sin of others, so don't make my boys suffer on account of my sin. Save them."

She wasn't surprised when she felt nothing; heard no answer. The night was completely still.

"Hannah."

The sudden male voice startled her. She turned around to look at Ennius. His features were barely visible in the dim light of the moon, but she was sure he was not pleased.

"Ennius."

"What are you doing out here in the middle of the night?" he asked in an accusing tone.

"I could ask you the same." She turned her attention back to the sky, back to the hope she had not found and searched for still.

"You do realize you have to leave in the morning," he said, coming around to stand in front of her. "I have to figure out what to do with you. You could at least show some appreciation."

She huffed and pulled her cloak tighter. "I'm not going to Rome. You aren't responsible for me. Just go to bed."

"I think you're a fool for turning down my offer to take care of you in Rome. But I wouldn't be much of a man if I said I cared for you and then let you starve or be stoned. Not when your only crimes are far less than mine. I'd be as corrupt as your people."

She sighed. "Sentiment doesn't feed my children."

She could tell she'd irked him with her response. But he steeled his jaw and continued on as if she hadn't spoken. "I'm taking you to

Yeshue."

"Are you crazy?" Her voice rose in the night stillness. "I've wronged him most of all!"

"I want you to tell me what he says. If anyone is going to have mercy, it's him. I've heard how different he is from your other leaders. How he argues with them and leaves them speechless."

Hannah shook her head, unconvinced. "If anyone has reason to show me judgment, it's him."

"Still, I think the best thing to do—the only thing to do—is go to him. Lysander has given me leave to do so."

"Why does he treat you with kindness? I've seen soldiers tied to that post and beaten until they passed out, all for ignoring a rule or missing a curfew. What makes you so special? Is your father in government? Is he wealthy?"

Ennius gave her a dark stare. She didn't think he would answer her, but finally he spoke.

"Lysander shows me kindness because he has owned me since the day I was born."

She wondered at his strange wording. "Owned you? What do you mean?"

Ennius's face went hard, as if he was preparing for battle in the simple act of speaking of his past. "In Rome, when a baby is born, the midwife places the child on the floor at the feet of its father. If the father picks it up, the child is welcomed into the family. If not, it is taken outside."

"Taken outside? I don't understand." But Hannah had the creeping feeling she did not want to know what he meant. Not with her own helpless newborn sleeping a few feet away.

"The child is left alone to starve or freeze."

Hannah felt her stomach turn. "How could anyone do something so horrible to their own child?"

Ennius shrugged and pulled his long red cape around him. He stared at the sky. "It mostly happens in poor sections of town, which is where I was born. If a family already has more children than they can feed, some see it as their only option."

Hannah felt a wave of anger. "Your people are cruel."

When Ennius didn't respond, she began to consider why he was telling her the information. It occurred to her.

"You?"

He stood still, not looking at her. "The day you had your son Yosef, I watched the joy on your face as you saw him for the first time. That day went very differently when I was born. My father, whoever he was, didn't want me. I was left out in the street where the refuse runs past. Lysander happened by and heard me crying. He was a young soldier then, completing his first guard duty. He took pity on me, saying I sounded heartbroken for being left alone."

"Did he care for you by himself?" Hannah tried to picture Ennius's childhood, curious.

"One of the women slaves at his father's home had a baby of her own. He asked her to nurse me. I was raised as a slave in his household, but he always treated me like a son, even after he had his own family. That didn't mean *they* saw me as family, though. It was a difficult life. When he offered me my freedom, I asked to join the army and serve under his command."

He gave her a quick, hard look. "I don't know why I am telling you this." His voice was gruff. He shook his head, as if he'd like to retract the story.

Hannah didn't know what to say. She'd thought of him as a strong, passionate man of honor. She would have never guessed he'd spent his life as a slave.

His cold laugh interrupted her thoughts. "You think less of me now, Jew? Now that I'm not an important man to Rome, I'm not important in your view, either?"

"I never said that," she huffed. "Don't speak for me."

"You won't look me in the eye. That says enough." He watched her with a wounded expression. "You are no more than an outcast from a poor Galilean family, and yet you look down on me."

"I do not!" she yelled in frustration, pushing him back. Her arms were not strong enough to move his person even an inch. She kept her hands on his chest, staring angrily into his eyes. "I only feel pity for you."

Her words were spoken too quickly. He narrowed his eyes. "You feel pity for the poor slave no one loved? And who has loved you, Jewess? Who has really loved you, other than for what they could gain from it?"

He pushed her hands away and turned. As he stalked off, his sword clinked against his iron breastplate.

She felt his words like a blow, but the answer to his question slipped from her mouth before she had time to fully think the thought. "Yeshue. Yeshue loved me."

Hannah thought she would never see Ennius again. But he was waiting outside her dwelling at dawn. His muscular brown arms were folded across his chest and he scowled at her from under his helmet when she came out with her boys and a few bits of food packed in a cloth.

"I didn't expect you to come," she said quietly.

He frowned at her. "Where are your things?"

"I have no things," she said with a shrug. "Only a jar of perfume I stole from my mother-in-law when I left. I thought I'd leave it for the next occupant."

"Egyptian alabaster? Long-necked bottle?"

She nodded. "I think so."

"Get the jar. It's valuable."

She was surprised, but she did as he said, going back into the house. She took the jar from the shelf and studied it, wondering where Reuben's mother had come across it and why she hadn't traded it in Sepphoris for more practical things. She ran her fingers over the smooth, cream-colored jar and the sealed stopper before she wrapped it in a cloth so it would not be broken as they traveled. She took Y'aqim's hand. He stared at her with wide, fearful eyes. She realized this was the only home he'd ever really known.

"It will be all right, my little Y'aqim." She squeezed his hand, not quite believing the words herself. She made sure Yosef was well-tucked into the sling across her chest and went back outside.

Ennius led her away without a word. Soon they had walked the path to the gate of the fort, and her heart started beating faster as she looked down at the bustling Jewish town beside the sea.

She was well-aware of the fact that Ennius wanted to take her to Yeshue. But she didn't know how she could face him. Not just for the sake of her life, but for the fact that only thinking about Yeshue made her feel guilty. She had no desire to look him in the eyes and feel that miserable.

Ennius must have sensed her slowing down, for he turned around. His face seemed to soften, if just a little. He walked back to her. "I will protect you. I have a sword and a spear. I won't let anyone harm you."

If only he had a weapon that would protect her from the guilt. But not having a better plan, she continued after him as they walked toward Capernaum.

Apparently just accompanying a Roman soldier was enough reason for condemnation among the Jewish residents. Their eyes narrowed and they mumbled insults as she went past.

Only one dared to confront her, a young Jewish man was loading a pack mule when he turned suddenly at the sight of Ennius. His eyes darted from Ennius to Hannah, and she saw the rage in his eyes. His hand hovered over his belt, and she saw he was reaching for something. Sicarii carried hidden daggers.

"Ennius, be careful!"

Ennius quickly grabbed the man's arm before he could withdraw the knife hidden in his cloak. The man turned on Hannah. "You are a traitor to your people! How dare you wear that veil? You and your children should be stoned."

Ennius produced his sword, and the people around them scattered like mice. Even Hannah stepped away when she heard the terrifying sound of the weapon leaving its sheath with a rush of metallic fury.

"Back away," he said, and let the man go. The man moved, but he continued to glare at Hannah.

"Don't think your pagan will protect you from Alaha," he muttered in disgust and spat on the ground.

Ennius grabbed her arm and pulled her through the market. If Hannah knew her people, word would spread of her and Ennius before sundown. And there were other zealots who would just as easily sacrifice their lives to administer the justice they felt she deserved by associating with the enemy. Ennius would also need to watch his back.

"This isn't a good idea," she said under her breath, but Ennius ignored her and pulled her on through the street.

They searched all morning, but found no sign of Yeshue or his disciples. Ennius asked around but only received silence and angry stares. Hannah overheard a conversation late in the afternoon from women standing around the well. She came close and took her time fetching water for Y'aqim and herself. The women talked of how Yeshue had traveled to other cities around the sea, teaching and performing his miracles. She felt relief that he wasn't nearby, but she was surprised to also sense disappointment. She missed him. She wanted to know if the unbelievable things she'd been hearing about her brother were true.

They made camp outside the town that night as it started to rain. Ennius created a makeshift shelter for her and the boys, pulling his own cape over the top of it to keep them out of the rain. Hannah tried to get him to go back to the fort and sleep in his own bunk, but he refused. He sat in the rain and folded his arms across his chest to keep warm.

"At least take my cloak," she started to pull her heavier covering off to hand to him. He held up his hand in refusal.

"You're so stubborn!" she said in frustration. "You'll freeze to death with those bare arms and legs, and then what good will you do us?"

He didn't answer. He only stared into the rain and blinked moisture out of his eyes.

She fumed. After she got the boys settled inside the dark, mostly dry shelter, she stuck her head outside. "At least come inside."

"There's no room," he growled.

"I'll make room."

"No. Get away from me."

"Fine!" What was the man proving by sitting in the rain? And why should she care if he chose to sit out there like the drenched street rat he was? She curled up by the boys and fell asleep.

Sometime later something startled her awake. She sat up and looked out, seeing Ennius had fallen asleep. His head lulled forward; his cheeks red from cold.

"No better than an ornery old donkey," she said in a huff. She took off her cloak and crawled out of the shelter. She found sticks and propped them up with stones around Ennius's sleeping form. She laid her cloak over the sticks. It wasn't nearly as strong a shelter as he had made for her, but at least he would have some protection. She returned to the boys and huddled close to her sons for warmth.

In the morning, the rain had stopped. The sun rose and filled the sky with rich color and life. The shelter was gone, and Ennius stood over her, extending her cloak. She expected him to chastise her, but he was silent. She took the cloak, and as she tried to pull it away, he held it, tugging her closer.

"Thank you." He let the cloak go.

Ennius decided they would walk to Bethsaida and look for Yeshue. Hannah noticed as he walked that his normally tan skin was pale. After walking for an hour, he began to cough.

When Bethsaida was in sight, she dared to ask. "Are you sick?"

He fidgeted with his sword and avoided her eyes. "Sometimes the weather gives me problems. It will pass."

"I'm not surprised you're sick after sitting all night in the cold rain," she muttered, but at the sight of his sweaty brow and glassy eyes, she felt a stab of pity.

"I won't take from a woman just to make myself more comfortable." He coughed again. "I've always been prone to sickness. Don't worry about me."

It wasn't a leap to wonder why. Being left out to die as an infant probably hadn't done his body any favors. She tried to feel annoyed again at his stubborn refusal of help the night before, but she only felt respect for a man who would give up his comfort, knowing he might be ill as a result, just to protect her. She could think of only one other man she was sure would do the same.

"I didn't expect you to be who you are," she said, though the words didn't really describe the depth of feeling she was experiencing.

He glanced at her. "You expected better or worse?"

She smiled and looked down at Yosef, asleep in his sling. "Definitely worse."

He almost smiled, but the thought seemed to sober him. "And has this caused you to trust me?"

She considered the question. She wasn't sure it was true until she heard the word come from her mouth. "Yes."

He raised an eyebrow. "That's something, I suppose."

Yeshue was not in Bethsaida. They started back to Capernaum, not arriving in the town until nightfall.

Hannah worried about Ennius. His cough was loud and tight, and as she reached up to brush her hand against his cheek, his skin was hot to her touch.

"You're on fire, Ennius. You need the doctor."

He waved her hand away as if it were a fly buzzing around his head. "I'm fine."

He took a few more steps before he collapsed in a heap.

She ran to him and tried to help him get up. He attempted to stand, but he didn't have the strength, so he fell back against the ground and closed his eyes.

"Please get up!" she pleaded, but he didn't respond. She scanned the area, realizing they were close to the military complex. Lysander would be there, and he would know what to do.

"I'm going for Lysander," she told him, running her fingers through his damp curly hair. "I'll be right back. Please don't die."

She picked up Y'aqim and ran as fast as she could with the two children toward the fort on the hill. The gate would be closing soon. She saw the guards and recognized them. One of them had been a customer in the past.

"Please let me in. I must find the Optio," she demanded.

"Go away, woman," the soldier closest to her pushed her back.

"It's Ennius! He's sick. Please let me by."

They ignored her. So she stood next to them and yelled as loud as she could. "Optio! Optio, please!"

After several minutes of her shouting, the guards tired of her and one of them came after her. But as he raised his fist, a voice from behind made him stop.

"Let her go."

The two men turned and bowed in respect. Hannah looked up and saw Lysander standing in the gate.

"My lord!" she cried with relief. "Please come with me. Ennius is very sick."

Immediately Lysander's features lit with concern. "Where is he?"

"Just to the east of here. He collapsed."

Lysander commanded the soldiers to bring him his horse. Moments later, he rode out of the gate, calling back to her to stay where she was.

In minutes he returned with the unconscious form of Ennius slumped over the front of his horse. The guards moved to help carry him inside.

"Put him in my house," Lysander said. They carried him to the house just outside the barracks hall. Hannah followed, Y'aqim in tow.

Once inside, Lysander had them put Ennius on his own bed and moved to grab a sponge and bowl. He poured water from the jug into the bowl and handed it to Hannah.

"Wash his face. Take off his sandals. I'm going for the doctor."

Hannah sent Y'aqim to the corner with a hunk of bread and turned back to Ennius. She loosened the thick leather bands of his sandals and set them aside.

Hannah rinsed the sponge and brought it to Ennius's face. She ran it along his fevered skin, rinsing the heated water from the sponge and exchanging it for cold several times as she washed his arms and legs as well. He shivered, so she pulled a thin blanket over him.

"Alaha," she said out of habit. "Would that you could make him well, despite how much you must hate me."

Lysander returned with the doctor, but after taking a look, the man shook his head. "He was sick as a child, was he not?"

Lysander nodded. "He was exposed as a newborn. He was ill much of his childhood."

"I'll give him some fenugreek, silphium and cold cucumber. If there's no improvement by this evening, I'll relieve him of blood."

"Do you think it will work?" Lysander asked.

"I think he's very ill," the physician said. Hannah noticed he avoided the question.

Later that night, when the doctor had done everything he could, he stood up. "I'm sorry, my lord. The fever has overtaken him."

"He's like a son to me," Lysander said curtly.

The doctor bowed in front of the centurion. "I'll come back in the morning and prepare his body for burial."

Hannah shuttered at his quiet words. The doctor left as Lysander watched Ennius with grief in his expression.

"I didn't save him to let him die like this," Lysander said without looking at her.

After a moment, he shook his head, as if waking up, and looked at her. "How did he become so sick?"

"We had to camp in the rain and he refused to share the shelter he built for me or to accept my cloak."

Lysander sighed. "Fool. He should have known better." He touched Ennius's brow with affection before he turned back to her. "Where did you go today?"

Hannah hesitated, not sure she should tell the Roman centurion who Ennius was interested in finding. "We were looking for Yeshue."

The Optio frowned. "Yeshue of Nazareth?"

Hannah nodded.

"He's a healer. I've heard of him." Lysander appeared to be deep in thought, and he didn't speak again.

As the doctor predicted, Ennius became sicker through the night. By dawn's light, he cried out in pain and terror. "What's wrong with my legs?" he demanded of Lysander in a panic. Lysander tried to calm him and sent for the doctor again.

But the doctor had no good news. "The fever has paralyzed him."

Ennius stared at the doctor in shock. Lysander took the doctor outside to speak with him while Hannah moved close to sponge his brow. She sang a psalm her mother had sung to her when she was ill.

"So shall all those that take refuge in you rejoice, they shall ever shout for joy, and you shall shelter them. Let them also that love your name exult in you. For you bless the righteous, Adonai, you encompass him with favor as with a shield."

Ennius wouldn't be able to understand the words, but she hoped her voice would comfort him. She wanted to pray for him, but she thought it might do more harm than good.

The hours turned into days. The fever clung to Ennius like a leech, sucking the life from his body, just as the doctor seemed to do every time he spilled Ennius's blood into the copper bowl at the side of the bed. After a week, it was obvious he was near death. His skin was ashen, his breathing ragged. He moaned in pain, but his thrashing had ceased, as if he had given up his fight and was resigned to his fate.

On the morning of the seventh day, Hannah and Lysander waited on either side of the bed. Y'aqim napped on the couch in the corner while Yosef nursed. Hannah had been dozing, but she felt someone looking at her and opened her eyes to find Ennius watching her.

"I'm going to die," he said in a weak voice. She shook her head, but she couldn't bring herself to disagree with him. He deserved to know the truth.

Lysander reached for Ennius's hand and gripped it firmly. "You must be optimistic. You'll get well."

Ennius turned to face him with great effort. "I don't want to live anyway. Not if I won't be able to walk."

Lysander sighed while Hannah wondered what to say that might change his mind. But how could she ask him to fight for his life when he would lose everything he'd worked hard to attain?

"The healer," Lysander said suddenly. "I'll find him."

"Yeshue?" Hannah panicked. "Here?"

"I must. I've seen his power. I know he can do this. Your God is powerful, Hannah."

She opened her mouth to protest, but nothing came forth. Of course he should go to Yeshue, if there was even a chance Yeshue could do something. Ennius' life was more important than her troubles.

"Go," she said. "Hurry."

TWENTY

Ya'achov

יעקב

Ya'achov stood by the tree at the base of a green hill covered with people who should have better things to do. He knew he had better things to do. He held his arms across his chest and twisted his mouth in irritation as he listened.

"Everyone therefore who hears my words and does them will be like the wise man who built his house on solid rock. The rain descended, the floods came and the wind blew. They rushed against the house and it did not fall, for its foundation was laid on rock. Everyone who hears my words but does not practice them will be like the foolish man who built his house on sand. The rain descended, the floods came, the wind blew, and they rushed against that house. It fell, and its fall was great."

Ya'achov sighed and cast Yose an impatient glance. What was that supposed to mean? All afternoon Yeshue sat on the hillside outside Capernaum, his disciples all around him like pathetic sheep eating up all the strange teaching that poured out of Yeshue's mouth. Who did he think he was, reinterpreting the laws of Moses? Who could really believe that anger was equal to murder and lust, adultery? What sort of nation would they be if they *loved their enemies* or *walked the second mile*, and generally let Romans trample all over their good name? Alaha had led them into this country and given them victory in many, many battles to make the land their own. Was Yeshue now saying they should cower at their enemy's feet as that enemy took everything away from them?

Ya'achov had heard enough. He would have left, but he wanted to admonish his brother first. He had almost been willing to consider the possibility that Yeshue was the M'sheekha after watching him heal and perform miracles. But if Yeshue was going to make them all into Rome-lovers, Ya'achov would draw the line. That didn't sound like the Jewish king for whom they had been waiting.

But what of the miracles?

Ya'achov shook his head in an attempt to clear the confusing thoughts. Maybe Yeshue had a demon that was doing those things through him. It would explain a few things.

But did demons heal and restore? He'd seen a few of the demon-possessed. There had been a woman from Magdala who had seven spirits controlling her. Before Yeshue had sent the spirits away, they had made her insane. Now, she followed Yeshue around everywhere like that devoted little dog he'd had when he was young.

What kind of trickster demon would spread renewal instead of decay?

Finally, Yeshue stopped talking. He rose to greet some who had been waiting to speak with him, leaning close to them as they whispered their needs or concerns. He prayed with some of them, his hand on their heads as they bowed before him. As if he was Alaha himself.

Disgusting. Irreverent. No wonder he was so unpopular with the leaders of the prayer houses.

Movement caught Ya'achov's eye and he turned to see a Roman centurion coming down the path from the military complex on a massive black horse. Two other soldiers rode behind him. A wave of protectiveness caught him by surprise. Well, what could one expect? Yeshue might be demon-possessed, but he was family. And no filthy Roman soldier was going to get past Ya'achov.

The man and his soldiers dismounted and began to talk to a group of rabbis Ya'achov recognized from the prayer house. Good. Hopefully they'd send him on his way. After a moment they started walking toward Yeshue.

Ya'achov stepped in front of them. "What do you want?" he demanded of the centurion. Ya'achov was startled at the look on the man's face. Humble. Grieved. Hopeful. Ya'achov took advantage of the man's apparent vulnerability and sneered at him, something generally not advised when approached by Roman soldiers.

The soldier wouldn't look him in the eye. "Please, sir, my name is Lysander. I am the centurion in charge at the complex. I need these men to speak to the healer on my behalf."

"Sorry. He has no time for the likes of you." Ya'achov curled his lip in disgust. Who did this man think he was?

"Ya'achov," Jairus said. "Let him by. This man has our blessing to talk to Yeshue."

Ya'achov was sure the lot of them had gone insane. He stepped back to let the man pass, but he glared at him as a warning that he wasn't going far.

But the centurion wouldn't move. "I'll stay here. I shouldn't get too close," Lysander said.

Jairus and several other prayer house leaders walked to the base of the hill, where Yeshue had just healed a small child. There were shouts of rejoicing and thankfulness. Ya'achov took a few steps closer so he could hear what the soldier wanted from his brother. Hopefully Yeshue would use the opportunity to show the Roman soldier what he thought of his paganism.

But Yeshue only gave them that infuriating, welcoming smile as he approached.

"Teacher, may I present Optio Lysander?" Jairus gestured to the top of the hill where Lysander waited.

"Sh'lam lak," Yeshue called to him with a wave.

The centurion only nodded and looked at his feet, as if he was afraid to speak to Yeshue.

"He has a servant called Ennius. This man is highly valued to the

Optio. Indeed, he is like his own son, and he's dying. We ask that you go with him to heal the man."

Yeshue eyed the centurion thoughtfully as another leader stepped forward. "This man deserves your help. He loves our nation and he's built our prayer house."

"You aren't going to find a better Roman than this man," someone else from the crowd.

Lysander continued to hang his head with a troubled expression. He wouldn't look Yeshue in the eye.

"Lead the way," Yeshue said mildly, following them up the hill. The crowd that had been waiting to speak to Yeshue curiously tagged along behind them.

But before Yeshue reached Lysander, the other two soldiers were sent to meet him.

"Optio says his servant is sick. He was rescued as an infant from exposure, and now he is lying in our commander's home—paralyzed and in terrible suffering."

"He was left to die?" Yeshue asked with sorrow, his eyes fixed on Lysander. Ya'achov wished his brother wouldn't show so much emotion all the time. People would think less of him if he appeared weak. Especially Romans.

"Yes," one of the soldiers answered. "Ennius has been a faithful servant. He has continued to follow the Optio even after he was given his freedom. He needs your help."

Yeshue moved past the soldiers and focused his gaze on Lysander. "I will go," Yeshue assured him.

The entire group started to move up the hill to the military complex, but Lysander quickly shook his head and held up his hands.

"My lord," he said, still not meeting his eyes. "I don't deserve for you to come under my roof. I'm not fit. But if you say the word, my son will be healed. I understand this because, though I'm under the authority of Rome, I also have soldiers under me. I tell this one *go*, and he goes; I tell that one, *come*, and he comes. I say to my servant, *do this*, and he does it."

Ya'achov doubted the man's sincerity. It wasn't like Romans to defer to Jews. The man probably put on the act so Yeshue would be impressed enough to help.

Yeshue apparently didn't share Ya'achov's doubts. The expression he wore spoke of amazement, which wasn't common for Yeshue.

Yeshue turned to the disciples and the group following him. "I'm telling you the truth—I haven't found anyone in Israel with as much faith as this man."

He walked closer to Lysander. The centurion lifted his eyes.

"Go. It will be done just as you believed it would."

He touched the man's arm. Lysander nodded, his expression full of emotion, and abruptly turned and motioned for his soldiers to mount. They rode back to the complex without looking back.

Hannah
חנה

Hannah sat beside Ennius, squeezing his limp hand as if she might will life back into his body. But his eyes stayed closed, and he barely breathed. She knew he was close to death. His ashen countenance reminded her of Abba just before he breathed his last.

Suddenly Ennius opened his eyes. A wild desperation lit them. "Will I perish?"

Hannah knew he was talking about whatever waited for him on the other side of death. She didn't want to consider it. She shrugged, unsure of what to say.

"Tell me if your God will forgive me," he said, panicked.

"I don't know," Hannah faltered. But the look of terror in his eyes was too much. "I'm ... I'm sure he will, Ennius."

"I'm evil," he protested, as he labored for breath.

"You're a good man," she said. "You took care of me and my children. I deserve death, not you."

Tears appeared in his eyes. They were irony from such an imposing figure. She swallowed with difficulty.

"I hope, wherever I go, that I can take your memory with me. You are my light, Hannah." Ennius paused to take a faltering breath. "I would have taken care of you. I hope you know that."

"Would that you could have, Ennius," she whispered. "Now, rest. Alaha has seen your good deeds."

"And the bad," he added.

She struggled for words. "Lysander has gone for Yeshue. He will help you."

"Are you sure?"

She hesitated. "I know him, Ennius. He is my brother."

Ennius coughed deeply before he suddenly fell back on the bed, still. She thought he had died, but he took another shallow breath a moment later.

Hannah was afraid he had spoken his last. Yeshue would be too late. She waited for his body to cease its struggle and give up the battle for life.

But several minutes later, Ennius opened his eyes again. Not only that, he sat up. She stared in amazement as the color seeped back into his face.

"Hannah?" His voice carried not a hint of weakness. He stared at her in shock, amazed at what was happening. Hannah had no idea what to make of it.

Throwing his legs over the side of the bed, he tested his feet against the floor. His eyes widened. He stood and took careful steps.

"Hannah, I can walk!"

She stood up so abruptly Yosef was jostled from sleep and fussed against her. Her heart surged with anticipation. She ran to the window, looking in every direction for Yeshue. Was he here? Was he coming? Her heart seemed to skip several beats.

But no one walked up the hill. All was quiet. She came back to Ennius, who swallowed her in a joyful embrace as he laughed in disbelief. He lifted her and Yosef from the tiled floor and spun them around until she was dizzy, with arms that only moments ago had been powerless.

"What is happening?" he asked, astonished. "I have never felt so strong! Praise the gods!" He set her down, smiling. "I mean, praise Yeshue."

"Praise Adonai," she said in awe.

His gaze softened and he reached for her, taking her face between his hands and lightly pressing his lips to hers.

The door burst open and Lysander entered. He laughed aloud as he saw Ennius. "The God of the Jews be exalted!" He came to the younger man and embraced him.

Hannah's heart skipped a beat when she saw the Jewish men standing outside the dwelling, peering in with curiosity. She had never seen Jews enter a Roman military complex before. It seemed even the hassle of purification rites was worth the trouble to find out what had happened.

She searched the group of gawkers from the window, hiding her face. No Yeshue. She was surprised at the stab of disappointment she felt.

She turned around. Ennius was well. He would live. A certain peace fell over her restless spirit.

Maybe it was time to face her brother.

Ya'achov

יעקב

Ya'achov stood in the doorway of the main house, his hands on his hips as he glared at his older brother.

"Are you calling me a liar?" Ya'achov demanded.

"You know I did not," Yeshue said firmly. "I believe you saw her."

"Our sister. In the house of the centurion, in the embrace of a soldier. You know as well as I what she is to him."

"You jump to conclusions, Ya'achov." Yeshue stood nearby, calm. "You cannot depend only on what your eyes see."

"She's a harlot!" Ya'achov tossed his hands in the air in frustration.

"She's shaming our family by parading around the Roman complex. She deserves to be stoned."

Yeshue flinched as if Ya'achov had struck him. Ya'achov shook his head in disbelief. "Do you think I'm enjoying this? It's our duty."

Yeshue stood and approached Ya'achov, his look severe. "It's *my* duty."

"Then do your duty!" Ya'achov flung the impatient words at him. "Or I'll be forced to do it for you."

"Shall I hold your sin against you as well, Ya'achov?"

Indignation welled up in Ya'achov' spirit. "Who do you think you are? How can you compare my sin with hers?"

"Sin is the same in the eyes of Adonai. It is all heartbreaking to him." Yeshue's voice remained calm. Ya'achov wished Yeshue would just yell. Then maybe they could settle it like men. But Yeshue never struggled. At least not in any way Ya'achov could win.

"What kind of M'sheekha ignores the law of God?" Ya'achov snarled back at him.

Yeshue didn't speak, but neither did he back down. Ya'achov turned in disgust and left the room. "I'm going to find her and deal with her before she ruins our reputation."

Yeshue didn't follow him, which made him even angrier. Maybe he really would find Hannah. That would show Yeshue who the holier brother was.

He left the house. His feet pounded the path, a drumbeat demanding justice.

Talia

טליה

Talia watched Yeshue that afternoon. He was quiet. Thoughtful. When the disciples had dispersed and Yeshue sat alone, Talia came and sat by her brother.

"Did you know Hannah was here?"

Yeshue nodded. "I saw her."

"Why didn't you say so?"

He gestured toward Ya'achov. "For this reason."

Nathanael had followed her and was listening to the conversation. He appeared troubled. "I know she is your sister ... but Ya'achov has a point. The law is clear. The girl is undermining your ministry, Yeshue."

Yeshue stood and went to the arched stones of the doorway, looking up over the rooftops to the Roman fort on the hill. He didn't speak for a long time.

"Is it wise to let her go?" Nathanael asked. Talia frowned at him, but he didn't look at her.

"Mercy, Nathanael," Yeshue said with a sigh. "*I desire mercy, not sacrifice.*"

"Even for a harlot?"

The room went silent again. Again, without warning, Talia saw images of Hannah dragged down the hillside with her son. Pummeled with stones. Bleeding, bruised, crying out for them ...

She gasped in pain at the thought of watching that scene. "Can I at least get her child?" Talia asked, standing. "I could raise him as my own son."

Nathanael looked to Yeshue, but Yeshue did not answer for him.

"Please, Yeshue, tell me what to do," he said quietly.

Yeshue watched him for a long moment, then nodded. He turned to Talia. "Go."

Talia flew out of the house and up the hill, throwing her veil over her face so Ya'achov would not see as she passed him. He had gone to the prayer house, probably to inform the leaders there would be a stoning.

She ran all the way to the fort. She was stopped by the guards at the gate, who pushed her back and ignored her as she begged to be let through.

Talia caught sight of Hannah standing outside a dwelling with two soldiers. "Hannah!" she called desperately.

Hannah turned, her beautiful face breaking into a smile at the sight of Talia. When she turned, Talia saw with dismay that she had a newborn in her arms. Her little son stood next to her, holding her tunic.

Hannah turned to the older soldier and said something. He motioned to Talia to come, and the soldiers stepped out of her way.

Talia ran to her sister and threw her arms around her, her tears breaking forth in bittersweet agony. How good it was to hold Hannah in her arms again, but how could she give her the awful news?

"Hannah, they're coming!" she cried, trying to catch her breath.

"Who? Yeshue? I think I'm ready to talk to him—"

"No, Hannah, you don't understand. It's Ya'achov. He saw you with the soldier earlier. He's coming with the leaders of the prayer house."

Talia didn't need to say anymore. Hannah looked wildly toward the gate. The sun had begun to set and the hillside was too dim to make out any figures if they didn't have lamps. Hannah looked to the young soldier standing next to her.

"Put a stop to this," he said to the older one, whom Talia assumed must be the centurion in charge. She trembled in their presence. Roman soldiers were to be feared. Avoided. How had Hannah ended up here? Was the baby fathered by this soldier?

If so, the night might become more complicated than it already was. Her entire family could be slaughtered by the Romans.

"We don't have authority to keep them from upholding their laws," the centurion said with concern.

Talia's eyes rested on the baby asleep in her sister's arms. "I'll take the children, Hannah. I'll raise them as my own—if need be."

Hannah glared at Talia, her countenance fierce, but desperate. She finally kneeled down in front of the little one standing beside her.

"Ama must say goodbye, my little Y'aqim. I love you. You are a good boy."

Y'aqim's large brown eyes watched her as his lower lip protruded. Talia took his hand, and he started to cry.

Hannah took her baby from the sling and lifted his soft head to her lips. "Go in the peace of Alaha, Yosef."

As Talia took the newborn in the crook of her arm, she wanted to linger. She wanted to hear Hannah's story. She could see in her eyes she was no longer the rebellious child who wanted her own way. Somewhere along the line, whether a year ago or a month ago or minutes before Talia arrived, Hannah had changed.

And the soldier did not look on Hannah with anything but love. Had she found love in the most unlikely place in the world for a young Jewish woman to find it?

Talia could not bear the sadness weighing on her soul. She hugged Hannah again. "I will pray."

She left the fort, her sister's two crying boys in her arms.

TWENTY-ONE

Hannah
חנה

Ya'achov wouldn't be far behind Talia. Hannah could see the lights of torches at the bottom of the hill.

She felt pressure on her arm. Ennius turned her to face him. "I will not let this happen. Come with me."

He grabbed her hand and pulled her behind him. They ducked out of the gate before Ya'achov arrived. Ennius practically dragged her down the far side of the hill in the twilight shadows.

He ran madly for a time, heading for the western hills that led to the rest of Galilee. But finally, she shook off his hand and stopped to catch her breath.

"I don't want to run anymore," she said.

He glared at her. "You'd rather die at the hand of your brother?"

She looked at him for a long moment. Then all that she'd done, all the ways she had gone against her family and searched for her own pleasure became too much to bear. She balled her hand into a fist and struck a tree as hard as she could. The pain and the blood were a strangely welcome sight.

"Ya'achov is right! I deserve to die. I have sinned," she yelled, angrier with herself than she had ever been.

Admitting it brought a rushing wind of relief that swept the weight of her burden away. She gave a long sigh and sank to the ground next to the tree. She felt Ennius's hand on her head. They were quiet for a long time. Eventually he sat down beside her and gathered her close to him, pulling her toward him. She hugged him back.

He shook his head. "I have done wrong, too. Why kill you when I am more at fault? The weight of my sin is impossible to pick up, Hannah. But your brother, Yeshue, didn't condemn me. He healed me! Why? Why should he care what happens to a sinful Roman slave? Wouldn't he treat his own family better than a pagan?"

Hannah considered his words with the tiniest thread of hope. But even so, she knew she didn't deserve mercy. She should have known better.

"Ennius, listen to me. I grew up in the same house as the M'sheekha. The Son of Alaha, Ama called him. He taught me the Scriptures. He warned me against the sins I've committed over and over again. I have no excuse."

Ennius wore an expression of awe. She'd never seen another like it on the soldier's face. "You believe your brother is the son of a god?"

"No. I believe my brother is the Son of the only true God."

He considered her words with a frown. "I've never seen power like his. He can heal even with a word spoken at a distance."

"Alaha's power is limitless."

Ennius stood up and began to pace. "All my life I have scorned religion, whether it be Roman or Greek or Jewish. It is all false. Pretend. But your brother is no statue or figurine being sold in the marketplace. I was dead, Hannah! My life was over, and here I am, breathing in and out – the very breath of your God."

She nodded through her tears.

"Tell me about him," he said, turning back to her once more and grabbing her hands, pulling her up on her feet.

"My parents always told us of his birth. We scoffed at them secretly. It seemed too ridiculous a tale."

"What tale?"

"My mother was with child before my parents were rightfully married," Hannah said.

Ennius shook his head in confusion. "Isn't that against your laws?"

She nodded. "But Ama always insisted she did not sin. That Yeshue didn't have an earthly father."

"Born of a virgin?" Ennius's expression was severe. "Do you believe it?"

"I didn't. I figured Ama would have said anything to save her reputation. In fact, I secretly wondered if she'd been attacked ... by a soldier."

Ennius nodded. "It happens. I'm sorry."

"You have nothing to be sorry about." She lifted her hand to his cheek.

He caught her fingers and kissed them. "I have plenty of shame, Hannah. Many regrets."

She nodded, understanding what he meant.

"But tell me the rest," he said suddenly.

"My parents still married. Abba said an angel gave him a vision and told him not to be afraid to marry her. Yeshue was born in Bethlehem during the census. King Herod tried to have him killed, so they had to escape to Egypt for a time. They came back when Herod was dead, and moved back to Nazareth, Ama's hometown."

"Did Yeshue do miracles there?"

Hannah shook her head. "Never that I remember. The first time I saw it was the night you took me into town to see him."

Ennius sighed. "We could just leave. Get the boys and go somewhere no one knows us. If we live in a Roman city and marry, you'll be safe. I'll be a good husband to you and provide for you."

Hannah reached up to put her arms around his neck. He kissed her nose. Her cheek. Her lips.

"It would make me happy to be your wife and raise your children. But I have a debt to settle." She pushed away from his embrace. "I have to face Yeshue. If I am to die tonight, I will repent of my sin first."

She turned toward the lights of the town. "Would that I had listened to Yeshue long ago. That I had followed him."

"If you had listened to him, we never would have met. You'd be married off to some farmer in Nazareth. I don't believe that was ever the plan of your God."

Hannah had never thought of it that way. She chuckled. "Maybe you're right."

Ennius grabbed her arm as she tried to walk away from him. "Not yet, Hannah. Ya'achov will get to you first and you won't have a chance to speak to Yeshue. You don't even know where he is! We'll give it a day or two, and then we'll go to him by night."

He pulled her close, and she wavered for a moment in his arms. This was where she wanted to be, always. Close to Ennius's heart. She would probably never be allowed to marry him, so the thought of enjoying one night together occurred to her. She'd never been with someone she loved. Wouldn't it be beautiful?

But even as she considered it, she knew it couldn't be. Yeshue had always said being sorry for sin involved turning away from that sin. She could not do it again if she was truly going to repent to Yeshue.

Ennius didn't make it easy. He reached for her. It took every bit of strength she had to push him away again.

"This is wrong."

"Your God calls love wrong?" he said.

"No. Alaha *is* love."

"Then come with me," he insisted, his voice thick.

"I can't."

He stepped back and she saw the familiar stubborn bent of his chin, the fists curling at his sides. "Fine. But don't expect me to go with you and watch you throw your life away."

Whether he was angrier that she was risking her life or that she had rejected his advances, she didn't know. But he stormed off in the direction of the fort and didn't look back.

Ya'achov

יעקב

"Get out of this house, Ya'achov!" Maryam cried, throwing down the jar of water. It broke in two pieces as she stood in front of him, crying.

"I'll find her," he refused to be swayed by his mother's hysterics. "If you are hiding her or you know where she is, may Alaha deal with you." Ya'achov felt shame at the way he was speaking to his mother. But she had chosen the wrong side.

"I don't know where she is, but I would not tell you if I did." Maryam spat on the ground.

"You don't think the Law applies to your own daughter? Because you have one perfect son, all your children can do no wrong except the one who is seeking justice?"

Nathanael hurried across the courtyard and put a hand of restraint on Ya'achov's arm. Ya'achov hurled him a look of warning. Nathanael dropped his hand, but the smaller man still stood up to him. "You must treat your mother with respect."

Ya'achov scoffed. "Stay out of my family's business. Go follow that worthless brother of mine who won't do what he should."

Nathanael took a step back, but he didn't leave. "Yeshue has spoken of the importance of showing mercy by not giving someone the punishment you think they deserve. He says this is pleasing to Alaha."

"Have you ever heard of such an idea before he said it?" Ya'achov shook his head in disgust. "I haven't. And I know the Law. Probably better than Yeshue."

"That may be," Nathanael said. "But Yeshue is special. He has the gift of new interpretations. The rabbis call it *s'mikeh*."

"I know what the rabbis call it. But I'll never accept that Alaha would have us change the fundamental laws of our religion," Ya'achov argued loudly. "Yeshue is going against what Alaha clearly told us hundreds of years ago. Thousands! And if you accept these false statements, you are no true Jew."

Nathanael shook his head. "You are acting out of anger. Give this decision more time."

"I don't have a choice! The girl has run off with her pagan lover to hide. Is that one who deserves mercy?"

"Ya'achov," Talia dared to speak from behind Nathanael. Her voice was timid, as if she expected him to strike her. She held that child—son of a Roman, no less—and dared to speak to him. "Hannah's different now. She is not the same girl we knew. And the soldier loves her. He took her away because he can't bear for her to be killed."

"Stay out of this!" Ya'achov yelled. He caught his wife's eyes from across the room and saw fear flickering there. Why was everyone around him being so unreasonable? Was he the only one left with the least bit of sense?

"I insist you speak to my wife with respect, Ya'achov," Nathanael warned, moving between them.

"What is it with you and Yeshue and everyone in your little group always talking about respect? Since when do we respect the opinions of women? They don't know how to make choices like these."

Nathanael's eyes rested on Nava. "Do you not respect the opinion of your wife, Ya'achov?"

"My wife would never think to subvert my authority. She stays quiet and out of my way, as she should. Alaha help her if she didn't," Ya'achov growled, only to look over and see the sadness that marred his wife's features. She didn't look up from the pot she was stirring.

"No one is saying the laws of Alaha are wrong. Only that Yeshue has brought us new angles to consider as we follow them. If Hannah is truly repentant of her sin, Yeshue says we should forgive her."

"Her groveling because she has been found out does not erase what she's done to disgrace our family. You know as well as I do what Roman soldiers do to women. How could we ever welcome her back into our family as defiled as she is now?"

Maryam shot him a look from where she stood by the wall, seething. "Watch your mouth," she said in a low voice. He recognized it as the one she'd used when he was in the most trouble as a child. He hated that it still had an effect on him.

He had to get out of this house and away from these people. He gave a menacing growl of frustration and left the house.

Y'hud

יהוד

Y'hud watched his brother go and sensed the relief that everyone felt as a result. He looked back and saw Nathanael reach out to Talia and squeeze her hand. "I'm sorry," he said.

She tried to smile. "Thank you for standing up for Hannah."

"No matter what I say, Ya'achov is within his rights to seek justice. We must pray he will have a change of heart "

"What does Yeshue say?" Talia asked as Maryam stepped forward to hear their conversation.

Nathanael sighed. "Not much. He prays for Hannah. But I don't think he'll challenge Ya'achov unless he sees that Hannah is changed. And if she really was different, she would have come to him already, wouldn't she?"

"Maybe she's afraid," Talia said in her defense. "Maybe she thinks Yeshue will agree with Ya'achov."

"If she's truly sorry for her sin, even that would not keep her away."

Y'hud wandered from the conversation to the Capernaum road, looking for Ya'achov. He must have gone to look for Hannah again. Y'hud wouldn't have admitted it to anyone, but he was glad Ya'achov hadn't found her. He didn't want her to die.

He felt like a traitor thinking that way. After all, he was a Jewish man now, having reached the age of twelve. He should be strong enough to face the hard decisions like Ya'achov did.

He wandered down the street. It was twilight, and neighbors were still standing about, talking. His eyes caught on a familiar face.

He started walking toward the girl from the prayer house who had asked him about Yeshue's ability to heal. She was sitting on the bench outside her house, one of the wealthier homes in the town. Her father was Rabbi Jairus, after all. He sat near her. Not very near her. After all, she *was* a girl.

"My name's Y'hud," he said, not looking at her as he spoke. When he dared a glance, he noticed she looked different than she had before. She was smaller and her bones stuck out in her face, which was white, except for around her eyes where there were dark circles.

"I'm Judith," she said. Her voice was raspy.

"You don't look well." He spoke before he thought about whether he should say the words. She didn't seem offended. She nodded and leaned back against the stone wall of her home and crossed her arms across her chest as if she was cold.

"What's wrong with you?"

"The doctor doesn't know," she said dully. "My father sent for a well-known physician from Jerusalem, but no matter what he does, I seem to get worse."

"My brother could help you," Y'hud said. "I'll go get him."

She shook her head, sitting up. "My father wouldn't like it. He's not sure about Yeshue's powers. He wonders if they might be from a devil."

Y'hud scowled. "My brother is the M'sheekha. You better be careful what you say, and you tell your father the same!"

Judith scooted away from him with a frown. "Why don't you just leave?"

Y'hud waved her off and went back down the street. Only fools didn't believe Yeshue was the king.

He peeked back at her home before he went inside his own gate. She wasn't on the bench anymore. The door of her home was closed and the lamps in the window extinguished.

"Y'hud, come inside," his mother called. He went inside, still sulking. He found Yeshue on the rooftop, praying alone.

He climbed the steps and went to sit next to him. "What are you praying about?"

"Didn't Ama call you to bed?" Yeshue opened an eye and frowned at him.

"I thought being a man would mean I'd get bossed around less," Y'hud said, kicking at a loose stick coming up from the dried mud.

"Being a man involves being able to be led. Obeying helps you obey Alaha later when *you* are the leader." Yeshue ruffled his hair. "Away with you. Obey your mother."

Y'hud stood up and started for the stairs. He looked back. "You are the M'sheekha, right, Abba?"

"Amen, it is as you say," Yeshue said. "And I will also be in the morning, when you will be free to ask me all of your questions. To bed."

Y'hud watched Yeshue return to his prayers, his mouth moving silently, his eyes closed tightly, his hands gesturing as if he were talking to someone.

Y'hud wondered if he prayed for Hannah.

Hannah

חנה

Hannah peered down the hillside at the village of Capernaum and to the see beyond. The orange sun kissed the edge of the waters. Colors painted the sky as if brushed by Alaha himself. She closed her eyes and felt the wind embrace her.

Could her sins be forgiven? She had never wanted to consider it before – the possibility of being washed clean. She was broken, deep in the very nature of her being. What was the point of hope if she couldn't be fixed?

But she could see there was only one choice, and it would involve her whole-hearted effort.

She was aware that she deserved death. She could look back and see the pattern of rebellion, starting when she was a girl flirting with evil. Sin had only led to more sin. And her wickedness had gotten her nothing but a few coins and a heart full of darkness.

What a waste.

"I'm a sinner," she said, because she couldn't say anything else. She lifted her arms toward the morning sky as she had seen Yeshue do. She pleaded with the unseen, all-powerful One.

"I have sinned!" she called in a louder voice. "If you require my life, I will give it. Only forgive my sin, Adonai!"

Heaven was silent. She felt silly for expecting anything but judgment. It was too late.

Ennius came trudging up the hill, a morose expression on his face. She could tell he thought her life was over. She knew he wanted to protect her.

"Ennius," she said when he came to her and took her hands in his. "I am making this hard for you."

"I don't understand why you won't just leave with me."

She shook her head. "Where is he?"

He glared, but he answered her. "He's at the house of Shimon eating supper. Wait till he goes home."

She looked down at the town, a thrill of anticipation surprising her as she saw the wealthy man's house lit up and full of people. Yeshue was there.

"Ya'achov will be at home. It's better this way. I will go now," she said, trying to tug her hands away from his. He started to argue, but she pushed him away. "The time has come. If you truly care about me, you will let me do this. Don't interfere with anything that happens at that house or in this village tonight."

"How can I agree to stand by and watch you destroyed? I can't imagine my life without you, Hannah. You'd have to kill me to keep me from coming with you."

"Then come," she said, turning toward the town and descending the hill. "But don't get in the way. Adonai will do what pleases him. Yeshue will, too. Trust the one who gave you back your life. He will do what is right with me."

"Wait," he said, grabbing her arm to make her stop. She turned and he brought out something from his pack.

She smiled. He had brought her the little alabaster jar she had taken from her husband's house. He'd even found a cord to thread through the handles so she could wear it around her neck.

"Take it. It may buy your freedom," he said, holding it out to her.

She took the jar and slipped the cord around her neck. She took a deep breath and walked purposefully toward the house of the Pharisee.

Ennius followed her down the hillside and didn't speak another word.

The house called her like a beacon in the darkening night. Music and male voices filtered into the night air outside the home. It was a well-attended party.

Her steps faltered. She imagined disgusted glances and calls for her death. But the thought of Yeshue kept her moving. Not even her life mattered as much as kneeling at his feet. Telling him she was sorry.

Ennius stopped outside the doorway. She glanced back. He watched her with his ever-furrowed brow. "I am not welcome here."

"I am not welcome, either," she said with a rueful smile. She gave him one final glance. His lean, muscled form that spoke of power and confidence competed with the vulnerable glint of moisture in his eye. She swallowed hard as she turned toward the house.

A few men glanced up at her as she entered. She scanned the room until she found the familiar form at the end of the table, facing away from her as he reclined with a few of the prayer house leaders.

Love overcame every other emotion. Her heart raced with expectation and she began to run to him. One of the servants stepped in her way, and she fell, but she crawled past him on her hands and knees, desperate to reach Yeshue.

Words failed her. She opened her mouth but could not form the sentences she had hoped to recite. She edged forward until she was close enough to kneel by his feet. She pressed her face against his feet hanging off the end of the couch. His face turned slightly when he felt her there, but he didn't look at her or speak to her.

Sudden clarity made her comprehend the truth. Her sin had hurt herself, had hurt her children, her family and Ennius, but she had hurt Yeshue the most.

Hannah felt a great pressure in her chest. Her eyes burned and her face felt like it was on fire. All the pent-up tears of a lifetime begged to be released in the realization of her great shame. The room had gone silent and everyone was staring awkwardly at her display, but tears cascaded down her face. She could do nothing to stop them.

She saw that she had made his feet wet with her crying and felt embarrassed. She saw her hair hanging loose around her shoulders. She had forgotten to cover her head before she came down to the village.

She slammed her fist on the stone floor. She couldn't even get her apology right. What a mess she had made of everything! She took the ends of her hair and dried his feet, bowing as low as she could get to the ground.

She remembered the jar hanging around her neck. That perfume could be her gift to Yeshue. A priceless gift, poured out in his honor. It would be her way of convincing him she was sorry. The remnants of her old life would fade away as the perfume dissipated, and whatever future she had would be lived differently. For him.

She quickly reached for the jar around her neck and broke the long-necked opening on the hard tile of the floor. A potent aroma filled the air around them.

Myrrh. It reminded her of the day Abba had died. The women had come and smeared the costly scented oils all over Abba's body. The smell of myrrh had permeated their home for days.

She stole a look at Yeshue as she rubbed the oil on his feet and wiped them again with her hair. Would he be angry that she had anointed him with oil meant for a funeral?

She placed every drop of the expensive oil on his feet. Then she kissed them and backed away from him, still on her hands and knees, her face prostrated to the floor.

Her voice would not work to tell him the things she wanted to say. *I'm sorry, Yeshue. I have sinned against you. I thought my way was better than yours. I was convinced you were trying to ruin my life, and I wasn't going to let you. I thought I knew a better way and I would do what it took to get what I wanted.*

You were trying to help me, not hold me back. I was selfish. My sin led me on a path that took me further and further away from your love. Now I am ruined. I am a sinner who has finally realized what that sin costs. I deserve death, and if it is your will, I will die for my sin.

"Shimon, I have something to tell you," Yeshue said. His voice interrupted her thoughts. He spoke to the Pharisee who owned the house. Shimon had been watching her with disgust from the moment she came in. She glanced up. His lip curled her as if she was a piece of refuse left on his clean floor. It wasn't hard to imagine what he was thinking. She heard commotion at the door. Someone breathed as if he had been running. She made herself look. Ya'achov pushed Ennius out of the way and stood in the doorway, seething at the sight of her.

She tensed with fear.

"Tell me, Rabbi," Shimon said in a falsely respectful voice. He exchanged looks with some of the other Pharisees in the room and at the table. Hannah had no doubt Ya'achov had spoken with at least some of them, and they were all in agreement that she should be stoned.

"One landowner had two debtors. One debtor owed him five hundred denarii and the other fifty denarii. And because they had nothing to pay, he forgave both of them. Which of them will love him more?"

"Five hundred denarii? Put the fool in prison or sell his children into slavery for a sum that huge," a man at the table laughed.

Shimon shrugged at Yeshue. "I suppose he who was forgiven most will love him most."

"You are correct." Yeshue sat up and turned around so he could look Hannah in the eye. She dared to meet his gaze, dared to search the familiar warm brown eyes of her brother for any sign that he might forgive. He didn't speak to her, but he smiled.

Yeshue smiled at her.

He spoke to Shimon again. "Do you see this woman? When I came into your house, you gave no water for my feet. She has washed my feet with her tears and wiped them with her hair. You did not kiss me, but, she has not stopped kissing my feet. You did not anoint my head with oil, but she has anointed my feet with an expensive ointment. On account of this, I say to you, that her many sins are forgiven her because she loved much, but he who is forgiven a little loves a little."

Yeshue hadn't stopped looking at her. What was he saying? Could he actually mean he forgave her? She searched his gaze. Love spilled from his spirit and kissed her soul.

He leaned closer. "Your sins are forgiven you. Your faith has given you life, go in peace."

TWENTY-TWO

Ya'achov

יעקב

Ya'achov searched house to house, asking if anyone had seen the Jewish prostitute from the army fort. When he came down the road and saw the Roman soldier standing in the doorway of Shimon's house, he smirked. He had her cornered.

He shoved the soldier aside. The man's hand went instinctively for his sword, but as Ya'achov was preparing for a very one-sided fight, the soldier released the handle and stepped out of his way with an ambiguous, seething glare.

Ya'achov bypassed him, giving him a wide berth and keeping his hand close to the dagger stashed in his robe. He turned his attention to the scene inside the house.

Shimon, the host, stood nearby with arms folded across his chest, watching Yeshue. Ya'achov followed his gaze to find Hannah weeping at the feet of Yeshue. She kissed his feet over and over, as if the number of kisses depended on whether she would be set free or not. Ya'achov narrowed his eyes. Whether Yeshue would or not, he'd be the first to throw a stone.

Then he heard Yeshue speak. "Your sins are forgiven you."

He gaped at his older brother, hardly believing the words had come out of his mouth, and yet knowing what Yeshue was going to say before the words left his mouth. Her sins forgiven? Who was he to forgive her sins? Alaha reserved that right. Ya'achov clutched the knife again, and the image of the blade plunged into Yeshue's chest appeared in his mind.

"Your faith has given you life. Go in peace."

With Yeshue's words, just like that, vindication was cancelled. Ya'achov realized there would be no stoning. Not with all of these witnesses to the elder brother's act of forgiveness. He wanted to take all the tapestries hanging in Shimon's gaudy house and rip them to shreds. He turned wildly and stomped into the street, swearing so loudly several turned to look at him, pulling loved ones away in fear.

Moments later, Yeshue and Hannah came into the street together. Their faces were lit only by the lamplight cast from the doorway and windows of Shimon's house. He seethed as Hannah ran into the soldier's arms.

"What do you think you're doing?" Ya'achov growled, going after Yeshue and pushing him against the side of the house. At several gasps from passerby, Ya'achov let him go, but he wanted to wring his neck. His hands ached with the urge. He clenched them tightly into balls and held his breath until his vision sparked and his head felt like it might explode like a pulsing timber in a hot oven.

"Ya'achov," Yeshue calmly said. Ya'achov heard the warning, but he didn't care anymore. He was done following his brother's shoddy leadership.

"What right do you have to forgive sins?" he demanded. "Are you in the place of Alaha, now? Should we all bow to you instead? A penniless teacher who depends on the good will of others to stay alive?"

Yeshue did not flinch. "Hannah's faith has saved her. Elohim forgives the repentant sinner."

"She should die! She's a whore for these filthy soldiers. You know it and I know it and everyone in this town knows it. You had no right to forgive her. She's humiliated our family."

"I had every right," Yeshue disagreed. "You add to your sin,

Ya'achov. Perhaps you should take some time to think before you say anything else."

Every shred of good sense left his mind, and Ya'achov pulled back his fist. He had every intention of pummeling his brother to the ground. But the cool steel of a blade touched his chin. He met the eyes of Hannah's Roman.

"Back away," the soldier said. "Go home."

Ya'achov wanted to rage with fury. But he was no match for a Roman sword with only a small hand-made knife to defend himself. Besides, all of Rome stood with the soldier. Ya'achov's death would be swift.

He swore again as he turned toward home. When he reached the house, he pushed past his dumbfounded wife and children and went out behind the house to the beach, where he picked up stones as large as he could manage and hurled them into the sea.

He wished every one of them were his unbearable, irritating, pigheaded donkey of a brother.

Hannah

חנה

After Ya'achov left, Hannah released a tense breath, thankful for Yeshue and Ennius. She turned to Yeshue with a shy smile, still scarcely able to believe he had forgiven her.

"This is Ennius of Rome," she said, gesturing. "Ennius, my brother, Yeshue of Nazareth."

Yeshue turned to Ennius and nodded, raising a hand to grasp the soldier's thick arm. Ennius stared at Yeshue's hand in surprise.

"You healed him," Hannah said to Yeshue. "You probably don't realize it, but Ennius is the centurion Lysander's servant. I was with him. He almost died, but you healed him. From a distance!"

Yeshue's smile widened, though he didn't appear surprised. "I am glad you are well. Your master has great faith."

Ennius swallowed and shifted his eyes downward. He cleared his throat. "I don't deserve what you did. I am in your debt."

Yeshue watched him with interest. "You have a burden you have carried far too long, Ennius." Yeshue's voice was tender and quiet, his words meant only for the soldier. "Elohim can forgive sin. Even sin you can't forgive yourself."

Ennius met his eyes with surprised confusion. "Master, I think you are mistaken. I am Roman. I don't know your God."

Yeshue shook his head. "How could Adonai not love the work of his hands?"

Hannah was surprised by Yeshue's unusual words, but she met Ennius's expression with a smile.

Yeshue spoke to her. "Sister, you have children who are missing their ama right now. Especially one who might be getting hungry."

Panic flooded her heart. Her boys! "Where are they?"

He motioned toward the path. "Come. Follow me and I will take you to them."

Talia

טליה

Talia opened her eyes. She shifted in the dark and felt the comforting arms of her husband surround her. He had come to Capernaum for a brief visit the week before, after Hannah had come to live with them, and she had begged him to at least allow her to stay with her family for the foreseeable future.

"I admit, it is nice having you closer," Nathanael said in a voice thick from sleep.

He hadn't been there when she had finally fallen asleep. Yeshue and his disciples had spent the day away and had not come back until the moon was high in the sky. Talia knew they would awaken at dawn and be off again.

Talia envied Nathanael's close relationship with Yeshue. She wished she could follow as closely as they did.

"Where's Yeshue?" Talia whispered.

Nathanael yawned. "He stayed in Peter's house. Said there were fewer little ones to risk waking up."

Talia smiled. That sounded like Yeshue.

She heard the soft whine of a newborn. Hannah roused behind the curtain to nurse her son. Talia shifted as she listened to Hannah's comforting tones. She had mixed feelings about Hannah's return. She was glad Hannah had repented and that Yeshue had forgiven her. Hannah's boys were precious and Talia enjoyed helping care for them. But the household was thick with tension between Ya'achov and Hannah. Ya'achov made barbed comments under his breath about Hannah and her children and her Roman lover. Talia worried when she heard strange noises at night. Ya'achov might sneak in with that dagger of his and mete out his own justice.

The Roman soldier, Ennius, came every day to see Hannah and her boys as if he were wooing her. It made the situation more uncomfortable. He came in the afternoon when Ya'achov was out selling wares in the marketplace, but Ya'achov could probably see him coming and going from his booth. Would Yeshue allow them to marry? How would Ya'achov react to *that* humiliation?

Talia felt safe when Yeshue was there, but he was often gone for days at a time, traveling through Galilee healing and teaching in the nearby cities. Talia sensed the soldier stayed close because he was concerned for Hannah and the boys. But his presence made everyone anxious. Everyone besides Hannah, that is. He was intimidating in size and disposition. He wore clothes that revealed his muscled arms and legs, and Talia could never quite guess what he was thinking beneath his ever present scowl. She prayed he wasn't a spy for Rome, or even for the Pharisees, who had begun making their displeasure known concerning Yeshue's ministry.

She had no idea what Yeshue would decide, and the uncertainty made the open affection shown between Ennius and Hannah uncomfortable to watch. Talia had never heard of a Jewish woman marrying a Roman, least of all a Roman soldier. Wasn't it against their laws?

Now Hannah's other boy, Y'aqim, was stirring. Talia knew Hannah would have a hard time tending to him while she was nursing. She got up and pulled her cloak on, quickly winding her headscarf around her head. Nathaniel stood and hugged her from behind, kissing her shoulder.

"I'll miss you," he said, and then he was gone, slipping on his cloak and turban as he left their sleeping space.

Talia washed and dressed Y'aqim and set him down to toddle off after his cousin, Amaris, who flitted around the courtyard in the pre-dawn, happy as a lark. She had taken two-year-old Y'aqim under her care and seemed determined to teach him everything she knew—such as it was. Would that her abba, Ya'achov, could learn to love his sister as much as Amaris loved Y'aqim!

"I wonder if Yeshue will decide today," Hannah mused aloud as she nursed. Yosef had become quite content since he'd been returned to his mother. Watching them together made Talia long for a baby of her own. Alaha had not seen fit to open her womb. Almost two years had passed since her wedding in Cana, and she was beginning to wonder if she was barren.

She hated even the thought of it, so she pushed the question away. "I don't know how long they will be away this time."

The summer had been long and full of monotony. Talia chafed somewhat under the constant routine of taking care of children, preparing food and cleaning. Her life had been much the same for as long as she could remember. She wanted to follow Yeshue like the women who stayed with them and saw to their needs. But something kept her from asking Nathanael again.

She sighed. Perhaps it was best to stay home. Look at Hannah. She'd gone out into the world. What pain could have been spared her if she had simply stayed home and obeyed Yeshue?

"I prayed to Alaha that Yeshue would let me marry Ennius," Hannah whispered eagerly.

Talia glanced around the dwelling to make sure Ya'achov or Nava weren't there to hear their conversation. But Ya'achov and Yose had left early to work in the shop down the road with the Capernaum tekton.

"Hannah, do you think that would be wise?" Talia asked.

Hannah's eyes flashed. "I don't care that he's Roman, and he doesn't care that I'm Jewish."

"Doesn't God care? Didn't he give us the law for good reasons?" Talia said slowly. She hated to start conflict with her sister, but Hannah's careless attitude worried her.

"Yeshue healed Ennius. Do you think he would have done that if there was no hope for him?" Hannah asked sharply. Her eyes seemed to take on the reflection of the stormy sea.

"Yeshue shows kindness to everyone. That doesn't mean he'll let his sister marry an idol-worshiper."

Hannah scowled. "Maybe if you weren't so afraid all the time, you would understand the risks someone is willing to take when they love someone."

Talia shook her head and stepped away from Hannah. She looked out the window.

"That's it. Run away like you always do," Hannah seethed under her breath.

Talia watched out the window as Ennius came sauntering down the road in his short red tunic and gold sandals. At least he wasn't wearing the breastplate or cape these days, but there was no doubt whom he was and from where he hailed. Hannah saw him and jumped up. She pressed Yosef into Talia's arms before she ran out the door and exuberantly jumped into her soldier's embrace.

Talia turned her attention to Hannah's abandoned children as she indulged a sting of envy. She might as well be the boys' mother. She did everything besides nurse. Why hadn't Alaha given the boys to her instead?

To Talia's delight, Yeshue came home that afternoon while the children were napping. She threw aside the hand mill and ran to the door to greet him.

"I'm so glad you didn't leave Capernaum again," she said as he hugged her shoulders.

Yeshue searched the room. "Is Hannah with her friend?"

Talia nodded. "She just left. I'm worried about her. She takes no thought for our ways."

Yeshue didn't comment. "I'll go find them. We'll talk later, sister. I miss your peaceful voice. Perhaps we'll walk on the beach tonight after supper?"

"I would love that," Talia answered with a smile. She was well aware how many people clamored for Yeshue's attention each moment of each day. Yet he wanted to sit and talk with *her*.

He stopped in the doorway. "Will you pray for me, Talia?"

Her heart went to him. Suddenly he seemed vulnerable as he stood in the doorway, all the weight of the world resting on his shoulders. Did anyone ever take thought for the burdens he carried without complaint? "Of course, Yeshue. Always."

He cupped her cheek with his palm before he left. She supposed he would make his way to the hill outside Capernaum where Hannah and Ennius liked to walk.

Hannah
חנה

Hannah saw Yeshue coming and her heart raced with anticipation. Surely, he would understand. Surely, he would see the love they shared and honor it. But as he came into clearer view, she saw his guarded expression, and she felt the same old disappointment of her youth when her ideas clashed with her older brother's plans.

She sighed as Yeshue sat down beside them in the grass. Ennius had been holding her hand, but now he let it go and scooted away.

"Sh'lam lak," Yeshue said to Ennius. He added a Latin greeting. "Salve."

Ennius nodded. "Salve."

Yeshue was quiet for a time, watching the busy waves of the sea continue at their task. He spoke in Greek for Ennius's sake. "You have seen each other through difficult times. I can see your affection is sincere. Ennius, thank you for watching over my sister."

Ennius nodded again, his eyebrows drawn together in ambiguous thought. Hannah remembered the times he had spoken against Yeshue for not taking better care of Hannah.

Yeshue sighed and shook his head slightly, as if it pained him to say what he must say. Hannah steeled her jaw and narrowed her eyes. She knew what was coming.

"I have prayed for you and for your unique situation. I hope you will hear my words and consider them before you discount my advice."

"I will." Ennius met Yeshue's eyes, his voice sure. "I'd be a fool if I didn't. Obviously, you're someone to heed."

Yeshue nodded. He watched them thoughtfully. "You care for each other, but your families know nothing but what the other's nation stands for. Hannah, that means all of your people will look at Ennius and see only what Romans have done to Jews and blame him."

"With good reason," Ennius said. "I'm not without fault."

"Ennius, hear me," Yeshue said, reaching a hand to his arm. "Elohim's arm is not too short to save *anyone*. Trust him."

Ennius gave a short laugh of disbelief, but he didn't argue.

Yeshue continued in a careful tone. "Ennius, your people will not understand your love for Hannah, either."

"They'd get used to it," Ennius said. "But I see your point, and I've considered it."

"I know you think I've come here to tell you I forbid your marriage," Yeshue said to Hannah. "But I won't tell you what to do. I leave the decision to you, Ennius. The road together would be a hard one, since you have both only begun to understand your Creator. And you both have sin in your pasts that has consequences, even if forgiven. You may not be able to find a place to call home."

Ennius's expression didn't lighten. Hannah ignored his frown and felt a thrill of excitement. Yeshue had not forbidden them to marry!

"If you decide to marry, do it soon, to prevent further sin between the two of you." Hannah didn't hear any condescension in Yeshue's tone as he instructed Ennius. "If you decide to wait, please do not see or speak to Hannah until you are able to make her your wife."

Ennius agreed.

"May I pray with you?" Yeshue smiled and reached for Hannah's hand, squeezing it. "Elohim, we are grateful for your blessings, and for love that still blossoms in the harshness of this world. You know what is best and we seek your wisdom. Reveal to Ennius who you are and the plan you have for his life. Show him what you would have him do. Let Hannah understand what it means to follow you with her whole heart, not holding anything back for herself. Be glorified in the path your servants take, and surround them with your mercies. In the name of Adonai, Amen."

"Amen," Hannah said automatically and sought Ennius's eyes for confirmation of his decision that they marry.

She was shocked to find his face hard. Uncertain.

"Sh'lam," Yeshue said, kissing Hannah's hand before he let her go. He went back down the hill, his face turned toward the sea, his hair and his tunic blowing in the breeze that whipped up from the bay.

"What's wrong?" Hannah demanded when Yeshue was far enough away. "Why aren't you happy?"

He shrugged. "I don't think I can marry you."

Her joy dissolved into fury. "Why not?" she demanded.

He stood up. "Because I'm not ready to be the kind of husband I should be. I know next to nothing about your religion, however interested I am. I need to learn. Maybe ... go to Jerusalem and study? I have no idea where to begin. But I can't ask you to join me until I know where I'm going."

"No!" she clenched her fists at her sides and felt the familiar rage build inside her. "We'll go together. I'll help you. Yeshue will teach you. Don't do this. Don't leave me."

He wiped his palms on his tunic as if he was wiping away every last remembrance of her. "I'm sorry, Hannah. It wouldn't be right."

She stood in paralyzed shock, willing him to change his mind, teeming with unspoken pleas for him to stay. But no words were spoken. Her voice wouldn't work. He watched her for a few moments, the glow of the red sunset reflecting in his curly brown hair and golden skin, making him seem more like one of the gods his people worshiped in their temples than an actual flesh and blood man. He might as well be now, for he would not be hers.

He cleared his throat as if to clear away the emotions that threatened his resolve. "Don't wait for me, Hannah."

As soon as he had spoken the words, he stiffly turned and walked back to the fort with heavy steps that seemed to weight his feet to the ground. Hannah clenched her teeth together and breathed in and out of her nose, furious.

The sunset brought a chill, but she hardly noticed. She knew Talia would have to feed her son with goat's milk again, but she didn't care. She had lost Ennius, and nothing else mattered.

Suddenly, in the stillness of evening, arms went around her from behind and she felt a gentle kiss on the top of her head. At first, she thought it was Ennius returning, but his scent was different. Ennius smelled like the scented oils from the bathhouse. She smelled sunshine and the breeze that rode on the waves of the sea and knew it was Yeshue.

"I know it hurts."

She let him pull her back toward him and rub her arms with his hands, but she didn't speak for a long time.

"Will he come back?" she finally asked.

"Ennius is seeking. All who seek Elohim will find him. You should take joy in that truth."

She noticed he hadn't answered her question. "I want him to be my husband," she said, sullen.

"Elohim has chosen a different path for you. In some ways, Ennius spared you heartache."

"But I love him!" she said, her chest aching with the emotions she refused to let go.

Yeshue reached for her hand and squeezed. "I know you don't want to hear this, but it is the truth, dear one. You must love God more than you love Ennius. Nothing else in your life will make sense until you do."

"I risked my life to make my confession to you. I believe in you. I believe you are the M'sheekha," Hannah argued. "What else do you want from me? Will you not be satisfied until every last thing has been taken away from me? Is nothing ever enough for you?"

She broke away from his grasp. He didn't try to stop her as she ran down the hill toward town.

TWENTY-THREE

Y'hud

יהוד

The hot sunshine greeted Y'hud as he came out of the prayer house after school. For the past hour he had thought of Talia's fresh baked bread with honey and fish frying over the fire. He was ready for his stomach to be full.

In his earnest desire to get home, he didn't see the burly soldier in his path and walked right into him. He jumped back. He'd been struck by a soldier before and it had convinced him to stay out of their way.

But the sword stayed in the scabbard. Y'hud lifted his eyes and realized the soldier was Hannah's friend. The friend she wasn't supposed to have. The one everyone in the house gossiped and "tsked" about. Ya'achov said it was men such as that one that had caused the disciple Peter to start wearing a sword himself. Someone had to protect Yeshue, since he didn't seem intent on protecting himself.

Y'hud wanted to believe his brother was the prophesied M'sheekha, as his mother and sisters seemed to think, but he had to admit it was hard to imagine Yeshue leading anyone into battle when all he did was walk from town to town and preach about the Torah.

But Y'hud didn't think this soldier was cruel. He trusted him.

"Y'hud." The soldier leaned down and grasped his arms, bearing a serious expression. "Is Hannah home?"

"I think so," Y'hud said as he looked around the man's large form to see if he could see her inside their complex. Hannah hadn't left home much since the soldier had stopped coming around. "Did you have a fight? I haven't seen you lately."

"No," he said, glancing around them. "You must give Hannah a message for me."

Y'hud nodded.

"Tell her I have decided to go to Jerusalem. Lysander arranged for me to be transferred. I am going to find out what it means to follow your God. Tell her to marry a good Jewish man. Tell her not to wait for a Roman fool."

"A fool is someone who doesn't believe in Elohim." Y'hud eyed him critically. "I'd say you believe in him if you are going to Jerusalem to learn about him."

The soldier considered his words. "I'm not sure what I believe. I have to know more first."

"It's not that hard," Y'hud said with a shrug. "Yeshue has all the answers."

"For me to follow your God means everything changes in my life, boy. I am a Roman soldier. I can't question orders to kill Jews. I could be executed for refusing ..." The soldier – was his name Ennius? – stopped and shook his head. "Just give your sister the message."

"All right," Y'hud huffed, glad he would be released to eat his dinner. Ennius squeezed his shoulder before he headed back in the direction of the fort. Y'hud watched him go.

"Adults make everything complicated," he said under his breath.

Hannah took the news much like Y'hud expected she would. She stomped around the house and acted as if the soldier had done it on purpose to spite her. Y'hud was happy when his mother said he could go down to the shore and ask if the fishermen had heard any news of Yeshue.

There was news, said old Zebedee, the father of two of Yeshue's disciples. He was past the age of fishing, but he still went to the harbor each evening to supervise all the younger men at their work of mending nets.

"What news?" Y'hud prompted the man who lost his train of thought when he saw a boy mending a tear the wrong way. He called out instructions while Y'hud waited.

Zebedee settled back on the bench. "Where was I?"

"You were going to give me news of Yeshue," Y'hud reminded him.

"Ah, yes, such a fantastic story. Who could believe it?" Zebedee muttered gruffly.

Y'hud sighed and stared at the sea, hoping to see what Zebedee meant in the water, stained crimson by the sunset.

"They say they were all in a boat with Yeshue. All the *talmidim*, his disciples. In the fishing boat I gave to my sons Yohanan and Ya'achov, no less. They were going across to the Decapolis, though who knows why they would want to go there. Full of sin and demons. Heathens."

His voice trailed off into sounds Y'hud could not understand. He wondered if the older man was as confused as Uncle Amos, who usually referred to Y'hud as Yosef, his dead father, and regularly asked if he'd seen Tabitha, Amos's wife who had died in childbirth many years before Y'hud was born.

"Not today, Uncle Amos," he always said as everyone else in the family did, to avoid difficult conversations. Yeshue was the only one who took the time to gently explain the truth. Everyone teased him about it, which bothered Y'hud, but it bothered him more that Yeshue kept talking to Amos when he knew everyone would laugh at him.

Zebedee started speaking sense again. "A great squall came up in the middle of the lake ..." He sat up straight and held his arm toward the sea. Y'hud closed his eyes. He could almost see the waves crashing madly against the sides of the boat and ominous clouds hovering over them. There had been such a storm only two nights ago. Perhaps it was the one

Zebedee meant. Storms were common on the sea. They would spin out of nowhere and leave a fisherman grasping the sides of the boat, praying to Alaha to keep them from capsizing. Many a fisherman had drowned, pulled into the bottomless murky waters.

"The talmidim were scared out of their heads. They thought they would die. My boys included. And where was Yeshue in all of this?"

"Tell me!" Y'hud wanted to tug on the man's arm and make him say the words.

"Asleep! In the bow!" Zebedee guffawed loudly and slapped his knee. He wheezed with laughter until he had a coughing fit. Y'hud sighed and crossed his arms over his chest as he waited for the rest of the story.

"He got up when they called him. They said he didn't care they were going to die. So he got up on the bow of the ship and ..."

"And what?" Y'hud felt a tremor of excitement run down his spine.

"He spoke."

"He spoke what?"

"He spoke to the wind and the waves. *Be still*, he told them."

"Then what happened?" Y'hud was breathless.

"The storm stilled. Everything was peaceful. Quiet."

Zebedee looked straight at Y'hud with his milky white eyes and weathered skin. "Coincidence? Or miracle?"

Y'hud smirked. "Miracle," he said. "My brother has powers no one has ever had before."

Zebedee smiled. "Time shall tell, young one. Time shall tell." He made a groaning sound as he moved to stand. "Now be off with you. You've made me tired and I must go home and sleep."

Y'hud ran all the way back to his house, anxious to tell the story. He was sure he could tell it better than old Zebedee. But when he arrived home, children were being put to bed and nightly chores accomplished, so no one had time to hear it. He finally got Talia and his mother to listen, but they laughed and waved him off when he told them about the sea rising to swallow Yeshue and the disciples and drag them down to Sheol. He went out into the street looking for someone younger who might believe it.

To his disappointment, all the boys were concentrated on a ball and stick game and wouldn't be interrupted for a story. Frustrated, he scanned the street until his eyes rested on Judith, sitting on the bench again outside her home. He shrugged, figuring she would have to do. She looked like she could use a good story.

She smiled as he gave his version of the events. She even shivered in all the right places and gasped as Y'hud told of how Yeshue had battled the head demon and sent him right back to Sheol.

"Is this really true?" she asked him doubtfully. He noticed her voice was weak.

"Sure, it is." The verse about lying lips occurred to him, and he squirmed on the bench. "Well, most of it, anyway. I made a few things up."

She nodded. "It's a good story."

He watched her eyes close for a moment. Her skin was white and her hands trembled. He wasn't a doctor, and he hadn't been around sick people much, but it was obvious Judith was more ill than she had been in the spring when he had spoken to her last.

"You're not well, are you?" he asked slowly, afraid he would offend her but too curious not to ask. She didn't say anything, she only lifted her eyes to look at him.

Her eyes were pretty, he noticed. He'd been doing that lately— noticing things he'd never cared about before – and it occurred to him that Judith's eyes were a rich brown on the outside, but that she had flecks of green closer to the center. He liked that she didn't look like anyone else. But it seemed a shame for someone with such pretty eyes to have to die so young.

He was struck by a sense of loss. He didn't want her to die. He would miss her. Who else appreciated his stories? When Yeshue wasn't around, no one else even listened to him.

"If Yeshue were here, he could make you better," Y'hud said. He wondered if her parents would let Yeshue help her. Jairus was a rabbi, and rabbis and Pharisees didn't like Yeshue very much anymore. They were probably just jealous they didn't have powers like him.

Judith nodded wistfully, watching the fiery golden sunset. The red hues lit up her face and made her look rosier than she really was. He liked looking at her face.

"I'm going to die." Judith turned to him. "My father doesn't want to admit it, but we all know it. The doctor told Ama so. And I know it, anyway. I can feel it."

Y'hud frowned, kicking a stone across the path. "I wish you didn't have to," he mumbled. He stole a quick glance at her. He hoped she didn't take his words the wrong way and think he wanted to marry her or something. Girls could be like that.

"Yishar, Y'hud," she thanked him quietly, staring out toward the sea.

"Are you scared?" It suddenly occurred to him that he had never once in his twelve years considered the prospect of dying. Now that he was thinking about it, it must be frightening, going off into that other world no one had ever returned from.

She sighed. "A little. I know Alaha watches over me, but will it hurt very much? Will I see myself laying there dead and cold and not breathing? Where will I go when I'm not in my body anymore?"

Y'hud had no answer to her questions. Surely if her father, the prayer house rabbi, could not answer them, he couldn't.

"Yeshue would know the answers," he said, frustrated. He tried to think of what Yeshue would say. Suddenly a passage he had learned when he was very young came to his mind. He spoke the words softly.

"He took me; He drew me out of many waters. He delivered me from my enemy most strong, and from them that hated me, for they were too mighty for me. They confronted me in the day of my calamity; but Adonai was a stay unto me. He brought me forth into a large place; He delivered me, because He delighted in me."

Judith's eyes were shining with tears by the time he finished the passage. He hoped she wasn't mad. He looked away in embarrassment.

"Do you think Alaha really delights in me?" Judith whispered.

"Yeshue would say he does."

She stared thoughtfully into the sunset. "Thanks, Y'hud. I'm not as afraid now."

They sat there a few minutes longer, until the sun had disappeared into the sea and the night grew chilly. Judith went inside and Y'hud wandered home, wishing he could have thought of better things to say. Like Yeshue did.

He missed Yeshue. Now more than ever.

Y'hud came into the house the same time Shimon came in from a game. Ama was laughing as she scrubbed his face with a wet cloth.

"You smell worse than the goats!" she said.

Y'hud came up behind them.

"And I suppose you are as smelly as your brother," she said, coming toward him with the cloth.

He wiped the back of his hand across his eyes lest she see the moisture that had gathered there. He didn't understand his sadness, and he certainly didn't want to talk about it.

"What's wrong, Y'hud?" Ama asked in concern, feeling his forehead as if he might be sick.

He kicked at the dirt floor with his weathered sandal and shrugged. "Nothing."

She led him to the table and sat him down, handing him some bread and pouring a cup of watered wine. "Tell me."

He hesitated for a long moment, feeling ashamed to appear so weak before his mother. But he couldn't bear the burden alone anymore.

"Judith is sick."

She rested her chin in her palm. "The daughter of Jairus? She's been ill for a long time. Has she become worse?"

He nodded, feeling the burning in his eyes again. He sniffed hard. "She's just a girl, anyway."

Ama smiled in a sad way and reached to brush the hair out of his eyes.

"When will Yeshue come back, Ama?"

She sighed. "I hope soon. Maybe he would be able to help Judith, if Jairus allowed it."

"He must," Y'hud said, determined. He'd convince him if the man had any doubt. "If only Yeshue comes home in time."

"I have extra food from supper tonight. We even have pomegranates someone gave to Yeshue in thanks for a healing. He gave them to me. Do you think we should take them to Judith's family tonight?"

Y'hud nodded. "I'll help."

He was glad for his mother's suggestion as they gathered the items and put them in a basket. At least he was doing something.

Word came two days later that Yeshue and his disciples were on a boat headed back to Capernaum. They would be arriving within the next day or two.

Y'hud thought of all the things he wanted to say to his brother and the things they could do together. Maybe they could go to the harbor and toss stones as they had when they had first moved to Capernaum. He and Shimon had begged Ama to let them run out and meet the caravan, but his older brother Ya'achov stepped in and said he needed them to help load the wagon.

They did the work as quickly as they could and then raced to the harbor.

"What's going on? Is Herod passing through?" Shimon stopped short, awed by the immense crowd that had gathered on the shore. There must have been a thousand people.

"They're trying to get close to Yeshue," Y'hud said, amazed.

"Our brother?" Shimon wrinkled his nose, as if he couldn't fathom why such a crowd would be waiting to greet Yeshue.

They pushed their way through the crowd, determined to get to the front of it despite the slaps to the head and the grunts of disapproval they received in return.

When they pushed through to the very edge of the shore and the water lapped their sandals, they could see the boat. Y'hud watched his brother stand at the bow with a smile and a wave.

"He's waving to *us*," Shimon decided, and Y'hud agreed with a smug feeling in his chest. The crowd must have thought he was waving to them, for they cheered in response.

It seemed to take forever for them to row to the shore. Y'hud and Shimon waded out into the water with other children and helped pull the boat in. Yeshue stepped into the shallow water and held out his arms to Y'hud and Shimon.

"Abba!" A lump rose in Y'hud's throat as he saw his brother's face for the first time in weeks. Yeshue seemed to understand his thoughts and hugged him tightly. He tussled Shimon's hair.

"My little men have come to greet me! Elohim has blessed my heart to see your faces again."

Y'hud clung to him for a long moment until he remembered all the men were watching him. He reluctantly let go.

He stood back. "Everyone's waiting for you at home."

Yeshue looked to Capernaum with a particular yearning in his eyes. He grasped Shimon's hand and put his hand on Y'hud's shoulder and they walked through the crowd. He tried to ask them how they had been and what they had been learning in the prayer house with Rabbi Jairus, but the noise of the crowd around them forced him to repeat his question several times. The people pressed against them on every side, even though the disciples were doing their best to keep them back so they would not be crushed.

"Yeshue, say a prayer for my land so it will produce more crops!" A man yelled insistently.

"Make my children provide for my needs!" an elderly woman cried.

"Back up!" Peter shouted in a harsh tone. "Would you injure the Master? I said *back up!*"

"Y'hud, what have you been thinking about since I was gone?" Yeshue asked patiently next to his ear. Y'hud almost laughed out loud. His older brother didn't seem to notice the chaos around them. He must be used to it by now.

Y'hud remembered then what he needed to tell Yeshue. "Judith, the daughter of Jairus, is very ill. You have to heal her."

Yeshue's eyes softened. He didn't answer.

"I don't want her to die," Y'hud said, pulling on Yeshue's hand.

Yeshue nodded. "Elohim loves Judith, my son. He will take care of her."

Y'hud didn't like his answer. He stopped and pulled on Yeshue's arm. "Will you heal her or not?"

"I will heal her if Jairus asks."

Y'hud fought the lump in his throat. He didn't want anyone, including Yeshue, to see him crying over a girl. "What if he doesn't ask?"

"Have faith, child," Yeshue said, resuming their walk and tugging Y'hud gently along behind him. "Trust me."

For the first time in Y'hud's life, he didn't know if he could.

TWENTY-FOUR

Talia

טליה

"Talia, Hannah, come quickly! Yeshue is home!" Talia heard her mother call from the window. They rushed from the courtyard.

"Nathanael!" Talia saw the dear features of her husband and her brother, but her heart sank at the sight of the crowd. Surely she would not see either of them for a long time. Maryam and Hannah pushed into the crowd to greet him, but Talia dejectedly turned back to the children playing in the courtyard.

An hour later, she bounced fussy Yosef in her arms and willed Hannah to return so he could nurse. She called to Amaris and Y'aqim to get off the ladder leading to the roof. As she did, she felt a kiss on the top of her head.

She whirled around and gave a cry of delight at the sight of her husband.

"Talia," he said, crushing both her and the baby against him, kissing her cheeks, her forehead and her mouth over and over. She laughed and pushed away long enough to set unhappy Yosef on the ground so she could jump into his arms.

"My love, how I've missed you," he whispered, his hands squeezing her sides while Yosef screamed his protest from the dirt floor.

"Where is Nava?" Nathanael asked, glancing quickly around the room.

"In her house." Talia smiled, realizing his thoughts. In one movement, he gathered up all three children and took them across the courtyard to Ya'achov's door. He deposited them inside despite Nava's protests. He returned to Talia and pulled her into the house, behind the curtain and into his arms, all in one breath.

"The people used to hang on his every word," Nathanael said as they walked to the harbor together later that evening.

"Judging by the crowd today, they still do," Talia said.

She felt a prickle of foreboding as she watched his reaction. He stared at the sea, his features pensive. He was troubled. Talia could only think of her old fears and the prophecies.

"They do, but it isn't a comfortable affection," he answered slowly. "I remember when we first started out, two years ago, it was different. The people were different. They were delighted with him, but now they seem to think they own him. Do you know what I mean? They want things from him ... desperately. They want him to change their circumstances so badly that they would do anything—even force him— to make it so."

Talia shook her head, as if the act might keep his words from being true. "May it never be," she whispered.

"Talia." Nathanael turned to her and held her arms. "I want you to be prepared if something should happen. I believe you should know that we are on a dangerous mission. But I still believe it is right. He is right. We live in such a world that takes righteousness and chews it up; spits it out. You should know the possibilities."

Talia pulled away from his arms, shaking her head. "You must protect him, Nathanael. Promise me."

He swallowed hard, as if he realized his words had upset her and worked to reign them in. He attempted a wobbly smile. "I'll do my best, love."

She allowed him to come forward and take her in his arms again, but the storms of her heart were not stilled. They raged on.

Ya'achov

יעקב

Ya'achov snarled at the crowd causing a commotion in the harbor. So much for being able to sell anything else in the market that day. Yeshue appeared, with the whole world following alongside, coming down the road into Capernaum. As if he wasn't a poor carpenter's son. As if he was a king.

Ya'achov turned back to the boat he was mending for Zebedee. Had the nail a voice, it might cry for mercy with his forceful banging.

"Ya'achov!" Jairus called behind him. The rabbi came down the hill, running at top speed. Something must have happened. Ya'achov straightened and jogged to meet him.

"Help me get to Yeshue!" Jairus's voice was panicked and his eyes were wide and full of tears. "She'll die if Yeshue doesn't come now!"

Ya'achov clenched his jaw. He only had to imagine his precious Amaris as sick as Judith to feel pity for the other father. Could he turn his own daughter over to the grave without a fight? He shuddered at the thought, but he knew better than to offer Jairus false hopes.

"I'm sorry, Jairus. Truly. I can imagine how you must feel, but don't make it worse. Go home and say goodbye."

"No!" Jairus stared wide-eyed at Ya'achov as if he were the devil himself. "What kind of father would I be? Yeshue is her only hope!"

Ya'achov watched Jairus turn and plunge into the crowd by the harbor. He struggled through the sea of people toward Yeshue. Finally, he broke through the center of the crowd and pulled desperately on Peter's arm.

"Please, let me talk to him!" Jairus cried. Ya'achov dropped his hammer and moved closer to hear the conversation as the crowd pressed in around them.

A collective gasp spread over the gathering as Jairus fell at Yeshue's feet and clutched the hem of his robe. "Please, Yeshue! My little daughter is dying! Please come and put your hands on her so she will live."

Ya'achov watched Yeshue's expression change, empathy straining his features. He tenderly put his hand on Jairus's head as the crowd murmured sympathies.

"Take me to her."

Jairus leaped up and turned toward his house. The crowd parted for them and they quickly made their way up the hill.

Ya'achov followed along behind the crowd, curious, though he wouldn't have admitted it. He had come to know Jairus during the time he was seeking to have his sister stoned, when he urged Jairus to overrule Yeshue's decision to forgive her. Jairus had expressed doubt that Yeshue had any true power to forgive sin, but he had not wanted to challenge him. Yeshue was the head of his household and capable of making such a decision.

What made this respected leader come to Yeshue and fall on his knees? He was a man known for his level head and vast knowledge of Scripture. To bow before a rebellious, possibly crazed rabbi and beg for healing? Even, Alaha forbid, if Amaris lay dying, he would not suddenly believe that Yeshue had any real power to save her. It was foolishness. The crowds had been deluded with beautiful lies. There had to be some sort of trickery involved. They had real laws to uphold, even if it meant losing your own flesh and blood.

What laws has Yeshue broken?

The voice of doubt within him whispered. He willed it away and concentrated on his anger toward Yeshue. His righteous anger. Surely, Alaha shared his feelings. The law had been broken. He was sure of it. All the Pharisees and leaders said so. He wouldn't be fooled like the simpleton crowds that followed Yeshue.

Ya'achov nearly stumbled over a woman crouched in the street as he moved with the crowd. He let out a sound of disgust. The woman had been sick for years and everyone knew she was impure. What was she thinking—joining a crowd like this?

She tried to stand and follow after Yeshue. Ya'achov saw her lean forward and grasp the end of his brother's robe.

Jairus turned, desperation in his eyes as Yeshue stopped and looked back at the crowd. "Master, please hurry. She's so sick."

Yeshue didn't seem to hear Jairus as he scanned the crowd with a furrowed brow. "Who touched me?"

No one knew what to say. What in the world was he talking about? Finally, Peter, receiving a pleading glance from Jairus, stepped forward and touched Yeshue's arm. "How can you ask who touched you, Rabbi? The crowd is thick. We all touched you."

Yeshue emphatically shook his head. "No, someone touched my robe. I felt power leave me."

Ya'achov twisted his mouth, annoyed. Trust his brother to not only let a little girl die because he was distracted, but to remind everyone of his *great power* at the same time.

The woman trembled as she came forward. "I touched you, Master," she said in a timid voice. Yeshue leaned down and took her hands, which seemed to give her confidence to continue. "I've been ill for twelve years, and all I did was touch your cloak, and I am healed. I can feel the life restored within me."

Ya'achov doubted it. And he couldn't believe Yeshue wouldn't chastise her for touching his clothes. It was far too bold. How would anyone respect him if he allowed everyone to come so close?

"Daughter, your faith has healed you. Go in peace."

Ya'achov sighed. She'd probably not even get back home before she realized it was just her imagination.

Although, she had been pale when she had first arrived on the scene. Deathly pale. And now her complexion was healthy. She looked twenty years younger, in fact. He shrugged away his doubts. He didn't want to think about Yeshue anymore.

A servant approach from Jairus's house.

"No," Ya'achov said under his breath.

The man seemed to have trouble speaking as he reached toward

Jairus. "Don't bother the teacher anymore. Your daughter is dead."

Jairus held his hands to his head and stepped back in shock. "No. No, no … please …"

Yeshue reached for Jairus's arm. "Don't be afraid. Just believe, and she'll be healed."

The crowd started murmuring as Jairus turned to stare straight into the gaze of Yeshue. They stood there for a long moment, looking at each other.

"My daughter has just died," Jairus said quietly. "But come and lay your hand on her, and she will live."

Ya'achov shook his head and sighed. His brother was an attention-seeking fool, using Jairus's grief for his own gain. No one, even the great so-called M'sheekha, could raise the dead.

The crowd was not as dubious as Ya'achov. They pressed forward, clamoring to see what would happen next. Yeshue motioned for his disciples to hold back the crowd as he moved forward with Jairus and three of his disciples.

Ya'achov had seen enough. He waved off the entire scene and returned to his boat, ashamed of his kinship to Yeshue. He felt powerless and frustrated. What had he ever done to have to be the brother of the crazy rabbi?

Everything would have been different if Yeshue had never been born. Ya'achov's life would have made sense. He would have been the great leader. He would have been the head of the household. Nothing would ever be right with Yeshue in charge.

Y'hud

יהוד

Y'hud watched with baited breath as Yeshue entered the rabbi's house. They could hear the tell-tale sound of the mourners wailing inside. Y'hud swallowed back his tears as he pictured Judith, white and cold and dead inside on her pallet.

He sat on the roof of his house which looked out over the street and the scene that had unfolded. He sniffed and wiped away a tear that escaped before he resolved to get up and see what Yeshue would do. He was probably just comforting the family. What else could be done if her spirit had already left her body?

He ran along the edge of the street until he came to the house. Yeshue was standing in the courtyard, frowning at the women who wailed and prostrated themselves on the ground and the men behind them who played funeral dirges with flutes. Y'hud had never liked the paid mourners. Their grief was false, based only on their desire to receive a reward. How did that help anyone, especially the one who had died?

Yeshue apparently felt the same way. "Go away," he said to them.

The women stopped crying and stared at him indignantly.

"Who do you think you are?" one of them said to him.

"She's not dead. She's sleeping. Now go away!"

They started to laugh, forgetting they were there for the opposite purpose.

"He thinks we don't know death when we see it," the woman said, mocking him. "Fool. You'll see how dead she is."

Yeshue ignored her and went to the door of the house where Jairus stood, shoulders sagging, a dejected look on his face. Yeshue touched his shoulder and disappeared into the dark room.

Y'hud sidled up through the courtyard. No one questioned him. Everyone was distracted by the tragic events of the afternoon. He stepped up to the house and peered inside the room.

Yeshue wasted no time. He stepped forward and gently kneeled beside Judith's body, taking the small, white hand in his own. "Little girl," he said with a tender smile, as if she was still in the room, listening to him. "Get up."

Y'hud couldn't breathe. He watched her still form, and for one agonizing second, he was sure nothing had happened.

Then, as he watched, her cheeks turned pink and her eyes fluttered open. She stared at Yeshue in surprise.

Yeshue helped her to stand up. "Give this girl something to eat! She's hungry. Aren't you?"

Judith looked around the room and found her parents standing to the side. They looked so shocked they couldn't move. Her mother covered her mouth with her hands. Then Judith looked back at Yeshue and giggled, as if the two of them shared some secret no one else could know. "I *am* hungry."

Her parents came to her then, enveloping her in jubilant embraces. Yeshue stepped back and motioned his disciples, who also stood with mouths agape, to follow him. He spied Y'hud in the doorway and winked at him.

"Sh'lam lak, Y'hud," he said as he passed him.

Y'hud walked beside him. "Abba, is she going to be sick anymore?"

He felt embarrassed for being so concerned, but Yeshue didn't seem troubled by his worry over a girl. "She is well, Y'hud. She will have some supper and a long life ahead of her."

Y'hud's entire body seemed to relax when he heard Yeshue's words. Even as the relief washed over him, he felt a shiver of fear as he stared at Yeshue. What kind of man raised the dead? He'd never heard of such a thing. It was unimaginable.

Yeshue gave him a final smile before he turned the corner of the courtyard and disappeared into the crowd waiting in the street.

Y'hud stared after him. Despite his misgivings, pride swelled in his chest.

"My brother is a king," he said to himself.

TWENTY-FIVE

Talia

טליה

Talia glanced at Yeshue as he moved about the room, helping her bring the sauce bowls and bread to the courtyard table. He didn't seem to notice the other men glancing awkwardly at him as they waited while he served. She hid her smile. Yeshue had never been opposed to helping with women's work when he could.

As he returned to the house for the wine, Talia held out the jug to him, but it was her face he reached for instead. She closed her eyes, reveling in the peace his touch brought. These hands that had healed sick, touched the untouchable – even raised the dead – these hands were her comfort.

He studied her face. "Your heart is troubled."

Her eyes stung. "May I trust in Alaha."

"You can't will away fear, Talia. Your anxious, churning thoughts must be forsaken."

She frowned and turned away from him. "It's not that simple. I have tried to think right. To pray more. But I can't. I'm not doing it on purpose."

He nodded. "The spirit is willing, but the flesh is weak. One day, you will have the power to overcome it, sister."

He took the jug and returned to the table.

"Talia, please take Amaris and Y'aqim out to play. They are under my feet and dinner will never be served this way."

Talia did her mother's bidding. She led the little ones outside into the street and tried to catch their interest with wooden blocks Y'hud had made with leftover scraps. She sat on the bench and watched them build towers and giggle with delight when they fell. She tried to remember the last time she'd laughed about anything. Life seemed so hard all the time.

"I'm sorry, Talia," Maryam said behind her, appearing in the doorway. "You were talking to Yeshue, and I interrupted."

Talia started to answer her mother, but suddenly a woman came to them.

"You are the family of the great teacher?" she asked eagerly.

Talia smiled politely. "We are."

"You are his sister? And his mother?"

Talia nodded.

"It's the mother of the healer!" the woman stepped back and cried loudly. People turned as the woman fell to the ground in front of Maryam, prostrating herself. Others followed suit.

Maryam dropped the bowl in her hands, and her face paled in horror. "Get up! What are you doing? Get up!"

"You are the mother of the M'sheekha," the woman spoke, not daring to raise her head. "You are to be praised above all women! Holy is your womb!"

Talia got up and ushered the children and her mother inside. Maryam was shaking her head, agitated. "Why would they do such a thing, Talia?"

"Don't think about it, Ama," Talia said, though she doubted her mother would be able to stop, since the people had gathered outside the window and door and were looking inside and murmuring to one another. Talia felt the same unease her mother did. It had never troubled her to see people bow before Yeshue. He was the M'sheekha. But Maryam and Talia were sinners as anyone else. It would be blasphemy to accept the worship of people.

"It's idolatry, Talia." Maryam held her hands to her face. "Alaha, forgive me if I ever did or said anything to encourage it."

Talia didn't know what to say. Her mother was right, and she knew Yeshue would not approve of the people's reaction. She didn't answer.

"Talia, I could not bear to steal glory that only belonged to Adonai."

"You haven't, Ama."

"They didn't listen. Still they wait outside for me."

"It is their sin. Not yours." Talia hugged her mother, even as the old panic rose up in her chest like bile.

Maryam leaned back. "You are a good girl. And yet you are pale. Do you feel sick?"

"I'm just tired," Talia lied. "I'll be fine."

Maryam brushed stray strands of Talia's long brown hair and tucked them back inside her headscarf. "Take a walk. Y'hud and Shimon can play with the children."

Talia didn't argue. She needed time alone. She needed to calm the raging within her, lest she choke on it.

She wished she could talk to Yeshue. Or at least Nathanael. They were both so busy – too busy to take time for her silly fears. She walked to the field on the hill outside town and covered her face with her hands.

She stayed too long. She fell asleep in the grass and didn't wake up until night was beginning to fall. She got up and dusted off her dirty tunic. Why hadn't Mother sent one of the boys to get her?

She hurried back down the hill until the soft sound of a voice caught her attention. She stood still and listened. A man was speaking in low tones nearby. She followed the dim path in the direction of the voice.

When she came closer, she realized the voice belonged to Yeshue. He must be praying. She turned to leave, but the melancholy ache she heard in his tone stopped her.

"Eloi, oh Eloi! Why have you forsaken me?"

She recognized the words from the psalm, written by David so many hundreds of years before. But the broken sound of Yeshue's voice didn't make sense to her. Alaha would never leave Yeshue.

"Why are you so far from saving me, so far from the words of my groaning? O, my Eloi, you are enthroned as the Holy One. You are the praise of Israel. In you our fathers put their trust—they trusted you and you delivered them. They cried to you and you saved them. In you they trusted and were not disappointed."

Talia leaned back against a tree and closed her eyes as she pictured King David in his throne room, on his knees as he called out to Adonai. What had inspired the words? And what inspired Yeshue to repeat them this night?

"I am a worm and not a man. Scorned by men and despised by the people. All mock me. They hurl insults and shake their heads at me. 'He trusts Adonai, let Adonai save him.'"

Talia sighed softly. Her clenched hands opened and her breathing slowed at the musical sounds of her brother's whispers.

"You brought me from the womb. You made me trust you even at my mother's breast. From birth I was cast upon you, you have been my Elohim. Do not be far from me. Trouble is near, and there is no one to help."

Didn't King David have armies of men to help him? Servants, wives, children? Had the king spoken the strange words for someone else?

"I am poured out like water. All my bones are out of joint. My heart has turned to wax and melted away within me. My strength is all dried up, like a potsherd. My tongue sticks to the roof of my mouth. You lay me in the dust of death ... evil men circle around me. They pierce my hands and feet."

David must have written the psalm for someone else. But for whom was it intended? She knew some psalms carried prophecies of the M'sheekha within them. Was this one of them?

Eyes closed, a sudden picture of hands and feet appeared in her vision. A memory she'd tried to erase. She was just a little girl. She'd been happy, excited to see the city, singing joyful songs with her sister as they danced along the path that led into Jerusalem.

From above her, she had heard a groan of agony and looked up to see the naked, bloody body of the young man. The image of his grotesque wounds were seared into her memory forever.

"Save me," the man had called in anguish, his breath strangled as he painfully lifted himself up at the feet to gasp the words. "For the mercy of Alaha—I did nothing but stand up for you. I tried to make ... a difference. Help!"

But no one had helped him. They had passed, heads down, as if they could not see him suspended on the wooden boards, broken, bleeding, dying.

Only Yeshue had looked at him.

They have pierced my hands and feet.

Talia shook her head, pressure building in her throat as Yeshue continued to softly pray the words of the psalm.

"*I can count all my bones. People stare and gloat. They divide my garments and cast lots for them. Be not far off, Adonai! Oh, my Strength, come quickly to help me. Deliver my life. I will declare your name to my brothers. I will praise you before them all. You who fear Adonai, praise him! For he has not despised the suffering of the afflicted one.*"

Talia could not listen to Yeshue quote the text any longer. She turned for home, the old fears following close at her heels. She heard Nathanael calling for her in the distance and ran to meet him.

Who could be safe if not even the M'sheekha was?

Hannah

חנה

Hannah half-heartedly uprooted prickly weeds from Ama's garden. Her mind wandered as she worked, returning to her favorite place. She imagined herself out in the field by the hill, in Ennius's arms. She could almost smell his familiar scent of bay laurel and pine and feel his curls and his oiled muscles beneath her fingertips. She closed her eyes and remembered how it had felt when he kissed her lips.

"Hannah?" Talia's voice interrupted her daydream. She sighed and returned to the present moment, complete with dirt and weeds.

"What are you thinking about?" her sister asked as she reached in to gather herbs for the lentil soup.

Hannah didn't answer. Ennius had made Talia uneasy, and she had no desire to argue with her older sister.

But Talia guessed. "The soldier?"

Hannah shrugged. "I know you don't approve. But I still love him. He's a good man."

Talia wore a doubtful expression, which made Hannah seethe within herself. What did she know? She was as narrow-minded as all the rest of their people.

"I'm sorry, Hannah. It's just hard for me to see any Roman soldiers as good. We've both witnessed what they are capable of."

Hannah scoffed. "You don't know anything."

Talia sighed and thoughtfully watched her. "Your soldier *was* different. And Yeshue did heal him."

Hannah was caught off guard by Talia's words, but she refused to show it. "He's not the average soldier," she said in a defensive tone. "Believe me, I've had plenty others to compare."

Hannah felt remorse at her sister's obvious embarrassment. "That's not what I meant, Talia."

But it was. She had allowed soldiers to come to her night after night and take what did not belong to them for the price of a few Roman coins.

"I'm not that girl anymore," she said. "I did those things because I had to feed my son."

Talia was quiet as she laid out the herbs on a towel. "He would have been cared for here."

Hannah's anger ignited. "What would you know about it? You've never been alone. You've never had a child. You're so afraid you can't even leave the house. You have no idea what it takes to survive on your own."

Talia wrapped the herbs and stood up. "I would never give myself to a Roman soldier, no matter how different he was." Talia turned toward the house before Hannah could fly at her.

Hannah yelled in frustration. "I did not give myself to Ennius!"

Talia didn't look back as she walked away, which made Hannah angrier.

"You have your sins as well, Talia! You have no right to judge!"

Talia turned at the doorway, her tone cool when she spoke. "Yeshue has forgiven your sins. Who am I to bring them up? I am only worried that you will return to them."

Hannah knocked over the bowl of produce on the ground beside her. "Why do you always assume the worst of me?"

Talia regarded her for a long moment. "Don't be angry, Hannah. I don't mean to make you feel bad."

Hannah locked eyes with Talia. She spoke slowly, her frustration evident in every syllable. "Imagine how you would feel if Nathanael were in Jerusalem and you were here and you weren't married or even pledged. Imagine if you didn't know if you'd ever see him again, and even if you did, would your people ever accept him?"

Talia's face changed. Softened. "That would be difficult," she admitted, stepping closer.

Hannah sighed again and flopped to the ground. The sun had risen to the highest point in the sky. "No one understands."

"Yeshue does," Talia said.

"He's a man," Hannah said doubtfully.

"He is the Son of Alaha," Talia reminded her.

Hannah frowned. "That doesn't help me, Talia."

She felt guilty for being harsh with her sister. It wasn't Talia's fault that Ennius was lost to her. But the frustration of being separated was wearing on her. She knew in her heart she belonged with him. She had no doubt. And it was only her people and her religion, of which Yeshue stood for, that kept them apart.

"I think you should follow Yeshue," Talia said quietly. Hannah wondered if it had cost her sister something to say it. "I will take care of your children."

Hannah didn't know what to say. She considered the offer. And as she did, she jumped up in excitement. "If I travel with Yeshue, we might go to Jerusalem, and I might find Ennius!"

She felt a rush of delight as Talia went into the house. Hannah immediately went to find Yeshue to ask if she might join the caravan the next time he left Capernaum.

She almost didn't hear Talia's quiet response as she passed her.

"I wish I had your courage, little sister."

Y'hud

יהוד

Rabbi Jairus had only proceeded halfway through the Torah memorization lesson before a stir spread through Capernaum. People were moving through the streets, leaving their market tables to walk toward the hill outside the town.

"Something's happening, rabbi," Y'hud pointed out the window. Jairus looked up on the hill and a smile pulled at the sides of his mouth.

"It's Yeshue. He's walking out to the wilderness where there's enough room for everyone. I think he's going to speak." Jairus looked back at the children. "What do you all say we stop lessons early and go listen to him?"

The children didn't need to be told twice.

The day passed quickly as Y'hud sat with the other school boys and watched Yeshue. He healed lame and made blind people see again. Y'hud laughed in delight while a man who had been crippled danced around, praising God.

The day became evening and the crowd of people still waiting to see Yeshue was so large that everyone decided to spend the night. They camped in small circles. Early the next morning Yeshue was up and meeting with people one by one, patiently instructing and healing everyone who came to him.

Y'hud lost interest near the end of the second day and went home for the night, filling in the women on what was happening. The next afternoon he went back with Talia to see if they were still there.

They were. And the crowds that waited were beginning to look haggard. Y'hud wondered if anyone had brought any food. They probably hadn't been planning to stay three days.

They pushed through the crowd and sat among the disciples. They watched Yeshue work until he suddenly turned to them with a torn expression.

"I feel sorry for these people," he said, motioning his disciples over. They got up and stood around him. "They've already been with me for three days and no one has any food. I don't want to send them away hungry. They might collapse on their journey. Some of them have come from quite a distance."

Peter shook his head. "I don't know where we'd find enough bread for such a crowd. This is a remote place.

"How many loaves do we have?" Yeshue asked.

Talia held up the basket of bread and fish she and Y'hud had brought.

"Seven," Nathanael answered. "And a few small fish."

Yeshue stood up and spoke in a loud voice. "Everyone sit down." He made motions with his hands for those who couldn't hear him. Eventually, the word spread across the valley and everyone did as he said.

Yeshue reached for the basket and held it up, saying a prayer of thanks to Alaha. Then he reached inside and began to tear the bread into pieces, placing some in seven other baskets they had collected.

"Yeshue has done this before," Nathanael told Y'hud and Talia. "Watch what happens."

Y'hud waited as the other disciples exchanged knowing glances. When Yeshue was finished, he passed the baskets to the disciples standing nearest. They looked inside and laughed.

Y'hud ran to Peter and jumped up to see inside. "It's full!" he cried.

Hours later, after the food had been distributed and everyone had eaten, Y'hud looked in the baskets and saw how much was left.

"Take them home," Yeshue said to Talia and Y'hud. "Give them to anyone in need, and then give the rest to Ama."

Y'hud frowned as he set the basket down. "You're leaving?"

Yeshue nodded, reaching for Y'hud's shoulder. "We are crossing over to Magadan. We'll be back in a few days."

Y'hud suddenly had a bitter taste in his mouth, no matter that the bread had been the best he'd ever tasted. "I thought we could go fishing."

He was determined to be a man about it, but it was hard to hold back the childish tears. Yeshue was *his* brother. His *abba*. Why did everyone else think Yeshue belonged to them?

One of the disciples scoffed at him, overhearing his words. "The boy thinks Yeshue has time for fishing."

Y'hud scowled when they all chuckled. He supposed Yeshue would laugh at him, too. But when he looked up, Yeshue wasn't even smiling.

Yeshue looked Y'hud in the eye. "I would love to spend that time with you, Y'hud. And I would if there weren't so many others that need my help. Do you think I should choose fishing over healing the sick and telling them how to know Adonai?"

Y'hud kicked at the dust. "You should help them."

"You take care of the women and children while I am gone." Yeshue squeezed his shoulder.

Then he was gone. Y'hud watched until they were out of sight.

TWENTY-SIX

Hannah

חנה

"Your babies aren't going to remember you by the time you return, foolish girl," Nava said to Hannah, condescension in her tone.

Hannah packed food in a cloth. She pulled her cloak over her tunic and tied the cloth in the sash around her waist. She flipped back her long hair and covered it with her headscarf. "You're just jealous," she said.

Nava laughed harshly. "Jealous of you?"

"You're jealous that I don't have a husband to order me around."

"You're a wicked little devil, and no one doubts it," Nava said quietly, so only Hannah would hear.

Hannah smirked. She leaned over to kiss her sons on the head.

"You better hope I have enough milk to feed your horrid Roman baby," Nava continued.

"Nava!" Talia protested as she came within earshot.

"Stay out of it," Nava said to her. "You don't know yet what it's like to have children."

Hannah saw the wounded expression on her sister's face. Nava could be a menace when she was angry. But Talia took everything too seriously.

"Be nice, Nava." She kissed Talia's cheek. "Don't worry about her. You'll have children soon. You're a better mother than Nava already."

Talia didn't seem comforted, but she said nothing. Hannah shrugged and gave Nava another scathing glance before she left the house.

Yeshue had been hesitant to let Hannah come along with them. He had been concerned about her sons' care, but Hannah had assured him they would be well cared for and that it had been Talia's idea. "I want to go with you, Yeshue. I want to learn."

It wasn't completely the truth. She knew she should take more interest in his teachings, but truly, she wanted to go to Jerusalem to find Ennius, and Yeshue had said he was going to be spending more time in Judea for the next few months.

"Hannah, if you are going to accompany me, you must be honest with me." Yeshue had given her a firm expression.

She had shrugged. "I am."

He had watched her for a long moment before he finally agreed. "Then you will come. But I do not think this trip will be what you are hoping."

She had laughed and jumped into his arms, embracing him. He had hugged her back, but said nothing else.

The first few miles of the trip to Bethsaida were exciting. Hannah walked alongside the other women as they followed Yeshue and the disciples. Sometimes Yeshue would begin to sing or pray, and they would all join in.

She liked most of the women. Maryam of Magdala was her favorite. Even though Maryam was a few years older, she had been rescued and forgiven just as Hannah had, so they shared a bond none of the other women understood. They walked arm-in-arm and shared many secrets.

The first night as they lay on their pallets in front of the fire, Maryam watched the other side of the camp where Yeshue rested with his men.

"Are you thinking about my brother?" Hannah followed Maryam's gaze and smiled knowingly.

"He is a good man," Maryam said. Her tone was casual, but Hannah thought she heard something more behind her words.

"He is," Hannah said with a chuckle.

"He is very good looking," Maryam admitted softly.

Hannah made a sound of disgust. "He is as plain as the grass in the field."

Maryam gave a laugh. "He is not!"

"He looks okay, I guess, but Alaha didn't give him the beauty of King David, to be sure," Hannah teased.

Maryam pouted. "You have to say that. He's your brother."

Hannah shrugged. "Maybe. But you shouldn't waste your time pining over Yeshue. He's not interested in a wife."

"I know," Maryam said with a sigh. "I accepted that months ago. I wouldn't be worthy of him anyway. But I still like to look at him sometimes."

Hannah glanced at Yeshue, who was snoring lightly with his mouth open. She giggled, as did Maryam.

The second evening when Hannah was almost asleep, she felt a light touch on her arm. She gasped and sat up quickly. Judas, one of the disciples, was standing over her, holding his finger over his lips to silence her reaction.

"Come with me," he mouthed and tiptoed out of the camp.

Her heart beat faster, and she almost ignored him and went back to sleep, but curiosity got the best of her and she followed him to the seashore, which was brilliantly lit by the full moon overhead.

He turned as she approached, smiling.

"What do you want?" She crossed her arms over her chest. She wasn't afraid of him, but she wasn't about to let him try anything. He was a man, after all.

She shivered in the cool night air, so Judas took off his cloak and handed it to her. "Nothing. I thought you might appreciate the view."

Hannah raised a skeptical eyebrow.

"I've been watching you share secrets with Maryam and wishing I was the one talking to you."

"How nice of you," she said. "But I really should return to the women's camp."

He gave her a rueful smile. "Stay. There's no harm in a young man and woman talking in the moonlight. I want to know about you."

She took a step back, but she did not return to camp. Surely if Judas was a chosen follower of Yeshue, he was safe. Besides, it felt good to have a man pay attention to her again. He made her remember how good it felt to be pursued.

She shrugged. "What is there to tell? I am Hannah. Sister of Yeshue, daughter of Yosef."

"You are young," he said.

"I'm sixteen."

"I am twenty," he said.

"An old man," she said, mocking him.

He smiled. "Where is your husband? I noticed you have two young sons."

Hannah shivered again, aware of his nearness. "I was married very young. My husband died of a fever."

"I'm sorry."

She shook her head. "Don't be sorry. I was relieved when he died."

Judas nodded and leaned closer. Hannah pushed him back and searched for words to continue the conversation.

"And who are you, besides a follower of my brother?"

"I am Y'hud, son of Shimon Scariota."

"Scariota? You mean the Sicarii? Is your father a Zealot?"

Judas shrugged. "He called himself one."

Hannah watched his eyes turn darkly toward the sea. "Is he dead?"

"Killed by the Romans in his first battle. Took a sword through his back." His tone was more ragged.

She heard the slight change in his voice and inched back. She looked back at the camp, wondering if she should return. He turned toward her and his eyes flashed.

"I won't be like him. I won't give up my life to a filthy Roman. I'll spill his blood first. I won't ask questions."

She didn't answer. She looked up at the moon.

"I'm sorry. I don't like to speak of my father."

"I should go," she said quietly.

"Hannah, please, don't go. My anger is with the Romans, not you. I'm sorry I spoke that way."

"It's all right," she said with a shrug. She threw his cloak back to him and went back to her pallet next to Maryam. Judas didn't follow her. She lay awake for a long time. It was only when she looked over and saw the form of her brother sleeping among his disciples that she was able to close her eyes and find rest.

She talked to Maryam about the encounter the next morning as they served breakfast.

"Judas asked me to come to the shore with him last night," Hannah whispered to her friend as they fried fish over the fire.

"Which one? Not the son of the Sicarius, I hope."

"Yes. Why?"

"I don't know. Maybe it's my imagination, but there's something about him. I've had an invitation or two away from camp as well. I think there's more to him than he's saying. Be careful."

"I have no interest in Judas." Hannah shrugged. "I love Ennius."

Maryam nodded. "Good." She laughed. "I never thought I'd be saying it was good that a woman was in love with a Roman soldier."

"Shh!" Hannah nudged her arm. "They'll hear!"

Hannah didn't attempt to speak to Judas again, but he tried to engage her in conversation. She ignored him most of the time.

"Did you see what Yeshue did outside of Capernaum? How he fed thousands with a few small pieces of bread and fish?" Judas asked as they went through a market one afternoon buying food for supper.

Hannah shook her head. "I didn't. My brother and sister told me about it."

"Your brother has great power. More than any rabbi has ever had."

Hannah nodded. "That is no secret." She moved away from Judas so he would leave her alone, but he followed. His nearness made her uncomfortable.

"This kind of power could defeat Rome," he said in a hushed tone. "I don't understand what we're waiting for. We should make him King. Now. Tonight. His power would defeat any armies that tried to come against him."

Judas's words brought a picture to her mind. Ennius, bloodied and still on the ground as Judas stood over him with a dagger. She shook her head in horror.

He looked angry at her response.

"Yeshue doesn't want to be a king," Hannah said, though she wasn't sure it was true.

"What kind of Jew are you? What else would he be here to do? With Yeshue as King, no one dies. Only the Roman pigs. Let them lay in their own blood and be eaten by crows. Who will care?"

He stalked off, leaving her there, shaking. She couldn't find Ennius. If she did, Judas would kill him.

Later, after supper, she came to Yeshue as he sat by the fire. He looked at her. "What is it, sister?"

"Do you know that some want to force you to be king?" she asked, her voice low.

He nodded, his expression sad. "I know of their plans. But trust me. My time hasn't come yet."

She leaned against him as he hugged her shoulders.

"Hannah, you are shaking. Did something happen?"

She forced a smile. "No. I'm fine."

Yeshue was silent, as if he knew she was lying, but she didn't say anything. It would do no good to trouble him.

He stretched out his legs. "We will set our sights on Jerusalem tomorrow. Passover is near."

Jerusalem. Jerusalem meant Ennius. She forgot about her worries of Judas and felt a surge of joy. "Ennius is there."

She realized she had spoken aloud and her face felt hot.

Yeshue hesitated before he spoke. "Hannah, look to me. Nothing else, nor anyone else, will satisfy your longings."

She felt a slight prick of irritation. Why did Yeshue always seem to know what she was thinking? "What are you saying? That I shouldn't hope to see Ennius again?"

"Seek after the things of Elohim, and everything you need will be given to you," Yeshue replied calmly. "That is what Ennius is doing. For his faithfulness, he will be rewarded."

"I'm here, am I not? Will my sin follow me around forever? Can you never believe that I have repented?" She pouted.

Yeshue took her arms and looked her in the eyes. She couldn't escape his gaze. "Nothing I have forgiven will ever be held against you." His voice was firm, as if he wanted his words to resound in her mind for the rest of her life.

And. if she were to be honest, they did.

That night as they camped, Hannah sat next to the fire, imagining herself running into the arms of Ennius outside the ornate steps of the temple. Yeshue and the disciples talked on the other side of the fire. Yeshue had walked off with Peter, Ya'achov and Yohanan and they had rejoined the group after supper, tight-lipped about where they'd been.

Hannah's attention was pulled from her daydreams only when things got quiet. Everyone was staring at Yeshue as they waited for him to speak. Hannah was surprised by the troubled look on her brother's face. He stared into the fire, his usually peaceful expression gone.

"From this point on, we will set our faces toward Jerusalem. We are going to Judea."

At first, no one responded. But as the words sank in, concern appeared on the faces of the disciples.

"Master, do you think that's wise? I'm sure all of these Pharisees you keep arguing with are reporting back to the temple. Judea might not be the safest place for you."

"There are more important things than being safe, Peter." Yeshue folded his hands over his knees and watched the fire thoughtfully.

"How is he going to declare himself king if he's hiding in Galilee?" Judas spoke up, glaring at Peter.

Yeshue didn't respond to Judas's words. He didn't look up.

Peter fumed. "Why would he tell us not to spread word about him if he wasn't trying to protect what we are doing? There is a time for everything, Judas, and not all of us are dagger wielding savages—"

"Ah, yes, Peter, the most cowardly disciple of all," Judas mocked.

"Peter, don't." Yeshue still didn't look at either of them.

"But Yeshue—"

"The Son of Man will be betrayed to the hands of men. They will murder him, and the third day he will arise."

No one spoke. The disciples looked at one another, horrified. Hannah sat up, staring at her brother's face. Was it just a story, meant to grab their attention and teach them something? But when Yeshue told stories, he wore an animated expression. He was somber. He wouldn't even look at them.

Surely there was another explanation. Surely, he hadn't meant it the way it sounded.

No one spoke. Hannah supposed no one wanted him to clarify the meaning of his words any more than she did. It was easier if they all believed what they wanted to believe. Yeshue would be king. Yeshue would defeat his enemies. Yeshue couldn't die. How could the Son of Alaha die? It was absurd.

Yeshue didn't speak again the rest of the evening. Almost as if he wanted his words to sink in. Meanwhile, Hannah did everything she could to forget they had ever been spoken.

TWENTY-SEVEN

Talia

טלה

Talia sat on the bench outside the house and enjoyed the sounds of her neighbors visiting and the children playing. She held up the tunic she was working on.

It was a special garment. She had decided to make it for Yeshue the last time he left. She noticed the one he was wearing was threadbare and it probably didn't keep the night chill away as well as it could. It was winter now, and the rains never let up. Talia wanted him to be as comfortable as possible. Yeshue had never taken much care with his own comfort. His thoughts were always on others.

Talia couldn't help but smile at her accomplishment. She had started weaving the material from the finest wool she could afford in the market. Maryam stood behind her throughout the process, exclaiming over her fine stitches.

"Talia, this is excellent work. Yeshue will be so pleased." Maryam had paused, studying the garment that Talia had started. "It would be something if we could weave it completely and not have to sew it, wouldn't it? Yeshue needs something special. It wouldn't tear easily and need repairing. And it would say something about him, too. That he is seamless. Sinless. Different than the rest of us."

Talia loved the idea, so she spent the rest of the day pondering how to construct the garment without seams. She decided to start from the top and work down. It would take much time, but what did she have but time?

She had spent the entire fall working on the garment, until her fingers were calloused and her back ached. But she was glad for the suffering. It made the gift mean something. Like King David had said. *I will not offer sacrifices that cost me nothing.*

And now it was finished – this work of art. She only needed to see Yeshue again to give it to him.

He'd been in Judea since the beginning of the fall season. They heard of him through travelers passing through, but the reports seemed vague and distantly removed. It wasn't the same as being with him. Fortunately, the Feast of Dedication was approaching, and the family would be traveling. She missed her husband. She missed Yeshue.

Talia watched Y'aqim and Yosef play in the street with the other young boys. She had come to dearly love her nephews. Hannah had come home once at the end of summer and had seemed happy to see them, but they still looked to Talia to care for their needs. It did nothing to satisfy the need in her heart to be a mother, though.

Her hands went to her tight, flat stomach, wishing it was soft and stretched like her mother's. She hated to think of herself as barren, but how would she ever have a child if Nathanael was never with her? When they had traveled Galilee, she had seen him often. Now she had not seen him in months. Was this any way to have a marriage?

Hannah had come home with the men and left again, traveling to Judea with them. Talia had wrestled with her jealousy. She knew her sister's motives for going with Yeshue were not pure. She wanted to find her Roman soldier. Talia wondered how Hannah managed to live so selfishly. Talia would be miserable if she were always trying to please herself.

Bitterness had crept into her heart where her sister was concerned. The last time Hannah had been home, Talia had listened to her laugh with the other young women at the well and despised her. Hannah had no right to be so cheerful. Not after everything she'd done. Talia had done nothing to deserve the constant struggle of her fears. It wasn't fair.

Ya'achov

יעקב

Ya'achov stood next to his booth of wares. It had been a slow day at market. He would be taking home nearly as much as he brought with him. He sighed and looked upward, blaming the rain and the cold for a lack of travelers and townsfolk willing to come out and buy.

A group of men nearby had formed a circle, discussing what Yeshue had been doing in the past few months. Ya'achov was irritated that they seemed to know more than he knew. Yeshue had never been much for keeping his family filled in on his whereabouts. So much for the family leader.

"Are you Yeshue of Nazareth's brother?" One of them caught sight of him and gestured to his stone and wood booth. "I heard he was a tekton before he became a rabbi."

"He's my elder brother," Ya'achov said, trying to sound polite in case he might be able to convince them to buy something.

"Do you know if he plans to go to Jerusalem for Dedication?" The man came closer.

Ya'achov shrugged. "I don't know. If he knows what's good for him, he'll go."

The man tilted his head. "You sound as if you do not approve of your brother. He is a miracle worker and a powerful teacher, no?"

Ya'achov knew he shouldn't respond, but his irritable spirit got the best of him. "I advised Yeshue to go to Jerusalem and Judea a long time ago. I told him no one who wants to be a public figure acts in secret. I said he should show himself to the world."

"And the world is in Jerusalem," the man agreed.

"He didn't listen to me at the time. But I guess he decided I was right after all, because he's been in Judea for the past few months."

"Amazing, that you are able to advise such a wise and powerful man."

Ya'achov smirked, enjoying the praise, whether it was true or not.

"Are you going to the feast?" the man asked, running a hand along the smooth edges of a stool Ya'achov had made.

Ya'achov nodded. "We will. Business isn't good this time of year, anyway. Our whole family is joining the caravan to Jerusalem."

"Well, if you see him, give your brother our regards."

Ya'achov thought back to the conversation he'd had with Yeshue. It had been months ago.

"What is it," Yeshue asked as Ya'achov and Yose approached him. He'd been praying on the beach.

Ya'achov cleared his throat and exchanged a glance with Yose before he spoke. "We've noticed you don't have as many followers lately."

"What you say is true," Yeshue said with a nod. He didn't appear to be upset over the fact.

Ya'achov hesitated. "Well, we think you ought to go to Judea. Let all these followers of yours see your miracles. Who cares what these people up in Galilee think? It's ridiculous to want to be a public figure but act in secret. Since you're going to do this whether we want you to or not, you might as well show yourself to the world."

Yeshue looked at his folded hands and the vastness of the sea beyond them. "You think I am trying to become a public figure?"

Ya'achov laughed harshly. "Well, why else would you choose this life? You walk all over the countryside performing tricks and gathering crowds so you can tell them your stories and theories about Torah."

"Ya'achov," Yose interrupted. "Maybe it would be better if I speak."

"Fine," Ya'achov said, waving his hand. He folded his arms and turned away from them.

"Yeshue, it's just that this is Galilee. The people here don't have any power to change anything. If you are the M'sheekha, as you say you are,

why wouldn't you want to reveal your powers in Jerusalem?"

Yeshue smiled in a wistful way. "My brother, how can I make you understand? The right time for me hasn't come yet. For you, any time is right. The world can't hate you. It hates me because I testify to its evil nature."

Yose didn't answer. Ya'achov turned back to see Yeshue reach out and touch Yose's arm.

"You go to the feast. I'm not going yet. Not until the right time."

Ya'achov sighed loudly. "Maybe the world hates you because you're an arrogant fool! Who would want to be told that they are evil? Our people are already subject to Rome and despised by everyone. None of us have the heart to constantly hear about our sinfulness."

Yeshue didn't respond, which made Ya'achov angrier. Why couldn't he fight like a normal person? Was he too holy to raise his voice like the rest of the human race?

"Why are you angry, Ya'achov?" Yeshue asked him.

"Because you are tearing up our family with this little spectacle of yours and you won't even do it right."

Yeshue got up and walked to him. He put both hands on Ya'achov's shoulders. Ya'achov tried to brush his hands away, but he held him firmly.

"I made you a promise, my brother. One day you will understand everything."

Ya'achov scoffed at the memory. He would never understand his brother's apparent need for constant attention, yet his secrecy about his abilities. Yeshue didn't make sense, and he was just going to wind up dead. Men couldn't say the kinds of things Yeshue did and not be strong enough to stand behind them with some kind of force.

Now, months later, he watched the retreating backs of the men. Their long prayer shawls with tassels nearly brushing against the ground told him they were religious leaders. Pharisees. They weren't local, so they must be traveling around, trying to find Yeshue.

There was an air of something false about them. Had he just given the enemy weapons against Yeshue?

It would serve Yeshue right, but did he really want to be the brother who caused the death of the man his people believed was their M'sheekha?

Talia

טליה

Talia had no thought for the journey until the moment she saw the shadows of familiar figures in the distance. Her mind woke as if from a dream, and she ran.

She flew into Nathanael's arms as he laughed at her exuberance.

"I have missed you!" she said, trying to hold back tears that suddenly made her throat ache.

"I have missed you, too, beloved," he said as he cupped her chin with his familiar hand. She kissed it and held her to her face.

"We weren't sure if you'd get here today or tomorrow." Nathanael put his arm around her and they rejoined the caravan as family members surrounded Yeshue and the disciples. Talia saw Ama and Hannah embrace as her boys clamored for her attention.

"We hurried. It has been too long." Her voice hitched as she finally caught sight of Yeshue. He was crouched beside Y'hud and Shimon, his eyes alight with affection as they spoke to him.

"It has," Nathanael said, kissing her head. "I hadn't realized just how much I needed you until I was holding you again."

Talia buried her head in his chest.

When she opened her eyes, Yeshue was standing before her, the smile in his eyes as warm as the smile that pulled at the edges of his mouth.

"Yeshue," she said, and went willingly into his arms.

"My gentle Talia," he said. His voice was quiet and full of emotion. As if they shared a secret, and he was reminding her. As if he had looked at her just then and felt a certain emotion he hadn't felt before. It was a wistfulness, a yearning. She put her arms around his waist and hugged him, hoping her love would give him the composure she sensed he was lacking.

"What's wrong?" she whispered as she gazed into eyes that crinkled so merrily in the corners, yet held the depths of the darkest well within them. She had always felt that Yeshue's eyes were vaster than the brightest, starriest night. The whole universe seemed to reside within them.

He held her face with his hands. "Nothing that can't be made right by one of your embraces, dear sister."

She hugged him again, trying to give him the entire amount of affection residing within her.

When he finally turned away to greet their mother, she swallowed hard and turned frightened eyes on Nathanael.

"What's wrong with him? He seems so sad."

Nathanael frowned. "He does? I guess I hadn't really noticed. He has moments when he speaks of things that are troubling, and he has been quieter, but I didn't know anything was bothering him."

Talia sighed. Her husband was a good man, but he didn't sense the emotions of others the way she did. He took everything as it was or appeared to be. She patted his cheek and accepted his kiss.

"What about you? Have you been able to stay away from the dark thoughts?" he asked as the caravan started to move again, heading in the direction of the Holy City.

She wanted to assure him she was fine, but it wasn't the truth and she wasn't a good liar. She chose not to answer him instead.

"You are always worried. Don't you think I can protect you? And even if I couldn't, Yeshue could. How can you be afraid?"

She gave him a sad smile and shrugged. "I don't know. I'm a foolish girl, I suppose."

He took her hand. "Are you worried about going to Jerusalem?"

"I am worried about what I always think about. The prophets –"

Nathanael interrupted her with a sigh. "Talia, you are a woman. These things are too much for you. Rest, and know that your men will consider these things for you. Leave it to Yeshue. Worrying that a prophet's cryptic words might be about your brother will do nothing except make you crazy with fear."

Talia stopped walking. *"They will look at me, the one they have pierced, and they will mourn as one mourns for an only child, and grieve bitterly as one grieves for a firstborn son. On that day the weeping in Jerusalem will be great ... the land will mourn ..."*

She saw the image in her mind again. Yeshue, bloody beyond recognition, nailed to the Roman torture device she had seen as a young girl. "Yeshue," she whispered.

Nathanael shook his head and she sensed the spark of impatience. "That prophecy doesn't mean Yeshue is going to die."

"On that day a fountain will open to the house of David and the people who live in Jerusalem, to cleanse them from sin and impurity," Talia continued, her eyes coming to rest on the Holy City in the distance, lifted up on the hill as if to meet Alaha halfway between heaven and earth.

"Of course he will save us from our sin and impurity. That's why he's here. But think about it, Talia! Wouldn't a man who can heal sickness, banish evil spirits, even raise the dead, be powerful enough to stop someone from killing him? Trust Yeshue. He is the M'sheekha, and he will be king. Just wait and see."

Talia appreciated his attempt to quiet her fears, so she didn't tell him they remained. She gave him a brave smile and a nod and then continued walking.

"Sometimes I think Yeshue made a mistake teaching you so much Scripture. Women aren't meant to carry such burdens. You don't understand what you are talking about."

Talia didn't contradict him. In fact, she hoped he was right. She hoped she was just a silly woman worrying about things that would never happen. After all, who knew what those prophecies really meant?

But another occurred to her. *"Strike the shepherd, and the sheep will scatter,"* the words came from her mouth before she could stop them.

"Yeshue will win," Nathanael said firmly. "You must have faith."

"I do," she said. "I believe Alaha means what he says. And as much as I want to see Yeshue accomplish what Adonai sent him here to do, I my brother to be safe more."

Nathanael gave a short laugh of disbelief. "As far as I can tell, you can have both. Evil will not win over your brother. I promise."

She let him lead her back to the caravan, where she presented her gift of the seamless tunic to Yeshue. As he exclaimed over the excellent stitching and the time it must have taken, the words went through her head, over and over.

Strike the shepherd, and the sheep will scatter.

Hannah
חנה

Hannah felt a surge of anticipation as they came through the Sheep Gate into the city. The main road flooded over with bodies. She held tightly to her sons' hands, afraid she would lose them in the swarm. After Yeshue had become lost one Passover many years before, the family had developed a plan should children become separated from the group. Every child old enough to understand knew to go to the temple steps in such an event, but Hannah's boys were too young to know how to get there. She held their little hands so tightly they whined in protest.

The festival had already begun. The market was full of optimistic vendors hoping to make a profit from the swollen crowds. Yeshue bypassed the market and went on through the city. Hannah could see he was headed for the temple. She had no interest in following them. The temple was interesting to look at, but the lambs bleating helplessly as they waited to be sacrificed bothered her. She wasn't going to cry over it like Talia did, but that didn't mean she wanted to hear it or explain it to Y'aqim.

The long, mournful shofar blast echoed eerily through the street and caused many to quiet and turn toward the temple. It was almost time for the afternoon sacrifice.

"Ama, take the boys," she said, turning Yosef and Y'aqim over to her mother. "I'll go back to the market to get food for supper."

Maryam didn't look appreciative, but she let Hannah go, firmly taking Yosef in her arm and holding Y'aqim protectively next to her. Hannah knew they would be safe, and they would enjoy seeing the grandeur of the temple for the first time.

She wandered back through the market, enjoying her freedom. She fingered a few beaded necklaces and dyed fabrics she would never have enough coins to buy.

"Do you have money to buy those things?" a voice spoke in her ear, and for one moment her heart stopped, thinking it belonged to Ennius.

She turned, disappointed to see Judas.

"Why aren't you with Yeshue?" she asked in irritation.

"I need to ask you a question," he said, shifting his eyes as if in guilt. He took her arm and guided her through the marketplace.

She tried to shake him off. "Let me go, Judas. I'll scream."

"No one will hear you. Just cooperate. I'm not going to hurt you."

She wished she believed him.

Music played loudly to her left, people haggled over cooing doves to her right. The smell of spices and bodies in need of washing made her feel sick. The sting from his fingers in her arm angered her.

What worried her most was the darkness of the small space between buildings where he seemed to be headed.

Everything became quieter as he pulled her inside the alleyway.

He looked around wildly. His tone was desperate when he spoke. "I need you to tell me whether Yeshue hid any money anywhere."

Hannah scowled. "You are the one that keeps my brother's money bag. Shouldn't you know that?"

Judas gripped her arms until they ached. "Your brother owes debts. You need to tell me where he hides his money for his sake, and for yours. You know as well as I do that the Romans could take you into slavery if he didn't pay his taxes."

"I don't know about any secret stash of money," she said, trying to push him away. Anger flared in his eyes and he pushed her back against the wall.

She kicked him, but it seemed to have the opposite effect she had hoped, and his grip tightened. The look in his eyes changed, from frustration to something else. Was he considering what she had been in the Roman fort? Would he try to take advantage of her? She couldn't let it happen. Not again. She tried to scream, but he covered her mouth with his hand.

Suddenly a tall, dark form appeared in the entrance of the alleyway.

"Get your filthy hands off her. Now."

Hannah could hardly believe her ears. "Ennius!"

Ennius glared at Judas. "Let her go. Last warning."

Judas let go, but he didn't retreat back into the crowd as Hannah hoped. He stood before Ennius, breathing hard through his nose, reaching into his robe for the dagger he surely had hidden there. Hannah remembered the things he had said about his father and about Rome.

"Ennius, be careful," Hannah said, but it was unnecessary. Ennius pulled his sword from its sheath.

"You're going to want to leave now," Ennius advised, his eyes dark and scathing. "And don't ever let me catch you alone with this woman again."

"Roman scum," Judas spat. He met Ennius's gaze with contempt. "Don't think I won't kill you. I'll avenge my father's murder, even if Yeshue won't."

Ennius didn't comment. He steeled his jaw and pointed with his sword. Finally, Judas disappeared into the crowd.

Ennius turned back to her. She was about to jump into his arms when she noticed the steely glint of his eyes. He glared at her. "What's going on here?"

Hannah heard the accusation in his tone. She supposed he thought she'd returned to her old ways. "Nothing," she said hotly, silently daring him to contradict her.

"Really?" His words were more challenge than question.

"I don't know," she said with a defensive shrug. "Do you think I was seducing him?"

He didn't answer.

"That's exactly what you think." She groaned in frustration. How could he be such a simple-minded fool? "Here I am, overjoyed at the sight of you–"

"I would have hoped to see you fight a little more," he interrupted in reproach.

"I can't believe you!" she bellowed, throwing her arms in the air in exasperation.

"See?" He gestured to her. "You know how to fight."

"I *did* fight back! When will you accept that I am not the same as I was in the outpost? I have been faithful to you."

"You'll pardon me if I don't believe you."

Anger set her face on fire, and she punched him as hard as she could in the arm. He seemed unperturbed as he returned his sword to its sheath.

"I suggest you scream louder next time." He waved his hand at her in irritated dismissal before he turned and headed into the mass of people. She ran after him.

"Ennius! Stop! I've missed you so much." She followed him.

He turned abruptly. She stepped back at the sight of him, formidable in his armor, helmet and sword. For a moment she forgot he was just Ennius, and saw the fearsome authority of Rome.

"Don't tell me you missed me, little girl," he said, his tone heated. "I have been here, studying Scripture with Jewish rabbis, enduring the mocking and disapproval of all my fellow soldiers as I try to find the answers concerning your M'sheekha brother. Meanwhile, you hide in the shadows and tempt men to pay for your time, just as you always did."

"That is not what happened, you stubborn man! I am here with Yeshue. He's at the temple."

Ennius scowled. "And you are not."

She shook her head. "Why have I wasted even a moment of time pining after you? Would that I could get those moments back!"

She turned on her heel and headed in the direction of the temple. She had no satisfaction when she realized he hadn't followed her.

Hannah pounded up the temple steps as fast as the crowd of people would allow, hoping not to meet Judas again before she rejoined the group. She spied Yeshue and his disciples walking through the covered walkway to the side of the temple, supported by massive pillars. The women and children stood to the side, talking in a circle. She ran across the courtyard to them. Her eyes avoided the bloody scene where priests sacrificed the lambs, but she heard their strangled bleats.

"There you are," her mother said with irritation, handing her Yosef. "Where are your purchases?"

"I haven't got any," Hannah admitted as she took Y'aqim's hand. "I ran into someone."

Maryam gave her a questioning look, but their attention was stolen by Pharisees who suddenly surrounded Yeshue, preventing him from walking any further.

"How long will you keep us in suspense?" One of them smiled at the crowd around them who had stopped what they were doing to watch. "Tell us plainly, Yeshue of Nazareth, are you the M'sheekha?"

Hannah frowned at the obvious false politeness. She hoped Yeshue knew it was a trick. Her brother regarded the man evenly.

"I *have* told you. What I do in my father's name testifies that I am who I say I am. You don't believe because you are not my sheep. My sheep listen to my voice. I know them, and they follow me." Yeshue gestured to his disciples and to the group of women.

Yeshue continued, but he seemed to be talking to Hannah and the rest of his people more than to the religious leader who had asked the question. "I give them eternal life, and they shall never perish; no one will snatch them out of my hand. My Father, who has given them to me, is greater than all. No one can snatch them out of my Father's hand. I and the Father are one."

To Hannah, the words sounded beautiful. Comforting. But the leaders and other Jews suddenly reacted. They gasped and produced stones from within their robes.

"No!" Talia cried. Nathanael held her back. Maryam tensed and looked desperately to Yeshue.

Hannah scowled. They were trying to trap him. Why else would they have waited until Yeshue was surrounded or have kept stones waiting in their robes?

"Hypocrites," she said under her breath. She hoped Yeshue would call down fire from heaven or command the earth to open up and swallow them. Hadn't there been a story in the Torah like that?

"I have shown you many good works from the Father. For which of these do you stone me?" Yeshue asked calmly, gesturing to their weapons.

"We are not stoning you for any good work," they replied, "but for blasphemy, because you, a mere man, claim to be Elohim."

"Why do you accuse me of blasphemy because I said I am Adonai's Son?" Yeshue asked, his voice still disproportionately composed compared to the tension around him. He shrugged. "Do not believe me unless I do the works of my Father. But if I do them, even though you do not believe me, believe the works, so you know and understand the Father is in me, and I in the Father."

They angrily rushed forward and tried to grab Yeshue. What happened next made no sense, and Hannah didn't know how it happened, but somehow, he got out of the circle and motioned for his family and disciples to follow. He calmly led them out of the temple and down the steps. Hannah looked back at the leaders and laughed as they stumbled around, disoriented, looking for Yeshue.

TWENTY-EIGHT

Y'hud

יהוד

Y'hud couldn't stop thinking about what happened in the temple. It was dark, and they had walked to Bethany to stay with Lazar and his sisters in their home. Lazar had a servant start a bonfire in the courtyard and the group sat around it, talking. The crowds outside the gate had finally died off for the night, and Y'hud was glad. He hated being watched by curious people wanting to catch a glimpse of Yeshue or talk to him. He hated that he always had to give up his brother so that the masses could have him.

Yeshue sat with his disciples and Lazar snacking on grapes. Maryam and Marta, Lazar's sisters, served them. Y'hud's mother and sisters helped them, and Ya'achov and Yose and the rest of the family sat separately with their own conversation.

Y'hud wanted to be with Yeshue. But every time he tried to leave the family, Ya'achov called him back with a harsh whistle. He sat sullenly and listened to Ya'achov and Yose talk about what had happened earlier.

"Well, at least he doesn't seem to be hiding anymore," Yose reminded Ya'achov as Nava brought a platter of dates and figs and set it in front of them.

"When I said he should show himself to the world, I didn't mean he should stand in the temple and taunt the Pharisees." Ya'achov made a sound of disgust. "Did you hear the talk in the street afterward?"

Yose nodded. "I heard a few who insisted there was no way M'sheekha would come from the north. Everyone else thought it was funny."

"Fools," Ya'achov said. "Though they do have a point."

Yose was thoughtful. "I heard one man say a Galilean couldn't be the M'sheekha because the Scriptures said he would be born in Bethlehem."

Y'hud's ears perked up. "But Yeshue *was* born in Bethlehem! And he also comes from David's line."

"They can't get past his accent," Yose continued, ignoring Y'hud. "Some of them think Yeshue was born in Alexandria."

"People don't like admitting that the village of Nazareth is filled with descendants of King David. Only the people of Nazareth talk about it."

Y'hud considered that. He looked at his hands. The blood that flowed through his veins was the very blood that had given life to King David.

Y'hud's eyes wandered over to Yeshue. The disciples were gathered around him, speaking in low voices. Maryam, Talia and Lazar's sister Maryam had stopped their serving to listen to what Yeshue said.

They all laughed at something Y'hud couldn't hear. He sighed loudly.

"I'm going to sit with Yeshue," he said to Ya'achov in a sudden burst of boldness.

"He's busy. Stay here with us." Ya'achov scowled at him and returned to his conversation with Yose. Y'hud fumed and considered disobeying his older brother. He was technically a man, wasn't he?

"Yeshue should leave here. He thinks he's safe because he's with friends, but he stepped on important toes today. They were ready to kill him."

Y'hud looked back at Yeshue. He would never forget his terror when those Pharisees pulled those stones out of their robes. He'd never seen anyone stoned publicly, but that didn't mean it didn't happen. They had been angry enough to kill him.

But Yeshue had escaped in a way that defied explanation. That was a comfort to Y'hud. At least his brother was stronger. He wouldn't let anyone kill him. He was the M'sheekha. It wouldn't make sense for him to die.

Y'hud watched Yeshue lean close to Lazar and smile at something he said, clapping his friend on the shoulder. Lazar and his sisters had been family friends for as long as Y'hud could remember. Lazar had been friends with Abba. Y'hud liked listening to Lazar speak of the father he'd never known.

Y'hud looked around at the familiar surroundings of the spacious villa. He felt a mixture of envy and wonder when he stayed here. Their home was so different than the two homes Y'hud had known. Sometimes he found himself wondering what it would be like to be as rich as Lazar, until he remembered how Yeshue felt about the love of money. He supposed being rich had its own set of struggles.

Yeshue left the next day. There was much gossip among the adults that stayed behind. Did he leave because he was afraid of the Pharisees?

Y'hud knew Yeshue would never leave out of fear. He'd never known anyone as brave and calm in the face of danger as his abba. He watched the retreating backs of Yeshue and the disciples – no one else this time – as they headed toward Jordan.

The days that remained of the festival were boring. Y'hud spent the time playing with Shimon or running in the streets of Bethany with other boys his age. One evening as he came home at sunset, he was surprised to find Lazar sitting outside on the stone fence that surrounded their villa.

"Sh'lam lak," Lazar said in a strange, thick voice. He smiled, so Y'hud came and sat next to him.

"Sh'lam lak. Are you well?"

Lazar lifted a pale face to the red sky that lit up the sky behind Jerusalem up on the hill. "It is a beautiful city, is it not?"

Y'hud nodded, suddenly speechless as he stared across the valley to the Holy City. "It is, Lazar."

Lazar lifted a trembling hand to wipe the sweat from his brow. "Do you see the door cut into the rock? There, by the well."

Y'hud squinted his eyes and caught sight of the small, dark entrance. "I see it. It is a tomb, no?"

Lazar gave him a sad smile. "It *is* a tomb. I think ... I think I may have need of it soon."

Y'hud felt a cold chill pass over him as he glanced wildly at the older man. "What do you mean?"

Lazar sighed, as if he knew he shouldn't say such things to a young boy, but he needed to speak to someone about his suspicion. "Y'hud, you will tell your brother not to worry that he wasn't here, won't you?"

Y'hud swallowed hard. Finally, as Lazar watched him expectantly, he nodded.

"Your father was a good man, Y'hud. One of the best. You should be proud to be called the son of Yosef."

"I am," Y'hud said in a quiet voice.

"But be prouder to be called the brother of the M'sheekha." Lazar coughed, the sound bitter and painful. It seemed to rise up out of the deepest part of the man, as if he had already been defeated by whatever was stealing his strength.

They sat in silence for long moments.

"Yeshue will comfort my sisters," Lazar said, nodding to himself.

"Please, Lazar, can't I find a doctor? Or I could run for Yeshue! He could heal you in a second, even from miles away! I've seen him do it."

"As have I, my son, as have I." Lazar gave a weak laugh. "But this time, I believe Alaha would have me go. There is a time to be born and a time to die. But don't say anything to my sisters. Their grief will begin soon enough."

Y'hud steeled his jaw. He didn't feel right about not telling anyone.

He watched Lazar for the rest of the day. When he realized the older man had disappeared, he went to Marta, who was busy grinding grain for bread.

"There are many mouths to feed!" She smiled at him and wiped her brow. "Can I get you something, Y'hud?"

Y'hud chewed on his lip and looked around to see if anyone would see him go against Lazar's request. "Your brother is sick."

Marta nodded. "He has not been well lately. I hope he is resting so he can feel better."

"He thinks he's going to die." Y'hud kicked at the dirt and looked away, not wanting to see the panic fill her face.

She didn't speak for a long moment. "Then we must send word to Yeshue," she finally said in a determined tone. Y'hud nodded.

She went to find her brother. Marta found Lazar in his bed, unconscious and feverish.

Messengers were sent not ten minutes later. They promised to get to Yeshue as soon as they could with the word of Lazar's illness.

Y'hud didn't want to say it aloud, but he didn't think they would get to Yeshue in time.

A week passed as Lazar lay unconscious on his pallet, barely breathing. The sisters said he was strong and he would stay alive until Yeshue could get there. They estimated the messenger would have reached Yeshue by that time, so surely, they would arrive any day. But much like a clay jug dropped to a stone floor, everyone's hopes were broken. Late one night Lazar breathed his last.

Maryam and Marta were beside themselves with grief. Maryam wailed and rocked back and forth near the fire, pouring ashes on her head. Marta paced, giving herself completely over to funeral plans and the preparation of the body. Y'hud saw the wild look of sadness in her eyes. He thought it would be better if she would cry, but it wasn't Marta's way.

"Yeshue will come," she kept saying, absently, to herself. "He'll know what to do."

"What is there to do?" Y'hud's mother held Marta's shoulders and spoke in a soft voice. "We must bury him. There is nothing else to do but grieve."

Marta shook her head. "No. Yeshue must come. He'll know …"

Ama gave Y'hud a sad look.

Y'hud watched in morbid curiosity as the women carefully laid Lazar's body out on the long table and washed it. The sisters poured myrrh and other spices onto his skin and rubbed them in until his body glowed with the sheen. Then they wrapped the corpse tightly in long strips of cloth that had been bleached in the sun.

People poured into the house. Lazar must have had many friends in Jerusalem, because the spacious villa seemed crowded and small with so many people gathered. Marta frantically prepared food for everyone while Maryam sat beside the body and cried. People brought gifts to console them – expensive perfumes and oils and household items. Y'hud didn't know what they would do with all of it.

Y'hud was asked to help carry the body to the tomb. He remembered Lazar telling him about the grave inside the rock – expecting to use it soon. They made a somber procession as they took the body down the hill and maneuvered into the small, arched doorway. There was another passage in the floor that had been opened. They carefully took the body below the ground and laid it out on a bed of stone in the lower chamber. When Maryam and Marta had ensured everything had been done, they all quietly left the tomb and the large circular stone was dragged over the entrance.

Four days passed. Every day seemed identical to the one before. Crowds. Gifts. Mourning. Wailing.

But late in the morning, a young man ran in to the courtyard, breathless. "Yeshue is coming!"

Marta immediately reached for her headscarf and ran to meet him. Maryam looked up, but her head returned to her arms and she began to sob.

Y'hud felt miserable as he watched her cry, but he didn't know what to do. Talia came and sat beside Maryam on the floor, enveloping her in an embrace. Y'hud followed Marta out and sprinted down the hill to the group barely visible on the eastern horizon.

Marta didn't waste any time. She fell on her knees at Yeshue's feet as soon as she reached him. "Adonai, if only you had been here, my brother would not have died."

She choked with sobs as she continued. "But even now, I know that what you ask Alaha, he gives you."

Yeshue leaned down and took her hands, pulling her up. Yeshue watched her sadly. His voice was soft and full of emotion. "Your brother will rise."

Marta nodded bravely, trying to contain her emotions. "I know he will rise in the resurrection on the last day."

Yeshue shook his head slightly, his warm brown eyes suddenly filling with tears. He grasped Marta's hands so firmly his knuckles turned white. "I am the resurrection and the life; whoever trusts in me, even if he dies, he shall live, and everyone who lives and believes in me shall never die." Yeshue paused. His eyes searched Marta's. "Do you believe what I'm saying?"

She slowly nodded. "Yes, Adonai. I believe you are M'sheekha, the Son of Alaha, who has come into the world."

Yeshue squeezed her hands. He looked around them. "Where is Maryam?"

"Still in the house. Her pain has been nearly unbearable." Marta's eyes fell to Y'hud. "Go and whisper in Maryam's ear, Y'hud. Tell her our Rabbi has come and asked about her. Don't tell all the others or we will be swamped with people when she tries to see him."

Y'hud ran back to the house. As usual, the gathering in the courtyard had grown, and he had to wiggle around the people to get to Maryam.

She lifted tearstained eyes to his face. He glanced around at the people who all waited to hear what message he had brought. He leaned forward and cupped his mouth to Maryam's ear. "Yeshue has come. He asked for you."

Maryam rose immediately and pushed her way through the crowd. Y'hud followed her, but to his chagrin, so did the rest of the crowd, curious.

"Maybe she is going to the tomb to weep," he heard someone say.

Maryam ran all the way to the valley outside of the village and fell at Yeshue's feet, sobbing. "Adonai," she wailed. "If only you had been here – my brother wouldn't have died!"

Yeshue watched her, his face contorted with sorrow. His mouth was open in an expression of surprise. As if their grief had caught him off guard. He searched their faces, looking from one sister to the other, reaching and touching their cheeks in turn. He tried to speak, but his voice wouldn't work.

Finally, he cleared his throat and asked, "Where have you laid him?"

"Come see, Adonai," Marta said, and gestured toward the tomb. Maryam followed, holding Yeshue's hand and leaning against his arm, still sobbing.

Yeshue suddenly stopped and leaned over, grasping his knees and breathing hard. He started to cry great sobs that threatened to tear Y'hud's heart out. He'd never heard anyone so broken, so dumbfounded by grief. Yeshue reached for the sisters and they tightly embraced, all three in tears.

"See how much he loved him," someone whispered.

"Was not the man able to open blind eyes powerful enough to keep him from dying?" someone else whispered. Y'hud turned around and glared at the naysayer. His brother was the most powerful man alive. But in the back of his mind, he wondered the same thing. Why had Lazar needed to die with Yeshue as a close friend? Why hadn't his brother come sooner, or at least spoken a word of healing from where he was? Surely he'd known his friend's time was short.

Yeshue took Maryam and Marta's hands and they moved together toward the recessed tomb. They went under the stone arch and down the stairs until the closed vault was at their feet.

"Take away this stone," he managed to Y'hud and several others who stood behind them on the darkened stairs.

Marta gave him a strange look. "Adonai, by now the body is decaying. It's been four days. It will smell awful."

Yeshue looked at her, and suddenly Y'hud saw the old determination in his brother's eyes. "Did I not tell you that if you would believe, you would see the glory of God?"

Y'hud helped Peter and Yohanan to pry the heavy stone from the opening. Y'hud stepped back, covering his nose. What would Yeshue do next?

Yeshue stood still and quiet for a long moment, his eyes closed and his hands open. Finally, he spoke. "Father, I thank you that you have heard me. I know that you always hear me, but for the sake of this crowd standing here, I said these things, that they may believe that you have sent me."

There was another long, silent moment. No one dared to breathe.

Suddenly, Yeshue called out in a loud voice, as if he was calling to a place beyond the close quarters of the underground tomb. "Lazar, come out!"

Y'hud gulped, his entire body tingling as if he'd been struck by lightning. The crowd around him gasped as if they had sensed the same thing.

Y'hud trembled all over as he peered into the darkness of the underground room.

A shadow appeared. Movement! The grave clothes glowed white in the dark. Several people screamed and those who had come down into the small tomb with Yeshue and the sisters suddenly moved back and climbed the stairs, frightened.

Y'hud made himself stand in one place, like Yeshue did. His heart beat with an erratic rhythm and his mind buzzed with fear, but he forced himself to look on the form of a dead man trying to stagger off the stone while bound with strips of cloth. Y'hud couldn't see his face because it was still bound by the turban.

He met Yeshue's eyes, but still his brother showed no signs of surprise or fear. He gestured toward the form stumbling around in the darkness as he held the sisters' shoulders to his chest. "Go, Y'hud. Unbind Lazar and let him go."

A small smile appeared on Yeshue's tearstained face. Y'hud gulped, nodded, and slowly made his way down the second level of stairs to the inner crypt.

"Hello, Lazar," he said as he stepped into the dark room and reached for the ghostly form to steady him. Lazar stood still while Y'hud pulled away the cloths. When he saw the surprised face of Lazar, he couldn't help the laugh of disbelief that escaped him. The fear fell away as he worked to free him. When they both realized the disoriented man was now naked, Y'hud took off his cloak and handed it to him.

Everyone had moved out of the tomb to give them room. Y'hud led Lazar up into the daylight, where Maryam and Marta instantly fell into his arms with tears of joy and relief.

Y'hud looked to Yeshue. His mind swirled with emotions and thoughts like a storm brewing on the sea. Had he really just watched his older brother raise a dead man to life? Could it be a trick? Had Lazar just been unconscious and was revived by Yeshue's call? But no, he'd been in the tomb four days. Too long to have passed out. Y'hud had been taught that the spirit hovered near a body for three days, trying to rejoin. Lazar's spirit should have already gone on to Sheol by now.

"Yeshue," he said, but he didn't know what else to say. He just stared at him, shaking his head.

"Remember this, Y'hud," Yeshue whispered for only him to hear. Y'hud didn't know what he meant. Yeshue turned to walk away from the tomb.

"Adonai," Y'hud whispered as he looked back at the dead man, now alive.

TWENTY-NINE

Ya'achov

יעקב

Ya'achov was tired of hearing the story.

"Give glory to Alaha," he always mumbled when someone praised his brother for raising a man from the dead. And so he said the same to Nicodemus, the Pharisee and member of the High Council, as he spoke to him by the temple three days after Lazar returned to life at the word of Yeshue.

"Who else could raise the dead but Alaha?" Nicodemus spoke quietly, obviously taken aback by Ya'achov's reaction. "Do you not believe your own brother?"

Ya'achov looked around, knowing that if the wrong people overheard their conversation, Nicodemus would be in serious trouble. As a member of the Sanhedrin, discretion was necessary since the other members had grown increasingly intolerant of Yeshue's antics.

Ya'achov leaned against the temple retaining wall and shrugged, refusing to meet the older man's gaze. "I know him better than you do."

Nicodemus shook his head. He leaned close. "Ya'achov, how can you deny what has happened?"

"I'm not denying it." Ya'achov crossed his arms over his chest and stared at the crowd moving slowly past them on the road. "I'm only saying that glory should be given to Alaha. What's wrong with that?"

Nicodemus shrugged. "Nothing, I suppose."

"What do the Pharisees say about it?" Ya'achov tried not to appear too interested. He didn't want anyone to think he was worried about his brother.

Nicodemus nodded. "The men are agitated. They can't come to a consensus. They worry we will gain Rome's attention."

Ya'achov nodded. He could see their point, though he wasn't willing to argue with Nicodemus over it, since he knew the other man was sympathetic to Yeshue's ministry. "What did Caiaphas say?"

"The High Priest seemed peaceful. As if he already knew what would happen and he was content with it."

"What does he think will happen?"

Nicodemus hesitated.

"I can handle the truth," Ya'achov assured him.

"He favors turning Yeshue over to the Romans."

Ya'achov wasn't surprised. He'd known it might come to this. Yeshue wasn't one for smoothing over his differences with the religious leaders. In fact, he instigated many of the fights that made them so angry, as if on purpose. What could Ya'achov do if Yeshue refused to respect their leaders and the tenuous position they maintained in a Roman world?

"I must tread carefully. I believe they are starting to suspect I have sympathies," Nicodemus admitted.

Ya'achov sighed. "What a mess."

"I am glad you came to see me. Is Yeshue safe?"

Ya'achov shrugged. "How should I know? We try to keep him safe. His disciples attempt to keep him away from Jerusalem. But he seems determined to be arrested."

"You speak as if you do not trust him. Surely his own brother would believe he is who he says he is," Nicodemus said softly, his tone of admonishment not missed by Ya'achov.

"Not this brother." Ya'achov clenched his jaws together.

"Do you wish to see him taken?" Nicodemus asked, troubled.

Ya'achov considered it. "No," he finally admitted.

"You know now what they are planning. Warn Yeshue. They will arrest him the next opportunity. Understand me, Ya'achov. There is no thought for mercy—they want him dead. Whatever differences you have with your brother, I expect you want to protect his life."

Ya'achov gave a short nod, though a part of him, deep within, ravaged by bitterness and jealousy he wasn't willing to admit, was not so sure he was altogether against Yeshue being removed from his life for good.

"I've tried to talk to him. He doesn't listen. He keeps making it worse."

Nicodemus heaved a sigh. "We are ruined if we kill our M'sheekha. Ruined."

For a brief moment, the weight of what Nicodemus was saying occurred to Ya'achov. The essence of truth residing in the words called to him, asking to be heard. But as quickly as he had the thought, he pushed it away.

"You hear the skeptics. How could M'sheekha come from Galilee?" Ya'achov shrugged.

"You and I both know Yeshue was not born in Galilee. You are the offspring of David."

Nicodemus was frustrated with him. Ya'achov didn't want to discuss it further. He pushed away from the wall with his foot and started off in the direction of Bethany. "It all comes down to Yeshue and whether he decides to stay away. No one can make him do anything he doesn't want to do."

Ya'achov knew that to be a fact, better than anyone.

Ya'achov met Nathanael coming back to the villa in Bethany. Which meant Yeshue hadn't left yet.

"Why is he still here?" Ya'achov asked him without stopping.

Nathanael followed him back in the direction of the villa. "Yeshue says we will leave at first light."

"Good," Ya'achov said with a short nod. "It's not safe here. The Council is looking for a reason to turn him over."

Nathanael walked beside him, quiet. He shook his head. "I don't understand their hatred. It can only be jealousy. What would they arrest him for? The healing? Bringing the dead to life again?"

Ya'achov frowned. "Perhaps for the disregard of traditions and his tendency to elevate himself to the level of Alaha." He felt Nathanael's questioning gaze on him, but he didn't look at him.

"Ya'achov, do you agree with the Pharisees? Do you think he is wrong?"

Ya'achov didn't want to answer the question. "It doesn't matter what I think."

"Could *you* do the things he has done?" Nathanael wouldn't let it go. His quiet question made Ya'achov burn with anger.

"I don't know. Maybe. I never tried. Can't you? Didn't he give you disciples the power to do the same things he does?"

Nathanael nodded sadly. "He did. But our progress is limited. It's to our shame."

"I don't know." Ya'achov sighed, hoping Nathanael would get the message and leave him alone. But his brother-in-law seemed determined to prove his point.

"He fulfilled the prophecies. I wouldn't have followed him if I hadn't carefully checked."

"Maybe."

Nathanael hesitated. "Yeshue said something on the way Jerusalem. We can't make sense of it."

Ya'achov stopped and looked at him. "What?"

Nathanael shook his head. "He said that all that had been written by the prophets about the Son of Man would come to pass. That he would be delivered to the Gentiles. Mocked, spit on, beaten and killed."

Ya'achov felt an unexpected stab of fear.

"Do you have any idea what he's talking about? We were all afraid to ask him what he meant."

"He was probably just quoting the prophets. You know what he's like."

Nathanael nodded, but Ya'achov could tell he wasn't any more satisfied with Ya'achov's answer than Ya'achov himself was.

"Still, I feel like there is some great truth here we are missing. It isn't the first time he's spoken like this. But something in the message seems hidden. Perhaps he is speaking in a parable."

"He does like to talk in riddles." Ya'achov started toward the villa again. "He's always been a storyteller."

"And a good one." Nathanael followed after him. Ya'achov didn't say anything else. He didn't trust his mouth to keep hidden what his heart was harboring. The bitterness and the hatred continued to fester. It ate away at him inside.

Talia
טליה

Talia would have expected to feel better than she did after witnessing her brother bring Lazar back from the dead. But as the family and friends celebrated around her, all she felt was unease. Something she couldn't identify plagued her. Something didn't make sense.

Why had Yeshue waited to come to Lazar until after he had been dead so long? Nathanael told her in confidence that Yeshue had waited two more days after hearing Lazar was sick before he came back to Bethany. So he'd done it on purpose. But for what reason? It wasn't just out of love for Lazar and his sisters. Yeshue was trying to say something, and judging by the sad look he'd worn all evening as the dancing and eating progressed into the night, she doubted the message was a happy one.

Lazar had never looked healthier or stronger. He was twenty years older than Yeshue, but he seemed to have the vitality of a much younger man now that he had been raised. He greeted his guests warmly and ate with them, but when she went to him and welcomed him home, she noticed that same indistinct sadness in Lazar's eyes that she'd seen in Yeshue's.

He saw that she'd noticed and smiled. "I'm sorry, Talia. I do not mean to frighten you. I am thrilled to be called back to this life, if only to see his face again. And yours." Lazar touched her cheeks with the warmth of a father. "It's only ... well, I can't remember what it was like there."

"In Sheol?" Her voice trembled as she spoke.

He nodded. "Yes. I can't remember, but I suppose I feel a certain disappointment at leaving it behind. Does that make any sense?"

"Are you saying we shouldn't fear death?" Talia asked softly. "That it is a pleasant place?"

"I'm sure that depends on the person experiencing it." He sighed and stared at the night sky. "I don't know, child. I just wish I could recall. I have the impression of freedom. Rest."

"Why did Yeshue bring you back if that place was a good one?"

He stared at the cup of wine between his hands. "Truthfully, I'm afraid to consider it."

When the guests had finally left for the night and the families and disciples had retired, there was a knock on the outer door of the gate. Talia hadn't been sleeping, and she sat up straight on her pallet.

She tiptoed through the courtyard and through the front house and peeked out the window.

Standing tall and fearsome in the light of the moon, with dark, furrowed eyes and unruly black hair ... was a Roman.

Hannah

חנה

"Hannah, wake up."

Dreams mingled with reality as Hannah tried to shrug off sleep at the sound of her sister's voice.

"Hannah, you must wake up. Someone is at the door."

Her first thought was that soldiers had come for Yeshue. She jumped up. "Is Yeshue safe?"

Talia pushed the wayward strands of hair away from Hannah's face as she had when Hannah was very young. She smiled. "Yeshue is fine. He is sleeping. But if your soldier keeps pounding on the door, no one in the household will be sleeping for long."

Hannah gasped and jumped to her feet. "Ennius? Here?"

She left Talia behind and ran down the hallway, pulling on her cloak and her headscarf as she ran. She didn't see anything in the dim light of the moon and stars until a shadow stepped out from behind the small sycamore tree that grew in front of the villa.

"Come with me."

Ennius said nothing more. He turned and left abruptly. Hannah pushed her feet into her sandals and followed him out of the house and down to the path that led out of the village.

"We're going to Jerusalem? At this time of night?" Hannah struggled to keep up with his larger stride. She noticed he wasn't wearing his uniform. He wore the simple tunic and cloak of her people. Did he hope to blend in wherever he was taking her?

He didn't speak until they had crossed the valley and climbed the stairs to the Temple. He bypassed the holy site and ducked into an affluent looking house.

A crowd of men gathered inside the main room. Hannah didn't recognize anyone, but she could tell they were religious leaders. Members of the Council. Others stood around the perimeter watching the meeting.

"Is this the Sanhedrin?" she whispered to Ennius.

He nodded. "Stay behind me where no one can see you. Hopefully they won't notice us."

Hannah stepped behind him and listened to the men argue.

"What are we accomplishing here?" One of the men stepped into the center of the circle, holding the sides of his prayer shawl and puffing out his chest. "This man performs miraculous signs. If we let him go on like this, everyone will believe in him. The Romans will come and take away our place and our entire nation."

"Everyone already believes him," a younger man said from the corner of the room. "After Lazar appeared to come back to life, they've started flocking to him like pathetic sheep. They believe he is M'sheekha."

Murmurs of disapproval sounded from around the room.

A man stood in the center of the room and cleared his throat. Everyone stopped talking and looked at him. Hannah peeked around Ennius.

"Is that the High Priest?" she asked close to Ennius's ear. He gave a short nod and motioned for her to be quiet.

"You know nothing at all!" The man scowled and brushed the front of his prayer shawl harshly, as if he was brushing off their ignorant conversation. He paused for a long moment, turning in a circle to look each man in the eye. "Don't you realize? It's better for one man to die than for the whole nation to perish."

Hannah gasped audibly. Ennius reached behind and grabbed her arm so hard it hurt. She put her hand over her mouth.

Her mind screamed a response. The High Priest of all of Israel had just declared her brother must die. Who did Caiaphas think he was? These supposed leaders of her people would kill the one who had proven himself to be who he said he was? *Kill* him? She breathed fast, her anger causing her face to heat. She eyed Ennius's sword in its sheath, tempted to grab it and see how many of them she could kill before they stopped her. Better they should die than her brother.

Ennius moved his grip from her arm to his sword, as if he read her thoughts. He leaned back and spoke softly into her ear. "Look in the back. Behind the pillar by the window."

She focused her gaze where he had directed it and almost gasped again. "Judas!" she whispered in disbelief. "Why would a disciple of Yeshue be here in this place?"

The disciple stood to the back, his arms crossed over his chest, his eyes narrowed and hard as stone.

"What is he doing?"

Ennius shook his head. "I suspect he is thinking about the personal benefits of betraying your brother to this sorry lot."

Ennius pulled her back through the door and led her across the quiet street until they were safely out of earshot.

"Why would they want to kill Yeshue?" she demanded.

"Because he's better than they are," he said.

"And why don't you stop them?" She pushed against his chest with her palms.

Her push didn't move him in the least. "If I had tried to stop them, you and I would both be dead right now. Did you not see the armed temple guards at every entrance?"

She sulked. "We have to warn Yeshue about Judas."

She started to turn around, her sights on the villa in Bethany, but Ennius caught her by the arm.

"Hannah, I already have."

She stopped and stared up at him. "Well, what did he say?"

Ennius shrugged and sighed. He looked back toward Bethany. "He said nothing would happen that isn't Elohim's will."

"You knew about this before now?"

"Hannah, I patrol this very street nearly every day. I hear conversations they don't think I can understand, because they don't realize I study their language and their Scriptures when I am not on duty. They have been talking long into the nights trying to come up with a reason to arrest your brother. And your friend the disciple has been with them the last couple nights. He is always silent. Always standing in the back."

"Judas is no friend of mine," she said, indignant. "But maybe he is spying on them for Yeshue."

"Has he warned Yeshue of these meetings?"

"I wouldn't know. But I don't think Yeshue knows he's there."

Ennius stared hard at her features. Did he doubt her sincerity? Was he trying to find her guilt in her expression? "Are you protecting Judas?"

She swallowed her pride and admitted the truth. "I'm not, Ennius. But I can understand why you might think of me that way. I have sought the attention of men before."

"Why?" Ennius glared, his jaw tense.

"I don't know," she said, shrugging. "Maybe I grow impatient waiting for Alaha. I think my plan will get me what I want, but it never does."

"Did you not think of me?"

She heard the hint of vulnerability crack in his voice, but it did not soften her answer. "Don't pretend you are innocent. You left me, even after I begged you not to go."

"I never said I was leaving for good." He curled his lip, as if he was disgusted with her for thinking it.

"You said I should accept an offer of marriage if it was given to me!" She gave a harsh laugh of disbelief. "You must make up your mind, you stubborn ox!"

"I didn't tell you to flirt with scoundrels in alleyways."

She sighed. What good would it do to try to explain again? He wouldn't listen.

"Go home," he said, turning away from her. "Warn your brother about the disciple. I can't guarantee his safety if he stays in this region."

"You would make me walk home through the streets of Jerusalem by myself?" she asked, indignant.

"I will watch." He nodded toward the house on the hill, dimly lit with torches at the gate.

She waited another long moment, hoping he would change his mind. Hoping he might take her in his arms and kiss her as he had in the past. But the determination did not leave his expression.

"Go, Hannah. I don't want to be near you right now."

"I heard them say it with my own ears." Hannah heard her voice raise in frustration as she glared at her brother. "Yeshue, they want you dead!"

Yeshue took another grape from the bowl Marta had set on the table in the main room. The disciples stood around him, watching Hannah with distrustful expressions. Talia seemed ready to faint. She held her hand to her mouth and leaned against the wall.

Yeshue's expression remained even. "Nothing will happen that is not –"

"The will of Alaha. I know." Hannah held up a hand in an attempt to stop him. "I know you believe that, but I'm not so sure. You need to get out of Jerusalem."

"Hannah, please speak with respect," Yeshue reminded her. "I appreciate your concern. I do." He looked around the room, making eye contact with every man, woman and child present. "I appreciate that all of you are concerned about what is happening in the city. But you must trust me."

"What will you do?" Peter, who stood next to Yeshue, asked, his hands on his hips. Yeshue didn't answer immediately. Hannah watched her brother's features. He'd just been told there was a plot on his life, but he looked at each person in the room as if his concern was only for them. Hannah felt a twinge of guilt at her attitude.

"We leave as planned. For a time."

"Where are we going?" Nathanael eyed Talia as he asked the question of Yeshue.

"To Ephraim."

"The village in the desert?" Judas stood in the doorway. Hannah fumed. How dare he come back here? She started to speak, but Yeshue caught her hand. When she looked at him, he shook his head.

"But –"

"No, Hannah. Let it go. Trust Elohim."

Talia came forward and took Hannah's arm, leading her out of the main room into the small room with the oven where the food was prepared. It was hot and Hannah impatiently wiped the sweat from her brow.

"What is it, Hannah?" Talia asked timidly.

"Judas was at the meeting of the Sanhedrin. Ennius took me. They are plotting to kill Yeshue."

Talia gasped and clamped her hands over her mouth, stepping back and moaning softly. "No …"

"Judas has to be a traitor," Hannah said. "What other reason would he have to be there? And Yeshue must know. Yet he is going to let him go with them to Ephraim?"

"It can't be true," Talia said softly. "One of Yeshue's beloved disciples – a traitor? How could any of them join a conspiracy against him?"

"I don't know." Hannah made a sound of frustration and paced the room. "We have to do something. We have to convince him, somehow."

Talia slowly shook her head. "You know Yeshue never changes his mind. It's pointless. We have to trust him. We can't do anything else."

"At least he's leaving," Hannah said. "Surely he'll be safe in Ephraim."

"As long as no one finds out he's there." Talia squatted by the oven and buried her face in her arms. "This can't be happening."

Hannah sighed loudly as a small figure came to the doorway.

Maryam, the youngest sister of Lazar, came into the room and knelt beside Talia on the tile floor. "Are you okay?"

Talia shook her head, unable to speak.

"She's fine. She's just worried about Yeshue."

"Yeshue was concerned for both of you. He sent me to check on you."

"He won't listen to reason, Maryam! He's determined to get himself killed." Hannah took to pacing the room again.

Maryam stood up as she considered Hannah's words. "Hannah, tell me about the moment you realized your brother was different than other men."

Hannah shrugged. "We always knew he was better. Ama made sure we knew that." She gave a short laugh. "But I guess I didn't see him as different until I sinned. Greatly. I gave myself to my husband before we were betrothed."

Hannah glanced at Talia. Her older sister didn't like her to speak of such things. But Maryam didn't seem shocked, so she continued. "Yeshue knew I had done it. Right away. I'll never forget the look in his eyes. He wasn't angry. He was disappointed. Heartbroken, even."

"But he forgave you?" Maryam asked.

Hannah nodded. "Though he could have had me stoned."

Maryam watched Hannah expectantly, as if she knew the story wasn't over. Hannah cast another wary glance at her sister before she told the rest. "Life was difficult for me in my husband's house. I hated every moment there, though I knew it was what I deserved. And I was glad when they all died from sickness." It had never occurred to Hannah how hard her heart had been. She frowned as she thought back to that day when she had celebrated their deaths. "I was *glad*."

Hannah walked to the small window and peered out over the garden. "I took my baby and ran away. I was going to find Yeshue and the family in Capernaum, but I was ashamed. I took a job at the Roman bathhouse instead."

"Is that where you met the soldier?" Maryam gestured toward the front gate where Ennius had been the night before.

"Yes." Hannah's voice became hushed and she looked down at the floor.

"What did you do there?" Maryam's tone suggested she already knew the answer.

Hannah shifted uncomfortably. "I sinned. Again. Over and over. I took all the love and forgiveness I'd already been shown and threw it back in Yeshue's face. I traded my body for coins. I thought of it as survival for my son and me, but my family was never more than a Sabbath's day's walk away."

The room became quiet except for Talia's sniffing. Maryam stayed by her side and held her close. "Oh, Hannah. You have known such sadness."

"Sadness I brought on myself," Hannah said dully. "Ennius saved me from my sinful life by loving me. He was the one who encouraged me to go to Yeshue and ask his forgiveness."

"Ya'achov wanted to have her stoned," Talia said suddenly, her voice breaking into the conversation, rough and teary. "He tried. But Hannah got to Yeshue first."

"I didn't know if he would spare my life a second time," Hannah added.

"The men were dining at a neighbor's house," Talia spoke again.

"Yeshue was at the head of the table. Hannah came in and fell at his feet, crying. I was with the women, but I saw what happened. She took a jar of expensive perfume and anointed him. He was moved when she washed his feet with her tears and dried them with her unbound hair."

"How beautiful," Maryam breathed, her hand going to her chest as she pictured it.

"I was anything but beautiful. But he still forgave me. I don't understand why he keeps forgiving me, Maryam."

"I long for this forgiveness," Maryam said, surprising them both. Hannah laughed aloud.

"How could you possibly need forgiveness?" Talia managed a small smile.

"You are convinced of your sin, Hannah, because of the consequences, are you not?" Maryam asked, looking at Hannah with a direct gaze. Hannah nodded.

"I am convinced of my sin because I know my heart. My attitudes. My selfishness. I do not deserve his mercy. Not if he can see what is underneath, and I know he can. I can feel him sharing my thoughts. Seeing inside my mind. Do you know what I mean?"

Talia and Hannah met each other's gaze. "Oh yes."

"But, Maryam, I've never known a woman as gentle and humble as you. I can't imagine you this way," Talia said.

Maryam sighed. "I've tried my entire life to be as good as my brother and sister. I've always obeyed the law. I did everything asked of me, but it didn't make my heart any different. I lied so people wouldn't know there was darkness in me. I confess I hated the men who confronted Yeshue in the temple. I have wished his opponents dead."

"So do we all," Hannah said with a shrug. "What's wrong with that?"

"I know what you mean, Maryam." Talia stood, reaching for Maryam's hands. "I don't claim to know the answers, but maybe that's the point. Maybe this inability we have to change ourselves is why Yeshue came in the first place."

Hannah watched her sister's face fall. "Are you thinking of the prophecies again?"

Talia nodded, inhaling deeply and fighting against the flashing images of her mind.

Maryam suddenly went to a niche in the wall and surveyed a row of small bottles. "The nard," she said softly, to herself.

Hannah studied the pretty jar Maryam took from the shelf. It reminded her of the alabaster jar she had stolen from her mother-in-law. "What is it?"

"This must be what it was for," Maryam said, taking off the stopper and letting the rich, heady scent free for just a moment so they could smell it.

"That's beautiful," Talia said. "It must have cost a fortune."

"I can only imagine. Someone gave me this jar after Lazar died. It was a woman. I didn't know her. But she said I would need this for a specific purpose, and I would know what it was for when the time came."

"What are you going to do with it?" Talia asked. Hannah watched Maryam's face and smiled, knowing what the other woman was planning.

Maryam placed the jar back on the shelf. "I'm going to do what Hannah did. Seek forgiveness. Before it's too late."

Part Three

MY BROTHER THE KING

Say to the daughter of Zion, "Behold, your King comes to you
meek and riding on a donkey."

Zechariah 9:9

THIRTY

Talia

טליה

Talia saw neither her husband nor her oldest brother for four months. The family went home to Capernaum, leaving Yeshue and his disciples about fifteen miles northeast of Bethany, in the village of Ephraim. Talia could only imagine what happened there during those long days between winter and spring.

It was not even a question of whether the family would go to Passover. They spoke of it as a surety, making plans long before it would be necessary. They were pulled to Jerusalem. They all wanted to see him again.

But after they had arrived at the home of the living Lazar and his sisters, and the familiar form broke the horizon, followed by twelve other forms, Talia could not shake her sadness.

When he was finally there, embracing them, kissing their faces, murmuring his joy at having them each in his arms again, Talia's tears flowed. There were lines on Yeshue's face she hadn't remembered. The haunted expression in his tender eyes had grown deeper. His smile wasn't as easy and his tears flooded his eyes more than once as he greeted them.

"My dear friends," he said, embracing Lazar and the sisters. "Your faces are so dear to me."

Talia hung back, waiting until he had greeted everyone in the group but her. He came to her, grasping her hands and kissing her forehead as gently as he had when she was a very little girl and in need of comfort.

"My dear Talia," he said in a soft voice. "See, I have worn your tunic. It has held up very well. You are a gifted weaver."

She smiled through her tears.

"I almost hoped not to see you," she said. She dipped her head in embarrassment for her strange words.

He gripped her hands tightly. "I know. I understand."

"She means it was foolish for you to come to Jerusalem," Ya'achov said behind them. Ama made a sound of disapproval, but it fell flat. Because everyone, whether they voiced it or not, agreed.

The neighbor, Shimon the Potter, had delivered some jars to the women earlier in the day and heard that Yeshue was returning. He offered for the family and disciples to join him at his house that evening when Sabbath was over. Marta and Maryam had made a special supper in honor of Yeshue's return, so the women loaded a cart to take the food to Shimon's house after sundown.

Maryam came to help her sister Marta and the other women, but she suddenly stopped. Her eyes fell to the jar on the shelf. Her gaze met Talia's briefly, and she wiped her hands on her tunic, purposeful in the act as she moved forward to carefully retrieve the treasure.

The men had gathered around the table in Shimon's home. They reclined and listened to Lazar report on the events in Jerusalem since Yeshue had left months earlier.

"It has been quiet," Lazar said with a shrug. Shimon nodded his agreement with the assessment. Lazar sighed. "Maybe they have forgotten their anger. Who am I to say you are not safe?"

Ya'achov made a scoffing noise from where he leaned against the wall in the corner, his thick arms crossed over his chest.

The conversation quickly quieted as Maryam entered the room, purposefully carrying the jar in her hands. Talia leaned against the doorway, watching to see the look on Yeshue's face. She had not been there when Hannah had done much the same thing, desperately seeking the forgiveness of Yeshue as Ya'achov went on a mission to take her life. Now Hannah smiled at Maryam, nodding in encouragement as she replaced the empty wine jug.

Maryam kneeled before Yeshue, whose smile pulled at the corners of his mouth. She took a small mallet and broke the neck of the jar with one firm tap. A pungent, earthy smell immediately filled the room. Talia wasn't sure she liked it. There was a sweet, floral undertone, but the heavy spice made her think of death. Tombs.

Abba.

Maryam took the jar and stood behind Yeshue as she poured it out completely over his head. She deftly rubbed her hands against his scalp until the ointment had been worked into his hair. Yeshue closed his eyes, the smile still apparent on his mouth.

Judas scoffed loudly. He aimed his accusation at Lazar. "Why didn't you donate this to the treasury? We could have sold it for a year's wages and fed the poor with that money."

Talia heard Hannah made a sound of disgust. "As if you care about the poor," she said under her breath. Maryam's hands stopped their ministrations, and her voice faltered as she tried to speak.

She thinks he's angry with her, Talia thought.

"Leave her alone," Yeshue said firmly. He said it to everyone, not just Judas, for some of the other disciples had indicated their agreement. "She has done a beautiful thing for me." He looked at her tenderly, and Talia saw Maryam's face relax. Perhaps she knew the forgiveness she desired. Talia was glad. Yeshue turned back to the disciples, sitting up. "She has been saving this for my burial. You'll always have the poor. You won't always have me."

Yeshue turned back to Maryam and squeezed her hand, still thick with the spiced oil. "Wherever my story is told, you will be remembered."

Maryam nodded, her eyes filling with tears and her lip trembling. "Thank you, Yeshue."

"Thank *you*, Maryam," he said quietly.

No one else seemed to notice what Yeshue had said. *Saving for my burial ... you won't always have me.*

Talia fled the house, fled the smell that seemed to climb through her nose into her mind and taunt her. *Yeshue smells of the tomb ... Yeshue is ready to be buried ... You won't have him anymore.*

Nathanael followed her back to the villa and caught her in his arms as she burst into the abandoned, echoing hall.

"How are we going to protect him?" She searched his face for some indication of hope. Reassurance. Her heart seemed to stop beating for a long second as she realized there was neither in his expression.

Nathanael shook his head. "We can't protect him, Talia."

It wasn't what she wanted to hear. She put her fists on his chest and pushed against him. He held her firmly, not letting her get away. "Settle down. You'll do him no good by having a fit."

She continued to struggle. "I'll do him no good anyway! I'm useless to him."

He sighed deeply against her. "So am I."

"What's going to happen?" she asked in a whisper, her mind frantically rehearsing the prophecies again, as if she might divine her answer from them. But she couldn't make sense of them. It was only blackness, swirling around her head, trying to get within her, trying to make her despair. For it would take Yeshue away, it reminded her. It would have the final say, and his life would be no more.

"I don't know what's going to happen, Talia," Nathanael said, his tone more vulnerable. "But I think you should prepare yourself."

Y'hud

יהוד

Maybe it was that Y'hud was older. A man now, even, at thirteen. Had this thick tension always been looming over his family – his brother – as it did now? And was time so malleable that it could slow down? He felt as if the events of his life had rushed by and suddenly everything was halted. Honed in on Yeshue. Waiting, breathless, for him to make his next move. It felt like all of creation paused and watched.

The scent of nard still clung to his clothes. He walked beside his brother – or as close as he could get for the crowd. They had come to the villa that morning looking for Yeshue, hearing he was there.

Yeshue had sent Nathanael and Thomas ahead, and the large group walking from Bethany met them just outside the temple gates. Nathanael led a mother donkey and her colt toward them.

"The prophecy," Y'hud heard Talia murmur. He only had to consider what she meant for a moment before he remembered the words of the prophet Zechariah. *Rejoice greatly, O Daughter of Zion! Shout, Daughter of Jerusalem! See, your king comes to you, righteous and full of salvation, gentle, riding on a donkey.*

Excitement made the flesh on his arms prickle, causing the hair to stand on its end.

Yeshue approached the donkeys, first going to the mother and gently running his hand down her neck. She bowed her head at him and brayed mildly.

"May I sit upon your little one, gentle Ama?" he asked. Some of the disciples glanced at one another with strange looks on their faces, but Y'hud liked that Yeshue talked to animals. He'd always done that. Once Y'hud had asked him why, and Yeshue had told him the story of Balaam and his donkey who talked back when he was mistreated.

"You never know when one might have something to say," he had said with a secretive smile.

Yeshue went to the foal, which skittered nervously away from Nathanael, but nuzzled Yeshue as he reached out his hands and patiently waited for the young donkey to come to him. "You are a special little one, aren't you? Don't worry, we will keep Ama close the whole time."

Nathanael spread his cloak on the donkey's back, and Peter followed suit. Yeshue wasted no time. He nimbly climbed on the back of the foal and clutched the mane. Nathanael led the mother toward the gate. Y'hud felt the excitement soar in his chest as the people around him realized what it meant. What Yeshue was saying by fulfilling so specific a prophecy. They began to cheer as Yeshue began to move forward.

The crowd continued to grow larger as people came to see what the commotion was about. Children danced and waved their hands while their parents praised God with hands lifted high to heaven. As Yeshue came toward the Shushan gate, people collected olive and palm leaves from the trees and began to wave them in the air. Y'hud followed the disciples' lead as they took off their cloaks and laid them in the path of the little donkey.

Singing began in earnest. "Hoshanna to the Son of David, to he who comes in the name of Adonai!"

Y'hud felt his chest puff with pride as he walked beside the foal and watched the people praise Yeshue as their king. This was the moment they had all waited for. Finally, Yeshue was being recognized for who he was. For his power against their enemies. It was as if Yeshue had just declared war on Rome, and their people would follow him into battle! They would take back their country and live as Alaha's free people once again.

He eyed the donkey. He wished it were something nobler. Why hadn't Zechariah foreseen a powerful stallion, ready for battle? Why a baby donkey?

Talia walked beside him, and she ran her hand over the animal's coarse fur. "Isn't it interesting, Y'hud? A donkey is what kings traditionally rode in times of peace, not war."

Her voice was dreamy, as she had been lately. But she was right. Donkeys were a symbol of peace. How could Yeshue hope to defeat an enemy as formidable as the Roman Empire with *peace*?

Y'hud stopped walking. He curiously watched the procession. The dancing and singing continued up the hillside toward the Eastern gate by the temple. In one sense, it was perfect. Exactly as they had hoped.

But Y'hud couldn't escape the dark look on his brother's face as

Yeshue watched the crowds. Why wasn't he happier? Why didn't he shout in triumph or at least sit regally? Why did he look so sad?

Why did Yeshue always look so sad these days?

Ya'achov

יעקב

Ya'achov leaned against the retaining wall of the temple and scowled at the ridiculous procession. Why was Yeshue humiliating himself riding a donkey? What a bunch of fools if they thought Yeshue was going to accomplish anything they wanted from him. Ya'achov wanted to tell the lot of them to go home and wait for a M'sheekha with some backbone. Or at least one who owned a sword.

He eyed the Pharisees, standing inside the gate and watching the spectacle with indignation. They wanted control more than anything else, to protect the city from a Roman rampage. Rome wouldn't hesitate to beat them back into place should one of them rise up. It had happened enough times before for the people to know what to expect. If Yeshue didn't have the power he claimed, he was essentially dooming them all.

Ya'achov rubbed his eyes with his palms. When he took his hands away, he was looking into the narrowed dark eyes of a Roman soldier. He reached for his dagger.

"You're that soldier of my prostitute sister." Ya'achov curled his lip in distaste. "You should be dead."

"I should," Ennius said without hesitation or emotion. "Fortunately, your brother disagreed."

"What do you want?" Ya'achov glanced around, hoping no one noticed him talking to the soldier.

"Yeshue is in danger," Ennius said without hesitation. "Hannah has warned him of the possibility of one of his disciples turning on him." Ennius gestured to Yeshue, who had climbed off the donkey next to the gate and was greeting the children who had been dancing and singing. "I don't get the impression he's heeded any advice to stay out of open areas."

Ya'achov shrugged. "We've tried to warn him. The man only listens to his own opinion."

"That's not all. The city is a bowstring right now. The people are ready for someone like your brother to come in and save them. Especially after he fulfilled the prophecy."

"What's your point?" Ya'achov wouldn't look the man in the eye. He didn't want him to know how surprised he was that the Roman had known of the prophecy.

"Your leaders fear another uprising. They don't want to die for your brother. They think it would be better for everyone if he was dead instead of them."

"Can you blame them? There have been so many M'sheekhas who have come and gone. I doubt Yeshue is different from the rest who have spilled their blood in Jerusalem in the name of freedom."

Ennius glared. "I would agree, except that every breath I take is a reminder that this body of mine should be rotting in a tomb." He took a step toward Ya'achov, claiming his attention. "I was a dead man, yet here I am—living and breathing. All because of your brother. What other M'sheekha could have done the same?"

Ya'achov couldn't think of an answer. He shrugged and covered his chest with his arms, looking down the hill. "My people still suffer."

"They do. And my people suffer in their sin. That's why I must believe your brother is who he says he is. He's not only interested in saving the Jews. He cares about a dying pagan uncomfortably close to his family. That says something."

Ya'achov sighed and shifted. "What's your point?"

"I want to protect him if I can. If your leaders offer him up as a sacrifice, the Governor Pilate will kill him. He's too afraid of revolt. And besides, Romans love to kill. We're good at it."

Ya'achov could tell by the hard edge to the soldier's voice that Ennius disagreed with the philosophy of his people. He wouldn't have thought a Roman capable of conscience or morality. And it made him uncomfortable to consider it. Which made him hate the man all the more for shaking his belief system.

"As you know, no one tells Yeshue what to do. If he's determined to pursue this, he'll bring down the consequences on us all, and he won't give us a say," Ya'achov said.

Ennius nodded and glanced over at Yeshue, who was entering the gate into the temple, lovingly touching the walls of the passageway and smiling. "If he's truly a king, he can do nothing less."

The statement bothered Ya'achov more than he cared to admit. He walked after the crowd, abruptly leaving the soldier's presence.

The temple courts were crammed with bodies. The Passover crowds had arrived and it seemed everyone in Israel was there to offer their sacrifice. Plenty of merchants were trying to take advantage of the situation. They had not only filled up the space along the streets outside the temple, but some of them had moved inside, right into the Court of the Gentiles with their loud, stinking animals and money boxes full of clinking coins. Men haggled, children cried, animals squawked in protest.

Ya'achov took it in stride. It was Passover. The city was swollen with pilgrims and there wasn't a free space in all of Jerusalem. What else were the merchants to do?

Apparently, Yeshue felt differently.

Yeshue went to the first table and pushed it over, sending coins flying in every direction and people diving for them. Ya'achov stared in surprise at his brother. Yeshue had always been maddeningly mild-mannered and the picture of self-control. Had he finally lost it?

"My father's house is a house of prayer!" Yeshue went to the second table and did the same thing. "You have made it a den of thieves!"

At the third table, they had already gathered up their coins and were trying to contain the doves they had in makeshift wooden cages.

"Get out!"

The merchants ran for the entrance. Ya'achov glared at Yeshue. "They're just trying to make an honest day's wage," he said under his breath.

He didn't think Yeshue would have been able to hear him, but Yeshue whirled around and pinned his indignant gaze on Ya'achov.

"This is a house of worship for everyone!"

Ya'achov didn't want to argue further. But a great well of rage deep within him suddenly broke free. "Who do you think you are?" He imagined taking the dagger from his belt and stabbing Yeshue in the heart. Then he'd be quiet. Then he'd give up this arrogant crusade. "This is just the court of the Gentiles! Who cares whether they worship or not?"

Yeshue's voice broke when he answered. "I care."

Ya'achov could handle his brother's outrageous display no longer. He covered the distance between them and pushed Yeshue as hard as he could. Yeshue was ready for it, as if he expected it. He stayed in place, never taking his eyes from Ya'achov's face.

"I'm done following you," Ya'achov said. "I'm done listening to you. You don't care about our people. You don't really care about our religion. You care about the Gentiles and the poor and that ragtag band of disciples who will betray you in the end when Romans hang you up. And they will hang you up because of spectacles like this, Yeshue. So go ahead. Get yourself killed. All you'll ever hear from me is that I told you so."

He was breathing heavily and his hands were shaking with emotion when he turned away from Yeshue. He could feel his mother and sister's sorrow, his wife's embarrassment, but he only felt apathy. Yeshue had gone too far. He seemed intent on not only getting himself killed, but dragging the family name through the sludge at the same time. He talked as if he were the Son of Alaha, but he made a fool of himself at the same time. Ya'achov was done with the least suspicion that his brother was M'sheekha.

Yeshue was a fraud.

"You're all fools if you keep following him," Ya'achov said, waving his hand at the sorry lot standing around Yeshue. "He's got you under a spell. Run while you can."

Ya'achov grabbed his young son and motioned for his wife and daughter to follow him. He left the temple by the same gate. He went back to Bethany without uttering a word.

Talia
טליה

Talia watched Yeshue with wary glances as he sat at the table with his disciples surrounding him. Passover had always been an exciting time – a happy time. It was the only time of year when every Jew believed in freedom and hope of a better future.

But she'd never attended such a somber Passover in her life. The disciples were mostly quiet, taking their lead from Yeshue, who had barely spoken since they'd sat down to their meal.

Was he still thinking about what Ya'achov had said a few days earlier in the temple? As each day passed Yeshue's brow creased further. He was easily brought to tears. He looked at each one of his family members and friends as if it was the last time.

Man of Sorrows … acquainted with grief …

Hannah had tried to warn Yeshue of the possible plot of Judas and the temple leaders. Ennius had reported everything that happened in the meeting of the Sanhedrin. They wanted to kill Lazar along with Yeshue because of how the people flocked to see Lazar, since he was proof of Yeshue's amazing ability to raise the dead. They worried about how the "whole world was going after him." But they said they shouldn't take him during the feast or the people might riot.

Yeshue didn't respond to the reports given him in secret. He just stared out the window or went to the grove of olive trees beyond Bethany to pray.

Yeshue … Talia stared at his face, trying to memorize every line, every curve of his dear features. She tried to remember when Yeshue had been happy and carefree. She closed her eyes and remembered toddling around the carpenter's shop after him. He would tell her the stories of Noah and Yosef and Moses in his animated and lively way. She felt as if she were floating down the river with Baby Moses through the bulrushes to the steps that led to the princess's rooms. She would breathe deeply and nearly smell the fire that burned as the Israelites wildly danced around their golden calf, sealing their fate with their betrayal of Elohim, who had led them out of slavery. She would lift her arms and feel the desert wind whip across her face as they plodded on in misery, hoping for a better day when sin had been atoned and their children were free.

Her people. So sinful. So lost. They couldn't even see their M'sheekha for who he was.

She admired the strong hands that held the Passover bread, fingering it as if he pondered the shape and texture. These were the hands that had comforted her when Abba died. Hands that had crafted beautiful things with wood and meticulous blocks of stone that held up massive buildings in Sepphoris to that very day. Hands that had touched and healed sick, dying, broken. Hands that had brought life out of death.

Her mind suddenly flew to that place outside Jerusalem as a girl. The young man in agony. Screaming. Begging for help. His hands nailed to wooden beams. She shuddered in horror at the pain he had felt, but even more so the mental torment he must have endured.

A flash. Now the hands that bled, nailed to the beam were familiar. Familiar hands that had held her.

She gasped and covered her mouth as Maryam and Hannah looked up at her.

"Come, Talia, take Yeshue the wine." Her mother urged her, pushing the jug into her hands. "Don't think on those things right now."

She went to the table, suddenly possessed by the need to talk to Nathanael. She gave the wine to Yeshue and went to her husband, kneeling next to him and whispering into his ear.

"Will you stand by him?" she asked, searching his eyes for signs of weakness. "Will you defend him when they come?"

Nathanael frowned at her, reaching a hand to wipe the tear escaping the corner of her eye. "Hopefully it won't come to that," he said, and she knew he was avoiding her question.

Her breath caught in her throat as she stood and went back to the room with the other women. He would abandon Yeshue if he was taken. Her eyes searched the remainder of the faces at the table. Familiar faces she had come to love. But she knew the truth as she looked into the heart of every one of them.

None of them had the will to stand with him in his hour of testing. They would run like scared rabbits when the treason and murder began.

Yeshue was doomed.

"Where is Judas?" Hannah asked. Talia looked back and saw the empty seat.

"He left," Maryam said softly. "I saw him get up and leave. Yeshue didn't seem surprised."

"I'm not surprised, either," Hannah said, her voice edged with irritation. "It's not like we didn't warn Yeshue. He should have sent him away long ago. I bet he went straight to the temple to tell them where Yeshue is."

Maryam shook her head. "Ah, my son! Why do you stay here in this city where men want to kill you?"

Talia watched him break the bread and pass it to his disciples. He poured the wine and passed the cup, urging every man to drink.

The men began to sing in haunting tones the traditional song of Hallel.

"The snares of death encompassed me, the pangs of Sheol laid hold on me; I suffered distress and anguish. Then I called on the name of Adonai, I beg you, save my life!"

Talia covered her face with her hands and wept as Yeshue led the psalm, his beautiful tenor voice heavy with unshed tears.

THIRTY-ONE

Hannah
חנה

Hannah couldn't sleep. She paced in the garden outside the villa, her glance falling often on Jerusalem. The city seemed deceptively quiet.

The chill of the night breeze rustled her tunic, making her wish she'd stopped to grab her cloak before she came outside. But Yeshue and the disciples hadn't come back, so they were in the cold somewhere. She shivered and crossed her arms.

She saw distant torchlight in the city. Temple soldiers, perhaps? They came from the Shushan gate. Her eyes darted to the garden on the Mount of Olives, between Jerusalem and the village of Bethany. She suspected Yeshue was there. He loved that garden.

And the crowd was heading there. A stab of foreboding struck her heart.

"Hannah!"

She whirled around as Ennius came through the garden gate. "What's happening?" she asked breathlessly as he came to her, grabbing her arms.

"Judas told the Council where he is. He is leading the procession. They're headed to the garden now with guards and weapons." Ennius shook his head. "Understand me, Hannah … they wouldn't be going after him in the night if their plans were honest. Or legal."

"No," Hannah felt the pressure of her anger as if she might explode. She clenched her fists and roared in frustration. "Take me there."

"Should we tell your sister?"

Hannah glanced back toward the villa. "Talia shouldn't know yet. Not until we have something to tell her."

"Let's go."

They ran down into the valley toward the garden where Yeshue liked to pray in the old olive grove.

"How can we fight them?" Hannah asked as they ran. "You're only one man against so many."

Ennius shook his head, his eyes narrowed and hard. "We can't fight them, Hannah."

"What about my brother Ya'achov? He's a Nazarite. They'd respect him – he's been under a special vow since birth."

Ennius stopped outside the garden, breathless. The sound of marching feet grew closer, the light from their torches glowed on the horizon. "I already asked Ya'achov to go to the Sanhedrin, Hannah. He refused."

"How dare he betray our brother?" Hannah stomped her foot on the ground. But their attention was stolen by the sound of Yeshue's voice speaking softly nearby.

"Arise, let us go. Here comes my betrayer."

Yeshue turned as the temple guards rushed through the gate and down the hill. Judas led the band of armed men.

Hannah narrowed her eyes as she watched Judas reach Yeshue. He gave a false smile, but she could tell he refused to look Yeshue in the eye. He leaned forward and kissed Yeshue on the cheek.

"Sh'lam, Rabbi," he said in a high-pitched, nervous voice. His wide eyes told Hannah he might be on the verge of madness. Had this been building in him all along? What had made him snap? Was he possessed by the evil one this very night? Could she be looking instead into the eyes of Satan himself?

"Judas," Yeshue said with compassion, holding the palm of his hand to Judas's face. "Do you betray the Son of Man ... with a kiss?"

The eyes of Judas went dark for a moment, and he stared at Yeshue in horror. Then, like a flash, his smile returned. "Rabbi," he murmured. "Rabbi."

"Have you come to this, my friend?" Yeshue voice was tender. Broken.

Guards came forward and took Yeshue's arms. Hannah could see that their expressions held fear. She didn't blame them. Darkness hovered over the garden. It was unmistakable.

Suddenly, Peter came forward. He looked terrified, but his sword was drawn and he went for the closest man, the one who had tried to take Yeshue's arm. He swung blindly, his sharp blade falling down the side of the man's head and shaving off his ear in one clean slice. The man cried out and held the side of his head in horror as blood spurted down his arm.

Yeshue turned to Peter. Hannah heard power when he spoke. "Put that away! Those who live by the sword also die by the sword. And don't you think I could call a legion of angels to help me?" He leaned closer to Peter's terrified face. "The Scriptures *must* be fulfilled! I *must* drink this cup."

Yeshue reached down to the ground and picked up the bloody ear. He dusted it off and held it in his palm as he cupped it to the side of the man's head. When he drew his hand away, the ear was restored.

Yeshue turned back to the guards. "Whom is it you seek?"

"Yeshue the Nazarene," a brave guard replied, sounding anything but bold. Hannah couldn't see who had spoken.

"I am he," Yeshue answered.

Hannah gasped and the entire company of Jews fell back as if the breath from Yeshue's mouth had been strong enough to blow them over.

"What just happened?" Ennius looked at Hannah in confusion.

"*I Am* is the holy name of Alaha," Hannah whispered. "He is saying he is God. They think he speaks blasphemy."

"Does he?"

Ennius's pointed question made Hannah consider it. She had never given much thought to whether her brother, as the M'sheekha, was divine. Could a simple man from a simple family really be the Creator who had spoken the world into existence?

The hair on her arms stood on end as a chill passed over her. She shook her head with determination. "No. He's telling the truth."

Ennius stared at her as she looked back at the tense scene playing out on the garden hill. The crowd of men stood back as if they were afraid of Yeshue, looking everywhere except straight at him.

"I'll ask you again," Yeshue said, his voice far more patient than he had a right to be. "Whom are you looking for?"

"Yeshue of Nazareth," someone finally spoke in a timid voice. Most of the guards and soldiers looked like they were ready to run away in fear.

"I told you I am he," Yeshue said again. "If you are looking for me, then let these men go."

"Surely they'll leave him alone now," Hannah said, relieved that Yeshue had demonstrated his power.

The disciples had all retreated, hiding within the old olive grove. Hannah sneered. "What a bunch of cowards," she said under her breath.

"Am I leading a rebellion that you come with swords and clubs?" Yeshue spoke calmly, gesturing to their many weapons. "Every day I've been with you in the temple courts, and you didn't touch me. Why now?"

No one answered. They looked at one another as if they'd been struck mute.

"But the Scriptures must be fulfilled," Yeshue said, nodding. "And this is your hour—when darkness reigns."

They hesitated another long moment. Then the two closest to Yeshue took him by the arms, chaining him by the hands and feet like he was an animal who might escape. As if he couldn't get away from them if he wanted. She'd seen him do it before. They led him out of the garden.

Why isn't he escaping?

"No!" Hannah came from behind the brush, intending to run after them.

Ennius grabbed her and held her back. "We'll follow, Hannah, but if you rush into that crowd, you'll be taken along with him."

"I don't care!" she said, trying to shake his hand away.

"I do." He kept a firm grip on her. Movement drew their attention to the darkness of the olive grove.

"They're all running away," Hannah said in dismay.

"Every last one of them." Ennius watched the disciples flee. "They're scared they'll be taken, too. For good reason."

"Cowards!" she yelled.

Ennius looked at her as if he might say something, but he shook his head and closed his mouth. He pulled on her hand. "Come on."

Hannah gulped back a lump in her throat as she watched them lead her brother out. She ached when she saw him stumble because of his chained feet. She hadn't felt such pain since the night she had sinned and he had come to find her. What had he thought as he looked at her, huddled and broken in the darkest corner? Why hadn't he condemned her?

"Born of a virgin," she mumbled as they walked. Her mother had said it so many times. The family scoffed at the story, but her mother wouldn't lie about it. Maryam was a far better woman than Hannah. She wouldn't have sinned like Hannah did. If Maryam said Yeshue had been born of the Spirit of Alaha, then that was exactly what had happened.

She shivered as another chill possessed her.

They went first to the house of the High Priest. The elders had gathered in the courtyard. They peered through the gate and Hannah saw Yeshue standing in the middle of them, still chained. His head down, he kept silent as angry voices called out around him.

"They've all deserted him. He's alone."

Ennius had a pained expression, but he didn't answer her. He tugged on her hand. "Let's go."

She let him lead her along for a time. They walked through the still, dark streets of the city. Ennius finally stopped in front of the governor's palace.

"Why are we here?" she asked. Beggars leered from the side of the road while others slept in pathetic, bedraggled heaps.

"We're going into the palace." Ennius didn't elaborate as he led her through the gates, nodding at the soldiers who stood guard.

"But why? They wouldn't bring Yeshue here. He'll have to stay with the Sanhedrin for his trial tomorrow. We need to go back."

Ennius kept possession of her hand and led her forward. "Trust me. They'll come, and they'll come soon. They have no authority to do to Yeshue what they want done. I've been listening to their plans, remember? They need to convince Pilate to do the deed. They'll bring Yeshue here."

"What if …?" Hannah didn't want to fathom it.

Ennius hesitated, his narrowed eyes dark under his furrowed brow. They had come to the large open hall – the Praetorium. It was dark and quiet. He leaned his head back against the stone wall and closed his eyes tightly.

"Hannah," he said slowly, his voice a whisper. "I'm on duty in the morning." His eyes opened, wide, as if he was fully grasping what his mouth had just uttered. "God help me, I'm on duty."

Hannah tried to understand. He was dressed in his uniform, carrying his helmet and spear. What if Pilate agreed to execute Yeshue? Would Ennius have to carry out the sentence?

"What are you saying?" she demanded.

"I'm assigned to serve the governor come sunrise. Crucifixions are one of my responsibilities." His voice was dull.

"Ennius …" she said, her voice wavering. "What will happen if you refuse?"

He shook his head and met her eyes. "I'd be hung up beside him."

"No!" She clenched her fist and paced the length of the wall. "Is this really happening? What in the world has he done to deserve this?"

Ennius gave her a long look. When she paced back to him, he grabbed her and pulled her into his embrace.

"Help us, Elohim!" she cried in desperation. "You must rescue your Son!"

They stayed there together in the dark silence for what felt like hours.

Finally, they heard a rumbling outside the wall. The gates burst open with a heavy line of people. The entire assembly hall was filled within a matter of minutes. Mostly men, they carried torches and spoke to each other with angry voices. Yeshue was led through last. He stumbled through the gates and toward the front. Hannah gripped Ennius's arm when she saw her brother's face. His lip was bleeding, his eye swollen shut. He had to shuffle with the leg chains, and he had trouble maintaining his balance with his wrists bound.

"They're treating him like a murderer," she protested.

"They're treating him like the leader of a rebellion," Ennius said quietly in response.

"Yeshue!" she cried over the din, but her voice was swallowed up by the noise of the crowd.

Pontius Pilate appeared and stood at the balcony. He grimaced as if an early morning trial was the last thing he was interested in doing at the moment, but there was fear in his expression as well.

Yeshue was pushed toward the foot of the stairs. Members of the Sanhedrin surrounded him and looked up at Pilate.

"Ama," Hannah said suddenly. "Ama needs to know what is happening."

Ennius nodded. "Go get her and the others. I'll stay here. I promise I won't leave him."

She took a long look at Yeshue, who stared at the ground. Hadn't the events of the nights shocked him? Why did he stand by so passively and let the drama unfold? With all the power available to him with so much as a word? It made no sense.

Hannah ran all the way to Bethany. The first hints of sunrise glowed on the horizon when she glimpsed the villa.

"Ama!" The stillness was broken by her voice as she burst through the door. "Talia! Y'hud!"

Maryam appeared in the doorway. Her eyes were red from crying and her hands were shaking when Hannah took them in her own.

"Is he ..."

Hannah shook her head. "He's appearing before the governor. On trial."

Maryam sobbed and Hannah took her in her arms, holding her tightly. Behind her she saw a familiar figure. Yohanan stood next to Y'hud with a hand on his shoulder.

"You!" Hannah let go of her mother and charged at the disciple she'd always respected in the past. "You traitor!"

She beat her fists against his chest, and he let her, a sad expression on his face.

"How dare you abandon him? You call yourself his friend. You should be standing with him to face Pilate!"

Yohanan hung his head as if he agreed with her, but Maryam pulled Hannah back. "Yohanan came to us as soon as they took Yeshue from the garden. He's taking us into the city."

Hannah looked at the disciple again. She sighed. He wasn't many years older than her. She shouldn't fault him for being terrified.

"Ama, they beat him," she said, her voice breaking. Maryam's eyes filled with tears. Y'hud glared at her, his mouth set in a firm line.

Yohanan took Maryam by the shoulders. "Let's go to him."

None of them were ready to make that journey back into the city. But they could do nothing else. Their son, their brother, their friend and teacher was on trial for his life.

"Get Talia," Maryam told Hannah as they prepared to leave. "She fell asleep about an hour ago."

"Do you think that's a good idea?" Hannah asked warily.

Maryam considered her words. "She'll be worse if she wakes up and finds she's alone. She needs to be with us."

Hannah nodded and went to wake her sister.

"Come, Talia. We are needed in the city." Hannah helped Talia with her cloak and headscarf. Talia gave her a wild glare that told Hannah she wasn't ready to hear why they were rushing into the city at dawn.

Hannah took Talia's arm and followed Yohanan, Maryam and Y'hud down the hill. Her mother's sorrowful but calm response to the news surprised her. Maybe Hannah had expected her to react with the same outrage she felt. Wouldn't she want to call down curses on the ones who were trying to kill her firstborn son? If anyone tried to hurt Y'aqim, Hannah was sure they'd have to do it over her dead body. But Maryam seemed to face Yeshue's arrest without a fight. Only with her grief. Almost as if she had already accepted that this would happen.

Hannah certainly hadn't accepted anything. She started to race back down the path to rejoin Ennius in the palace, but the form of her sister next to her stopped her. Talia could barely walk for her grief. She leaned heavily against Hannah. What was she going to do with her? She would surely die of a hysterical fit if she saw Yeshue as he was now.

"Where's Nathanael?" Hannah asked her, angry once more at the cowardly way the disciples had responded

"I don't know," Talia said with difficulty.

Traitor, Hannah thought, but she didn't say it to her sister.

"Did Lazar and the sisters go into the city? Where are the children?" Talia asked.

"Lazar left. There was talk of his life being threatened. Friends took him to Jericho. Maryam and Marta are with friends in the village. They have my boys and Shimon with them."

Talia seemed to bolster herself. "Where are we going, Hannah?"

Hannah hesitated, but she knew she couldn't hide it from her forever. "Yeshue has been arrested. He's standing trial at the governor's palace."

Talia's face went ashen with anguish, but she seemed no more surprised than their mother. "Yeshue," she whimpered.

"Don't let go of my hand," Hannah said. "We'll stay together."

They hurried to the city. First light dawned as they passed through the gate, already crowded with people. Since it was both market day and Passover, vendors had set up booths all the way down the narrow streets. They pushed their way through the crowds until they came to the palace.

When they arrived, people were spilling out into the street. They became separated from Maryam and Yohanan in the unrest.

"Hannah, why has he been brought to the Roman governor?" Talia asked as they fought against the crowd to gain entrance.

Hannah hesitated to tell her. "The Jewish leaders are seeking a harsher sentence. They are not allowed to carry it out on their own."

"Death?" Talia cried, inhaling fast and nearly choking.

Hannah nodded, steeling her jaw against the tears. "The governor won't see any reason to sentence him to death. He can't."

The sisters glanced at each other and then at the crowd. It was no secret that Pilate was afraid of losing his position for failure to keep order. And the crowd struggling against each other and screaming angrily wasn't a good sign.

The governor stepped into view. The unrest of the crowd grew at the sight of him.

It took several minutes for the crowd to quiet enough for Pilate to speak.

"Here is your king," Pilate said loudly, pushing the prisoner forward, clothed in a purple robe with a string of thorns pressed into his brow.

"Yeshue!" Talia gasped in horror.

Hannah squinted her eyes at the same moment Yeshue looked up. "It can't be," she gasped, her stomach turning in revulsion.

Pilate shouted in a loud voice so that the whole courtyard would hear his words. "What evil has he done? I have not found any fault in him that deserves death. I shall punish and release him."

But the crowd yelled again, a hollow, remorseless cry that caused Talia's knees to go weak. Hannah caught her and held her close, feeling both of their bodies tremble.

"CRUCIFY! CRUCIFY! CRUCIFY!" they screamed.

"Shall I crucify your king?"

"WE HAVE NO KING BUT CAESAR."

"No!" Hannah shouted with rage until her voice was hoarse.

Pilate showed the crowd his hands and deliberately soaked them in a bowl of water. He held them up. "I am innocent of this man's blood. It is your responsibility."

The men around them began to shout. "Let his blood be on us and our children!"

The mob suddenly began to yell as one, their words cold and evil and final. "Take him away! Crucify him! Crucify him!"

Pilate abruptly disappeared from the balcony, waving his hand toward the soldiers without looking at them. They stepped forward and took Yeshue by the arms.

"It's over," Hannah said, stunned. "He's going to be crucified."

"This city has gone mad!" Talia sobbed. "We are possessed by evil! Can't you feel it, Hannah? It's everywhere. It's cold and black. We'll never escape our punishment for this. Our people are doomed!"

THIRTY-TWO

Hannah clung to her sister as Talia cried. They were nearly trampled as the crowd exited the courtyard. They watched until Yeshue had been led out of their view.

"Hannah!" Ennius pushed his way through the crowd.

"How could this happen? Why aren't you doing something to stop this?" Hannah demanded.

"I'm sorry," he said, and the uncertainty that infected his tone made Hannah's hopes plummet. "I have no power here. God will have to stop this—it is beyond human control."

"But they're going to kill our brother!" Hannah held Talia up as she went limp. He only shook his head, his expression vacant of hope.

"What are you going to do?" she finally asked, hearing the defeat in her own tone.

Ennius shrugged, helpless. "My job. Or die with him."

Hannah made a sound of disgust. "He's not worth that?"

Ennius didn't answer, so she continued "He healed you. You'd be dead if it weren't for him. How can you turn on him now?"

He nodded. "Yes, he did heal me. And if he's powerful enough to do that, I'm trusting he can do the same for himself."

"What if he doesn't?"

Ennius sighed and looked away. "Then he isn't who he said he was, and that's not a man worth giving your life."

Hannah roared in frustration. "A healer and teacher being condemned to die? What about justice?"

"Your brother says sin is sin. Hate is murder, lust is adultery. Right?"

Hannah shrugged. "So?"

"So lying is sin. And if your brother lied about being God, then he deserves what he gets."

A fresh torrent of sobs wracked Talia's form as Ennius turned away from them.

"Get out of the city. I don't want you harmed." He only turned long enough to speak the words.

"As if I'll ever do anything you say again," Hannah called angrily after him. She took Talia by the shoulders and made her sister look her in the eye. "I'm going to follow the crowd. Do you want me to get you home first? Maybe Nathanael has come back to the villa by now."

Talia suddenly bolstered herself. As if her grief had been possessed by an acceptance born of necessity. "No. Yeshue needs us."

She took the end of her headscarf and mopped her tears, then took Hannah by the hand. "Let's go. We'll hold each other up."

Hannah nodded, squeezing her sister's hand. They followed the crowd and ended up outside the gate next to the courtyard. Yeshue was pushed into the smaller courtyard. His chained hands were attached to a wooden pillar in the center, stained with the blood of many others before him. One of the soldiers stood behind him with a menacing whip in his hand. Without ceremony, the soldiers stripped Yeshue of his tunic and the purple banner used to mock him, casting them to the side in a heap.

"I made Yeshue that tunic," Talia said in a faraway voice, her hand reaching for the bars of the gate. The tunic lay beside the post, covered in blood.

"He's already been beaten. How much can he take?" Hannah said the words to herself, not expecting Talia to answer.

The crack of the whip and the sickening sound of flesh ripping open made Hannah's stomach heave in protest. She grimaced as she heard the familiar voice of her brother grunt in tremendous pain.

Talia stiffened as if the whip had hit her instead of Yeshue.

"Adonai," she called weakly. "How can they do such a thing?"

The tiles were quickly soaked with precious blood, blood that ran through their very own veins. Hannah felt dizzy as she watched familiar hands grip the post, fingernails digging into the wood. Her ears burned as the sound of her brother's groans and the murmuring and laughter of some of the crowd members.

"Close your eyes, Talia," Hannah instructed. Talia did so, burying her head in her sister's shoulder. Hannah forced her own eyes to stay open. Yeshue deserved her attention. He shouldn't have to face this completely on his own.

When Yeshue went limp at the post, long moments later, the soldier overseeing the whipping raised his hand. Yeshue was taken from the post and pushed out of sight again.

Hannah stared hard at the smear of blood he left on the pavement.

"Why doesn't he stop them?" she whispered. "He raised the dead. Why can't he stop them?"

Ya'achov

יעקב

"Ya'achov, we should do something," Yose said, his voice thick.

It was nearly nine in the morning. The brothers were waiting in line at the temple, their lambs secured at their sides. From the look of the Passover line to the stairs of the Holy Place, they had hours of waiting ahead of them. They had done their best to go about their business. Ya'achov knew his brother had been arrested by the Sanhedrin that morning, but he hadn't tried to find out more information. Yeshue deserved a scare. Maybe it would help him wise up.

But the brothers had been listening to the talk of the other men in line with them. Not only that, they could see for themselves that something was happening. The city was eerily quiet. As if it was ashamed of something that lurked within its walls. As if they were trying to hide their evil deeds from Alaha.

Ya'achov worked to keep his voice even. "We aren't his family. His disciples are his family. Let them see to him."

"The rumor is that his followers have all deserted him," Yose reminded him. "How can we live out our lives if we let our brother die alone?"

Ya'achov forced his mouth into a hard line. "He's done nothing for us."

"That's not true," Yose argued. "He did what he could."

"It wasn't enough."

Yose sighed, his expression as firm as Ya'achov could ever remember. With sudden decision, he handed Ya'achov the lead for his own perfect white lamb. "I'm going. If you don't come with me, you'll regret it the rest of your life."

Ya'achov didn't answer. He took the rope, but he wouldn't look Yose in the eye. He wanted to go with him. He wanted to support his family and see them through this trial, but he felt like a statue, glued to the polished tiles of the temple courtyard. It was an odd feeling, as if time were standing still, holding him captive.

I am the way, the truth and the life. No one comes to the Father except through me.

Had Yeshue said the strange words at some point? What had he meant? If he were the way, why was Ya'achov standing here in an endless, tedious line waiting to slaughter an innocent lamb to cover the price of his sin? Were all these lambs dying for nothing? The blood that flowed at the altar an exercise in futility?

It was too hard to accept. Too hard to believe that Alaha would change the rules.

Yose could go, because he didn't consider whether Yeshue could be the M'sheekha. He went because he felt a duty to his older brother, the leader of their family. Yose wasn't interested in spiritual things. Ya'achov couldn't go, because he knew there was an all-or-nothing decision to be made when it came down to who Yeshue really was. Either he was the Son of Alaha, or he was a ridiculous joke of a man who would cast a shadow on their family for generations to come.

I am the way, the truth and the life.

Ya'achov felt his breath leave him, like someone had punched him in the stomach. His hand almost let go of the leads of the lambs, but stubbornness hung on.

"My son just came from the Praetorium," he heard a man near him in line say. "The one from Nazareth has been sentenced to die."

Other men clicked their tongues and shook their heads. "I can't say I'm surprised," someone else replied. "He wouldn't try to get along with the Sanhedrin. I'd hoped he was really the Promised One."

Ya'achov felt his mouth go dry. *Sentenced to die.*

"The Romans showed him no mercy. Beat him nearly to death. My son said he'd never seen someone so striped with bloody wounds."

By his stripes we are healed …

"I just came from there." Another man behind Ya'achov joined the conversation. "It was awful. He didn't put up a fight, and no one was there to stand up for him. They shoved a crown of thorns on his head and put a purple robe on him to make a mockery of him. I've never seen such a humiliation. It's really too bad. No one deserves to be treated like that."

"It just goes to show you no one should attempt to go up against Rome unless they really are the M'sheekha," the first man said, his hand on his boy's shoulder. "A quick way to get yourself killed."

He was oppressed, and he was afflicted, yet he would not open his mouth; like a lamb to the slaughter he would be brought …

Ya'achov's eyes fell to the lambs at his side, nervously bleating as they stood together, helpless.

"He took his suffering with honor," an older man spoke, even further back. "He didn't curse or fight it. Just stood there and took it. Shows his character."

The words triggered a memory.

"Where's Yeshue?" Maryam asked Ya'achov, coming from the house with her grinder in hand. "I haven't seen him all morning."

Ya'achov rolled his eyes. "How should I know? Am I in charge of him now? He's thirteen, isn't a man old enough to look out for himself?"

"Ya'achov!" his mother said harshly. "Enough of your foolish talk.

Go find your brother."

Ya'achov wanted to argue, but he didn't want a reprimand from his father. He got up from where he stacked stone against the wall in the shop and went outside to call for his brother.

The last time he'd seen him, Yeshue was helping Yosef haul rough stone to be chiseled in the shop. Ya'achov went down to the side of the hill where they harvested their stone. Yosef wasn't there, and the area looked abandoned.

That's when he heard the sharp intake of breath. The whispered prayer.

He found Yeshue under a huge stone, pinned against the rock face by the boulder. It had landed on his leg. Ya'achov took one look at the funny way Yeshue's leg was bent and the blood pooling under the injury and felt sick to his stomach.

He took a stick and tried to use it as a lever to free his brother. It took several tries, and every time the heavy boulder moved, Yeshue gasped with pain. But he didn't cry out.

When Ya'achov finally freed him, he had to put his brother's arm around his shoulder and drag him up the hill toward their house. Judging from the severity of the wound, it must have caused Yeshue immense pain. Unlike anything Ya'achov had ever felt. The only thing he wondered during that silent trip up the hill was how Yeshue could take the pain so quietly. Ya'achov would have been yelling loud enough to scare all the birds away.

"Yeshue isn't afraid of pain," Ya'achov said, muttering more to himself than to the other men in line. "If he's suffering, it isn't from the pain."

Indeed, he bore our illnesses, and our pains – he carried them, yet we accounted him as plagued, smitten by God and oppressed.

Ya'achov swallowed hard. He closed his eyes tightly and willed away the emotions that suddenly swarmed in his head.

"Have I been a fool?" he whispered. He hadn't wanted to consider that dark place in his being, where all his fears resided. He had refused.

But now he could look nowhere else. The darkness beckoned him. Urged him in. It was time to think the unthinkable.

Y'hud

יהוד

Y'hud stood next to his mother and Yohanan the disciple, his eyes wide and unblinking. He rubbed them when they began to ache from the dust.

How could that bloody, broken man be his abba?

"Ama," Y'hud breathed a desperate whisper to his mother.

Maryam turned her tear-stained face toward him and reached for his hand, squeezing. "Don't look, Y'hud," she said, her throat tight with emotion.

But he couldn't tear his eyes from the scene playing out in the street before him. His beloved brother carried a wooden beam on his shoulders. Every exposed area of his body bled freely. His face was unrecognizable for the thorny crown that pierced the skin of his forehead, causing blood to run rivulets down his eyes and cheeks. One eye was swollen shut.

"He's not afraid of the pain," Yohanan said, brushing away his tears and staring in horror at his rabbi. "But something haunts him."

"Our sin," Maryam said. "The weight of it."

Y'hud looked from her face to Yeshue's. He didn't understand what was happening. He couldn't fathom why they were standing in the crowd at the side of the narrow road, within reaching distance of Yeshue, letting him be treated like this.

"We need to help him," he said to his mother, tugging on her arm. "I'm brave. I'll go to him."

Maryam looked on him with love, heaving a heartbroken sob. "No, my son. There is nothing we can do. The soldiers won't let us come near."

Y'hud looked and saw the Roman soldiers standing on either side of Yeshue, roughly pushing back the unruly that tried to get past.

Y'hud had never seen anyone crucified before. He'd heard tales of it from other boys who had spoken with smiles on their faces, their blood lust obvious. Were the things they said about crucified men true? Would that happen to Yeshue?

Fear thumped in his chest, manic and out of control.

"Ennius," he whispered, recognizing the soldier who walked to Yeshue's left.

"Oh," Maryam said as she saw him. She covered her mouth with her hands.

Yeshue fell then, his strength giving way and his body slamming into the pavement. Trails of blood smeared the path as he tried to lift his body and failed.

Ennius watched him, his eyes dark and narrowed. Y'hud wondered how he could be so cruel, but when another soldier started to lift his whip to beat Yeshue, Ennius stopped him.

"You," he said to a dark-skinned man who stood at the side of the road, his arms across his chest and his face troubled. He was a tall, strong man. "Carry his cross for him. We're wasting time."

Y'hud clenched his jaw as the man, eyes wide with fear of Ennius's drawn sword, took the beam from Yeshue's shoulders and rested the weight of it on his own.

"Thank you," Maryam whispered, reaching a hand toward Ennius as if she wished she might kiss his hand for the small gesture he'd shown her son.

As Y'hud's eyes fell on his brother's face, it seemed that everything and everyone else faded away. He didn't hear the shouts of the crowd or the soldiers, the cries of the women and the other condemned men who cursed and railed against their captors. He heard only the voice of Yeshue, praying in the early morning as dew lay softly upon the earth. Singing in the moonlight as he walked to the garden. He didn't see the blood that soaked the tunic Talia had made, but instead he saw the hand Yeshue lifted toward Judith when he raised her from the dead.

How could they kill him? He was their king! He was there to save them. Why was this happening? Why did Yeshue allow it?

He struggled to understand. Had it been only a few days ago that he had danced with the children in the road outside the Shushan gate, calling Hoshannas to the King of Kings? He had waved branches, laid his cloak down in front of the donkey and bowed to his brother as the king of the Jews.

Now Yeshue would die? How had they come to this?

Abba!

Talia
טליה

"Traitor. Filthy Roman." Talia heard her sister's wrathful tone. Hannah spat in disgust as Ennius passed her. Ennius's eyes darted Hannah's way, but he didn't stop.

As Ennius passed and the procession continued, Hannah's hand dug into Talia's arm. Both of the women stared in horror as the form of Yeshue came around the corner. He fell, grimacing in pain.

Talia's eyes were drawn to Yeshue's hands as he pushed himself up from the ground. They were familiar hands. How many times had she stared at the long, tapered fingers and neat, short fingernails marred with wear from the stonework and wood dust?

Now they were dirty and bloodied. They would not come to her or comfort her. They had only one job left, the one she had known deep down would come. She'd known her entire life. Those hands would be nailed to that inevitable cross.

Hannah tugged on her arm, and the sisters followed the procession. The crowd thinned when they reached the Damascus gate. Yeshue walked through, but many lost interest and turned back toward the temple. It was nine in the morning of Passover, and preparations would have to be made if the meal was to be ready in time. Besides, who wanted to view a Roman crucifixion? There was little in life that was more brutal and disturbing to watch.

Talia and Hannah followed the smaller crowd outside the city.

Something was familiar in all of this. There was a theme, a feeling in the horror that she could barely trace but knew was there. The words of the prophets swirled in her mind, appearing as parchment in her searching soul. An image came to the center. Before he had been beheaded by Herod, Yohanan the Baptizer, her cousin, had always called Yeshue "The Lamb" when he saw him.

Behold the Lamb who takes away the sins of the world.

Talia's brow furrowed as she considered it. It had never made sense to her. Why hadn't he said *Behold the king*, or *Behold the Son of Alaha?*

She pictured the lambs that would be lined up in the temple now, awaiting sacrifice on the altar in front of the Most Holy Place in the temple. They would be white, beautiful, free from blemish. She'd always hated the thought of them being slaughtered. She'd covered her ears so she wouldn't hear the desperate bleating before their throats were slit. But now, she only saw her brother.

Like a lamb to the slaughter.

The tiniest thread of faith occurred in her sorrow-infected soul.

Maybe—just maybe—there is a plan in all of this, she thought in wonder. *Maybe Adonai is not surprised by the evil overwhelming Jerusalem.*

Maybe there's hope.

THIRTY-THREE

Y'hud

יהוד

The crowd thinned as they left the city. There were lambs to slaughter. Passover meals to eat. More important considerations.

Y'hud noticed two things about the people who stayed on with the procession. First of all, most of them were women. Besides the soldiers and some of the Sanhedrin members who remained, probably to see that the job was done, the rest were mostly grieving women.

Y'hud climbed the hill behind them, staying as close as he dared. He had seen the side of this hill – the appearance of sunken eyes, a nose cavity and an empty space where a mouth should be. No wonder they called this place *Galguta*. Place of the skull. Legend said there was a demon who resided in the skeletal façade. He could believe it was true. What else but a demon was at work this day, putting to death the holiest man who had ever walked the face of the earth?

He watched, unable to tear his burning eyes away as the soldiers stripped Yeshue of his bloodied tunic again. They readied the cross.

Y'hud had never seen a man crucified before. He'd only heard tales. He hadn't wanted to believe there were men capable of such cruelty. But he knew there had not been a single bit of exaggeration in the stories he had heard. A soldier stretched Yeshue's hand toward the end of the beam and quickly tied it. Y'hud looked away as the soldier unceremoniously took a large nail and pounded it into the skin of Yeshue's hand. Y'hud heard his mother and sisters cry out as he did the same with the other hand. Yeshue clenched his teeth and suppressed an agonizing groan. It was almost as if he'd expected the pain and torture. As if he had prepared for it years before it actually happened.

"Abba," Y'hud said, hearing his own voice and thinking he sounded much younger. A scared child. That was really all he was – not a man.

"This one doesn't make much noise. Perhaps we should think of something more painful to impress him," the soldier said as he drove another nail into Yeshue's feet. The soldiers working on the other two men laughed.

Y'hud stood, paralyzed. He could hardly breathe. As the cross was raised up and dumped into a hole already dug, Yeshue's body shuddered involuntarily and the sound he made was like a dying animal.

"Some king," a man spoke behind him. Y'hud turned, glaring, to see a group of Pharisees standing at a distance from the scene, holding their prayer shawls up away from the dirt and curling their lip in disgust.

Disgust at what *they* had done.

"Aloha curse you," Y'hud muttered. He clenched his fists so tightly that his fingernails cut his skin and started to bleed.

The men hardly glanced at him before they turned and made their way back down the hill. Even as Y'hud called curses on them, he heard Yeshue speak, soft and labored. "Abba … Abba, forgive! They don't know what they are doing."

Y'hud shook his head. He didn't want Alaha to forgive any of these poor excuses for men. They didn't deserve it. No one who killed the M'sheekha should get away with it. Why would Yeshue ask Adonai to forgive?

A woman's crying pulled Y'hud's attention away from Yeshue's tense, bloody features. His mother stood near the foot of Yeshue's cross with the disciple Yohanan and the woman called Maryam Magdalene.

Y'hud forced his feet to move, to approach the graphic scene so he might have the comfort of his mother's embrace.

"Ama," he said, his voice high and childish as he fought sobs.

"Oh, Y'hud," Maryam reached for him, holding him so tight he could hardly breathe. He didn't mind. He wanted to feel something other than the torture raging within him. To know even a small taste of the suffering his brother endured only a few feet away.

They held each other without speaking. The wailing of the women died to whimpers and sniffles. It was quiet at place of the skull, so that they could hear the drip, drip, drip of Yeshue's blood, falling from his feet to the gravel below. His labored breaths echoed in their ears. Did all that were present sense the evil that hung over this hill?

The soldiers who had done the work of getting the men on the cross apparently thought they were entitled to the men's belongings. They laughed as they argued over the tunic Yeshue had been wearing, now stained crimson.

"All the countless hours Talia spent weaving that tunic for him," Maryam said, regret shading her voice.

Y'hud fumed, hating them with every part of his being. He would never forget this. He would grow up to be a freedom fighter. He would take on the Caesar himself. Run him through with a dagger hidden in his cloak like the Sicarii.

His eyes fell on a familiar face. The soldier who Hannah had befriended stood to the side of the hill, leaning on his spear. He was pale, his eyes narrowed and focused on the ground beneath him. He looked as if he might be sick.

A deep sigh drew Y'hud's attention again to the top of the cross. Yeshue peered at them, his eyes blinking away the blood so he could focus on them.

"Dear woman," Yeshue spoke with broken, gasping words. "Behold ... your son." He nodded toward Yohanan, standing on the other side of Maryam.

Maryam nodded, reaching her fingers to her lips as if she meant the contact to be a gentle kiss on her dying son's forehead. Y'hud wondered how she could be so calm. So accepting.

Yeshue caught the gaze of his disciple. Friendly, compassionate, unassuming Yohanan. Y'hud had always liked him for his funny stories and the way he had of making even children feel as if they held some value.

"Yohanan," Yeshue managed. "Behold your ama."

Yohanan gave a brave nod and put his arm around Maryam, his jaw working to control his emotions. Y'hud wondered at the strange words Yeshue had spoken. Did he think Yohanan was Ya'achov or Yose?

Then Y'hud understood. He glanced around. Ya'achov and Yose weren't there.

He turned around, looking at every face that stood beneath that cross. Stunned, he realized that of all Yeshue's disciples and brothers, only Yohanan and Y'hud himself were present.

Talia
טליה

Talia's mind screamed with each pounding against the spikes that pierced her brother's hands.

Behold, I have graven thee upon the palms of my hands.

She heaved, wanting to look away, but unable to keep her eyes from searching Yeshue's face. She thought of the crucifixion she had seen as a child. She had always known the road would eventually lead to this cursed hill.

She knelt in the dust and retched.

On that day, a fountain shall be opened for the house of David and for the inhabitants of Jerusalem, to cleanse them from sin.

She took a deep breath and dared to peek up at the cross. She remembered the first time she entered Jerusalem. The young man who had suffered on the cross – how the boy had screamed! How he'd begged for mercy. Yeshue did neither. His determination grew with every labored breath. As if he were hauling some impossibly heavy stone and had no choice but to see it back to the workshop. He seemed to be doing something that must be accomplished entirely.

She recalled the day Yeshue had stood up in the synagogue in Nazareth and read the passage from Isaiah. She closed her eyes and saw his perceptive smile pulling at the corners of his mouth. The kind of smile he had when he watched Y'hud and Shimon playing or his mother opening her arms to him.

"Elohim has sent me to bind up the brokenhearted. To proclaim freedom for the captives and release from darkness for the prisoners. To comfort all that mourn ..."

Talia's mind stilled. The torrent of despair and grief that had swirled in her mind as a storm suddenly fell silent, as quickly as Yeshue had calmed the storm that raged over the Sea of Galilee. Suddenly, she understood what he had been saying. She caught a glimpse of the plan of Elohim, and her breath caught in her throat.

"I am here to provide for all those who grieve in Zion. To put on their heads a crown of beauty instead of ashes. The oil of gladness instead of mourning. A garment of praise instead of a spirit of despair."

She whispered the words he had spoken as she lifted her eyes to his dear face. She had only known grief when she had looked at him as her brother. As a man. As far less than he really was.

"Adonai," she said, lifting her hands in worship, bowing her head as she kneeled in the dirt before him.

Now, she looked at her Savior. And she realized that his entire life had led to this very moment. This was what he had been born to accomplish. He wasn't born to sweat in a workshop or solve family arguments or even to teach Torah to followers.

Born to bleed. Born to suffer.

Born to die.

Hannah

חנה

"It was the will of Adonai to crush him and cause him to suffer ..." Hannah heard Talia mumble beside her as she suddenly went still and

lifted her arms in the air.

"What are you talking about?" Hannah wondered if the stress of the event had finally caused her sister to go mad. But the words she had spoken sounded familiar. Like Scripture.

"After the suffering, he will see the light of life. He will be satisfied."

Hannah shook her head. "I don't know what you're saying, Talia."

"Don't you see? Don't you remember everything he taught us?"

Hannah didn't answer her sister. She looked back at the cross. No, she didn't remember. She hadn't been paying attention. She'd been a selfish, immature fool. It was the only thing she'd ever been good at.

"I can't tell you why or how, but I believe it's going to be okay," Talia said, reaching for Hannah's fingers and squeezing.

"I don't know how you can say that," Hannah said, pulling her hand away and covering herself with her arms.

Talia gave a soft sigh and returned to her prayers, closing her eyes and moving her lips.

Hannah glanced at Ennius through narrowed eyes. Though he had done nothing to contribute to her brother's pain – she had watched carefully – he had also done nothing to stop the progression of this unthinkable act. Now he stood next to the cross, trying not to look Yeshue in the eye. Turning away from the stupidity of his fellow soldiers instead of defending the very one who had saved his life.

She was surrounded by fools and cowards. Why did no one, including his own mother, protest this murder?

She moved closer, stepping around her little brother and her mother. She stepped in front of Ennius and put her hands on her hips.

"Stop this," she said hotly.

He didn't look at her or respond, so she took a step further and raised her eyes to Yeshue. She had not known just how beaten and bloody he was until she came so close. Her stomach lurched, threatening to bring up her hurried breakfast.

"Yeshue," she whispered desperately. "Why don't you do something to stop this? The Son of Alaha should be able to raise up an army and defeat the miserable cowards who are taking your life."

Her words were quiet, so no one but Ennius heard them. He finally looked at her with a dark expression. "What have *you* done to help?" he muttered.

"Me? You say that to me as you stand here and murder him, you Roman pig?"

"My people are not responsible for this killing." Ennius captured her eyes with his scowl. "Where are his men? Where are his brothers? Where are all the people who made him believe they were devoted to him? I see a lone follower and a child who called him father. I see a few crying women. No one who has power to do anything. Where are the vast crowds who followed him around Galilee begging him for miracles?"

Ennius's words were spoken only for Hannah to hear. She sighed; her zeal suddenly punctured.

"I don't know," she said flatly.

Yeshue interrupted their conversation with a sudden gasp for air. He turned his eyes toward heaven, searching the skies as if trying to understand some sudden revelation. "Eloi! Eloi!" he called as if someone had left and he was trying to call them back. "No ... why have you left me?"

Hannah stared at her brother. His sudden panic caused a chill to run down her spine. Yeshue had always maintained perfect composure. She had never seen him afraid and vulnerable. As if in that moment, suddenly Yeshue himself didn't understand the plan anymore.

"Please don't leave him," she said, examining the anxious face that stared heavenward, still searching. Then, as Hannah watched, he looked down at them.

"I'm thirsty," he managed hoarsely.

Hannah gave Ennius a wild stare. "Help him!" She prayed that Yeshue would start fighting now. That he would turn this whole thing around, as Talia seemed to believe he would.

Ennius quickly reached for a sponge and soaked it in a dish of sour wine. He stuck it on his spear and lifted it to Yeshue's mouth.

Yeshue drank and then gave an exhausted sigh. He closed his eyes and gave a little nod.

"It is accomplished."

His whole body sighed as if it were giving up possession of something so vast and so perfect it was difficult to expel. Then he went completely still.

Hannah stared at the peaceful expression on his lifeless face. *This is why. This is why he could forgive my sins.*

"He's gone," Ennius said, his voice choked with surprise. Hannah shook her head as a collective wail sounded around her. She stood back as the sky suddenly went completely black. The air felt heavy – oppressive and hopeless. Though it was beyond strange for night to fall at three in the afternoon, it felt right. As if it could be the only response of nature to the death of Yeshue the M'sheekha.

One long, haunting blast from the shofar sounded, the sound echoing through the city from the highest pinnacle of the temple. The sound eerily filled the darkness with the reminder that the Passover lamb was being sacrificed.

"*The Lord is my strength and song; he has become my salvation,*" Talia spoke near her from the thick blackness.

Three short blasts from the ram's horn followed. "*The cords of death entangled me, the anguish of the grave came upon me. I was overcome by trouble and sorrow. Then I called on Adonai ...*"

Hannah finished the verse for Talia. "*Save me.*"

Nine quick tones flowed from the shofar. "*In my anguish, I cry to Adonai.*" Talia's whisper was followed by a moment of absolute silence.

Then the screaming began.

The ground shook so violently that the rocks on the top of the hill split. Ennius grabbed hold of both of them and held them steady as the very earth beneath their feet objected to Yeshue's death.

It would only be later that Hannah and her family members would learn what had happened in Jerusalem the moment her brother died. The thick, impenetrable veil that separated the Holy of Holies had ripped from the top all the way through to the bottom, as if heaven were making some sort of dramatic declaration. Nothing of that magnitude had ever happened before. Everyone had fled in fear.

If that weren't enough, dead people rose from their graves! Some newly dead, still laid out on their sickbed, when life returned to them. Some raised from their tombs. They walked through the streets as if on a mission, their returned life a mysterious testament to an unjust death. And though it should have been a happy thing, to receive back their dead, everyone who told the story had been terrified. A force moved through the city, so strong it was able to knock them all over with a single blow. It was the spirit of the Passover angel. It threatened to have its revenge for the murder of the Son of Elohim.

Hannah realized that life would never be the same again. Not after this dark hour. Humanity could not recover from the blow they would receive for killing the one sent from heaven to rescue them.

"You're wrong, Talia," she said, reaching in the dark to grab her sister's arm. "It's not going to be okay. Ever again."

THIRTY-FOUR

Gradually dim light returned, and Hannah could make out the forms around her. Talia had gone to their mother and Y'hud. She held their younger brother in her arms and rocked him back and forth, singing a soft song of Hallel.

Ennius's forehead furrowed. His eyes sought something to focus on but found nothing.

"What are you thinking?" she asked.

He met the eyes of the centurion who had been overseeing the crucifixion. The other man shook his head and looked down as if he was ashamed. He approached Ennius, his hands shaking as he glanced nervously toward the cross.

"I should have listened to you. Surely this man was righteous."

Ennius grimaced, unimpressed by the confession, though Hannah stared at the high-ranking soldier in astonishment.

"He was the Son of God," Ennius said. The other soldiers turned to look at him.

Ennius stood up and shook his fists. "This man was the Son of God!" he shouted as loud as he could. He threw down his spear and helmet. He stomped down the side of the rocky hill, not slowing though his legs were scraped by the jagged edges of the outcropping of stone.

Hannah watched him go. She turned and viewed the scene, wind still blowing, ground still shaking with occasional tremors, sky still dark and menacing. A sense of wild foreboding caused her to gasp. Would Alaha judge them now?

Talia
טליה

Talia felt the next hours pass as long and arduous years. The Council members complained to Pilate that the bodies needed to be removed before Sabbath began, in order to observe their laws. Their hypocrisy reminded her of so many of Yeshue's stories Hadn't Yeshue called them white-washed tombs? Beautiful and ornate on the outside, but full of dead men's bones within.

Few men were present for Yeshue's crucifixion. Mostly soldiers and Council members. But after Yeshue had breathed his last and the Sanhedrin had left, two Council members came up the hill.

The older one approached Maryam and bowed his head in respect. "My name is Yosef. I am from Rathma. I have been to see Pilate to ask for the body of Yeshue. I would like to bury him in a tomb I have purchased. It was a tomb hundreds of years ago, but there are no bones within it now. I had a new niche cut. It's just behind this hill and it is hidden within a peaceful garden."

Maryam's strength and her tears had been spent. Yohanan and Talia supported her on each side, practically holding her up.

"You are of the Sanhedrin?" she asked, wary. "Are you not of the men who had him killed?"

Yosef met her eyes with a troubled look. "Forgive me, dear woman. I did not support their decision. But ... I was afraid. I didn't attend the meeting in the city last night. If I could go back, I would stand up for him."

Maryam shook her head. "If you had, you'd be dead as well. Evil possessed them and no one could stand in their way."

Yosef nodded. "But Yeshue stood up against evil. I should have as well. Giving you this tomb is a sign of my repentance."

Maryam nodded. "Thank you."

The other man stepped forward. "I am Nicodemus. I spoke with your son and found him to be a just and holy man. I am devastated at what has happened."

Maryam sighed heavily and closed her eyes as fresh tears fell from the corners of her eyes.

"If you will allow me, I would like to provide spices to prepare his body. I've bought as much as the vendors had tonight, seventy-five pounds, but I will buy more tomorrow for the final preparation after Sabbath."

"Seventy-five pounds?" Yohanan stared at him in disbelief. "That's enough for a king's burial!"

Nicodemus nodded. "As it should be. I only wish I could have bought more."

Yosef held up a length of pure white linen. "Let's get the body down and go to the tomb."

Yosef and Nicodemus had the body taken down and carried to the entrance of the tomb. They stood back respectfully as Maryam, Talia and the other women who had been followers of Yeshue quickly began the process of preparing the body. Sunlight was fading.

Maryam held up the long strips of cloth they would wrap around the shroud. Her voice trembled as she spoke. "This is the same kind of cloth I wrapped him in when he was born."

"We must hurry," Yosef said, looking toward the sky. "It's nearly evening."

Talia hated to rush the process. Did it matter if they observed the Sabbath anymore, since they had killed their M'sheekha? She wanted to say goodbye, to touch his hands and his face one more time before they were wrapped in the shroud and never seen again.

They anointed his broken body with the expensive ointments. The smell was so rich and heavy Talia's stomach lurched in protest, reminding her she had not eaten all day. But how could she think of food now? Her brother, beloved and good and kind and a sort of tether keeping her grounded, was dead. His skin was cold and pale, his chest still. It seemed every drop of blood had been drained from his body, yet when she covered his head with the cloth, blood still soaked through where the thorns had pierced him.

Hannah had been right. How had she imagined this could end well? It was her foolish wishful thinking, always expecting that good would triumph and right the wrongs evil inflicted on the world.

She knew death when she saw it. And even if Yeshue had been able to reverse the death process, he was not here to do so now. She glanced at Yohanan, Yeshue's disciple, and knew from his expression he had no idea how to fix this.

Hope was dead. Buried in a stone chamber. Sealed with a massive blocking stone and a wax seal, protected by temple guards to make sure no one disturbed the tomb. Hope was a distant memory.

Maryam, Yohanan, Talia and Y'hud walked silently back to the city in search of the other followers of Yeshue. They found the upper room where they had eaten the Passover meal, but the door was locked.

Yohanan banged on the door, shouting for them to open it. "They have to be here," he said to Maryam. "Where else would they go?"

Eventually, someone pulled the door open a crack. Then the door opened.

"Maryam," Peter said, his voice heavy with emotion. And shame, Talia suspected. "Come in. Come in, all of you."

Talia stepped through the door to see the remaining disciples, aside from Judas. As she looked at her husband, sitting next to the far wall, his arms on his knees as he studied a piece of bread in his hands, she felt betrayal so staggering she thought she might be sick. Her breath came faster as she went to him and stood over him.

"Where were you?" she seethed, forgetting everything she had ever been taught about treating her husband with respect, especially in the presence of other men.

Nathanael seemed to understand her anger. He hung his head and closed his eyes. "I'm sorry," he said in a vague tone.

Angry tears flooded her eyes. "Do you know where I've been?"

Nathanael didn't meet her eyes or answer her question.

"I just buried my brother. I poured spices on his body and helped to cover him with a shroud and watched them seal up his tomb. After I watched him tortured and murdered. Every last drop of blood drained from his body." She inhaled quickly, and felt pressure rise in her chest. "Where were you?"

He pressed his lips into a thin line and stared at the bread.

She shook her head, disgusted. "You are nothing like him. You're a fraud. I despise you."

Still, he said nothing. She left him and went back to her mother and brother. She determined she would never speak to him again.

The day that followed was the bleakest, darkest, quietest Sabbath Talia had ever known. They ate little and murmured prayers that seemed to go no higher than the ceiling. The disciples jumped every time they heard a noise. Yohanan quietly filled in the other men on the details of the crucifixion while they told him that Judas had hung himself in apparent regret over what he'd done. Talia felt ill at the thought of what it must have been like to realize thirty silver coins had purchased the death of M'sheekha.

Talia eyed the disciples with frustration, especially her husband whom she had always considered brave and capable. How ridiculous that the Council had gone to such lengths to protect the body in the tomb, afraid that these men would come and steal the body and create a resurrection hoax. They were too scared to even unbar the door. It was pathetic.

Exhausted, Talia fell asleep on a pallet with her mother early in the evening after Sabbath. She awoke briefly when Nicodemus brought the rest of the spices. The scent of them was already heavy on her clothes. The scent of death. She would have to find the strength to stomach them again in the morning. They would have to figure out a way to get past the guard and sealed tomb in the morning. She fell back to her exhausted slumber.

The next thing she knew, Maryam of Magdala was shaking her gently by the shoulder.

"Come, Talia," Maryam said softly. "We are going to anoint the body."

Talia jumped up, reaching for her white headscarf. She followed the other women out of the room where the disciples slept. She left her mother to sleep. The woman was completely spent and she would be ill if she didn't rest. Talia pulled the curtain around her and hoped she wouldn't be disturbed. She wondered where Y'hud had gone. He'd been sleeping nearby when she had fallen asleep.

When they stepped outside, yellow light was barely beginning to appear on the horizon. The city was still. Peaceful. The air was cool and clear, as if it had been cleansed. They made their way out of the Shechem Gate, speaking little, and passed the hill with the skull impression, around the side to the little garden where cheerful birds sang. A Rose of Sharon bush bloomed near the steps that led to the tomb. Talia reached for a blossom to keep as a memento.

She closed her eyes. *Why do I feel joy? Is it the peace of this place? Is it because Alaha still watches us, still cares?* But a stronger feeling tempted her, called to her to have faith and look at the tomb. *Has the unthinkable actually happened?*

Her heart suddenly lurched in fear as Maryam Magdalene screamed, the sound tearing through the early morning quiet, ripping it to shreds.

"No, no, no ..." Maryam passed Talia, running back in the direction from which they had just come.

Talia turned slowly toward the tomb and saw a fellow follower, Johanna, gasp and drop a jar of spices. It hit the tiles of the pavement in front of the tomb and the heavy scent permeated the air.

Her skin crawled with prickles of exhilaration as the other women fell back in fear.

Nothing could have prepared her for what she saw when she set eyes on the tomb.

THIRTY-FIVE

Ya'achov

יעקב

Ya'achov banged on the door of the upper room, but heard nothing inside.

"Open the door! It's Ya'achov. I'm looking for my mother, Maryam, and my brother, Y'hud."

It hadn't been his choice to come into the city. He wanted to pack up his family and head home to Galilee after he heard what had happened to Yeshue. Part of him was ashamed he hadn't been there to support his mother. Part of him was angry at himself for wishing it on Yeshue. Now that he was dead, none of the things for which Ya'achov had hated him seemed important any longer.

But Nava had made him feel guilty for not caring for his mother. "It is your duty as the eldest son now," she said in her quiet, wise way. "If you want to be seen as the leader of the family from now on, you will have to fulfill your duties."

So he had come into the city to collect his mother and take her home with them.

Finally, the door opened and a sheepish Peter squinted his eyes at the light of the sun. He said nothing, but opened the door wider and ushered Ya'achov inside.

"Your mother is resting. Wait for her and have some bread."

"We are going home today. We need to start out with the caravan soon." Ya'achov looked around the room for his mother and brother.

Peter sighed and pointed at the curtain behind which Ya'achov could see his mother's form lying on a pallet on the floor. But where was Y'hud? Ya'achov surveyed the room and snarled in contempt. "You all just hide here? Is that what he taught you to do?"

"We don't know what else to do." Peter sat at the table and put his forehead against his folded hands.

"Where are the women?"

"They went to the tomb. To anoint the body."

Ya'achov nodded. The smell of spices hung in the air. He felt an unexpected lurch of emotion deep within his being. His brother was really dead. He would never set eyes on him again. His throat felt swollen and he coughed.

Yohanan poured a cup of wine and offered it to Ya'achov, who held up his hand in refusal.

"That's right. You took the vow." Yohanan poured water into another cup and handed it to him. "I was there, you know. When he was crucified."

Ya'achov swallowed hard. "I thought you had all left him alone."

Yohanan nodded. "I ran, at first. I went back to Bethany to find Maryam and tell her what was happening. But they wanted to go to him and I couldn't let them go alone."

"And was it as bad as they say?"

Yohanan's eyes filled with tears. "Worse. It's … it's hard to put it into words, Ya'achov. Never have I seen good men turn so evil and nature so protest a murder."

"Did he suffer?"

Yohanan met his eyes. "More than you could imagine. But the physical suffering didn't seem to be what caused his anguish."

"He was always strong when he was in pain," Ya'achov acknowledged.

"It was almost as if he died not so much from his wounds, but from a broken heart. He said Elohim had left him."

Ya'achov felt a rush of nausea rise up from the pit of his stomach. Yeshue had said Alaha had left him? He couldn't even imagine it. "If anything were to break Yeshue's heart, it would be that."

Yohanan nodded sorrowfully.

Sudden pounding on the door made the disciples jump and their eyes grow wide with fear.

"They've come for us," Peter whispered in a strangled voice.

Ya'achov frowned. "Or it's the women coming back from the tomb." He went to the small window and peeked out. "It's Maryam. The one from Magdala."

He opened the door and Maryam burst into the room, sobbing hysterically.

"They've taken him from the tomb! We don't know what happened to the body."

Peter watched her with doubt. He exchanged a glance with Yohanan, and the two of them seemed to bolster their courage. They went through the open door.

Maryam ran after them, but Ya'achov stayed put. He wasn't about to run all over the city at dawn based on a woman's frenzied visions.

A few minutes after they left, the rest of the women returned. Ya'achov watched the exultant look on their faces with suspicion. They all began to talk at once, and Ya'achov only heard pieces of their story.

"Angels ..."

"Tomb was unblocked ..."

"Risen ..."

Eventually, the disciples, who had gathered with curiosity, dispersed, dismissing the claims as female madness from grief. Ya'achov sat with the disciples, eyeing the women doubtfully as they talked excitedly to each other.

Peter and Yohanan returned within the hour, walking at a normal pace. Ya'achov wasn't surprised. He opened the door for them and they entered.

"What did you see?" Ya'achov crossed his arms over his chest, trying to speak in a casual tone.

"His body wasn't there." Peter appeared confused.

"Did the thieves leave any evidence?" Ya'achov asked.

Yohanan hesitated before he answered. "Ya'achov, the grave clothes were still there. The separate one they put over his head was ... folded up. Set aside."

"What?" Ya'achov shook his head, trying to make sense of the information. "Why would a grave robber take off the grave clothes and bother to fold them?"

Yohanan hesitated before he spoke. "I know none of us want to consider it, but Yeshue did say many times that he ... would rise again."

"Ridiculous," Ya'achov said, waving his hand. "Men can't raise themselves from the dead. It goes against reason."

"He told us it would happen by the power of Elohim," Peter murmured, watching Yohanan.

"Then where is he?" Ya'achov demanded. He didn't want any of them holding on to false hope. It had been a hard enough loss as it was.

Yohanan and Peter went silent. Long moments passed as the men stood there, quiet.

"Let his spirit rest," Ya'achov continued finally. "After such a gruesome death, he deserves to be left alone. Cursed be the fools who stole his body. We'll find them and bring them to justice. Then we will bury him properly."

While he was still talking, they heard Maryam's voice again outside, screaming.

"I've seen him!" she shouted with excitement as they opened the door. "I've just seen Adonai. He's alive!"

She laughed and twirled around the room, her face radiant with pure joy. The women joined her in her celebration.

Ya'achov shook his head, sure the woman had gone mad. Hadn't she been possessed by evil spirits before she'd met Yeshue? But whether they wanted to hear her ramblings or not, she poured out the whole story, her eyes shining and her breath coming in short gasps.

"I went back to the tomb. I was standing in front of it and crying when a man came up behind me and asked me what was wrong. I said that someone had taken my Adonai away, and if it was him, to tell me where he was and I'd get him. I thought he was the gardener." She laughed. "I thought Adonai was the gardener!"

"And how are you sure he wasn't?" Yohanan took her shoulders, trying to make her stand still.

"He said my name. I turned around, and there he was! Our Yeshue – alive! I practically leaped on him and he laughed and told me to come and tell you all the news."

Ya'achov sighed with impatience. "This is ridiculous." He exited the door and slammed it behind him. He'd had enough of these people and their hallucinations.

He walked the street toward Bethany, wanting nothing else but to get his family and go home. He had almost made it the length of the path when a hand suddenly rested on his shoulder. He thought it must be Yohanan, coming to call him back.

"Yohanan, I know you want to believe this crazy story, but ..."

He turned around, holding up his hands in front of him, but when he beheld the face in front of him, his mind could not comprehend what he was seeing.

"Yeshue?" he said in a hoarse whisper. His legs began to shake and he felt for a moment as if he might faint dead away on the stone pathway.

Yeshue smiled. "My brother."

Ya'achov took a step backward, overtaken with fear. Had the ghost of his murdered brother returned to judge him for his hatred?

"I'm not a ghost, Ya'achov," Yeshue said, holding out his hand. "Here, touch me and see."

Ya'achov stared, wide-eyed, at the hand Yeshue held in front of him. A large hole scarred the middle of his palm. The other palm had a matching wound. *Look, I have engraved you on the palms of my hands.* Isaiah's prophecy flashed through Ya'achov's mind.

Other than that, Yeshue looked fine. His color was good—radiant, even—and his clothes were white and new. His hair was neatly combed and trimmed.

Yeshue still held out his hand, patiently waiting for Ya'achov to respond. Finally, Ya'achov lifted trembling fingers to touch the skin of what he thought was an apparition. What he felt was warmth. Life. Reality.

"Oh," Ya'achov whispered, staggering back. Yeshue took hold of his arms and held him up.

I've been wrong. He was the Son of Alaha all along. I didn't believe him. I disrespected him. I wished him dead.

"Adonai," he managed, falling to his knees, not caring about the bruises he would have later, bracing for the judgment this divine being would surely give him.

But Yeshue only chuckled. He pulled him up by the hand and embraced him for the first time since they had been children.

Ya'achov sputtered in disbelief. "You … you really were the M'sheekha. You *are* the M'sheekha!"

Yeshue watched him tenderly and gave a nod.

"I didn't know, Adonai. Please have mercy on me." He tried to fall on his knees again but Yeshue held him up.

"I did. When I died for you. For your sins and for the sins of the whole world."

All the pieces of the puzzle that had never seemed to fit suddenly fell into perfect cohesion. "It was why you came. All along, you were following the plan, and none of us could see it."

Yeshue touched his face with affection. "Elohim has opened your eyes today. Your whole life is going to change."

"It has already," Ya'achov said, tears stinging his eyes. He couldn't remember ever being moved to tears as a man. It was as if he could feel his heart within him, once stony and cold, melting and becoming flesh. He gave in to the love he hadn't known was within him. Maybe it hadn't been. Maybe Yeshue had put it there.

"You rescued me," Ya'achov said through his tears. "I was so proud. I didn't want you to save me. I wanted you to be a fraud. But you rescued me anyway." His breath caught in his throat. "How can I ever thank you?"

"You will. You'll thank me with your life. Yes, you will make a fine leader of my church here in the city." Yeshue smiled. He turned toward the upper room Ya'achov had just left. "I'm going to the disciples now. Will you come with me?"

Ya'achov, still trying to understand Yeshue's surprising prediction, started to follow him, but then remembered Y'hud. "I didn't see our brother Y'hud up there with Ama. I'm going to look for him. He has to be upset."

Yeshue nodded. "Find him and bring him to me."

Ya'achov watched until Yeshue had reached the top of the stone stairway. He waited for him to knock on the locked door, but Yeshue didn't reach for the handle. He turned and gave Ya'achov a grin that reminded Ya'achov of their youth. Then Yeshue walked through the door, vanishing completely from his sight.

Ya'achov rubbed his eyes and looked again. Had he just imagined the whole exchange?

He considered it. Did he believe? And if he did, was he truly ready to let go of the bitterness he'd gathered and stored all these years?

He gave a short laugh and shook his head. All along, he'd thought this was all about him and his feelings. But it had been so much bigger than their family. Yeshue hadn't come to take care of them or be the eldest brother they thought he should be. He had come to pay the very price for their sin. He was the ultimate Passover Lamb.

And he'd done his whole duty, and proved who he was by returning to them.

Finally, he saw Yeshue for who he was, Almighty Elohim. Finally, freedom flooded his being. He gave in to faith, and it flooded his soul and made him new. Changed.

Changed forever.

Hannah

חנה

Early Sunday morning Hannah sat in the courtyard of the villa and fed her sons their breakfast. They were fortunate to be too young to understand the things that had happened. They could still play and laugh, unaffected by the sorrow and fear that had taken over the followers and family of Yeshue.

The more she thought about Ennius and how he had stood aside and let her brother be savagely murdered, the more she began to hate him. She hated him more than she hated Judas, though she couldn't say she was sorry the betrayer had killed himself. At least he had felt some remorse over his part in it.

"Hannah."

She whirled around. He stood over her, his gaze as hard as ever. But when he spoke, there was regret in his tone. "I killed him."

Hannah looked at him, unable to speak for her anger.

"I killed the Son of God. Knowingly."

She stood up. "Yes, you did. And you have the nerve to come here and remind me of it?"

He shook his head, reaching for her arms before she could stop him. "I'm sorry, Hannah. I'm so sorry. If I could go back …"

She shook off his hands and took steps backward. "I don't want to see you again. If I do, I'll kill you with your own sword."

His face fell, but quickly hardened back into his usual dark glare. "That won't be necessary."

He left her, but his words didn't sit well. She had a sinking feeling in the pit of her stomach. What had he meant? Did he intend to solve the problem of his guilt as Judas had?

Only minutes later, Talia came, flushed and excited. Hannah stared in disbelief. What could her sister be so happy about two days after the death of their Yeshue?

Talia was still a good way down the hill when she began shouting her news. "He's alive! He's alive! Yeshue is alive!"

Hannah came out to the gate and stared at her sister as Talia closed the gap and reached for her, pulling her into a joyful embrace.

"What are you saying? Have you finally gone mad, Talia?" Hannah pushed her away.

Talia laughed a cheerful giggle Hannah hadn't heard since they were children. Talia's cheeks were pink and her eyes bright. Hannah shook her head, confused and angry at her sister's manic joy.

"He has risen! He said he would all along, and the prophets foretold it, but we were all too senseless to see it coming."

"How do you know, Talia?" Hannah asked, still doubtful.

"I saw the empty tomb! And angels – Hannah, there were angels sitting on the stone! I saw them!"

"Angels?" Hannah remembered her mother's stories from long ago. "Like Ama saw?"

Talia nodded enthusiastically. "Yes! They said Yeshue wasn't there, that he was alive. We couldn't believe it at first, we were sure someone must have stolen his body. But as we turned around and went back to the city, there he was in front of us! I've touched him, Hannah! I've felt the scars on his hands. He's alive! He's really alive! Hurry, come and see him!"

"I've got to find Ennius," Hannah said, dazed. "Can you watch the boys?"

Talia nodded and urged her on. "Go. Find him and take him to Yeshue."

Hannah started to run, then came back to Talia. "Are you sure?"

"I'm sure." Talia held her sister's cheeks between her hands and smiled. "Go."

Hannah ran in the direction Ennius had gone. She came to the Shushan gate and nearly pushed early morning pilgrims out of the way as she rushed into the temple area. She went directly to the gate of the Antonia fortress, which was guarded by soldiers, a place she had always avoided like any other Jew.

The fortress was larger than the garrison in Capernaum where she had lived. These soldiers wouldn't let her past the door.

"Please! I'm looking for a soldier. His name is Ennius."

They ignored her. She looked more closely at one of the men guarding the door.

"You were there. You killed my brother, Yeshue." She stepped up to the man and accused him.

He frowned at her. "You're a bold one for a Jew. And I don't want to talk about that man."

"He's my brother. I'd like to talk about him."

"Are you looking for a bribe?" The man narrowed his eyes. "You think because I followed my orders and killed your rebel brother you deserve something from me?"

Hannah shook her head. "I don't want your filthy money. I want to know where Ennius is."

The guard sighed. "He's in his barracks."

"Then let me in!"

"Maybe we could let you in. If there's something in it for us." The man reached toward her unbound hair. She felt the top of her head. She had forgotten to put on her headscarf!

"I'm not that kind of woman anymore," she seethed.

"Anymore?"

"Please just let me through to see Ennius."

He glanced at the other soldier smirked. "Will there be something left for us when Ennius is done with you?"

She gulped back her disgusted response. "He might be willing to share."

She was ashamed of herself, but her trick gained her entrance. The guard nodded and opened the gate. "Last bunkhouse, left side."

She ran to the end of the row, ignoring every lurid glance she received on the way.

Please don't let me be too late, Adonai!

She threw open the door. The large room was empty except for a lone soul, kneeling on the floor, his spear in hand. He was weeping.

"Ennius, no!" She leaped forward and grabbed for the spear. He held it away from her.

"You were right, Hannah. I deserve death," he snarled.

"I don't want you to die, Ennius," she said. "I have good news."

"What news could possibly change my mind? I betrayed the Son of

God."

Hannah laughed softly. "So did I."

He lifted his dark eyes.

"The first time I betrayed him I was just a foolish little girl, giving myself to a boy who didn't love me. I hurt Yeshue terribly. I'll never forget the look in his eyes."

"You didn't kill him." Ennius was not impressed.

"I betrayed him to live in the garrison and play the prostitute. He should have had me stoned. I didn't understand why he didn't until this very day."

Hannah listened to her own words, surprised as she spoke them. "I think he spared me because he knew he was going to cover the price for my sin."

Ennius shook his head. "You are his sister. A Jew. I am a pagan who helped kill the M'sheekha. How could he forgive me?"

Hannah kneeled next to him and put her hand over his, holding the spear with him. "Don't you see? You didn't kill him. He gave his life. Willingly!"

"Either way, he's dead." Ennius pulled the spear from her grasp and stared hard at it. "It's right for me to die."

He pushed her to the side and stood.

"Ennius," a voice said behind her.

Hannah's heart began to pound at the familiar sound. She turned, and her heart nearly exploded with the joy she felt at the sight of his face. She had believed Talia, but there was nothing like seeing him in the flesh.

"Yeshue!" She ran to him. He hugged her tightly before turning his attention back to Ennius. He went to him, leading Hannah by the hand, and kneeled on the ground.

"You have much to do." Yeshue took the spear and set it aside.

"How ..." Ennius stared at Yeshue in confusion. "You were dead. Oh, God ... you were dead ..."

"I was. And now I am alive." Yeshue shrugged as if it were a common occurrence. "Believe."

Ennius said nothing for a long moment. Finally, he bowed low to the ground. "I am your servant, Adonai."

"As am I," Hannah said. "Adonai, please forgive me."

Yeshue touched their heads with scarred hands and spoke tenderly. "I forgive you both. With all my heart. With my very life."

When they looked up, he was gone. Ennius stared at her with wide eyes a moment before he pulled her into a crushing embrace.

THIRTY-SIX

Y'hud

יהוד

Y'hud woke, finding himself lying on Yeshue's cot in the villa. His brother's scent still lingered on the soft fleece skin. He buried his face in the warmth and cried new tears. How would any of them go on without him? How would life ever make sense again?

"Y'hud!" Y'hud heard Ya'achov call to him, but he didn't answer. He hoped his brother wouldn't find him.

He wasn't to have his wish. Ya'achov peered around the plastered wall. Y'hud was surprised when he saw Ya'achov's usual hard stare replaced with a certain light he'd never seen before.

"Are you happy that Yeshue is dead?" Y'hud accused as he turned his face to the wall.

He felt Ya'achov sit on the edge of the cot and touch his arm. Ya'achov had never touched him before. Something was different. He turned and sat up. "What has happened?"

Ya'achov smiled slowly. When he finally answered, his voice was as hushed, as reverent as the rabbi when he read from the scrolls on Sabbath. "He's alive."

Faith burst through the walls of Y'hud's grief like the sun's light after a storm. He sat up, a grin spreading across his face and into his spirit.

"Of course he is," Y'hud said with a shrug, causing Ya'achov to chuckle. "He's the M'sheekha, after all."

Talia
טליה

Talia's heart had not stopped soaring since the moment she saw Yeshue alive, forty days before. She had been transformed. She was able to forgive her husband, who had also been altered by the events. By Yeshue.

There was a twist of bitterness in the sweetness this morning. For it was the day Yeshue would leave them.

"You don't understand," he said with compassion as they mourned for him. "I'm only going away because I will be able to send you my Spirit. He will live within you! I will be with you and all who follow after you in faith. Forever! And then when my church is complete, I will come back."

They stood in the morning sunshine. It was Yeshue's favorite time of day. He led them all to the highest part of his beloved Mount of Olives. They could see Lazar's villa from their vantage point. She glanced around his garden, his special place of prayer. She promised herself she would pray there every time she came to Jerusalem.

She held on to Nathanael's arm, and he smiled at her. He knew it was hard for her to say goodbye, but they both felt strong enough to face this change. After all, they had already experienced the worst. What was anything else in comparison?

She glanced behind them as they reached the top of the hill. Hundreds of people gathered, and not just Jews. Hannah stood next to her new Roman husband, Ennius, with their sons on either side. Ama stood with Y'hud and Shimon, Yohanan standing nearby. Talia knew that they would be well looked after as the family divided, going into all the world and telling the story, just as Yeshue had instructed them to do.

Ya'achov stood with his family, tall and strong and more confident than Talia had ever known him to be. He smiled at Yeshue. He had already made it known he would be staying in Jerusalem to lead the flock of believers gathering daily in the temple. She knew he would do well.

Yeshue sighed, a wistful smile pulling at his mouth. He spoke in a loud enough voice that everyone could hear him. "All authority has been given to me in heaven and in the earth. As my Father has sent me, I am sending you. Make disciples of all the nations and baptize them in the name of the Father and the Son and the Spirit of Holiness. Instruct them to keep whatever I have commanded you. You will know them by my signs."

Talia watched his beloved face, trying to memorize every detail, when his eyes suddenly met hers. "Remember – I am with you every day, even unto the end of time."

She could not hold back her tears. Nathanael held her close. As they watched, Yeshue rose into the air like he was riding on a cloud. They stood and stared long after he was a tiny speck in the sky above. Suddenly, two very bright men stood in front of them on the top of the hill.

"Those are the angels from the tomb," Talia whispered to Nathanael.

"Why are you standing around staring at the sky?" one of them said with a smile. "He'll come back, just the way he left. Go, hurry and do what he told you to do while you wait!"

A rush of joy rippled through the crowd of believers. Some started to cheer. Children began to dance.

Nathanael turned to Talia. "We have work to do."

She smiled through her tears and laughed as he picked her up in his strong arms and swung her around. He kissed her, setting her down and holding her face gently between his hands.

She closed her eyes. "Help us always follow you, Yeshue. Our Adonai."

"Amen," her husband whispered.

EPILOGUE

Indeed, the family of Yeshue fulfilled their mission because of the new Spirit who took up residence in their hearts. While the events of the past three years were still fresh in their minds, the family gathered with the disciples and wrote down the things they had witnessed. Peter wrote a rough account of events, which helped the others to remember the details they had forgotten. His words were used as a pattern for the other gospels. Yohanan wrote his last, later in his life when all of his fellow disciples were gone, filling in details he found to be missing from the others and providing the seasoned perspective of a man who had lived his life for Yeshue the M'sheekha.

Ya'achov and his family stayed in Jerusalem, and Ya'achov became a prominent leader of the church, elected bishop of the first Christian church. He earned the title of Ya'achov the Just, and went often into the Holy of Holies in the temple to pray. They said of him that his knees were as calloused as a camel's because he was so often on them, praying for forgiveness for their sins.

When he was in his sixties, Ya'achov was asked by other leaders at the temple to go up to the pinnacle—the highest point of the temple, and tell the people that Yeshue was dead, because they knew the people would listen to him. So Ya'achov climbed to that pinnacle.

"The people respect you as just. Tell them the truth about Yeshue your brother. That he was crucified. That he's dead, and they should worship Alaha instead."

Ya'achov called out in a voice of authority, with a smile on his face. "He was crucified, but he's alive! He's sitting at the right hand of Elohim, and you'll see him come back! I know it, because I saw him alive. I touched his scars. Adonai be praised, Yeshue is alive!"

For his testimony, many people believed. But it cost him his life. The men pushed him off the pinnacle, and when that didn't kill him, they stoned him to death there in the street, only a short distance from that beautiful little hill called *Galguta*, blessed with the remnants of a cross, and an empty grave standing open.

"Father, forgive them," Ya'achov prayed as he died. "They don't know what they are doing."

Y'hud lived a long life of service to Yeshue his *Abba*. He mourned the death of his brother, Ya'achov, but took over his position as bishop in the Jerusalem church that quickly grew into the thousands. He taught his family the truth so well that his great-grandchildren testified of Yeshue to the emperor Domitian. They were martyred during the reign of Trajan, gladly giving their lives in honor of their M'sheekha. His grandson, Judah Kyriakos, was the last bishop of Jerusalem before the city fell.

Hannah and Ennius took the story of Yeshue to Rome and helped build the church there. They raised Hannah's two sons as well as three more of their own to be followers of the Way. A spy infiltrated their small house church and reported them to the governing officials, who approached Ennius and Hannah and ordered them to publicly give worship to the gods and to the emperor.

"My only God is Almighty Elohim – Yeshue my M'sheekha." Ennius said, and Hannah agreed. They gave their lives for their unwavering faith, fed to wild beasts during an intermission at the games in Circus Maximus.

Talia and Nathanael wasted no time in obeying Yeshue's instructions. They went first to India, taking the disciple Matthew's written account of Yeshue's life, and they led many to believe. They went other places as well, traveling with Nathanael's childhood friend and fellow disciple Philip, spreading the gospel like wildfire wherever they went. They came to Armenia and found a home. The people there became so fond of Nathanael he was brought to the king, who asked the disciple to heal his daughter. Nathanael did so, and both the king and queen professed faith in Christ. But this angered the king's brother, who ordered Nathanael, Philip and Talia to be killed.

Talia faced the cross where they would hang her husband after ripping open his flesh, but she did not feel that familiar horror and panic she used to know. She was grieved that he suffered, but peace calmed her. After he had faithfully given his life and gone to Yeshue's open arms, it was Talia's turn. Since she was a woman, she was not tortured, but she was made to kneel at a block where she would be beheaded.

She breathed her final words. "Adonai is with me; I will not be afraid. What can man do to me?"

The next moment, she found herself in the familiar circle of Yeshue's strong embrace.

The End

AUTHOR'S NOTE

Tackling a project about Jesus is always risky. I have been working on this story for over ten years, hoping somehow to get it perfect. I've accepted that's not going to happen.

Jesus is personal. We each see our own unique version of him. How do you choose one perspective? How do you mold him down into a person that lives and breathes and speaks?

Jesus did breathe and speak. He lived among us. So there is a reality there, perhaps buried, perhaps obscure, perhaps not always what we would want to hear. Yet there is plenty of Jesus to go around.

While I'm sure I did not get every detail right, I prayed throughout the thirteen years of pondering and writing this book that I would get the impression right. That you would sit down to read and fall back through time to a tiny village in a Roman-occupied world. A difficult life, but rich, simple and wonderful in many ways. I wanted you to see Jesus through fresh eyes. I wanted you to think of him in ways you may never have considered before. I wanted every reader to be surprised with an incredible sense of familiarity to these people, enough that we could see their perspective.

After all, that is the purpose of the gospels. If we read them and study them and experience them deeply with our hearts and emotions engaged, we will see the divine.

That is my prayer for you. That you will be inspired to follow Jesus, to love him and to share him with your world.

FURTHER STUDY

You may be wondering what was truth and what was fiction. I invite you to discover this for yourself as you go back and read the gospels, the Prophets and the Psalms again with a fresh perspective. Fiction opens our hearts and causes our emotions to come into line with knowledge and facts. You may be surprised at the exciting truths that will come alive to you as you revisit these places, or maybe come to them for the first time.

Some places to start:

Old Testament

- Isaiah 7:14, 9:6-7, 11, 40:1-5, 43, 52:13-53
- Zechariah 9:9, 11:12-13, 12:10, 13
- Psalm 22
- Psalm 113-118 ("Hallel" Psalms, sung by Jews on holidays for praise and thanksgiving to God.)

New Testament

- Matthew
- Mark
- Luke
- John
- James (Ya'achov)
- Jude (Y'hud)

I encourage you to read a good translation of the Peshitta (Aramaic New Testament.) Understanding Jesus's story in his own language has many benefits. The version of the Peshitta I used is listed in the copyright information at the beginning of this book.

Talia was fictional. We know Jesus had sisters (Matthew 13:55-56) but we are not told their names. I asked Adonai's help in creating these characters, and I was careful to establish every detail of their lives and their thoughts credibly, within the firm structure of the gospels. I tied my fiction to Scripture in every case. For instance, Nathanael the disciple was from Cana, and Jesus and his mother and disciples did participate in a wedding in that little village.

Hannah and Ennius were semi-fictional. I have no reason to say for sure that Jesus's sister was the woman who came to seek his forgiveness, but there is nothing to prove she wasn't. There truly was a servant of a centurion in Capernaum who was sick to the point of death, and that centurion was brought to Jesus for help. The point is not so much that this is exactly how these Bible characters' stories went, but that they were real people with real stories, and that their lives were undoubtedly changed by their interactions with Jesus.

The timeline and many of the events I used in this story are given to us, sometimes in multiple perspectives in the gospels. It was my goal not to tamper with these or use any artistic license to change anything I found in the Scripture. That meant sometimes going back and adjusting and rewriting things I discovered were not represented correctly.

Harmonizing the gospels is always a blessing, because it inevitably falls into place when you think about it with the correct perspective.

I pray you will go on and discover many new things on your own. Let Yeshue guide your path to a greater understanding of his heart and his love for you.

Y'va-reh-ch'-cha Adonai v'yish-m'reh'-cha, Ya-ayr Adonai pan-ahv ay-le-cha v'yi-chu-neh-cha, Yi-sa Adonai pan-ahv ay-ley-cha v'ya-sem l'cha sh'lam.

(Numbers 6:24-26)

ACKNOWLEDGMENTS

All praise to Yeshue my M'sheekha for granting me the privilege of spending so much time in his story, and allowing me to see it from so many distinctive viewpoints. It sounds cliché to say I am humbled, but how can I be anything else in his presence?

My capable editor, Tanya Dennis, labored through this manuscript not once, but twice in the years it took me to write it. She didn't hesitate to challenge my thinking or my conclusions. I am indebted to her on so many levels. I can't thank her enough for her honest, intelligent evaluation. I pray God's blessing on her family and her ministries as a writer, editor and Bible study leader.

ABOUT THE AUTHOR

Miranda Shisler grew up in a pastor's household. She inherited both a love for the Bible and a love for writing from her father and began writing as a way of thinking from an early age. She attended Cornerstone University to study vocal music and music education, but after marrying her love and becoming a mother, she clearly sensed God's call to write.

These days, when not writing or reading, she can usually be found serving in the music ministry of her church, leading women's Bible study or homeschooling her four children.

Connect with her online!

mirandashisler.blogspot.com
facebook.com/authormirandashisler
pinterest.com/mirandashisler/ (See the *My Brother the King* board!)
goodreads.com/mirandashisler

Please remember this is an Indie project so you can have the best reading experience. You can help (far more than you might think) by leaving a review for *My Brother the King* on Amazon and Goodreads today!

OTHER BOOKS BY MIRANDA SHISLER
Available on Amazon Kindle or in print

The Midwest Maidens Series

Where We Belong

Whiter than Snow

This is My Song

Coming soon

My Good Name

www.ingramcontent.com/pod-product-compliance
Lightning Source LLC
Chambersburg PA
CBHW050538260626
47157CB00002B/343